THE LITTLE GIANT

THE LITTLE GIANT

A Life of I. K. Brunel

ALAN BUCK

DAVID & CHARLES
Newton Abbot   London   North Pomfret (Vt)

For Pamela
And to Sim, John W., and so many others –
for their belief, much thanks!

British Library Cataloguing in Publication Data

Buck, Alan
   The little giant: a life of I. K. Brunel
   I. Title
   823'.914[F]   PR6052.U241

   ISBN 0–7153–8793–6

ⓒ Alan Buck 1986

Photoset in Linotron Plantin by
Northern Phototypesetting Co Bolton
and printed in Great Britain
by Redwood Burn Ltd Trowbridge Wilts
for David & Charles Publishers plc
Brunel House Newton Abbot Devon

Published in the United States of America
by David & Charles Inc
North Pomfret Vermont 05053 USA

PART ONE

January 1828 – November 1831

Chapter One

'AGAIN, again, again!' The piping voices shrilled an insistent duet as their diminutive owners danced wildly up and down like a pair of animated but ineptly operated marionettes.

'Ben! Sophy!' their father admonished. 'For Heaven's sake! Don't get so excited.' His tone was meant to communicate extreme displeasure. But Benjamin Hawes found it quite impossible to keep a straight face when the children failed to take the slightest notice of him. And when he caught his grinning brother-in-law's eye he burst out laughing, a lapse that immediately brought forth another chorused shriek.

'Oh please do it again, Uncle. Please, please, please!'

'Children!' This time the voice of maternal authority, and not to be trifled with quite so freely.

'But Mama . . .'

Sophia silenced her six-year-old son merely with a look, and in deference to her the two men also subsided. 'It's already long past your bedtime. So that's enough.'

'Jutht onthe more,' lisped Sophy appealingly. She was only four, but already she knew how to make full use of all her charms.

'Pleathe Mama?' her uncle immediately added as the golden-haired tot reached up at just the right moment to clutch his hand.

Sophia sighed her defeat. 'Oh, very well. But once only mind. Then it's off to bed with you.'

With a shout of triumph the children turned to the small figure in front of the fireplace as he crouched to their level.

'Now, watch very carefully indeed,' he told them gravely.

Wide eyed, open mouthed, scarcely daring to breathe, the two concentrated all their attention on his slim long-fingered brown hands. A walnut, lightly held between his right index finger and thumb, disappeared with a flourish into his left palm. But when the palm was opened, there was nothing to be seen.

7

'Gone. Watch again.'

A second nut, this time held between his left index finger and thumb, disappeared into his right palm. But, again, when the palm was opened there was nothing there.

'Magic,' breathed Ben, his eager face a mask of puzzled delight. Sophy giggled nervously.

'Now, I wonder where . . .' their uncle murmured, making a pretence of looking for likely places to which the nuts might have flown. Then, holding a loosely clenched fist in front of each child's expectant face, he told them to blow gently on his fingers and at the same time make a wish. When they'd done this he slowly opened his hands and there, on each palm lay, not a walnut, but a gold coin, new minted and gleaming in the firelight.

It was a fitting climax to that New Year's Eve performance which had lasted almost two hours and the children were ecstatic, so much so it then took all their mother's persuasive powers to get them off to bed.

When at last they'd gone upstairs, Benjamin Hawes produced cigars and the two men settled themselves to enjoy a well-earned smoke. 'You know, you've a grand way with youngsters,' he commented, easing his bulk into his favourite armchair and stretching his long legs towards the fire. 'Isn't it high time you found yourself a wife and started raising some of your own?'

Isambard Kingdom Brunel smiled a slow, rather sad, smile. It was something he had thought about often of late. He was young still, not yet twenty-two at this dawning of 1828, and time was on his side. All the same he was aware, sometimes almost painfully aware, of a growing desire, nay a need, for a domestic security comparable to that long enjoyed by Ben Hawes and his eldest sister. And, deep within his being he was ever more conscious of an even more acute desire – to father a son, who would one day be to him what he now was to his own father.

Marc Isambard Brunel – the unusual Christian name had recurred regularly in the Norman farming family for nearly six generations – had been destined, as traditionally were all such younger sons if they were sufficiently intelligent, for the priesthood. Indeed, he had initially proved to be one of the most promising pupils ever to have attended the St Nicaise seminary in Rouen; for Marc Brunel, whatever his other failings, was far from unintelligent. To the utter disgust of his paternal and spiritual fathers, however, he'd made no secret of the fact that he hated the prospect of eventual ordination, that he loathed Latin, even more detested Greek, and was determined, come what may, to indulge his preference for mathematics, his aptitude for drawing and his quite remarkable manual dexterity. Nor could any amount of verbal persuasion or even physical bullying deter him from haunting blacksmiths' and carpenters' workshops either when at home or at school. So, disgustedly, his despairing parents had agreed to their shameless sixteen-year-old son going off to the West Indies where, to them a despised naval *voluntaire d'honneur*, he was to become, amongst other things, an expert hydrographer and surveyor.

He was twenty-two when he returned, to find France much changed and not at all to his liking. Almost immediately he fell foul of the Revolutionary authorities in Paris. He fled to Rouen, which still proclaimed its Royalist sympathies, there met and at once fell in love with an English girl, Sophia Kingdom, and would have married her had he not been forced to flee for his life again, this time to America.

In the course of the next six years he conducted the first detailed survey of Lake Ontario, mapped the course of a projected canal to link the Hudson river with Lake Champlain, submitted the winning design for the proposed new Congress House in Washington – which was never built though the plans were later adapted and used for a New York theatre, was appointed chief engineer for the city of New York and there built a new cannon foundry and laid out the defences of Staten Island and Long Island. He had turned his back completely on France, becoming a citizen of the newborn republic immediately on arrival. But he had never forgotten Sophia Kingdom with whom, after many frustrating disappointments, he'd eventually managed to re-establish contact, and to whom he'd once more proposed, this time by letter, and again been accepted.

By then Marc had acquired something of an international reputation, both as an engineer and as an innovator of considerable genius. One of his most impressively successful projects so far had been the perfection of a mass-production process for the manufacture of ships' blocks – those simple but absolutely vital items of marine equipment which still had to be made laboriously and most inefficiently by hand. With the war against Napoleon still being waged, Nelson's victories notwithstanding, this was something that could well affect the final outcome of the conflict. Armed, therefore, with a letter of introduction from the British secretary in Washington to Earl Spencer of Althorp, the First Lord of the Admiralty, Marc arrived in London where, in St Andrew's church, Holborn, he at last married his beloved Sophia. During the next six and a half years she gave him two daughters, Sophia and Emma; then, on 9 April 1806, a son – Isambard.

It was the deplorable condition of the tattered remnants of Sir John Moore's peninsular army that led to Marc adapting his now highly successful blockmaking enterprise – the machinery built with the assistance of Henry Maudslay, one of the rising generation of mechanical geniuses – to the manufacture of army boots. It was therefore no exaggeration to say that Marc Brunel was largely responsible for keeping the Royal Navy's fleets afloat and Wellington's armies on the march.

As long as the war lasted, the now naturalised British engineer prospered. He was constantly expanding and diversifying his activities. With a partner he established a highly successful sawmill in Battersea, its mode of operation revolutionary; he conducted a series of exhaustive experiments involving screw and paddle marine-propulsion systems; he invented a stocking-knitting machine; devised new machinery for the printing trade; designed and built docks and bridges, as well as engaging in extensive experimental work at Woolwich Arsenal and both Chatham and Portsmouth dockyards.

Consulted in 1818 by no less a personage than Alexander, Czar of all the Russias, about the problem of effecting a permanent crossing of the ice-plagued Neva at St Petersburg, Marc considered the possibility of a tunnel under the river as an alternative to a bridge – a feat yet to be accomplished anywhere. It was then that he designed what he called his 'tunnelling shield'. This, without doubt, was his most remarkable invention, inspired, whilst working in Chatham Dockyard on something entirely different, by his casual observations of the depredations of what is perhaps the most efficiently destructive creature nature has yet managed to evolve – *Teredo navalis*, the ship worm.

Just three years later came disaster! As innocently simple as he was brilliant, Marc Brunel was totally unconcerned about money. Always he had lived as if there were no such beings as rogues in this world. Suddenly he was overburdened with debts – so much so that he found himself ignominiously committed to, and promptly confined in, the King's Bench Prison. Refused adequate recompense even for the development cost of his wartime inventions, let alone their use, by Lord Liverpool's niggardly government, then callously swindled by his sawmill partner, he was faced with the dreadful prospect of perhaps an indefinite stay behind bars. Only after the Duke of Wellington's personal intervention on his behalf was he granted a miserly sum barely sufficient to pay off his creditors and restore his freedom. From then on the near-penniless engineer was forced to labour in a tiny office in Poultry in the City of London in an attempt to salvage at least something, somehow, from the shambles of what had once been a successful career.

As for his son, from the moment he'd been able to hold a pencil properly young Isambard had displayed such astonishing natural talent that by the time he was four years old his father had been able to teach him the principles of mechanical drawing as evolved by Gaspard Monge of Mézières in 1765. For thirty years this revolutionary method of representing a three-dimensional object in a two-dimensional plane had been a closely guarded military secret; even now there were comparatively few engineers outside France who had completely mastered it. The lad had further proved himself a true son of his father, for before his sixth birthday he'd known his Euclid by heart.

As soon as he was old enough he'd been placed in Doctor Morell's boarding school at Hove. As a means of amusing himself in his spare time he'd wandered the streets of the town compiling his own accurately detailed and illustrated survey of its principal buildings. To the astonishment of his teachers he'd one day calmly announced that a newly completed edifice near the school was in imminent danger of collapse. No one, of course, had taken this precocious, not to say crass, prediction at all seriously until, less than a week later, the structure had indeed fallen in ruins.

To complete his education Isambard had been sent to France, first to the college at Caen, then to the Lycée Henri Quatre in Paris where he'd won distinction as a star pupil in mathematics. Finally he'd served a brief but valuable apprenticeship with Louis Breguet, the doyen of all scientific instrument makers and horologists.

Marc's financial troubles, always darkly referred to by the family as 'the Misfortune', had not been allowed to affect young Isambard in any way. But on his return from France he'd immediately gone to work in the newly opened Poultry office and found himself busily engaged, principally with the preparation of drawings for the Ile de Bourbon suspension bridges – a small enough but to Marc then, a life-saving commission. In addition he'd been allowed to spend so many hours each week in the Lambeth workshop of the firm founded by his father's old friend and sometime associate, Henry Maudslay. Maudslay, Son & Field was now recognised throughout the world as one of the great practical schools of modern engineering, whilst Henry Maudslay himself was acknowledged to be to the craft of machine-tool making what Louis Breguet was to horology. No aspiring, talented young engineer could ever have wished for two finer mentors.

To start with there had been a certain amount of friction between father and son, as is nearly inevitable even in the best-regulated families. But the youngster's enthusiasm for his work, though it be dull and routine, had been boundless, and once he had learned to discipline the natural ebullience of his talent he and Marc had begun to work together not as father and son nor even as master and man, but almost as equal partners.

It was in the depth of the winter of 1822–3 that a certain Mr I. W. Tate had come to the Poultry office with a proposition that simply could not be refused. Twenty years before, Tate explained, he had been one of the principal promoters of the Thames Archway Company formed to back Richard Trevithick's ill-fated tunnel under the Thames from Rotherhithe to Wapping. That attempt had failed so miserably and so disastrously, Tate contended, primarily because of the want of sufficiently sophisticated equipment – a want that could now be supplied by Marc Brunel's tunnelling shield. Though fully patented, the shield had yet to be actually constructed, even as a prototype. But interest in Tate's idea rapidly caught on and in no time at all resulted in the formation of the Thames Tunnel Company with Marc Brunel appointed chief engineer.

Thereafter events had moved even more swiftly. It was the dawn of a new era of engineering enterprise with major undertakings, the like of which had never been seen or even contemplated before, becoming almost commonplace. George Stephenson, having now nearly completed his Stockton & Darlington rail road, was to start on another between Canterbury and Whitstable in Kent; work was about to begin on John Rennie's new London Bridge; the London docks were being extended, developed and modernised in a way that still made laymen blink; throughout the country, ashore and afloat, things were happening that people looked upon as miracles about to materialise, and it seemed nothing less than natural justice that someone like Marc Brunel should have a major share in what was going on, and that his son should be involved also.

Work on the Thames tunnel had commenced in the spring of 1825 with the sinking of a shaft, forty-two feet deep, fifty in diameter, in Cow Court, Rotherhithe. By November the shield, a massive cast-iron construction, was in position at the bottom of the shaft and poised to start its stupendous quarter-mile journey beneath the murky depths of London's historic waterway – now, alas, little better than a huge, noisome sewer. But on the very day that actual tunnelling operations were due to start, Marc was taken seriously ill. Less than three months later William Armstrong, Marc's resident engineer, also fell ill and promptly resigned. Which left Armstrong's nineteen-year-old assistant, Isambard Brunel, to carry alone the full burden of responsibility for what was already acknowledged to be one of the greatest engineering epics of modern, if not all, time.

To prevent his indefatigable son literally working himself to death the still ailing elder Brunel managed to persuade his reluctant directors, who from the start had never ceased in their badgering to cut expenses to the bone, to authorise the engagement of three assistant engineers. Edward Riley, Richard Beamish and William Gravatt were all healthy, mature men of sound engineering experience and strong physique; indeed Will Gravatt was a veritable giant, possessed of almost Herculean strength. But small though young Brunel was – he stood in his shoes at little above four inches over five feet – he had soon worked all three of them to their knees. Poor Riley lasted a bare three weeks before he succumbed to the same affliction that had laid Armstrong low. He was the tunnel's first fatality, and he was not replaced. Beamish, too, was badly affected. Luckily, he recovered, though the sight of his left eye remained permanently impaired. Big Will Gravatt was more fortunate; but fever, of a particularly noxious and virulent nature, was soon to become the main occupational hazard of the enterprise.

To identify the strata and establish the condition of the ground through which the great excavation was to be made, a team of supposedly expert geologists had made a number of exploratory borings through the river bed. That the accuracy of their findings was absolutely crucial to the entire enterprise was ominously evidenced by the still visible ruins of the Thames Archway workings which had been so calamitously flooded out as the result of a totally unexpected encounter with uncontainable quicksand. But the geologists confidently claimed they had incontrovertible proof of the presence of a more than adequately thick bed of heavy blue clay perfectly situated at a working depth that would place the crown of the new tunnel's arch fourteen feet below the maximum depth of the river. It was exactly what had been hoped for. It seemed almost too providential to be true. It was!

All had gone well enough until the shield was actually under the river bed. Then, almost at once, water began to pour into the workings. Flooding was never bad enough to make the already difficult job of the face workers impossible; but conditions there soon became barely tolerable, the truly appalling pollution posing a constant and ever increasing threat to the very lives of all who were in any way involved. Nor was there any prospect of improvement for, above their heads, where they had been assured there would be clay, the Brunels found nothing but gravel.

Vehemently Marc now cursed his own weakness in having given in to his directors' insistence that, in the interest of economy, he dispense with the elaborate drainage and ventilation systems he and Isambard had so painstakingly planned to install. If ever economy was to be proved false! But it was too late now, the die was cast. Gravel or clay, drainage system or no drainage system, fever or not, there could be no going back. They could only toil, hope and pray, and make the best of it.

The first hundred feet had been completed within six months without any further loss of life, though men falling sick were constantly having to be replaced. A hand-picked élite of Durham miners manned the working face of the shield. Gangs of masons and bricklayers constructed the actual fabric of the tunnel, its thirty-eight-foot width divided into twin arches. Stone, bricks and mortar were brought in by an ant-like army of Irish labourers who also carted away the spoil and endlessly strove with bucket pumps to control the incessant inflow of foul water and stinking mud.

In just over a year the 350-foot mark had been passed. Despite the terrible, near impossible conditions and the countless unforeseen difficulties constantly plaguing what was still a pioneering venture, not to mention the unthinkable dangers to which he and his men were continually exposed, Isambard had somehow managed to achieve the impossible – the work was actually ahead of schedule! For a coming-of-age present and a belated mark of appreciation for his efforts, the directors of the Thames Tunnel Company at long last confirmed the young man's position as resident engineer in succession to the now long departed and almost forgotten Armstrong. But less than six weeks later had come catastrophe. Without warning the ground at the working face had suddenly collapsed and the Thames had poured in unchecked. Miraculously no one was killed, though a few of those who were trapped for many hours before their rescue could be effected never recovered fully from their truly ghastly ordeal.

The enterprise, it seemed, must surely be at an end. In a sermon the following Sunday the curate of St Mary's, Rotherhithe, a stern critic of the work from the very beginning, had preached with thinly disguised satisfaction on the just judgement the Almighty, in His infinite mercy and wisdom, had seen fit to pass on the presumptuous folly of mere mortal men. In so doing he spoke for those, and there were many, who regarded all engineering works, be they tunnels or bridges or rail roads or steamboats, as little better than the works of Beelzebub himself.

The Brunels, however, had been neither impressed by such glib paralogy nor daunted by the apparent impossibility of recovery. Nor did they waste time fruitlessly bewailing their situation. It took a full half year of truly incredible effort finally to seal off the hole in the river's bed with tons of clay, to drain the tunnel, to clear away the slough of foetid silt left behind by the flood and to repair the shield which, mercifully, had sustained only minor damage. And that operation in itself was rightly regarded as an unparalleled achievement, well worthy of celebration. This took the form of a grand nine-course banquet in the tunnel, its walls hung with crimson draperies for the occasion, the diners serenaded by the band of His Majesty's Coldstream Guards. It was all Isambard's idea and on that memorable November Saturday night in 1827 he had delightedly and unashamedly basked in the glory he rightly shared with his father.

But for all the adulation, and however much he was involved, to him the tunnel remained essentially Marc Brunel's creation. It was he who had designed and built the tunnelling shield; in that Isambard had had no part at all. The successful completion of the work would be the climax of his father's career; it would be scarcely the beginning of his. All he would have achieved would be the practical realisation of another's ideas. What he needed, what he craved, was recognition as a creative engineer in his own right not mere acceptance just because he happened to be Marc Brunel's son. Above all else he yearned to create.

Oh, the bounding ambition that seethed within him! He would design a fleet of steamships such as never sailed the seas before, build a new bridge over the Thames with an arch spanning three hundred feet, he would build more tunnels – bigger and better than his father's – one at Gravesend, another under the Mersey at Liverpool. He would be rich, as no other engineer before him had been rich, and build his own great house to his own original design. He would be the premier civil engineer of the age, an example of industry and ingenuity to all who would follow. And he would do all this, when? Before his thirtieth birthday? Well – why not? Had not the great Billy Pitt been Prime Minister of England when he was only twenty-four? Dreams, all dreams, but glorious dreams; nor were they entirely idle ones. 'Castles in Spain' he called them, and what magnificent castles they were.

But, dedicated as he was as far as his career was concerned, Isambard had always tried never to neglect the purely social side of life. A firm believer in that age-old wisdom about all work and no play he delighted in the company of people, his well-groomed but natural charm, quick wit and ebullient if at times outrageous sense of fun, putting him in constant demand with hostesses. Regardless of the hours devoted to his exacting and exhausting work, he seemed never too tired for a party or a ball; to go riding, rowing or driving; to attend a concert, a play, the opera. He was ever ready to be entertained, or to entertain if requested, for as well as being a superb draughtsman he was a talented graphic artist more than willing to sketch a picture or paint a portrait to order, while as a performer of clever sleight-of-hand tricks with either cards or coins he found himself often called upon. He was no musician, nor was he much of a singer, though he possessed an appreciative ear. But he was frequently involved in amateur theatricals, both as a player and as an ingenious deviser of impressive stage effects. Universally popular, he was regarded as an extremely eligible bachelor and, though far from being a philanderer, it was a status and a role he thoroughly enjoyed.

He'd had his first affair during his student days in Paris where he'd also developed a taste for good wine, strong tobacco, the art and architecture of what had come to be called 'Le Grand Siècle', and a fondness for indulging in dramatic impact. To begin with, his eye had been as bold as his ideas. But 'would I make a good husband?' he'd asked himself on more than one occasion. And the answer had always been the same – doubtful, very doubtful. His ambition, or whatever it might be called – it was certainly very much more than just a mere desire to be rich – was rather too extensive. At first, therefore, he had seen himself as a lifelong bachelor, his profession his only fit wife. As long as health continued, his future prospects were tolerable and his present efforts reasonably successful, a bachelor's life could be deemed luxurious. Fond as he was of female society, he found the contemplation of such 'selfish comfort' wholly delightful and infinitely satisfying. His 'Castles in Spain' were surely founded on a conscious premise of complete and total independence. If he were ever to distinguish himself as he hoped in the eyes of the public, such freedom was surely essential.

As time had gone by, however, he'd begun to wonder. Life could never be that simple. 'Selfish comfort' would be all well and good as long as things were going as they should. But in times of sickness or disappointment, how much more delightful to have a companion whose sympathetic understanding one could be certain of possessing. And, of course, there was the little matter of the son he wished for – the fulfilment of that desire which had come to mean so much to him. Thereafter he had begun to regard his various attachments far more seriously. Each, in turn, had seemed to be the true one – until, that is, he had met and fallen hopelessly in love with Ellen Hulme.

She was the only child of a widowed Mancunian cotton magnate who was anxious to acquire a suitable business associate, to whom he would eventually hand on his booming enterprise, as well as a

17

suitable husband for his daughter. Ellen had been, as the saying goes, swept off her feet by this already famous son of a famous father. They'd met at a ball at the height of the London season when Isambard was only nineteen, and when they'd danced together Ellen had found herself gazing ardently into the depths of a pair of shrewd, dark, fathomless eyes. They were fascinating eyes, their positively magnetic brilliance accentuated by finely arched black brows. Thick, crisp, black hair, of a precisely fashionable length and cut, framed not a handsome but an arrestingly interesting face, its complexion dark, almost swarthy. It was a face that instantly revealed a forceful intellect and character – the forehead high, wide, well moulded; cheekbones also high and inclined to prominence; the nose large and, though undoubtedly aquiline, tending to be slightly fleshy. Above a small but firm chin the smile on his full-lipped, rather sensual, mouth displayed perfect white teeth, and told his partner exactly what he felt towards her.

Fully aware of this, and above all conscious of the warmth of his gloved right hand through the fine material of her new ball gown, Ellen Hulme's still somewhat provincial pulses had raced far ahead of the measured three-four beat of the Lanner waltz. There were still not a few narrow-minded reactionaries even in the upper strata of London society who continued to disapprove most strongly of the German dance, once described by Doctor Burney as 'this riotous modern invention', considering it but a flimsy excuse for the unashamed public indulgence of unseemly intimacy, and therefore a totally disgraceful spectacle. At first Ellen had identified herself as one such, for this young man's frighteningly forthright approach to the dance quite robbed her of breath. But, following his sure, expert lead, she had forced herself to relax. Her fears once conquered, the two had complemented each other perfectly in the precision of their movements and, as they'd whirled and twirled over the smooth, well-chalked oaken parquet, they'd thoroughly enjoyed themselves.

But Ellen's home was in Manchester, and since that momentous meeting they had been separated far more than they had been together. Nevertheless, through a regular written exchange of increasingly passionate outpourings, their love had blossomed. Nor was this exchange appreciably abated during Ellen's subsequent visits to London when she and Isambard met, albeit closely chaperoned and sometimes only fleetingly, almost every day.

Eagerly they had laid their plans for a future which had seemed delightfully rosy and practically within reach. But, of course, that had all been before the disaster in the tunnel. Now that future seemed to Ellen Hulme more distant than it had ever been.

Nearly a year and a half of courtship had left them with nothing but plans. They were grandiose plans to be sure, well laid, ambitious, wonderful plans – but still no more substantial than wishing could make them, and no nearer realisation. And Ellen knew full well that until Isambard formally asked for her hand and received her father's consent, they never would be. Had it not been for that cursed hole in the ground that stank so abominably, they could and they would have been married by now. It was no comfort that the attempt to tunnel beneath the Thames had captured the imagination of the entire civilised world, and that people came from near and far, from all over Europe and Asia and the Americas to see it for themselves and to marvel at what they saw. Ellen wasn't the least bit interested in engineering miracles. All she wanted was to set up a home of her own, with Isambard Brunel as her husband.

Their last meeting had been all but disastrous. Ellen's father had been one of Isambard's guests at the tunnel banquet. The following week he'd squired her, in company with his sister and brother-in-law, to a ball at Holland House. The two had skilfully managed to flout the convention that young unmarried persons should always be closely chaperoned, and had escaped unnoticed for a time from the crowded ballroom. In the other luxuriously furnished, elaborately carved and painted public rooms of the old mansion, ablaze with a multitude of candles and hung with mirrors to reflect the prismatic dazzle of priceless crystal and glass, they had managed to remain undisturbed for nearly an hour.

But the atmosphere between them was very strained. For much of the time they merely wandered aimlessly, admiring without really seeing the superb collection of furniture ranging from massive oak and walnut Elizabethan antiques through the best of French baroque to brass-inlaid Egyptian-motifed modern pieces in mahogany and rosewood. Exquisite examples of fine porcelain and the craftsmanship of famous gold- and silversmiths ornamenting highly polished surfaces amidst a profusion of ancient Greek and Roman statuary, went unnoticed.

To a secluded corner, effectively screened by the marble plinth of a decorously undraped figure of Aphrodite, they eventually retreated, there to reconcile their differences at last in a fond embrace. But Ellen was soon near to tears at the thought of their imminent parting and the long months of separation to come. Suddenly it all seemed too much to bear.

'Oh, why must you be so stubborn?' she had demanded in a bitter outburst of long suppressed frustration.

'Not stubborn, Ellen. Practical.'

She pushed him from her angrily. It was the same old ground they had been over and over so many times before, and always with the same result. But why, she pleaded, would he not agree to make at least some firm arrangements for their marriage?

With infinite patience he sought to quell her mounting emotion. Firm but gentle, he calmed her with words and soothed her with his caresses. For perhaps the hundredth time he tried to make her understand that his work must come first, before everything else. It was all-important to him – to them both. It was a fact of life she, for the moment, simply had to accept. To this they had long ago agreed, had they not? True, the last six months had, in a way, been a complete waste of time. It had taken from June to November just to make good the damage, six months during which the tunnel could well have reached the northern bank, so fast and sure had been their rate of progress just prior to the catastrophe. As it was, the working face had not been advanced by a single inch. But that, he told her, was all in the past. They were going forward once more. And with all the practical experience they had gained, the second half of the tunnel must be a far easier prospect.

'It can't possibly take more than two years,' he reassured her.

Another two years! Cold comfort indeed to poor Ellen's ears. She did her best to put on a brave face, but to her at that moment two years might just as well have been two lifetimes. He smiled in sympathetic understanding at her ill-concealed despondency.

'Oh come now! It sounds a lot, I know, but it's really not all that long. It will soon pass, you'll see. With luck it could well be less.'

Did he really believe it could all be finished in two years, she wondered, or was he just saying that in order to smooth things over between them? Would he be saying the same thing for the same reason another twelve months from now? She stared at him in silence for a long moment and he read the wordless question in her eyes.

'Two years, no more, I promise you.' He gave her another, this time irresistible, smile of encouragement. Slowly she responded. He took her in his arms. In a tender lingering kiss he told her all she could wish to know of the depths of his feelings for her. Would she wait for him until the tunnel was finished? Of course, of course she would wait, she whispered. She loved him so much she would wait forever, if need be.

'But pray Heaven nothing else will happen,' she added with more practical fervour.

'Amen to that,' he had agreed, no less warmly.

Chapter Two

THOUGH the country, under the totally ineffective leadership of George Canning's successor, Lord Goderich, appeared to be reeling helplessly towards a political crisis of unprecedented proportion, 1828 started well for the Brunels. During the first ten days of January the shield moved forward nearly as many feet. It was the first advance for more than seven months and, therefore, just cause for celebration. Everything, however, now depended on rapid results. The company's coffers were just about empty, and in the obviously deteriorating economic climate the possibility of further financing would become ever more remote.

As usual the work went on round the clock, Dick Beamish, Will Gravatt and Isambard sharing the supervisory duties underground with Marc as co-ordinator. But it was Isambard who set the pace. It was little short of killing. Where in his diminutive frame he managed to find the energy to sustain his never-flagging stamina and dynamic drive was a mystery. But find it he did and there were times when it was this and this alone that kept things going, the power of his personality and strength of will having never yet failed to inspire every single individual on the work-force.

Young he might be, yet already, having inherited none of his father's still often naïve faith in the natural goodness of human beings, he was a shrewd observer of men. In only a few instances had his judgement proved to be at fault. He was the sternest of stern taskmasters. And though he would never order anyone to do anything he himself could not or would not dare – he was a leader, never a driver – he expected the result of every man's labour to be at least comparable with, if not better than, his own. For this truly incredible capacity for hard work, for the painstaking attention he was always willing to devote to the smallest detail despite the constantly soaring vision of his mind, above all for his dogged persistence in adversity, his men respected him. But if he demanded much he was also prepared to give much in return. To all with whom he worked he became a firm and constant friend whose loyalty knew no bounds. And it was for this sterling and all too rare quality that they loved him.

Even so, all went in awe of him. Woe it was to anyone foolish enough to betray that mutual trust, or in any other way default. A tongue lashing from an irate Isambard Brunel was a rare occurrence indeed, in both senses of the word, but an experience not soon to be forgotten either by recipient or witness. Nor was there ever a second chance for a transgressor. Any man who showed himself to be lacking in any way was finished.

At ten o'clock on the night of Friday, 11 January, Isambard relieved Will Gravatt. Nothing untoward having occurred during the shift just ending, little verbal elaboration of the official reports and analysed soil samples were either necessary or indulged in. These two, and Beamish, had worked together so closely for so long now that communication concerning anything to do with the tunnel was almost telepathic. Big Will was grey with fatigue – twelve hours below ground was a very long time indeed – and looked sadly in need of a shave and a bath. Only a few years older than Isambard, he did his best to match the other's speed of thought and action. But, clever engineer though he might be, and always the most dependable of assistants, Will lacked that essential imaginative flair which immediately distinguishes genius from mere exceptional competence. At heart Gravatt was as aware of this limitation as he was of Brunel's superiority. But there was no bitterness in his knowledge, and such was the spirit of the man that he never gave up trying.

'Pressure increases in One, Two and Three up to high tide, both last night and this morning, were negligible,' said Will as he gathered together his personal odds and ends preparatory to leaving the tiny wooden cabin which was situated in the Western Arch a hundred feet or so back from the working face. It followed the shield at that distance, being portable enough to be moved with ease, serving both as a site office and, not infrequently, a bedroom for Isambard. When things were not going well he would spend anything up to forty-eight hours or more at a stretch below ground, and then he would curl up in the battered old armchair which was a permanent fixture in one corner of the cabin. He had the enviable knack of being able to sleep perfectly soundly whenever he chose, never for longer than forty or fifty minutes and, notwithstanding the most atrocious conditions of noise, damp and cold, waking as rested and refreshed as if he had enjoyed a full eight hours in the most comfortable of fourposters.

'No troubles at all then?' He was surprised by the news. Though progress had been excellent, one of their many problems had been the curious behaviour of the ground in front of frames One, Two and Three.

'Nary a one.' Gravatt yawned hugely, displaying a great cavern of a mouth, then scrubbed at his stubbled face and tousled head with a ham-like hand. 'Looks like it could only have been a small forest after all. We're back in open fields again.'

'Hmm. Looks like,' the other agreed, but without too much conviction. If they really were out of the forest as Will put it, then it was very good news indeed; but he preferred to wait for more positive evidence before getting too excited. He was no pessimist, quite the reverse in fact. But if he had learned anything at all in his thirty months under the bed of London's river, it was that nothing save the imminent possibility of being suddenly confronted with the totally unexpected was ever to be taken as a certainty. 'Well, we'll see what the next tide brings.'

'I'll wager you'll have as clear a run as I've had.'

'Half a guinea?'

'I'll even give you odds.'

'Done. Goodnight, Will.'

As soon as Gravatt had gone, Isambard went to the logbook in which was kept an accurately detailed record of every shift worked. He turned back six days. Though he already knew practically every word by heart, he carefully scrutinised each entry once more, just in case he might somehow have overlooked a clue, even the tiniest glimmer of a clue, that might throw some light on the mystery that had baffled them all for the past week.

There was evidence of what was presumed to be a considerable subterranean spring which rose somewhere near, though its exact location was even now not determinable. Also, there appeared to be a corresponding soft spot in the river bed. Presumably as a consequence of both these factors, there had been a disturbing sequence of curious and wholly unpredictable variations in the condition of the ground, especially on the extreme western edge of the face. As the tide rose to about half flood, dry hard clay would be forced through hardly observable openings. Then silt and water began to run with rapidly increasing pressure, but always in irregular fits and starts. At high water the pressure could, with no warning at all, become almost uncontainable, then, for no known or imaginable reason, just as suddenly fall off. On the ebb the rate of flow, if it hadn't already ceased, generally just petered out, though sometimes it seemed to take an inordinately long time to do so.

It really was all very perplexing and not a little unnerving, for everything seemed to be happening at the wrong time. This meant that any attempt to forecast conditions was not only impossible, potentially it was highly dangerous. The first encounter with the phenomenon had been so completely unexpected it had taken the combined efforts of a full mining crew just to hold the faces of the three frames affected, so enormous and rapid had been the pressure increase. But there had been no comparable crisis since.

Having failed to garner anything new, Isambard left the cabin. He picked his way through the busy two-way traffic of burly labourers trundling their enormous barrows along the raised plank walk that ran the full length of the tunnel to afford reasonably dry access to the working face. Below the plank walk a bucket-pump gang toiled endlessly, most of its members stripped to the waist and running with sweat despite the raw, bone-chilling cold of that awesome, echoing tomb-like vault of dripping stone and brickwork.

To the first-time visitor, however, even if fortunate to be blessed with the least sensitive of noses, it wasn't the size or even the location of the tunnel that made the greatest initial impression. It was its unbelievably foul stench. Indeed, in the dim light of lanterns suspended from the apexes of both arches it was almost possible to see the thick vile air which seemed to hang with sound-deadening effect over that grim scene of watery desolation and frantic activity like a grey, all-enveloping shroud. In sharp contrast, the shield, luridly illuminated by a pair of flaring gas jets, had the appearance of the maw of some monstrous hellish furnace.

Josiah Corby, recently appointed general works foreman and an old Brunel employee, was on the plank walk, and Isambard paused to have a quick word with him. Marc might, at times, be extremely gullible, but to some extent this failing of his was more than counterbalanced by his ability to hang onto a good man once he had

25

the good fortune to find him. Corby had been senior face foreman – the position now held by Sam Hall, another old hand of similar calibre – but had been trapped in the flood and his nerve as far as face work was concerned had been completely broken. But he had been by far the best man on the job and rather than lose him Isambard had, with Marc's agreement, put him in overall charge of the labourers.

A fully manned shift numbered some 190 individuals: 36 miners, plus 6 boys, 30 masons and bricklayers, and 120 labourers. All face workers – miners, masons and bricklayers – were hand picked and were one hundred per cent reliable. Not so the labourers, however. The majority were immigrant Irish and there were times when they tended to behave like overgrown children. They could work well enough when they had a mind to, in fact none could match them for sheer physical strength and endurance which was, of course, why they were employed. But unless constantly and rigorously disciplined they could quickly get hopelessly out of hand. There had been troubles a-plenty with them in the past, particularly in the immediate aftermath of the irruption, when for weeks at a time everybody's nerves had been stretched to the very limit. Panic would soon reduce this reasonably close-knit team of mutually co-operative if rough-hewn comrades to a screaming stampede of terrified animals. One of the first things they would do if they thought danger threatened was to make an already perilous situation infinitely more perilous by putting out all the lights, in the belief that the flood waters would not be able to find them in the dark.

One painfully memorable night, not so very long before, Kemble, the surface nightwatchman, had come to Isambard barely minutes after the latter had finished a shift in the tunnel to tell him the Thames had flooded in again and that water had already risen high into the Cow Court shaft. Scarcely able to believe what he was hearing, but convinced by the man's stupefied fear it must be so, Brunel wasted no time in argument. He raced to the shaft to find, sure enough, a mob of terrified 'Irishers' fighting to escape from its Stygian depths. Expecting every minute to splash into the rising flood, he forced his way down the pitch-dark staircase in an effort to reach those who, the fleeing men were screaming, were trapped below. He'd found himself well inside the completed length of the Eastern Arch before he'd realised the distance he had come. There was no flood. Since that episode Corby had ruled the labourers with a rod of iron, and by so doing had managed to keep his own, at times obviously shattered, nerves under control.

Work on the face was a dull, laboriously repetitive routine performed for a full and continuous twelve-hour shift by the three dozen miners – the toughest, most phlegmatically disposed and experienced men it had been possible to recruit from the Durham coalfields. To the uninitiated outsider they appeared little better than savages, speaking a language and living to a strange, apparently brutal code of behaviour entirely their own. But to Isambard Brunel these men were the salt of the earth.

Each of the twelve, three-storied iron frames – which were numbered from west to east and together made up the tunnelling shield – was held firmly in position against the working face by massive rearward-facing screwjacks at top and bottom which abutted against the leading edges of the arches. They stood on huge independently movable cast-iron feet, the ground above supported by a series of narrow iron plates. The shield was thus divided into thirty-six separate working cells, seven foot high by three foot wide and nine foot deep. The miners were responsible for the operation of what were called poling boards – fourteen to each cell and so numbered from top to bottom. These were three-foot lengths of hard timber, six inches wide and three inches thick, held horizontally against the earth by independent screwjacks secured at either end to the sides of the frame.

Their actions strictly co-ordinated by a foreman, all the miners simultaneously removed one poling board at a time, excavated the ground to an even depth of six inches, then replaced the boards, adjusting the screwjacks to put them firmly in contact with the earth again. It was essential for the men to work together in this way to minimise the stress variation on the shield's component frames, the structure as a whole being continuously subjected to truly enormous pressure. When all 504 boards had been so repositioned, the process was repeated. Then the shield had to be advanced, its frames, each weighing many tons, being manhandled separately. This was done by a series of huge wedges hammered home between the frame and the leading edge of the arch as all its poling boards were gradually retracted. Then fresh abutments for the main jacks had to be constructed.

To move the whole structure in this way – even under ideal

conditions, which were rarely encountered – was the work of one shift, the actual excavations and preparations for the move having been done, again in theory, during the previous shift. The advance completed, and with the frames once more accurately aligned, the bricklayers moved in followed by masons to face the newly laid courses with stone. A timber staging dismantled from the rear as it was no longer required had to be re-erected immediately behind the advanced shield, and from this the bricklayers and stonemasons worked while the miners pressed on with the next series of excavations.

It was at best a painfully slow process. To gain a full twelve inches within the allotted span of two full shifts was considered little less than a fine achievement. So a total advance of nearly six hundred feet in just over nineteen months of actual forward operation was therefore something approaching a minor miracle. In nine or ten days' time, a fortnight at most if the present rate could be maintained, the shield would stand exactly halfway under the river. Isambard had in no way exaggerated when he'd told Ellen Hulme that the stupendous project could be brought to a successful conclusion within the next two years – all things, of course, being equal.

In spite of the recent setback, the ever growing worries about money and the almost daily increasing numbers of less confident faces and voices, there remained a small but effective hortative faction of the company's proprietors who remained staunchly undaunted. Had he been of more mature years, young Brunel might perhaps not have shared their optimism quite to the extent he did, though given the strength and resilience of his complex personality this is by no means certain. After all, a pioneer without an inexhaustible measure of hope in his basic make-up to sustain him in times of trial and tribulation, and to fall back on when all else failed, must surely be doomed irrevocably.

The long night proved totally uneventful. High tide, shortly after midnight, brought no increase at all in pressure. It looked as if Will Gravatt had won his wager. As was his habit, Isambard had spent most of the shift in the frames with his miners. He was accepted as one of them, sharing their jokes, their discomforts and dangers, even, on occasion, joining in their boisterous horseplay.

At six o'clock on Saturday morning the new shift came on. While the crews were changing over he took advantage of the comparative quiet to write up the log and to breakfast on a foul-tasting sandwich and an equally foul-tasting cup of coffee; everything in the tunnel tasted the same, but everyone had long since ceased either to notice or to care. He had barely finished the entry when Michael Lane, the foreman bricklayer, stuck his head round the open door of the cabin.

'Sorry to bring you bad news, but it looks as though numbers One, Two and Three may have started their tricks again.'

The expression on Brunel's face did not change as he automatically checked the clock and noted the time in the logbook before reaching for the tide tables. But Lane knew that inwardly he must be cursing. His own language when he'd been told had been prime. Just when it looked as if the wretched problem had solved itself, here they were right back to the beginning again; it really was enough to provoke a saint to blasphemy, and Michael Lane was certainly no saint. Nor was Isambard Brunel, come to that. It was just that he managed to exercise a little more self control.

'Ball thinks you'd best have a look at it before they start.'

'I'll get along there straightaway.'

Lane knew that Brunel would not now leave the tunnel until he was satisfied all was well once more, even though it might take days. He, too, had been on duty all night and was dog tired. All the same he readily volunteered to remain below if he could be of any use.

'Probably no more than a repetition of last week's fun and games,' Isambard declined Lane's offer with a genuinely grateful smile.

'Do you want me to mention it to Beamish?'

'No, I'll send up a message after I've looked things over.'

Lane nodded and left. With a grimace Isambard gulped down the remains of his now cold as well as foul-tasting coffee, then hurried out of the cabin.

Sam Ball's familiar round-shouldered, long-armed, stocky figure (he had known Isambard since the day he'd been born) was silhouetted against the gas light and he knuckled a beetling black-haired brow as Brunel approached.

'Mornin' Master Isambard.'

'Morning Sam. We've got trouble again I hear.'

Ball shook his head and scratched absent-mindedly at a misshapen ear. 'Don't rightly know as it's trouble or not as yet. But she'm a definite bit of mystery still. You lookit for eeself.'

The cells of One, Two and Three stood empty, their erstwhile

29

occupants looking unusually shaken and extremely wet and bedraggled. The rest of the crew were still at their posts, but had not yet started on the preliminary work of moving the shield. 'I 'ad 'em 'old off till you'd gave the word,' Ball explained.

All nine cells bore evidence of what had clearly alarmed the foreman and his crew. And understandably, for it looked to be far more serious than anything so far encountered. Malignant gobbets of glutinous ooze had been forced in vast quantities through the narrow gaps between the poling boards of the top cell of number One. The others were still dripping water. The magnitude of the sudden pressure surge was all too obvious and Isambard did not like the look of things at all. He gave no outward sign; but he knew perfectly well that Sam Ball and every man present was just as capable as he was of interpreting the testimony of his own eyes.

'Poor old Collins 'ere got a phiz-full, didn't you old covey,' Ball chuckled, as much to break the mounting tension of the moment as anything else.

Collins, squat, hugely muscled, bull necked, who, as crew leader, occupied number One top, must have since dunked his close-cropped head in a bucket, for Isambard could not recall ever having seen him looking quite so clean before. The effect was immediately spoiled, however, by Collins rubbing the grimy palm of a horny hand over his still wet visage, thereby restoring its customary hue.

'What did it taste like, Collins?' Brunel enquired, smiling.

'I just ain't got the words to describe it, sir,' came the growled reply. But the vehemence with which the miner spat into the puddle at his feet spoke volumes and brought forth a ripple of unsympathetic laughter from his now grinning fellows.

'All right, Sam. Let's get the muck cleaned off. Then we can see exactly what's happened.'

Josiah Corby was still on duty and one of the boys was sent to fetch him. Rarely was he to be seen anywhere near the frames now. He would come if summoned, but the effort it cost him was at times pitiful to behold. Isambard simply did not know the meaning of fear. He could not recall having been afraid of anything in his life. During and immediately following the flood he had, quite without thinking, risked his life again and again – sometimes, he later willingly admitted, utterly foolishly. However, it was in no small measure because of that foolishness that six men, including Josiah Corby, were still alive. But his most reckless escapade had been in the diving bell. He and Will Gravatt had gone down to survey the breakthrough in the river bed. In order to get a closer look at the exposed head of the shield, Isambard had casually dived off the bell's footboard completely disregarding the fact he had made no provision for his return. He could swim like an eel and, able to hold his breath quite comfortably for two minutes or more, he had indulged a leisurely examination. It was not until he tried to return that he realised that going down was one thing, getting back without a safety line was something else again. He had succeeded, but only with the greatest difficulty, and only just in time. Even so, he had experienced no feeling of fear at all, either during or after the episode.

'Get your men clear of the tunnel please Jo,' he told the foreman when the lad had brought him. There might be nothing to worry about after all; equally curious things had happened before. And if such did turn out to be the case – and pray God it did – he would bitterly regret the time wasted. Anything, however, was preferable to another panic.

Alarm immediately kindled in Corby's pale watery eyes. 'Just a precautionary measure, that's all,' Isambard gave the man no time to voice his fears. 'As soon as you get back to the surface, I want you, personally, to report to Mr Beamish and give him this.' He handed Corby a hurriedly scribbled note. Beamish would probably be in the site office at the head of the shaft.

The foreman took the note with a shaking hand, his lips trembling and eyes wide and wild with terror. Then, masking his fear by a visible effort of will, he nodded shortly and abruptly turned away.

'All ready Master Isambard.'

'Thank you Sam.'

Forty-one pairs of eyes watched him intently as he climbed nimbly to the second tier of the masons' staging. It was his responsibility to tackle the problem in number One personally. Even if it hadn't been he would have insisted on doing so, just as Sam Ball now insisted on helping him. And he knew perfectly well that as soon as he called for a dozen volunteers to remain in the frames, all the others, including the four boys, would raise their hands. They did. Only after Collins who threatened to fight any and all for the right to stay and eleven other equally determined belligerents had eventually sorted themselves out, did the remainder reluctantly retire.

While the rest stood by on the staging ready to act the instant their assistance might be called for, Isambard, Ball and Collins entered number One top. The flow of water had ceased. There had been no further percolation, not even the suggestion of any seepage, absolutely nothing to indicate that anything might be amiss. After carefully probing the gaps between the poling boards and listening intently but in vain for the sound of movement, they cautiously released, then removed, the first board. Behind it they were amazed to find the ground hard and dry. Equally cautiously the board was locked firmly back in position. In the same way the second poling board was removed. Here, too, the ground appeared hard and dry. The second board was replaced. Nor behind the third, fourth and fifth did they find anything that could be interpreted as evidence of even a potential source of trouble. All seemed perfectly normal. But as the sixth board was about to be re-secured the ground behind it, seemingly as dry and as firm as before, suddenly surged and swelled like a live thing. Then a tremendously powerful jet of thick mud tore one end of the heavy board loose.

By ducking quickly to one side Ball just managed to avoid being decapitated. Collins immediately flung his weight against the flailing timber, but was unable to keep his feet. Brunel, caught by the full force of the jet, was hurled hard against one of the right-hand uprights of the frame. Completely winded, he collapsed through the narrow gap and was sprawling helplessly in number Two top, its poling boards too by now beginning to creak and strain alarmingly.

For several seconds the lethal barrage of gravel-loaded mud made it virtually impossible for anyone even to move. Then came the water. As soon as they were able the miners swung into the frames to do what they could to stem the flood. Shaken, but unhurt, Ball and Collins tried frantically to get the loose board secured. Still gasping for breath, Isambard could only hang on grimly to prevent himself being swept bodily out of number Two top by the truly frightening force of water that had begun to jet between its boards. But it was only too clear that already the pressure behind the flood was far too great to be contained even with a full crew. It could be no more than a matter of minutes before the whole working face must give way. Realising with sinking heart there was nothing they could do to prevent a second major irruption, Isambard ordered his men to abandon the frames and run for their lives.

Chapter Three

'JE..US God above! The Thames is in again!' That horrified cry finally convinced Dick Beamish and sent him racing, white faced and fearful, for the shaft from which panic-stricken men were beginning to fight their way out.

Alone in the site office, the general works foreman began to sob hysterically, until, finally sapped of all strength, he collapsed. Despite all efforts to keep a grip on himself, by the time he'd got to Beamish, Corby had been wild eyed, deathly pale, and only just in control of ragged nerves for too long stretched too far. Desperately he'd tried to think clearly and calmly. But the nightmare memories which had never ceased to haunt him since those terrible hours in the tunnel just seven months before suddenly became too vivid to be bearable any longer. A thousand times and more he had dreamed dreams so hideous he had long since grown too terrified to sleep, to face being left alone, even to close his eyes. And when he'd burst in on Beamish he'd scarcely known for certain whether what was happening was real, or whether it was all another horrifying dream.

In spite of Corby's insistence that his message came from Master Isambard himself – he had by this time lost and forgotten the note he had been given – Beamish, who was busy checking his clerk's returns for the issue of gin and warm beer to the miners who had just come off shift, dismissed it all as yet another false alarm, the deplorable state of Corby's nerves being no secret. Indeed, to Richard Beamish he seemed in an even worse state of mortal funk than Kemble and the Irishers on the night of the notorious panic. And as if to confirm that not altogether unreasonable conclusion the already unnaturally high-pitched voice cracked into an inarticulate scream as the foreman gabbled frantically at him. Then came that dreadful cry.

Josiah Corby lay where he had fallen, whimpering like a terrified child. Paralysed by imagined terror, tormented by nightmare memories of the past, his feeble grip on his last remaining shreds of

33

sanity was slowly and inexorably being prised loose.

Such was the force and quickly mounting magnitude of the flood, that by the time Collins and the other eleven miners got clear of the scaffolding behind the frames, the water was already lapping over the plank walk. Their danger was acute, and they knew it. If the shield held and the rate of flooding did not increase further they might, with luck, just have time to gain the safety of the shaft before the rush of water made it impossible for them to keep their feet, assuming, of course, the plank walk remained intact that long. But should the shield collapse they were already doomed, for then something akin to a tidal wave would engulf them. And in such a maelstrom no man, no living creature could possibly survive.

All Isambard had to do to leave the top cell of number Two was relax his grip on the side of the frame. Immediately he was swept down onto the staging beside Sam Ball, who broke his fall and helped him keep his feet on the wildly plunging timbers. Torn from its anchorage, the structure, substantial and extensive though it was, had been twisted sideways, jammed hard against the outer wall of the Western Arch, and was beginning to disintegrate like so much matchwood. Ball was bellowing something at him, but the combined cacophonies of rushing water, creaking snapping wood and screeching metal were so deafening that, though the man's lips were only inches from his ear, Brunel could not make out a single syllable. He assumed Sam was telling him that all the men were safely away, and with a hurried nod he indicated they should follow, and just as quickly as possible. Isambard might be fearless, but he was no fool. Nor was Sam Ball.

The first twenty feet or so of the plank walk plainly being in imminent danger of collapse, they had no alternative but to plunge into the already waist-deep water. It was a violently whirlpooling, foam-topped, debris-laden welter of menacing black turbulence which sucked and pulled at their bodies like quicksand. Still dazed and sore from the blow he had taken to the chest, Isambard was grateful for the support of Sam's long and powerful arm. But they had managed to struggle only a few short yards when a violent surge knocked him off his feet tearing him from that life-preserving grasp. Floundering helplessly, he was vaguely aware of anxious staring eyes and vainly clutching hands. Then a viciously numbing blow to the small of his back again drove the breath from his body and he went

34

under. Somehow he managed to claw his way back from what would surely have been the fatal depths of unconsciousness. But before he was able once more to gulp at the foul but still life-giving air above, his lungs were near to bursting point.

When at last he did surface it was pitch black. The gas jets had been blown out and every single lantern had failed. The wonder was they had stayed alight so long. Once he'd controlled his spluttering and could breathe again, Isambard's first thought was for Sam Ball. Where was he? Had he managed to get out or was he, too, floundering about helplessly? Or worse, was he injured and in need of help? He tried calling. But it was useless. He had no breath to spare. In any case, no one could possibly hear another's voice in that hideous, ear-shattering, mind-destroying hell. He could only trust to Sam's oft-tried and proved toughness of body and spirit, and hope for the best.

Exactly how, Isambard would never be too sure, but somehow he himself managed to survive. At least he was still alive – if only just. But now his lungs were no longer being tortured he was acutely aware of even more agonising pain in the small of his back, and he'd done something to his right knee which meant his leg was next to useless. Again he was knocked down, though he managed to save himself from being sucked under. But in that murderous torrent, threatened both by its wildly tossed flotsam and a constant rain of debris from above, he could do little more than try to keep afloat.

Suddenly he found himself being swept sharply to his right, the abrupt change of direction taking him completely unawares. Under he went again. But now the water was calmer. He surfaced almost immediately and was able, at last, to swim a little. Once he realised he'd been carried through one of the connecting archways and was now in the Eastern Arch he knew he had a chance – a slim chance to be sure what with the drag of his injured leg and his now fast-waning strength, but a chance nonetheless. And a chance was all he needed. But scarcely had he succeeded in thus orientating himself than an enormous wave which filled the tunnel to the apex of its arch, crashed down on him and he was once more fighting desperately for air, for life itself.

The works staircase in the Cow Court shaft was jammed solid with terrified men. Beamish could get no sense out of any of them. No one could tell him exactly what was happening below. He did his best to restore some sort of order, but panic had taken far too strong a hold. The mining crew was still somewhere at the bottom of the shaft, and to get down that main staircase was impossible.

There was a second, smaller stairway reserved for important visitors, the door to which was kept locked. Beamish carried a key. In his haste, however, he somehow managed to jam the lock. Cursing at his clumsiness, he struggled furiously to free it. In the murky dawn of that dark January morning the anonymous figures flitting with noisy but aimless urgency through the black shadows were all deaf to Beamish's shouted commands and appeals for assistance, heedless of his blasphemously impassioned imprecations. Finally, with a sledgehammer hurriedly obtained from the nearby engine house, he smashed the heavy door open, the sudden release of air trapped behind it filling his eyes and lungs with stinging grit and dust.

Momentarily blinded, he paused to listen in horror to the roar and splash of the raging flood below. Having experienced some of the worst moments of the previous flood he knew, or thought he knew, what to expect. But if sound alone was anything to go by, that catastrophe would seem to be as nothing compared to the magnitude of this one. With trembling fingers he fumbled with flint and steel to light the gas jet and the emergency lantern that was kept at the head of the staircase. By their light his worst fears were confirmed. The tunnel appeared to be completely flooded.

He picked his way down the slippery staircase. A huge surge boiled nearly halfway up the shaft, drenching him with spray. Still he could see only dimly what awaited him below. It wasn't until he got down to the level of the water that he realised that what he had taken to be just another piece of floating debris was, in fact, a body. Powerless to reach it he could only watch helplessly as it was tossed about and rolled over and over by the capriciously swirling water. When at last he did succeed in dragging it clear, Richard Beamish stared in horror at the apparently lifeless form of Marc Brunel's son.

Brunel was more than half drowned and deeply unconscious. Once he'd discovered Isambard was still breathing, Beamish wasted no time trying to revive him there and then – the water was icy and the morning bitterly cold – but got him at once to the life-giving warmth of the engine house. Old Toby, the engine-house keeper, whose proud boast it was to have been apprenticed to a blacksmith who had once worked with none other than the great John Smeaton of lighthouse fame, promptly produced blankets, dry clothing and even a flask of rough but welcome brandy from the dark recesses of a secret cubby hole behind the coal bunkers. His expert ministrations soon brought at least a vestige of colour back to Isambard's bloodless features. Once satisfied he was out of immediate danger, Beamish had no hesitation in leaving him in the old man's care while he went off to see what the situation was outside. A lifetime spent in every imaginable field of engineering had taught Old Toby as much and more than any practising physician could have learned when it came to caring for a victim of practically any sort of accident or mishap.

The surge of water that had torn Isambard from Sam Ball's grip was caused by the side shores of number One giving way. Seconds later Ball's head had been smashed by a baulk of timber dislodged from the disintegrating staging. Had he succeeded in holding on to his companion both must surely have been killed. When all the lights had been blown out the fleeing miners had plunged on through the darkness; but before any could gain the safety of the shaft they were overwhelmed as the plank walk collapsed. Nine of the twelve survived. One of those killed was Collins. In the shaft two labourers were drowned in the backwash of the surge that had drenched Beamish. Meanwhile, Josiah Corby had cried himself into a peaceful, mercifully dreamless sleep, the first he had known for more than half a year – a sleep from which he was never to wake.

But already Marc Brunel was on site and had taken charge. Will Gravatt and Michael Lane had been sent for, as had as many face workers as could be contacted, and a doctor had been summoned. Relieved and reassured by the news of his son's rescue, Marc, with the faithful Beamish at his side, set about tackling an all too familiar but nonetheless melancholy task.

Once it was known for certain that all survivors were clear of the tunnel and the shaft, some sort of disciplined order began to emerge from the chaos which had reigned unchecked since the irruption. A hurried roll-call established exactly who was missing. Six men, excluding Corby, were presumed to have lost their lives. The rest were issued with warm clothing and a double ration of hot rum. Then the least dependable among them were dismissed and the remainder put to work in an attempt to make some sort of assessment of the extent of the damage. But it was not possible even to get to the bottom of the shaft, let alone gain access to the tunnel.

When Marc finally got around to visiting the engine house it was to find Isambard engaged in a noisy quarrel with a Doctor Morris, a large florid man with a very loud voice and no bedside manner. Purple of visage and positively pop-eyed with indignation, the doctor turned on Marc as soon as the latter had identified himself.

'Sir, your son is, without question, quite the most unco-operative and obstinate patient it has ever been my misfortune to be confronted with.'

Looking at Isambard as he lay white faced and exhausted on the blankets Toby had piled for him in front of the furnace, this statement, to an outsider, would have been difficult to believe. But, as a wise father, Marc Brunel knew his son only too well. He acknowledged Isambard's painfully nodded greeting with a faint smile before giving his full attention to the irate physician.

'I take it you have completed your diagnosis, Doctor?'

'I have, Sir,' Morris snapped back, wiping his brow and his hands on a large, none-too-clean coloured handkerchief fished from his coat-tail pocket, 'severe and extensive bruising, both external and internal, to the middle and lower lumbar region; and incipient and probably highly dangerous fever resulting from exposure; and a badly sprained knee.'

The knee – the least of the young man's injuries, the doctor went on to explain tersely – required urgent treatment with both hot and cold compresses. The fever, if its effect was to be successfully minimised, necessitated immediate and drastic bleeding. But the lumbar injury, potentially the most dangerous by far, demanded instant confinement to bed if the worst was to be avoided. In short, unless so compressed, cupped and confined, without further delay – for several hours had already elapsed since the injuries had been sustained – no physician worth his salt, and most certainly not he, James Jeremiah Morris MD, could reasonably be held responsible for the consequences. 'Which will be dire!' Morris warned in sober conclusion. 'I do not exaggerate when I tell you this foolish young man, by his refusal to do as I say, may well be killing himself.'

But Brunel fils, equally as stubborn as Brunel père would have been in similar circumstances, was adamant. He flatly refused either to listen to reason or to leave the site.

Once recovered from the shock of his ordeal and his grief over Sam Ball's loss, Isambard had quickly grasped the seriousness of the situation. If there was to be any chance at all of saving the tunnel this time, both the cause of the irruption and the full extent of the damage had to be ascertained as quickly and as accurately as possible. That would mean using the diving bell again, with the operation of which only he and Will Gravatt were really fully conversant. And although even he had to concede that it was unthinkable for him to attempt a descent he could at least, he maintained, advise and, if need be, direct operations from the surface.

The bell and its barge had to be manhandled upstream from the West India Docks on the Isle of Dogs. Fortunately it was available. But by the time it had been manoeuvred into position above the breach in the river bed and securely moored, the day was far advanced and the bleak winter light beginning to fail. Nothing more could be done until next day. In the hope that the weather which alone had so far favoured them would continue to do so, the weary toilers settled to pass a long night as best they might.

Still Isambard insisted on staying. More irate than ever, Doctor Morris had him bedded down in the site office. They made him as comfortable as they could, but he had a wretchedly sleepless, restless time, and during the next seemingly endless day there were long periods as he lay on the deck of the barge when he appeared to be barely conscious. Nevertheless, his continued presence seemed to serve as a source of inspiration to Beamish, Gravatt and the others – inspiration sorely needed in the face of the damnable luck which persistently dogged all their efforts that black Sunday. Everything, it seemed, that could go wrong did go wrong before the diving bell could finally be lowered.

It was the moment of truth. If the shield were still in position the tunnel could be saved. But if it had collapsed, was too badly damaged, or even if it had shifted by more than the smallest fraction – and the odds must surely be that it had – then it was all over. They were finished.

For what seemed an eternity the workers and watchers on both banks of the river waited in silence and growing apprehension. By the time the bell surfaced the light was again beginning to fade. The shield, Gravatt reported, was still there. It was almost totally exposed; but it was undamaged. And it had not moved.

Supported on his father's arm, Isambard heard the news through a barely penetrable fog of pain and fever and a mind-warping delirium in which the ghosts of Corby, Ball, Collins and the others, every one of whom he recognised and knew by name, were reaching out for him. His final confused memory was of Doctor Morris's face, which seemed to fill his whole field of vision like some huge purple sun, its gruff-voiced owner at long last issuing an order his patient could not countermand.

As they picked up the mattress on which he lay he was briefly conscious of never before having felt so miserably, so abominably, ill. The slightest movement caused him unbearable agony, as if his body was being slowly and deliberately broken into a thousand separate pieces, each piece an independent source of dreadful torment.

Then mercifully, he fainted.

Chapter Four

WHETHER the efficacy of Doctor Richard Russell's celebrated sea-bathing 'cures' first practised more than fifty years before had ever matched their popularity had never been, and probably never would be, satisfactorily resolved. But while the actual imbibing of sea water was by the 1820s rarely advocated, there was still an ever growing number of medical practitioners more than ready to recommend that their convalescent patients take advantage of the restorative benefits of sea air whenever possible. One such was Doctor Travers, the Brunel family physician of many years' standing. He had relieved Doctor Morris of all responsibility for the injured Isambard and, as soon as the young man's recovery was judged sufficiently advanced, packed him off to Brighton for a fortnight.

Not since his early schooldays had Isambard travelled the Brighton Road. Vividly he remembered wretched road surfaces which made any progress in excess of a moderately fast walking pace a near impossibility, even under the most ideal weather conditions. Then, every journey from the Blossoms Inn in Lawrence Lane in London to Brighton's Castle Square had been a tedious bone-shaking nightmare interspersed with numerous and necessarily prolonged stops en route for refreshment, rest, and, above all, recuperation. Hostelries at Sutton, Banstead Downs, Reigate, Handcross, Staplefield Common, Cuckfield, Clayton Hill and Patcham had afforded the weary travellers respite from the torment of aching limbs, bruised bodies and utter boredom. But for all that, it had never been a journey to be lightly ventured upon. Even the eleven-mile haul from the Blossoms to the Cock at Sutton had meant a two-hour incarceration in a cramped and stuffy pair-horse coach. But now, even in the depths of winter, as long as the road was clear of snow and ice, the whole fifty-two miles could be covered in less than three hours with but five stops to change horses, and during only one of these did passengers find it necessary, or indeed have time, to partake of any form of substantial sustenance.

The Bristol–Bath Turnpike had been the first public highway to be completely 'macadamised'. But the construction techniques since perfected by Thomas Telford – whom Poet Laureate Robert Southey had dubbed the 'Colossus of Roads' – topped by John Loudon McAdam's truly superb surfacing, had made the Brighton Road one of the, if not the, finest in the world.

After ten days in bed at Blackfriars, to young Brunel the journey down from London proved to be a tonic in itself. Not for him the slow and stately progress of *The Sovereign,* that most comfortable and reputedly safest of the many coaches which plied the Brighton route and on which his doctor had advised him to travel. Quite openly trading on his current fame, having been publicly commended by the directors of the Thames Tunnel Company and prominently featured in the many dramatic newspaper accounts of the disaster, he easily acquired the always much coveted box seat beside the coachman of *The Comet,* foremost among the crack Brighton 'flyers'. On one of the fastest stretches between Cuckfield and Patcham he had 'handled the ribbons' for nearly the whole of the run. The four fresh thoroughbreds had gone magnificently; not for many a day had he known such marvellous exhilaration. And the best was yet to come, for Brighton, which was now to English society what the Georgian city of Bath had once been, turned out to be brilliant, even in winter. But instead of the intended fourteen, his holiday was to last a mere five short days.

The morning of the fourth he spent in composing a long letter to Ellen Hulme. She already knew all about the accident, of course, so he told her in detail everything that had happened since, doing his best to make the prospects for the future sound a little less bleak than he suspected they really were. He then went on to describe Brighton to her. He wrote of the pleasant company he had found there, of his strolls before breakfast on the famous Chain Pier – the first of its kind in England – and of the splendid ball he had attended the night before, but making no reference to the delightful young lady in whose company he had spent most of his time.

Late that same afternoon he first began to feel unwell. Reluctantly he made his excuses to his intended companions of the evening and went to bed early. During the night he was taken quite violently ill, and by the middle of the following morning was in a serious state of collapse. He was far too weak to travel alone so Dick Beamish came down in a hired chariot to take him not to Blackfriars but to the Barge House in Lambeth, the home of his sister and brother-in-law, where Doctor Travers was awaiting his arrival.

This time the diagnosis really was alarming. The blow to his back which had so nearly caused him to drown in the flood, had inflicted serious kidney damage. Both were malfunctioning. Obviously they had been since the accident; but because the symptoms of such injury took time to manifest themselves clearly, the true extent of the damage had gone unsuspected. His condition, though not yet critical, was serious – very serious indeed, Travers emphasized. If not improved, and improved quickly, there could be but one outcome. However a cure was possible. But, it would take time, and it could only be effected by strict adherence to a prescribed diet, by complete rest, which meant a protracted period of confinement to bed, and no argument!

The prospect utterly dismayed Isambard, but quite delighted his sister Emma. In striking contrast to her vivacious elder sister and highly intelligent young brother, poor Emma had all her life been the odd one out. She was plain, slow witted, and prone to be easily hurt through being too anxious to please. She should have been married in her tender teens to a none too rich, elderly but virile roué who would have treated her to a moderate measure of mild brutality before leaving her with a brood of harshly begotten young to enjoy her martyrdom of widowed motherhood. In such a role Emma would have been truly superb. As it was, her limited talents had so far been completely wasted and in lieu of being weighed down with a burden of genuine woes she was perpetually plagued with ailments mostly imagined.

At times she could be tiresome to a degree, displaying all the worst possible traits of an embittered, over-emotional old maid. But at heart she was a genuinely selfless angel of mercy who delighted in ministering to the needs of the sick – and the sicker the better – becoming in such circumstances sweetness itself and kindness personified. Emma really had but one hope of salvation, and that was marriage to a totally undemanding, totally moral man, totally devoted to good works in which she could totally share and thereby find total fulfilment. For the nonce, however, she kept house for her parents at Blackfriars, but willingly volunteered to move

43

immediately to Lambeth to stay for as long as she might be needed to nurse her adored young brother back to health.

Much to everybody's surprise and relief he proved to be if not a model, at least a manageable, patient. Stoically he consumed his plain unappetising daily fare with little enthusiasm, but without too much protest; he obediently swallowed the most nauseating concoctions; and he meekly submitted to being leeched sometimes twice in a day, and never less than five times a week. But in total and infuriating disregard of all orders, pleas, cajolery, threats or warnings he refused point-blank to stop smoking, insisting on having his four pipes of canaster a day, come what may. Apart from that there was no argument.

Three months were to pass before the invalid was allowed to leave his bed. Until he was able to do so Doctor Travers forbade all visitors. Not even his father was permitted to see him, so it was not until mid-April that he learned what had been happening at Rotherhithe. 'We had to dump four and a half thousand tons of clay into that hole in the river bed before the pumps could start lowering the level of flood water,' Marc told him soberly. 'And we still haven't finished clearing the tunnel.'

Once again the shield had done all and more than could ever have been expected of it. Naturally Marc was delighted that his invention had proved itself yet again, and his son said nothing to detract from this delight. But the cost of restoration before had been more than £12,000. How much would it be this time? 'Possibly as much as double that figure,' Marc told him. Which meant that once all repairs had been effected, out of the initial £180,000 subscription against the original estimate less than £10,000 would remain, with half the excavation and the constructional work, as well as the whole of the access shaft on the Wapping bank, still to be done.

It was a gloomy picture, unbelievably gloomy when compared with the high hopes entertained at the beginning of the year. But quite apart from anything else, costs had shot up far beyond any reasonable expectation, especially over the last six months – hence the huge discrepancy between the current actual and the original estimate, even allowing for that massive total of unbudgeted expenditure. And as things were, they were likely to go on rising. The country was deep into yet another trade depression, the fifth of its kind since the war. Prospects were uncertain, markets unstable, money was tight and getting tighter with each passing day.

Faced with the growing certainty that any immediate injection of fresh capital into the ailing Thames Tunnel Company was a near impossibility, the fainthearts among the directors were already talking in terms of cutting their losses and abandoning the project for good. Wellington had been Prime Minister of a new government since 25 January and there were hopes that in view of his past efforts on behalf of the company he might be persuaded to use his influence in its favour now. But everything was so terribly vague and dreadfully uncertain.

Though Marc did his best to avoid depressing Isambard too much, he did not altogether succeed. As always, he himself seemed remarkably unconcerned, even cheerful about it all. In the course of his long and adventurous life he had known so many disappointments and frustrations that whatever fate now had a mind to throw in his face he was supremely confident of his ability to throw it right back and survive. 'Have courage,' he said as he finally took his leave, his brown eyes bright behind the polished lenses of his small round spectacles. 'You will learn, my son, as I have learned, that a man who can do something and keep a warm sanguine heart will never starve.'

But despite his father's excellent advice and the buoyancy of his own natural optimism, there were days during his long illness when Isambard's spirits inevitably flagged and black clouds of utter despair gathered about him. On such days almost his only solace was the company of his eldest sister. Emma was a darling in her way and he loved her dearly. She never spared herself in her instant attention to his every need and slightest want, and he was by no means lacking in gratitude. But poor Emma was so terribly dull. She simply could not understand his need for almost constant intellectual stimulation.

Fortunately, for this he was able to rely on Sophia. Not for nothing had Ben Hawes jokingly dubbed his wife 'the Brunel in petticoats', and rarely did Sophia fail to live up to her well-deserved reputation. In so many respects she was like her mother. Sophia Brunel had always taken an active and comprehending interest in all her husband's multifarious works and activities. For his part, Marc never tired of repeating that whatever success he had achieved over the years was due entirely to the inspiration he had received from his beloved spouse. As a married couple they were surely unique – truly

45

a match in a million. Sophia Hawes's devotion to her husband was equally strong, and as loyal. But there was a part of her that had always been, and always would be, given up exclusively to her brilliant brother. Five years older than he, she had taken a pride in his development almost from the cradle.

By the time the slowly lengthening April days at long last dragged into May it became clear that the faint hearts had won. It was Sophia who broke the news that all work on the tunnel was to be suspended immediately, and indefinitely. Prepared as he was for the disappointment, it nevertheless came as a bitter blow. Overnight his wonderful Castles in Spain had become no more than phantom castles in the air. It seemed to him it must be the end. His career was over even before it had properly begun. He had learned enough about human nature to realise that the many flattering promises he had been given in the past would be instantly watered down and then further devalued until they were no more than meaningless friendly wishes for the future. In the harsh world of modern engineering nothing, but nothing, succeeded like success. No matter how glorious or how ignominious it might be, a failure was a failure.

The young Rennies would soon have completed the new London Bridge, he brooded miserably. That achievement alone would give them such a connection with Government as would defy any and all competition. Palmer had recently finished his work on the new London docks, so his future was likewise assured as was that of George Stephenson's son Robert and the Old Man's brilliant star pupil, Joseph Locke, to name but a few. What then of the future of Isambard Brunel? For five years, nearly a quarter of his existence on this earth, he had worked on the magnificent Thames Tunnel, undoubtedly one of the greatest of modern engineering feats, the 'eighth wonder of the world' it had been called. But it was a wonder abandoned whilst still only half complete; what sort of a recommendation was that?

'Damn the Thames Tunnel Company directors! And damn the white-livered proprietors too!' he swore silently. It wasn't only the disappointment over the tunnel that so galled him. To be sure, that was bad enough; but the utter waste of these last five years and the loss of future opportunity that must result was, in many ways, worse. As he saw it, this spineless want of courage on the part of others was the direct cause of all his chances slipping through his fingers like a pig's tail that had been soaped.

Try as he might, he could see himself as no better than an itinerant engineer, sometimes employed, sometimes not. Appalled by the vision, he contemplated the prospect of an income of at most two to three hundred pounds a year. That would scarcely be sufficient to provide the bare essentials of life. Certainly it would by no stretch of the imagination be anywhere near enough for the sort of existence he had always envisaged for himself, for he was unashamedly fond of those luxuries that only money in substantial quantities could provide.

And what of Ellen? I ought to break it off with her, he told himself, for now he could not hope to be in a position to marry for God knew how long; and to continue in the present state of uncertainty would surely be wronging her. There was always her father's firm, of course. Hulme & Company could provide him with a future, and a comfortable future, of sorts. But he knew full well that, much as he was in love with Ellen, he could never reconcile himself to such an abject act of surrender.

That night he insisted that Ben and Sophia and Ben's brothers, Tom and William, took wine in his room, a pleasure he was still denied. They came, solemn faced, and ready to commiserate. 'But I really can't work myself up into being down-hearted,' he assured them brightly. Then he launched into an hilarious monologue of what it meant to be a bedridden invalid. 'I give you a toast,' he concluded, when he had exhausted them all with laughter and it was time for him to take his evening dose of quite revolting medicine. 'Here's to bleeding, sugar of lead, and starvation forever!'

From all but Sophia he successfully concealed his feelings, but not even she could know the true depth and bitterness of her brother's almost hopeless despair.

Chapter Five

THE invitation to spend the summer at Clifton, a residential suburb of Bristol, was one which Isambard accepted with eager gratitude. By mid-June he had progressed sufficiently to be able to think in terms of a change of scene. Cobbett's 'Great Wen' he was finding increasingly unbearable; and Brighton had quite lost its appeal. So when Nicholas Roch, a well-to-do Bristol merchant, a close friend of Ben Hawes and a frequent visitor to the Barge House, suggested the West Country, the problem of where to spend his convalescent holiday was solved almost before it had been posed.

Until the closing years of the previous century Bristol, the second city of the kingdom and still its second largest port, had been supreme in the west, her vast trade with Africa and the Americas in slaves and tobacco, sugar and rum the firm foundation on which her merchants had amassed their fortunes. Such was their prosperity that even the sudden removal of American colonial markets had been accepted with comparative equanimity, the loss being more than compensated by rapid development of equally lucrative Spanish wool and wine trades. For centuries, sturdy broad-beamed West Country merchantmen had ventured far and wide, over near and distant seas, though every voyage completed had begun and ended in the same way. From the Severn Estuary to the Float – the city's docks – along a six-mile stretch of tidal Avon between the looming limestone crags of Clifton Heights on the Gloucestershire side, where the black mouth of the Giant's Cave yawned starkly against the dazzling white of the cliff, and the more gently rising slopes of verdant Somerset, the ships, with sails tight-furled and leadsmen in the chains, had to be hauled by hobblers.

But in recent years steam power and the factory system had revolutionized all manufacturing industry, and none more so than the cotton trade of Lancashire. It was only then that competition from the ancient but never developed port of Liverpool had been taken seriously by the complacent Bristolians. Ideally situated at the mouth of the Mersey – no necessity here for the expensive maintenance of navigable channels – the merchants of Liverpool were able to offer ship owners increasingly superior port facilities, and at considerably less than the extortionate Bristol rates. Small wonder the furiously expanding Lancashire borough, already a boom town like so many of her northern and midland sisters, had become a boom port. And in two years' time, or less, the rail road to Manchester, under construction since before the Stockton & Darlington had been operational, must inevitably pose an even greater threat to Bristol's future.

One of the few seemingly fully alive to this impending danger was Nicholas Roch. A member of the famed Bristol Society of Merchant Venturers, and of the board of the Bristol Dock Company, he was a regular visitor to London. He had been a founder member of John Wilson Croker's recently established Athenaeum and it was there he had met Ben Hawes, a fellow supporter of what had come to be called Reform politics.

Thirty years had passed since Charles Grey – now Earl Grey of Howick – had founded the Society of the Friends of the People, its purpose to promote peaceful constitutional change. Unfortunately, Grey had chosen his moment badly, and until the conclusion of the French wars he and his friends had fared far from well. But now things were different. Thirteen years of postwar industrial upheaval with its accompanying political turmoil had wrought changes in the social order not thought possible. Whole new cities had come into being where before there had been nought but a huddle of hovels. Tens of thousands of their inhabitants, middle- and working-class people, were clamouring for parliamentary representation – their demands, in essence, no different from those of the erstwhile American colonists. While ancient townships euphemistically termed 'rotten boroughs' and others – the gifts of a few great landowners in many instances peopled by no more than a dozen or so enfranchised freeholders – regularly returned mostly nominated Members of Parliament, citizens of the new industrial towns had no one to speak for them.

The truistic leitmotif of the Society of the Friends of the People, originally voiced by just a few scattered soloists, had become an ever swelling ground-base for an increasingly menacing chorale of almost universal protest, the volume of which, if not soon heeded, many feared might shortly shatter forever the glass-brittle foundation of the nation's very existence – for never before had the monarchy and all it stood for been held by so many in such low esteem. It had been hoped Grey would be invited to join Wellington's new administration. But this hope was dashed when the prime minister, though persuaded to accept long overdue legislation to further Catholic emancipation, doggedly declared that the present system of representation deservedly possessed the full and active confidence of the country.

But time was running out. The fires of disaffection were already burning, were spreading rapidly, blazing ever more fiercely. Should they flare out of control the result might well be nothing less than open rebellion.

There was nothing at Clifton to compare with the diversity of delight Brighton had had to offer. The Roch residence was an unpretentious but luxurious mansion built by Nicholas's grandfather in what was now a fashionable suburb. Even of ordinary social activity, there was little, save for the occasional exchange of visits with neighbours and friends. But the superb scenery – from its terrace the house commanded one of the finest views of the Avon Gorge – more than compensated for such trivial paucities, and the weather could not have been bettered. Day after golden day the sun blazed down out of cloudless skies. It rained with sufficient regularity to preserve the lush green of downland and woods, but the majority of the sometimes quite heavy showers seemed obligingly confined to the hours of darkness.

Margaret and Nicholas Roch and their twin six-year-olds made their guest so welcome he was quite overwhelmed by the genuine warmth of their hospitality. From the start his stimulating host and charming hostess made sure that he was made to feel like one of the family and the absolutely delightful boys were soon revelling in the company of this new-found, always merry uncle who, with a nonchalant flick of his fingers, would produce coins and all sorts of things out of thin air and make them disappear again. At table he held them all spellbound with tales of his adventures in the tunnel, while Nicholas in turn enthralled him with the stories he would tell of old Bristol and her past glories.

At first he was content to spend his days simply lazing in the sun, luxuriating in the sheer pleasure of a progressive return to health. Having felt as weak as a kitten for so long, his satisfaction knew no bounds as, day by day, he could actually feel his strength being restored. Free at last from the claustral restriction of his sickroom he was able to assess his situation at least a little more objectively. Once the works had finally been cleared of debris and the shield secured against the possibility of any further incursion by the Thames, the majority of the workforce had been dismissed. Only Dick Beamish and a few labourers remained with his father at Rotherhithe. Talks about the tunnel's future were still going on, although to what ultimate end was anybody's guess.

But though by no means as despondent as he had been, his mind still seemed clouded. Uppermost was the thought of Ellen Hulme. She had taken his decision to come to the West Country well enough and was apparently reconciled to the fact that it would be Christmas before they would see each other again. By then, therefore, he had to find some solution to the problem of his, of their, future.

As soon as he was strong enough he took to clambering about the fantastic gorge the river Avon had gouged into the towering white limestone escarpment. Armed with pencil and paper he sketched it from every conceivable angle, then painted it from memory. He was by no means the first artist to be inspired by its rugged beauty, but he was surely one of the most enthusiastic. After the filth and the foul stench under the Thames, the dreary months of illness and the near annihilating disappointment he had suffered, the dramatic beauty with which he now found himself surrounded was the vital spark needed to rekindle the fire of his imagination. For the first time since the tunnel débâcle the leaden pall of mental weariness which had so clogged his mind in defiance of all attempts to break through it began to lift at last.

It was then that Nicholas told him of William Vick's bequest to the people of Bristol. As he listened, his all but forgotten Castles in Spain slowly emerged from the mists of doubt that had so long shrouded them. And to those long-familiar visions of steamships and tunnels and houses and honours there was now added another – that of a bridge.

William Vick, wine merchant and would-be public benefactor, deceased 1753, had left £1,000 in trust to the Society of Merchant Venturers to be invested at compound interest until the proceeds totalled ten times the original investment. It was then, his will had stipulated, to be used to finance the building of a bridge across the Avon Gorge. Though still £2,000 short of that figure, the Society had decided the time had come to launch Vick's project and realise his dream. So a Grand Competition was shortly to be announced, open to engineers from all over the country, the winning submitted design to be selected by an appointed panel of judges. It would be an opportunity, almost unprecedented, for a rising young engineer to make a name for himself.

'Wouldn't it be wonderful, Nicholas, if Isambard were to build that bridge,' Margaret Roch had remarked as they bade their guest good-night later that same evening.

'If he did that,' observed her husband, regarding Isambard with a curious gleam in his eye, 'it could be the salvation of Bristol, as well as the making of Brunel.' And in that instant, though still beset with the same problems, and as far from their successful solution as ever, Brunel somehow knew he was free once more.

Rarely, even when he'd been so ill, had he found it impossible to sleep; but that night he could not close his eyes. Next morning he rose, dressed and slipped out of the house long before it was light, to witness, from the vantage point of the terrace, one of the most magnificent dawns he could ever remember seeing. As he watched the majestic scene materialise, his mind became a confusion of vague optimism and utterly baseless but sure conviction. Was this the opportunity he had been waiting for? Was this to be, at long last, what he had always dreamed of, his gateway to fortune, his open-sesame to everlasting fame – a bridge to span the Avon Gorge, Brunel's bridge!

Assume, he told himself, assume for the moment it was; for what better way to cultivate a possibility, however remote, than devote otherwise idle moments to indulging the fancy that might one day bring it about. The problem was how to cross that huge, truly awesome 300-yard gap. Stone was quite out of the question, even though the original Vick bequest had stipulated a stone bridge. Apart from anything else, it would make the cost prohibitive. Besides there was no room here, no need, for added grandeur. Nature had provided it in plenty. Who was mere man to think he could do better?

No, it had to be a suspension bridge, a broad-based tower to crown the soaring cliff and provide an anchorage for the suspension chains, an abutment on the opposite bank to complement the almost vertical wall of the gorge, but that was all. Under no circumstances must anything be allowed to intrude into the gorge itself. Here was no place for massive structures. No ugly central pier should ever disturb the placid serenity of the silver-threading Avon. And the bridge itself would have to be a thing of the air – light and simple, delicate even; but bold!

'A suspension bridge with a span of nine hundred feet!' he murmured aloud. Immediately his mouth went dry and he felt his heart beat faster at the thought. Was it possible to construct an unsupported span of such incredible length, he asked himself. He had no idea. All he did know was that it would be half the length again of Thomas Telford's Menai Bridge – the most modern, the biggest and the most superb suspension bridge ever designed and built. 'Nine hundred feet,' he said the words aloud once more. Yes indeed, that would truly be a stupendous bridge – if it could be done.

The subject was not raised again until nearly a month later. Roch had had to go to Plymouth and invited Isambard, whose extended holiday was at last drawing to its close, to accompany him. While the businessman discussed policy, profit and loss with his agents, the engineer took the opportunity to see for himself the achievements of two of those rightly judged to have brought honour to his profession.

Like a monument to its maker, the Eddystone lighthouse is clearly visible from Plymouth Hoe on a fine day. Standing where John Smeaton must have stood seventy-five years before, Isambard Brunel looked out over historic Plymouth Sound, beyond the bristling fortifications of Nicholas Island and the densely wooded rearing mass of Mount Edgecombe Park. Through a powerful telescope he watched in fascination as the endless procession of long Atlantic rollers vainly sought to destroy even the natural rock formations which dared impede their mighty progress. And closer inshore, between the twin bluffs of Redding and Staddon Points, John Rennie's magnificent mile-long breakwater boldly denied those same rollers access to the Sound, thus preserving inviolate the safe calm of its placid waters. The sight of these two great masterworks fuelled the fire of ambition which once again had begun to consume him. These were indeed monuments for posterity. Some day he, too, would have his monument.

The river Tamar at Saltash, which he and Nicholas visited prior to their return to Bristol, is nearly twelve hundred feet wide and seventy-five or more at its deepest. Some years before, the Brunels had been consulted as to the feasibility of bridging that vast tidal expanse.

'My father advised against it,' Isambard explained, 'because the Admiralty had stipulated there must be no obstruction, not even a temporary one, to the main navigable channel, and that the roadway had to be so many feet above high-water level to allow safe passage at all times for a fully rigged man-o'-war.'

'I don't wonder at it,' commented Nicholas. To his untutored eye any sort of bridge there, even without the additional problems posed by such prohibitive provisos, would seem to be quite out of the question. 'But you didn't agree,' he added, catching sight of the amused expression which had suddenly flitted across his companion's features.

Isambard was smiling at the memory of the one violent professional disagreement he and his father had ever had. Young, brash, precociously self-opinionated and not yet mature enough to know when to hold his tongue, he had persisted in expounding his theories on the subject until the argument, suddenly escalating out of all proportion to the issue, had culminated in Marc for once losing his temper and cuffing his son's ear.

'No,' he said quietly, 'I didn't agree.'

'And you still think it could be done?' Roch was watching Brunel closely now that the subject of bridges had finally come up, a moment the shrewd businessman had been waiting for and was determined to make the most of.

'Indeed it could. It would be difficult, mind, damned difficult; but certainly not impossible. Given justifiable requirements, the guarantee of adequate financial backing – that's where most projects come to grief – and, of course, sound basic engineering and planning, practically anything is possible.'

'And the Avon Gorge bridge . . . ?' prompted Roch.

The question came as no surprise. Isambard had been anticipating it ever since Nicholas had first spoken of William Vick. His reply, however, caused the Bristol merchant's heart to sink momentarily.

'Frankly, I don't know. But,' and the other's hopes instantly rose once more, 'as soon as I get back to London it's one of the first things I intend to find out.'

Chapter Six

IT was possible – a 900-foot span could be constructed! It took
nearly a year to amass the data he needed and work his way
through it all and, on paper at least, prove it to be a perfectly feasible
proposition to extend a single unsupported span, if need be, to a limit
of 1,000 feet, and more. But not until he was completely satisfied that
his theories were sound did he confide in anyone – not even his
father.

He had returned from the West Country to find the shield bricked
up, a large mirror installed in front of it, and sightseers admitted
though a turnstile at the head of the great Rotherhithe Shaft on
payment of one penny to what was now being called the 'Visitors'
Arch'. The capital's erstwhile 'Pride of Progress' had been reduced
to the ignominious status of a common peepshow.

Within days of its opening as such, the popular humorist Thomas
Hood had published his 'Ode to M. Brunel' in which he had wittily
and irreverently advised that the tunnel be turned into a wine cellar
under the sign of The Bore's Head. Inspired by this example, all the
would-be wits of Fleet Street, clever, competent and otherwise –
regrettably, mostly otherwise – had proceeded ad nauseum to pour
journalistic scorn on the Great Bore they had recently been so
anxious to outdo each other in extolling as 'the Wonder of this or any
other Age', while the fickle general public read and quoted them
avidly. There had been but one small crumb of personal satisfaction
for the Brunels in the whole sorry business. An attempt by a clique of
disaffected proprietors to oust them and bring in some ambitious
quacksalver had been well and truly scotched by the Duke of
Wellington, who thereby demonstrated his still active interest. His
Grace had put the instigators of the plot decisively in their places by
pointing out with characteristic pithiness that the problem, in case
they had not so discerned it for themselves, was not the lack of an
engineer but the means by which the engineer, any engineer, could

be enabled to complete the work. After that there had been no further talk of the Brunels being replaced.

But it in no way altered the fact that both of them were now unemployed. Fortunately, despite the bite of the depression, there was work to be had. Marc was soon involved in a proposed improvement programme on the Oxford Canal & Medway Navigation, while Isambard managed to obtain a commission to design a new system of drainage works at Tollesbury on the Essex coast.

'If your calculations are correct,' Marc opined gravely but with eyes twinkling mischievously when he returned Isambard's bridge thesis, 'I believe your reasoning is sound.' Even before he'd looked at it Marc had known the mass of figure work that made up the bulk of the fat sheaf of papers he'd been asked to examine would be correct down to the very last and most minute particular. Everything his son did always was.

As a youth Brunel junior had, at times, been something of a trial to his parent. In addition to his outstanding talent, most likely because of it, he had been possessed of a degree of irresponsible conceit which, coupled with an unashamed love of approbation, had often trapped him into showing off quite outrageously. There had been times when he had done the most stupid useless things just to appear to advantage before people he scarcely knew and about whom he really cared nothing. As he'd grown older he'd fortunately discovered this weakness in himself, and had had the good sense to guard against it and control it. Gradually self-conceit had metamorphosed into what was now a thoroughly justified self-confidence.

Once he'd matured he'd also discovered there were far too many so-called experts only too willing gratuitously to put forward what purported to be authoritative opinions on subjects about which they knew palpably little in theory and considerably less in practice. Also there were some rightly acknowledged experts who were so intent on protecting their own particular domains that they did not hesitate to condemn out of hand anything they considered likely to bring credit to another which would perhaps eclipse their own reputations. So the young Brunel had taught himself to keep his own counsel until he'd subjected every single constructive thought he might have, or any professional decision he might be called upon to make, to dispassionate objective scrutiny and exhaustive critical assessment.

He was by no means infallible, no man could ever be that; but he was rarely wrong.

Because of this carefully cultivated discipline, there were many who did not care for Marc Brunel's son. Too often he gave the impression of being cold and proud, aloof and too devastatingly impervious to criticism, altogether too infuriatingly self-assured. But Marc knew this to be a deliberately projected public image, a convincing impersonation of someone who really didn't exist. Behind the image was a curiously self-conscious, extremely sensitive, exceedingly complex and utterly private man of, as yet, untapped genius.

Soon after Marc's opinion on Brunel's ideas for a single-span bridge had been confirmed by Joseph Field, Henry Maudslay's partner and a recognised bridge expert, Nicholas Roch turned up at the Barge House with the news that the Bristol Society of Merchant Venturers, in collaboration with the Bristol Corporation and Chamber of Commerce, had officially announced the bridge competition. A fifteen-man committee chaired by the mayor had been formed, and an application to Parliament for a bill to authorise the venture was to be made immediately. Already there had been an enthusiastic response to a public appeal for funds to augment the Vick bequest.

'It is to be a suspension bridge,' Nicholas confirmed over dinner at the Barge House that night.

'Well after Telford's Menai, it couldn't be anything other than a suspension bridge, could it,' commented Ben.

'Not if Bristol hopes to derive any sort of benefit from the enterprise,' put in Isambard.

'And I for one am determined that she shall,' Roch declared.

'That's very important to you isn't it, Nicholas,' said Sophia.

'My dear,' was the reply, 'I've never made any secret of that aspect of the exercise being as important to me as designing this bridge is going to be to your brother.'

The closing date of the competition was to be Thursday, 19 November 1829. That was more than four months hence, but Isambard wasted no time. First he spent two hectic days in north Wales minutely examining every detail of every aspect of Telford's famous bridge over the Menai Strait.

Only for the last forty years had it been possible to construct a suspension bridge. Not until Henry Cort had discovered that by simply stirring molten pig-iron – a process called 'puddling' – could wrought iron of sufficient tensile strength for the manufacture of suspension chains be produced. Since then, however, a number of bridges of various designs, some good, some bad, but most mediocre and many considerably worse, had been erected in Scotland. Here fast-flowing rivers made the construction of central-support piers too difficult, too expensive and, following several catastrophic mishaps in flood waters, altogether too risky. The most successful of these structures, the work of Captain Samuel Brown RN, was less than ten years old. Crossing the river Tweed at Kelso with a single span of 300 feet, it had been opened in 1820. Telford's Menai, begun the previous spring, had been completed just six years later.

That single unsupported span of 575 feet had been, and was still, regarded as an engineering miracle which had taken the art and science of bridge building to the very limit of the possible, in its way as great a pioneering venture as the Thames Tunnel. At least so said all the experts – Brown, Tierney Clark who had just completed his new suspension bridge over the Thames at Hammersmith, and Thomas Telford, the Grand Old Man, the unchallenged master of them all. Twenty-three-year-old Isambard Brunel was quietly confident he was about to prove each and every one of them, including the unassailable, almost god-like Telford himself, wrong.

He returned to London via Manchester. But he made no effort to acquaint Ellen of the fact. Nor had he yet told her of his involvement in Bristol, merely that he was busy once more and that he would come to her just as soon as he could. He would surprise her with his triumph in the competition; then he would ask her father for her hand. Then, they would marry.

He even denied himself a visit to Rainhill on the nearly completed route of the Liverpool & Manchester rail road, where a series of trials were in progress to prove once and for all the still controversial claims of the Stephensons and others that steam locomotives could indeed be economically viable and superior to the horse-drawn passenger trucks still in use on the Stockton & Darlington. Instead he went to Broughton, just south of Manchester, where a suspension bridge had recently collapsed. The cause had not been an engineering fault, but one of those glaringly obvious phenomena which someone should have had the foresight to think of, but no one actually had. A company of foot soldiers marching in step across the bridge had set up a violent harmonic vibration, causing a retaining pin in one of the suspension chains to fracture. Henceforth notices instructing officers and NCOs in charge of troops to order a break of step when crossing were to be clearly posted.

The Bristol Bridge Building Committee had allowed a wide choice of sites, practically the only limiting factor being a minimum roadway height of 215 feet above the Avon's high-water mark. Though he had originally thought in rather conventional terms of suspension between towers, Brunel had radically altered and simplified his initial concept by developing the engineering techniques he now proposed to employ – techniques which were, in a word, revolutionary. He prepared drafts of four separate designs. When he saw the first rough drawings Roch was positively ecstatic and, thus encouraged, Isambard settled to his work with a will.

The simplest of the four required a span of only 720 feet between 70-foot-high towers. He considered this the most economical but the least aesthetically satisfying. Even so, the span, by currently accepted standards, was extreme. Some way down river he sited a similar structure with a 900-foot span. But this too he felt was aesthetically lacking.

But where the rocky wall of the gorge rose almost vertically to its maximum height above the roadway level he selected a third site for which he offered two separate designs, one calling for a span of 980 feet, the other going to an extreme of 1,160. With neither would suspension towers as such be necessary. He also discarded land ties, for he proposed hanging the suspension chains directly from the natural rock formation. But to complement the suggestion of Gothic gloom occasioned by the proximity of the forbidding maw of the Giant's Cave, twin massive but squat and purely decorative crenellated towers would glower at each other across the gorge.

Apart from the length of span, the only other major difference between the third and fourth designs was that the latter did away with the necessity of excavating a short approach tunnel through the Gloucestershire cliff. This last was without doubt the most ambitious of the four, and the one he recommended most highly.

Each design, executed with a draughtsmanship of such exquisite perfection as to make both drawings and the accompanying illustrations acceptable as works of art in their own right, was presented as a separate portfolio complete with comprehensive codex plus a wealth of additional explanatory information. He considered all this essential because, as well as the lengths of span proposed, the ideas he was putting forward for the suspension chains were likely to be regarded as equally revolutionary. Telford had used eight-foot links for his Menai chains, the largest ever made. But, as had always been accepted practice, they had been joined by short connecting links. Isambard reasoned that such connecting links in no way contributed to the overall strength of the chain itself. By doubling the length of Telford's chain-links and joining them with simple pins, it would be possible to manufacture a chain of comparable strength not only much lighter but at far less cost.

All in all the theories he was advancing represented as great a step forward in the techniques of suspension-bridge construction as Thomas Telford had achieved a mere three years earlier. The burning question was – how were they likely to be received?

Chapter Seven

'THE maximum permissible, or indeed possible, length of any unsupported span of any suspension bridge of whatever design,' declared Thomas Telford in his still distinctive Dumfriesshire drawl, 'is, at most, 600 feet, and not one solitary inch more.' For nearly an hour a packed audience in the committee chamber of Blaise Castle, Bristol had listened to the great man as he'd systematically dismissed as totally unacceptable the eight competition entries short-listed by the selection committee from a total of twenty-six. Brunel was the only entrant to have submitted more than one design and all four had been included in the short list. One by one Telford had mercilessly humiliated each design's author. But he had saved his most scathing remarks for Isambard.

'Mr Brunel is, without question,' he went on in a silkily sarcastic tone, 'without doubt, one of the finest young engineers this country has yet produced. His work for his father has proved it if, indeed, proof be needed. But,' and here the sarcasm hardened into concrete condemnation, 'as far as bridges in general, and suspension bridges in particular, are concerned, it is patently obvious that he knows nothing whatever. Oh, his theories are most ingeniously conceived, I grant you; and his plans most perfectly illustrated.' Then with all the bravado of self-delusion he declaimed, 'Any suspension bridge built to the specification he is advocating would be dangerously unstable and liable to collapse without warning at the first puff of wind.'

Outwardly unperturbed by this outrageous attack, Isambard retired for a few days to the seclusion of the Roch residence in Clifton. Calm he may have appeared, but in fact he was seething with rage at the way the prize – and until Telford's arrival on the scene it had been a foregone conclusion he had won the competition – had been almost literally plucked from his grasp. It had all been a disastrous waste of effort and of time, a fiasco, just like the tunnel, only worse, much much worse. This failure was not the result of a lack of cash, or want of courage on the part of others. This was due entirely to the petty naked jealousy of someone fearing for his own reputation, and he damned the aged engineer as vehemently as ever he had damned the Thames Tunnel proprietors. For how long, he asked himself despairingly, must he continue to languish in obscurity so that this selfish old fool, who had once been a great genius, could continue to cling to his precious pinnacle of solitary glory.

Having been specifically invited to make the final choice from their short list, Telford's sweeping condemnations now left the acutely discomfited selection committee with no alternative but to ask him to design the new bridge; and to this, after considerable hemming and hawing, which was interpreted as commendably modest reluctance, he eventually agreed. His drawings, he promised, would be ready by the middle of January. They were. They detailed a suspension bridge comprised of three separate spans: two of 180 feet each, flanking a central span of 360 feet. The suspension chains, of eight-foot links with connecting links, were supported at the two intermediate points by a pair of massively towering stone piers which rose like enormous stalagmites from the banks of the river in the bed of the gorge. The architectural style was a florid Gothic, the four faces of the piers decorated in a riot of elaborately panelled stonework, the suspension chains festooned with heavily ornamented frets.

In spite of persistently foul weather, which since the turn of the year had kept Bristol and the surrounding countryside blanketed beneath the worst snowfalls in living memory, people from near and far flocked to see the plan as soon as it was unveiled, with suitable ceremony, in the great hall of the Mansion House in Queen Square. All seemed to be absolutely captivated by what they saw. They gushed over the ornate style, they enthused about the wealth of elaborate ornamentation, they expatiated at length on the obvious stability of construction. Here, they said, was a bridge that could be called a bridge. And, almost without exception, they revered the sure, if unadventurous, touch of the master whose creation it was.

Telford Bridge favours and Telford Bridge ribbons were being offered for sale in the streets within hours of the plan being on view, quickly followed by commemorative bookmarks, embroidered scarves, flags, handkerchiefs, tablecloths, painted table mats, platters and plaques – the enterprising proprietors of the city's sweat shops driving their ill-paid drudges as they'd seldom been driven before in frantic efforts to squeeze all profit possible from what had developed literally overnight into a commercial boom of fantastic proportions. Thousands of copies of an artist's fanciful impression of the finished structure, in a setting bearing scant resemblance to any known part of the Avon Gorge, were printed. All were sold before the ink had time to dry properly. Soon there was hardly a public building or a private house either in city or suburbs that did not boast one. All other personalities previously associated with the bridge competition conveniently forgotten, Thomas Telford became Bristol's undisputed man of the moment.

When Nicholas saw the plan for the first time he very nearly rubbed his eyes in disbelief. Being neither engineer nor architect he could make no claim to be heard as a competent critic. But it seemed to him scarcely credible that a mind that had conceived such past wonders could possibly have brought forth this grotesque monstrosity. 'The damned thing is nothing but a folly!' he ranted to Margaret in a bitter, outraged outburst. 'What in God's name can the old fool be thinking of? Senility surely must be the only possible explanation.'

But what was even worse, what was the bridge committee thinking of? Roch began to wonder if all its members had suddenly gone senile as well. They were actually recommending acceptance of this ridiculous plan. And they were doing so with an apparent unanimity that was, in the light of the individual opinions they had so recently and so freely voiced, scarcely believable.

'Can't you do something to bring them to their senses?' demanded Margaret Roch, as outraged as her husband by the callous injustice that was being daily so brazenly heaped on their banished friend and protégé.

'I'm not sure it isn't already too late,' said Nicholas sadly. 'But by Heaven and by Hell, I intend to try!'

To the mass of the astonishingly involved and still wildly enthusiastic general public, the committee seemed to be a reassuring exemplification of sound civic solidarity. Safe within the sanctum of its Blaise Castle chamber, however, it was, in fact, a veritable bear garden of violently opposed views. Its members were hopelessly divided. Some favoured Telford's design. Some openly disparaged it. Some demanded that notwithstanding the gentleman's unfortunate intervention, even though it had been at their invitation, the original short list be recompiled and a final selection made from it by some other, less contentious, means. Some continued to press for adoption of the Brunel plan which had been most favoured from the start. Some contended that as the affair had already gravitated to the level of farce, the only sensible course of action was to declare all proceedings since the competition's closing date void and start again. And there were even some who just wanted to forget the whole wretched business and give up any idea of building any sort of a bridge anywhere.

But effectively nullifying each and every argument, was a cowering reluctance on the part of its advocate to risk incurring personal unpopularity by any outward display of opposition to what was seen as an overwhelming tide of public opinion. So, following hours of heated debate, Telford supporters began to impress the weakest among the waverers with the cogency of their argument, which was nothing if not pragmatic. The elderly engineer's plan might well be all its most hostile critics claimed it was, they conceded. But, they were also at pains to point out be that as it might, it was still a plan, a usable plan. And what was more, it had Thomas Telford's name on it. Now, did it really matter, they asked, if his talent had sagged a little? That his reputation was still intact was surely proved by the warmth of the reception he had been accorded by the city. As far as the general public was concerned Telford was as great a national hero as he had ever been. And that being so, his bridge could do as much for Bristol as his earlier works had done for Scotland and for north Wales.

Eventually it was the mayor's casting vote that carried the day. The Telford plan was formally adopted and, in accordance with normal parliamentary procedural requirement, immediately submitted for consideration by the appropriate House of Commons committee. The lavish civic junketings which celebrated this event, though betraying a hint of being more than a little half-hearted, did manage to engender one final euphoric fling.

Then, curiously, but perhaps in the circumstances understandably, practically everyone who had been in any way involved, from the highest to the lowest, apparently forgot all about it. Six months later the Bristol Bridge Building Committee, on the flimsiest of pretexts, withdrew its application to Parliament and announced a second competition.

Chapter Eight

AT first Margaret Roch sensed rather than actually observed anything fundamentally different about their guest. It was, after all, more than half a year since they had seen him, and to begin with she was inclined to dismiss the impression of change as a figment of her imagination. But as she watched him more closely and listened to him talk, she gradually became convinced that the difference, though it remained indefinable, was undoubtedly there. Isambard Brunel was, to all appearances, the same light-hearted, witty, charming young man he had always been, the personable friend and companion she and Nicholas and the twins had known and grown to love. But there was, nevertheless, a distinct hint of something in his bearing which most certainly had not been there before.

'Very well,' she said to her doubting husband when they were alone together in the early hours of the morning following Brunel's arrival from London, 'you can put it down to what you choose to call female foolishness if you like. But you see if I'm not right.'

That she was right Nicholas soon discovered. Whereas before he had always found his young friend a ready listener and, though firm in the opinions he held regarding his work, open to suggestion and willing to debate the detail of what was involved, Isambard now proved to be quite adamant in his declared intention. He was totally impervious to argument, averse even to any form of discussion. Which left the older man at first at a loss to know exactly how to deal with the situation.

At the first mention of the new bridge competition, Brunel bluntly declared he'd already had his fill of all such and would take part in no more. 'I've proved to everyone's satisfaction, except Telford's of course, that even the longest Giant's Hole span would be well within future limits,' he told Nicholas with a finality that seemed to preclude any further discussion on the subject.

With which statement, of course, Roch could only agree. Indeed, had the situation been other than it was, he would never have presumed even to suggest that an alternative to either 'Giant's Hole' design be contemplated. 'But what I am suggesting,' he attempted to explain, though because of the doggedly unreceptive attitude with which he found himself confronted, not at all successfully, 'is that we, that you, play Telford at his own game.'

'And how, pray, do you propose I do that?' came the sarcastic rejoinder.

'By presenting a completely new design for the same site Telford has used.'

Such was the truly astonishingly violent reaction, Roch was forced to exert all the power of his not inconsiderable personality to counter the other's scornful dismissal. 'Will you please hear me out?' he demanded, curbing his own rapidly rising temper with the utmost difficulty. Nicholas was not by nature a patient man. 'That's all I'm asking you to do.' For the moment the clash of wills made the atmosphere electric. Only by a supreme effort did Brunel in turn manage to control his temper. With a curt gesture he signified his willingness to listen.

'Yesterday Telford put out a statement to the effect that his plan was going forward as a competition entry.' Roch spoke quietly but with brusque deliberation. 'The statement also said he was not going to alter that plan in any way.'

'I'm sorry, but I fail to see . . .' Isambard attempted to interrupt but Roch stopped him.

'If you produced a new plan, a comparable plan, and for the same site, one that would make the old man's look as ridiculous to everyone as you and I and a great many other people now know it to be, then . . .'

'Nicholas, I am not in the least bit interested in revenge.'

'Who's saying anything about revenge?'

'He made a fool out of me, and now you're suggesting I try and make a fool out of him. Now what's that if it isn't revenge?'

'Not at all.'

'Then what do you call it?'

'I call it acting in accordance with a sound policy, being, I suppose the word would be, politic.'

'Oh, come now!'

'All right, playing politics if you will,' Roch snapped, his patience at last beginning to ebb, though he still held himself firmly in check. 'But you mark what I say. The only way Bristol is going to get an Avon bridge is by holding this competition. And, no reflection on the quality of your work, my friend, the only way we can be absolutely certain you will be the winner of that competition is to make sure of Telford's elimination.'

'You told me in your letter the way was clear,' Isambard flashed at him almost petulantly.

'So I did,' Nicholas agreed. 'And so it will be, providing we are careful. True, an awful lot of people have already turned against the old man, but you probably know better than I that it in no way alters the fact that, regardless of the worth of his plan, he will still command a great deal of popular support which certain members of the bridge committee may be only too ready to exploit. But if you can alienate that support, if need be by ridicule, once and for all, then, in my opinion, the result must be in your favour.'

The letter to which Isambard referred had been delivered to the Barge House only hours before a long-arranged departure for Manchester. Having had to forgo a visit to the Rainhill trials the previous autumn, in which the Stephensons' *Rocket* had triumphed so magnificently, he was determined not to miss the grand opening of the now completed Liverpool & Manchester rail road. He had also decided it was high time he faced up to reality. All his efforts to court success during the past two and a half years had come to precisely nothing. Furthermore, despite his repeatedly professed optimism – and to all except his sister Sophia he still appeared the perfect optimist – his prospects were nil. He had failed miserably to keep the promise he'd made just before the accident in the tunnel. So he'd decided he must now either marry Ellen Hulme and reconcile himself to a comfortable if dull future working for her father, or forget her.

Exactly what he was going to do once he got to Manchester he was still not sure, even after long hours spent in soul-searching debate.

'My dear Isambard,' Nicholas had written, 'the committee has at last come to its collective senses. As a result of the public's now total apathy, almost to a man its members have changed their minds. Telford's wretched plan is to be discarded. The application to Parliament has already been withdrawn. Our way is now clear.

Margaret and your many friends here join me in asking you most earnestly to return to Bristol just as soon as you can.'

The letter had come as a complete surprise. For many hours following its arrival Isambard had paced restlessly up and down in the garden of the Barge House smoking one cigar after another, brooding on what he should do. He had given up his pipe in favour of cigars and, though he always strenuously denied that he smoked far too many, he was now rarely to be seen without one.

'Though he'd never admit it,' Ben Hawes had commented to Sophia after the two of them had been watching the pacing figure for some time, 'that boy needs help. And you, my love, are the only one he'll ever be likely to listen to.' Sophia knew this. But anxious as she was to help if she could, she had no wish to interfere in her brother's affairs. Neither she nor Ben had any idea of the contents of the letter, though knowing it came from Nicholas they assumed it must have something to do with the bridge. But Sophia also knew that when he'd returned from Bristol following the Telford incident, Isambard had sworn never to go back, under any circumstances.

'On the other hand, of course,' Ben went on casually after watching in silence as his brother-in-law lit another cigar, 'he's just as likely to tell you to mind your own damn business and go to the Devil.' It was a challenge Ben knew no Brunel could ever refuse, and he smothered a smile as Sophia, bridling visibly, rose to the bait.

'For Heaven's sake don't tell him he smokes too much,' he'd admonished in a hoarse whisper as she gathered her skirts and marched down the steps from the terrace to the lawn.

'But you have no alternative,' she told Isambard emphatically when, following a certain initial reluctance to take her into his confidence, he'd finally finished unburdening himself. She suspected his decision would mean the end of his affair with Ellen Hulme but she had no compunction in advising him to cancel all his arrangements and go at once to Bristol. 'You must do as Nicholas asks. Ellen will simply have to understand. But go back to Bristol you must, and at once.'

For what seemed an age he'd sat in silence, lost in thought. 'Thanks Sophy,' he'd smiled at last, giving her hand a grateful squeeze, 'I think I'd already come to that conclusion myself. But you have given me the extra push I needed.'

Silently she'd sighed with relief. He'd been so depressed when they'd first started talking that for a long moment she'd feared even she might not be able to persuade him to be sensible, for instinct told her that to have ignored Roch's letter would have been fatal.

'Ben's a very lucky fellow. You'll never know how much I envy him.' And such was the obvious sincerity of Isambard's tone that for the first time in her life his sister found herself blushing.

He'd penned a hurried apology and rather lame explanation of his sudden change of plans to Ellen, despatched the letter in time to be franked for the evening mail to Manchester, then left for Bristol by the midnight stage from The Bell Savage on Ludgate Hill.

It had been a damp, cheerless journey; he'd travelled outside as was his custom, and by the time he got to Clifton he was miserably wet and thoroughly depressed. A hot bath and a change of clothes restored his physical comfort, but his depression persisted and, in no way alleviated by his heated altercation with Nicholas, grew steadily worse.

Determinedly the practical man of business sought to mollify and to reason with the outraged artist whose pride, in spite of repeated protests to the contrary, was still much in evidence. After long hours of protracted argument Nicholas eventually managed to persuade him at least to experiment by substantially altering the basic Giant's Hole design and resiting it as suggested. But the agreement to do so was considerably less than half-hearted. Still in too stubborn a frame of mind to appreciate fully the point Nicholas had been striving to get across, and in a mood as gloomy as the miserable weather which, since his arrival, had kept the gorge either shrouded in mist or veiled by heavy showers of rain, Isambard retired to his rooms.

Though his host had provided him with a fully equipped drawing table, it was several days before he was able to commit one single constructive line to paper. But once he got started, instead of adapting either Giant's Hole design, he set about the task as if it had been presented to him for the very first time. He found that by making a feature of a huge abutment on the Somerset side at Leigh Woods, which was virtually as he had first visualised the bridge, he was able to reduce the span to just over 630 feet. The abutment would, of course, add enormously to the overall cost. That apart, however, and even taking into consideration the fact that the much shorter span would make the overt technical achievement of the project less impressive, the result was in no way inferior to either previous design.

In happier circumstances he would have been more than satisfied with the first rough sketches. But he simply could not bring himself to view what Nicholas had termed a political compromise as anything other than an act of abject surrender of principle. As he saw it, he was being asked to make what amounted to a tacit admission that Thomas Telford's outrageous criticism of his theories had been justified. Suddenly the whole sordid business seemed utterly abhorrent, and before he could stop himself he had torn his sketches in shreds and hurled them across the room.

Instantly he was ashamed of himself. Momentarily satisfying though his absurd action might have been, it had served no useful purpose at all, save to make him feel more frustrated than ever. Desperate now to clear the confusion of uncontrollable emotion so hampering him, he impetuously stormed out of the house.

Heedless of the wet – the rain was still beating down and the evening already well advanced – and but partially protected by a far from adequate travelling cloak, he tramped up the muddy path leading from the far corner of the grounds to what had been his favourite spot from which to view the gorge. Just below the summit of the cliff he made himself as comfortable as he could beneath the sparsely leaved branches of an aged oak. He lit a cigar. As he smoked he contemplated the scene, colourlessly desolate in the dismal haze, the scene which had so inspired him when fortune had seemed to beckon in that first golden dawn. But on this occasion, try as he might, he was quite unable to marshal his thoughts into any semblance of order. The light faded and the sky grew more leaden as the evening dragged on. Dolefully he smoked another cigar, then another, and another. Not until it was dark, by which time he was thoroughly soaked and shivering with cold, did he return to the warmth and comfort of the house.

He had not expected to, but he slept extremely well. He woke early to find the morning bright with watery sunlight. And with that new day came a welcome release from his black depression. He walked once more to the cliff summit, marvelling at the transformation nature had wrought in both the scene and himself. Then he returned briskly, consumed a huge breakfast, made his peace with his host and retired to his rooms to work.

He quickly reproduced, and in doing so greatly improved, the sketches he had wantonly ruined the day before. Slowly the detail of the new design began to materialise on the drawing table. At first, progress was uncharacteristically uncertain and hesitant, even diffident. But as the structural unity began to emerge, his instinctive sense of the dramatic reasserted itself. From then on time ceased to exist, as with increasingly firmer and decisive strokes his pencil started to fly over the paper.

The first full drawing was completed. It was critically assessed, altered, reassessed, altered again, then ruthlessly discarded, replaced by another, and another and another – each in turn incorporating or excluding this detail or that, sometimes elaborating, sometimes simplifying, but always consolidating a steady and logical progress towards the ultimate goal. The process went on, tirelessly and without interruption all through that day and well into the night until the original idea had been developed into the complete entity which at last satisfied its demanding creator.

He had chosen an Egyptian architectural style, its massive monumental character serving admirably to emphasise the aerial grace and delicacy of the new span. The towers were squat, but they straddled the roadway on such firmly planted feet that they conveyed the impression of being huge and impregnable without detracting in any way from the natural splendour of their setting. Topped by a crouching sphinx, which glared balefully at its fellow on the other side of the ravine, each tower was encased in great plaques of cast iron. In keeping with true Egyptian tradition, the plaques were decorated with sculpted panels depicting the whole of the work of construction of the bridge itself and the quarrying, mining and manufacture of all its materials and components.

It was a perfect concept, a spark of pure inspiration. While rejoicing in the long-lost grandeur of Philae and Thebes, at the same time it invoked the true spirit of contemporary genius and endeavour and was as modern as the rail road locomotive and the steamboat. It was nothing short of masterly.

Chapter Nine

M ARCH 1831 stormed in like the proverbial lion. The winter, by no means as severe as that of the previous year, had nevertheless started early, and it seemed as if it was set to continue indefinitely. There had been no snow for several weeks, but the ground had stayed hard and the air was continually sharp with frost. Incessant northerly winds had kept temperatures hovering at best but a few degrees above freezing point, and the weather generally miserable with never more than the odd day's respite.

On that first bleak day of the month the wind, icy as usual and at times with the force of a full gale, fairly whistled round corners. It howled through the narrow thoroughfares and swept the open wharves of Thames-side Westminster. Gusting over the river, it whipped the murky waters into short angry waves which seemed from the shore to threaten imminent disaster to the frail-looking craft which plied their busy trade on its uninviting surface. But despite all the discomforts of cold and wind, from midday onwards the approaches to St Stephen's were crowded with all manner of people hopeful of obtaining entry to the House of Commons public galleries. For that evening Lord John Russell, Paymaster General in the new Whig Government, was to present at last the long-looked-for Reform Bill.

The fall of Wellington's Tory Government had come far sooner than even the most pessimistic of its supporters feared. An attempt had been made to persuade the duke to form another more broadly based administration. But he would have none of it. So Earl Grey accepted the royal invitation. Almost immediately the serious civil unrest – which had broken out six months before in Kent, spread rapidly through Surrey, Sussex, Hampshire, Wiltshire and Buckinghamshire, then to the industrial complexes of the Midlands and North where extremist agitators seemed more dangerously active with each passing day – came to an end.

There had even been signs of open rebellion and the military had been alerted. Troops in the capital had been substantially reinforced, the Tower placed in a state of defence, the guard at the Bank of England doubled. As a consequence the Funds had suffered an all but disastrous three per cent fall. Then shocked Londoners had woken one morning to find the walls of their city daubed with inflammatory slogans and plastered with seditious posters: 'To Arms!' 'Liberty or Death!' 'Away with Peel's Bloody Gang!' they exhorted. Rumours had been many and frightening, the most alarming being that an attack on Apsley House, the Duke of Wellington's private London home, was to signal a general uprising.

Naturally the criminal element everywhere had not been slow to take every advantage of the concomitant confusion, thus stretching the already strained resources of the new police to the very limit. Nor was their task made easier by the strong feelings of resentment shown by the citizenry in general for these still unpopular and largely unwanted guardians of law and order – the 'Peelers' as they had been disrespectfully dubbed after their founder, the former Home Secretary.

During the first two months of 1831 over eight hundred persons, men and women, involved in the various outbreaks of violence, criminal and otherwise, had been arrested. Several had been hanged, many transported and the rest crammed into already seriously overcrowded prisons at home. But the severity of the sentences seemed to have had little if any deterrent effect. The threat of even worse violence remained, and a recent attempt on the life of the Duke of Wellington had only been narrowly foiled, the would-be assassin – an Irishman by the name of Silk – being arrested actually in the lobby of the House of Lords.

'It will be my intention,' Grey had declared on taking office, 'to create a House of Commons that is really to represent the intelligence, property, and the feelings of the people.' The moment so many Englishmen had been waiting for, and so many had been dreading, had finally arrived. The winter of discontent appeared, to the optimists, to be at an end.

The result of the second bridge competition was to be announced on Friday, 18 March. Confident this time there could be no doubt that Brunel would be declared the winner, Nicholas Roch had insisted he be there. So Isambard booked an outside seat on the

Bristol *White Lion* and travelled down on the sixteenth.

The coach, a rather decrepit affair compared to the more fashionable Bath vehicles, but eminently roadworthy for all that, set off fully laden and with much creaking of springs and the grinding of iron tyres over protesting cobbles, from the Bull in Mouth on the stroke of six in the morning. With the guard, no mean performer, lustily trumpeting their approach, they had passed Kensington Church and Holland House, the home of the Whigs, well before the sun was fully up. Hammersmith Mall they found still almost deserted. But by the time they reached Brentford, the county town of Middlesex, the day had begun. Then past Sion House – the home of Lady Jersey, the uncrowned queen of Almacks, across Hounslow Heath with its great mansions and fine orchards, the coach sped, and so to Maidenhead for breakfast at the King's Arms.

Barely thirty minutes later – one needed a strong constitution and good digestion to appreciate to the full the joys of coaching – they were on their way to Reading where a change of team was effected without their even coming to a halt. The day was cold, but the air was crisp and clear and they made excellent time along the northern bank of the river Kennet to Newbury where there was another change, then to Marlborough in time for dinner and another thirty-minute stop.

The twenty-mile haul to Chippenham past Maerl's Barrow from which red-roofed Marlborough takes its name, the Avebury stone circle, second in mystery only to Stonehenge, and the equally mysterious and probably even more ancient man-made mound of Silbury Hill, took just over two hours. Here the horses had to be rested for twenty minutes, the team having been changed at Calne, while those passengers who felt the need partook of hurried refreshment. A final change was made at Marshfield. The last long climb up Tog Hill brought them to Kingswood's Heights from which, the evening being crystal clear, the distant twinkling lights of Bristol were plainly visible.

First thing the following morning Isambard was taken by Roch to see the solicitor who was acting for the bridge committee. 'I've no idea what it's about,' was the only answer Nicholas could give to his questions. 'All I know is I had a visit yesterday from Somers, Osborne's clerk, with a message that I was to get you there just as soon as I possibly could, and that the matter was damned urgent.'

William Osborne – a tall stately man of seventy or more whose old-fashioned gaitered garb, courtly manners, slow deliberate style of address and antique pronunciation concealed a professional acumen and natural perspicacity in no way impaired by the weight of his years – welcomed them to his soberly furnished but comfortable chambers with a characteristically effusive greeting. He had not had the pleasure of meeting young Mr Brunel before; he had naturally heard much about him, and in connection with enterprises other than the bridge; and his esteemed father, of course; he had admired the work of them both for a very long time – and so forth. Roch, who knew the old man too well to attempt to interrupt or even hurry him, fortunately managed to catch his not so patient companion's eye with a look of well-timed warning. At last the loquacious lawyer came to the point.

'What I have to impart to you gentlemen is, of course, in the strictest confidence,' he prefaced judiciously. 'Further, it must be clearly understood I am, under no circumstances, to be named as your source of information.' Nor would he proceed until he had received their individual acceptance of his conditions. He thanked them courteously, explaining at length the reasons for his seemingly excessive caution before going on.

'Gentlemen, I have to inform you that Messrs Gilbert and Seaward not four and twenty hours ago in this very room communicated to me, though, fortunately, not in confidence, their intention of recommending to the Bridge Building Committee that the winning entry of the competition should be, not that of Mr Brunel here as everyone, including myself had so hopefully, and I may say confidently, predicted, but the design submitted by Mr W. Hawks.'

Davies Gilbert, a past president of the Royal Society and once a close associate of the ill-fated Richard Trevithick, was undoubtedly one of the foremost experts on long-span suspension bridges, having acted as Telford's principal consultant on the Menai. As author of the first exhaustive analysis dealing with the construction of suspension bridges – it had been published five years before and its postulations were based on the theory of the catenary – no one seemed better qualified for the task of judging impartially the Clifton competition. However his fellow judge, John Seaward, though a marine engineer of some distinction, was, by his own admission, almost totally lacking in both theoretical knowledge and practical experience in this most highly specialised subject. His appointment had been, and remained, a complete mystery.

Of twelve entries this time, five had been short-listed – Telford's and those of W. Hawks, J. M. Rendel, S. Brown (the same Captain Brown who had been responsible for the Kelso bridge) and Brunel. But the design over which Bristol had so enthused had since been discarded, ostensibly because of the prohibitive cost of raising those two enormous towers. It was suspected, however, that the real reason was Isambard's brilliant exposure of its basic weakness and its elderly author's now obvious and tragic timidity.

Osborne's bombshell was greeted with stunned disbelief. Isambard sat motionless in his high-backed rather worn leather armchair, one of the pair placed for the occasion in front of the lawyer's vast and ornately carved black oak desk. His expression had not changed. He gave no indication of the inner turmoil he was suffering. But dear God above – if indeed there was a God, which in moments like this he sometimes doubted – fate could surely not be so damnably perverse as to have brought him yet again so nearly within the reach of the fruit of success and still snatch it away. Or could it?

In contrast to Brunel's apparent composure, Roch immediately blew up. For several minutes he stormed round the room, quite beside himself with rage. Osborne waited patiently until he had exhausted a truly impressive vocabulary of rare expletives before continuing.

'It would appear our two worthy judges have had some sort of last-minute disagreement regarding the total acceptability of Mr Brunel's design.'

'I was under the impression they had been in complete accord throughout,' Nicholas grated between tightly clenched teeth, the while furiously drumming his fingers on the mantelshelf.

'So were we all,' Osborne agreed. 'Right up to the moment they spoke with me yesterday it had seemed so. Indeed, on more than one occasion and in Seaward's presence I, and others, have heard Gilbert declare categorically his whole-hearted approval of Mr Brunel's plans.'

'Then why?' And Roch brought his fist down with such force that the heavily gilded French clock in the centre of the mantelshelf, Osborne's pride and joy, jumped perceptibly with a noisily discordant jangle of chimes.

'My dear Roch!' Osborne cast an anxious eye in the direction of his disturbed timepiece. 'All I can tell you is that Seaward suddenly raised three major objections.'

'Three objections. Just like that. Right out of the blue.'

'So it would appear.'

'But why?' Nicholas again demanded, this time of no one in particular, but once more threatening the clock.

'Can you tell me what the objections are?' Isambard spoke for the first time, and the quiet steadiness of his voice seemed to calm Roch's still flaring anger.

'They were, one,' Osborne ticked them off on his fingers, 'the method of attaching the suspension rods; two, the method of anchoring the suspension chains; and three, the use of pins instead of connecting links in the suspension chains.' Both business man and lawyer looked to the engineer for comment.

'Well, I suppose all three are reasonably valid points for Seaward to raise,' Isambard said after a pause. He was desperately trying to keep an open mind so that he might see the objections from what would be Seaward's obviously limited point of view.

'Yes, but not at this late stage,' said Roch bitterly, his suspicion apparent.

'You think Mr Seaward may have been – er, shall we say, influenced?' Osborne asked in a tone which seemed to indicate the thought was no stranger to his mind.

'Do you?' Roch challenged.

But Osborne refused to be drawn. Instead he said, 'I think it might perhaps prove more beneficial to our cause in the long run if, for the moment at least, we content ourselves merely with keeping an open mind.' At which Nicholas grunted disconsolately while the lawyer turned his full attention to Isambard once more. 'Continue, Mr Brunel, if you please.'

'Of the three objections the first two are relatively minor. Little more than quibbles, in fact.'

Nicholas snorted in disgust, taking this statement as confirmation his suspicions were by no means unwarranted. 'But the third is vital,' he growled.

Osborne looked again to Isambard.

'It is. Absolutely vital.'

'How so, Mr Brunel?' Osborne asked. 'Please explain. But in

layman's language, if you possibly can,' he hastened to add.

'Basically it is the one essential element common to this and my previous designs. Admittedly it is something of a revolutionary proposal to use pins instead of connecting links for the chains. It's never been done before.'

'But it *can* be done?'

'Of course. Precisely because it has never been done, it is one factor I've been particularly careful to verify – as far, that is, as is humanly possible.'

'Of all the experts who have examined those calculations,' put in Roch unable to keep quiet any longer, 'Mr Marine-Engine-Builder Seaward is – apart from Telford, of course, who probably didn't bother anyway – the only one who has raised any objections. Not Gilbert, mind – Seaward!'

'Which means?' Osborne asked mildly.

'That the wretched man obviously can't understand a set of simple mathematical calculations,' said Isambard tartly, the thought of being at the mercy of what he regarded as Seaward's abysmal ignorance at last getting the better of him.

'Or that he damn well doesn't want to understand them,' Roch concluded bitterly.

Osborne merely grunted and thoughtfully examined his immaculately kept fingernails. Then he said, 'Let us, for the sake of argument, suppose Mr Seaward's objections to be genuine, and entirely his own – the result, if you wish, of his inexperience in such matters. Also that, apart from these three specific points he has raised, both judges are still agreed that Mr Brunel's design remains superior to any of the others but, because of this use of pins in place of the more conventional connecting links in the suspension chains, both are prepared to drop it in favour of a poor second choice.'

'Damn Seaward!' Nicholas swore, making another vicious assault on the mantelpiece clock by way of emphasis.

'Gentlemen,' Osborne's eye once again strayed apprehensively in the direction of those painfully jangling chimes, 'as far as I am aware this information is known to no one outside this room – apart from the two judges, of course. It may, however, be made public at any moment; then the fat, I think, will really be in the fire. There is, I'm sure you will both agree, no time to be lost. For what it is worth, it is my opinion, Nicholas, that our brilliant young friend here is about to be robbed of his hard-earned and well-deserved success, not necessarily by Mr Seaward's unfortunate ignorance, nor even by his possible treachery, but by Mr Davies Gilbert's apparent inability to stick to his own decision without the whole-hearted support of his colleague. Such being the case, I regard the attitude of both individuals reprehensible and equally deplorable.'

'Well there's certainly no argument on that score,' Roch agreed warmly. 'But the question remains, what the hell's to be done about it?'

'Mr Brunel?' prompted the lawyer, his eyes suddenly twinkling.

'The sooner the one is disillusioned and the other reassured, the better it will be for all concerned,' said Isambard emphatically.

'Which is precisely why I was so anxious to have you call here just as soon as you had returned to Bristol. Thanks be to Providence, and Nicholas, that you came when you did.' Osborne beamed at them both before continuing. 'It is, furthermore, for that very reason that I have already taken the rather unforgivable liberty of arranging through an anonymous intermediary – needless to say one cannot be too discreet in matters of such a delicate nature – for Mr Brunel to meet and confer with Messrs Gilbert and Seaward this very afternoon. And, need I add, in the strictest privacy, of course. But, naturally, only if this admittedly somewhat irregular course of action is agreeable to you, my dear young Sir?'

Chapter Ten

THE house was a blaze of light, and the merrymaking within clearly audible above the leather creak of springs and the clatter of hooves as Brunel's carriage entered the wide sweep of its tree-lined drive. Even Porson, the Roches' normally taciturn coachman, was moved to remark with a wide grin that he had never experienced the like. 'Never in all my forty years with the family, Sir. Why, bless me! not even the Trafalgar and Waterloo "dos" was up to this lot,' he observed cheerily.

Brunel was overwhelmed by a veritable mob of wildly excited well-wishers before he had even crossed the threshold. He was shaken by the hand, shaken by both hands, clapped on the shoulders, slapped on the back, even unashamedly hugged and kissed by his delighted hostess whose example was instantly followed by all the other ladies present, young and old. He was plied with glass after glass of ice-cold sparkling bubbling champagne. Then he was chaired as if he had been the most important and popular candidate ever to have won an election. Eventually they stood him on a table and refused to let him down until he'd made a speech. Breathlessly he did his best to demur, but there was no escape.

That afternoon he had been summoned to Blaise Castle to be officially informed of his triumph. Then, not wishing to waste any more time – for it had taken the better part of two and a half years just to get this far – the full fifteen-man Bridge Building Committee under the chairmanship of the mayor had gone into working session with Isambard co-opted as a special member. There had followed several hours of lengthy totally inconclusive argument and hopelessly muddled discussion on this or that aspect of the undertaking, none of fundamental importance; but eventually a unanimous vote of confidence had given him virtual carte-blanche. The necessary applications to Parliament were to be made just as soon as the plans could be finalised, and the actual construction work was to commence no later than 20 June, next.

Though there was to be nothing to compare with the civic reception accorded Thomas Telford when his plan had been adopted the previous year, Brunel was in no wise disappointed. It was the substance of success, not the show, that was important. And with that, plus the fact he had also been voted a fairly generous expense allowance, he was, for the time being, perfectly satisfied.

'Speech! Speech! Speech! Speech!' chanted the throng surrounding him.

'For he's a jolly good fellow!' sang out a powerful tenor from their midst before it was quiet enough for Isambard's voice to be heard.

'And so say all of us!' agreed a lusty chorus to a thunder of applause and foot stamping.

'Hip-pip-pip', came an anonymous but equally commanding call from the rear of the serried ranks of singers. 'Hurrah!' roared the response. And twice more were the calls so answered. Then followed more applause, more foot stamping, yet more cheers, until the insistent chant of 'Speech! Speech! Speech! Speech!' was renewed.

Drawing himself up to his full five feet four inches, face flushed with excitement, wine and pleasure, eyes shining happily and chest puffed out in a mock magniloquence that thoroughly delighted his audience, Brunel did his best to make himself heard above the barrage of cheers, laughter and applause.

There was another celebration when he returned to London. But that was not until the second week in April, it having taken him a good three weeks of non-stop labour to complete the final plans for the bridge and have them engraved, printed and delivered to Osborne for despatch to Westminster.

Ellen's reaction to his news had been a letter much longer and loving than any he'd had since his failure to go north to see her the previous September. Poor Ellen! He could imagine how much she'd been hurt by what she must have seen as his continued cavalier neglect of her. He had tried so hard not to hurt her, even harder to explain. But now all that was going to be changed. Once the actual construction work was in progress he would have time, dammit he would make time, to go and see her and to put in hand, at last, all the necessary arrangements for their marriage.

The delay in getting back to London in no way impaired the spontaneity, nor cooled the warmth, of the welcome when he finally arrived. Emma's greeting was, of course, entirely predictable. Curiously though, his mother too shed a few tears, which was rare indeed, and even Marc's eyes seemed to be somewhat brighter than usual as he proudly embraced his son in true Gallic fashion. Then he soberly shook him by the hand in a manner far more in keeping with the less demonstrative custom of his adopted country. Sophia kissed him on both cheeks in staid sisterly fashion. But she smiled at him with a wealth of understanding, and an air of conspiratorial empathy apparent to no one else. Ben in his typically bluff, no nonsense, John Bull manner, thumped him so heartily on the back that for hours afterwards Brunel was ruefully conscious of the impact of that large heavy hand.

It being his first real independent success, his family naturally did their best to make the most of it. 'Let's hope,' observed Sophia a trifle sombrely when, to conclude the formal celebratory dinner at the Barge House, the final toast had been drunk, 'let's just hope none of this wretched nonsense in any way interferes with the building of Isambard's beautiful bridge.'

The 'wretched nonsense' to which Sophia referred was the renewed outbreak of civil unrest that had followed the near defeat of Grey's Reform Bill in the Commons. The government having survived by just a single vote, it seemed the prime minister now had no alternative but to ask the king for a dissolution. But King William, notwithstanding his previously professed support for Grey, was apparently proving no more trustworthy than his late unlamented brother, George IV, had been. Since coming to the throne, it was said, he was daily being more influenced by the hated Duke of Newcastle and his cronies Sir Robert Finch and Sir Charles Wetherall – the latter Recorder of Bristol as well as the sitting member for one of the duke's many Yorkshire pocket boroughs – and other equally hated anti-Reformers.

Also, rumour was rife that the Tories had already spiked Grey's guns, as it were, by having persuaded the king to call upon Wellington to form another administration instead of granting a dissolution. It would be perfectly constitutional for the sovereign to do this. But, many opined ominously, in the circumstances decidedly inadvisable. But no one really knew anything for certain, and such was the blur of chaos obscuring the political scene that few, even among those who could claim to be best informed, were capable of hazarding more than a guess as to how things were likely to stand from one day to the next.

On the twentieth Ben and Sophia were to dine with old friends of theirs, William and Elizabeth Horsley, and when their hosts learned that Isambard was at the Barge House, they insisted he accompany them. Having so much to do in London before his intended return to Bristol on the twenty-fourth, he was at first reluctant to spare the time. But, as things turned out, he was very glad indeed he did.

The moment he set eyes on Mary Horsley he decided she was, without the slightest doubt, the most exquisitely beautiful creature he had ever had the good fortune to meet. Truly her mother's daughter, as her father always proudly described her, she was, at seventeen, a most striking looking young lady already possessed of a perfect combination of classic features, natural charm and a poise which, like her mother's, would become all the more regal with the passage of time. It was not for nothing that Mary Horsley was known to her friends and her many admirers as the 'Duchess of Kensington'.

Mary had two sisters and two brothers. Fanny was fifteen, John just a year younger. Adult for their ages, though not in the least objectionably precocious, both were talented artists. John, it was hoped, would one day follow in the distinguished footsteps of his great-uncle, Augustus Wall Calcott, to become the family's second Royal Academician. Sophy and Charles, on the other hand – twelve and ten respectively – took after their father, a well known composer of anthems and popular glees, and were obviously destined to become musicians of note. Their eldest sister, however, displayed talent for neither music nor painting nor, for that matter, anything else. But with her own rare gift, of which she was undeniably conscious though not unduly vain, she seemed utterly content.

The Horsleys lived at 1 High Row in the village of Kensington Gravel Pits, only a mile or so from Piccadilly. Here the parents had raised their talented family, and in recent years their home had become one of the recognised meeting places for artists and musicians from home and abroad. Among the latter was Felix Mendelssohn-Bartholdy. Now twenty-two, Felix had been a child prodigy and the composer of many famous pieces, his incomparable 'Midsummer Night's Dream' music to name but one. He had first come to London two years before and had stayed at High Row, having been introduced to the Horsleys by Karl Klingemann, an attaché at the Hanoverian Embassy, and Friedrich Rosen, Professor of Oriental Languages at the newly founded University of London.

The young composer had been expected on the nineteenth; however news of the sudden illness of his father forcing him to abandon his trip had been received but a few hours before Ben, Sophia and Isambard arrived. The evening, nevertheless, was most enjoyable, especially as far as Isambard was concerned. To his delight he found himself next to Mary at table, then seated between her and her eldest brother in the drawing room afterwards. Once the two youngest children had withdrawn, after entertaining their parents' guests with a most expertly performed recital of piano solos and duets, the conversation had inevitably and depressingly gravitated to a general discussion of the political situation. But in this Isambard participated as little as politeness would permit, contriving instead to divide his attention between John and Fanny, who were talking art, and a covert but intense appreciation of the charms of the beautiful Mary. For him that evening ended all too soon.

The dissolution did, in fact, come two nights later. London promptly went wild with delight, as did all cities and towns throughout the kingdom as soon as the news reached them. 'Gaffer Grey – with the King's help, God Bless Him!' – had won the day. Down with the borough-mongers and up with the People! Now, they said, the Tories and their friends would really be put to rout.

The following night, and with the authority of the lord mayor, the capital was illuminated by fires, by lanterns, by torches, and by countless thousands of candles burning in countless thousands of windows. During the day banners and favours celebrating the dissolution had been displayed everywhere, and in streets thronged with triumphant processions of cheering chanting people, the opponents of reform had wisely chosen not to show themselves. On the whole, however, things had been relatively orderly.

But once darkness had fallen the situation soon began to get seriously out of control. Street-corner orators appeared as if from nowhere to urge their listeners, of whom there was no lack, to storm what they called the bastions of reaction; to seek out those they capriciously identified as the enemies of the People; to destroy their property; to round them up in the name of liberty; to plaster their persons with muck and mud and throw them into the nearest horse ponds. And once violence as a consequence of such outrageous exhortations began to erupt, it soon became rife and totally uncontainable.

All public buildings and private houses which failed to display what was arbitrarily considered to be requisite brilliance of illumination, had their windows smashed by gangs of toughs who roamed the streets only too eager to hurl their brickbats and wield their bludgeons with much abandon and little discrimination. Genuine reformers stood aghast at the appalling excesses perpetrated in supposed support of their movement. But they were as powerless as the police to prevent the hooligans from running amok and doing more or less as they pleased.

The residences of the Duke of Gloucester, Sir Robert Peel, the Marquis of Londonderry, the hated Duke of Newcastle and the Duke of Wellington were the first and most popular targets. Every visible pane of glass in Apsley House was shattered by a shower of stones. Inside the duchess lay critically ill. Two days later she died, her end undoubtedly hastened by the shock of the terrible riot. All night long the senseless rampage went on. When at last order had been restored it was only too apparent that it would be a good many days before the city's harassed glaziers would be able to obtain glass in sufficient quantities even to begin to make good the damage.

In Bristol, as elsewhere, election fever now disrupted practically every aspect of normal existence. With the new Parliament due to assemble on 14 June, the hustings began immediately – more violent than any within living memory. Everywhere the Tories were in the minority, and when it was all over there was many a long-serving member of the House of Commons who found himself unseated, even among those who for years had represented what had always been regarded as the safest of pocket boroughs.

Slowly at least a semblance of normality was restored. But there remained a uniquely curious undercurrent of excitement, an expectation that seemed to pervade every stratum of society. After such an emphatic declaration of the People's will, it was said, there surely could be nothing to prevent the passage of any future Reform Bill through Parliament.

Fortunately all this seemed to have had a minimal effect on the arrangements for starting work on the bridge. In fact the first turf on the site of the tower on the Gloucestershire side of the gorge was cut on Waterloo Day, two days before the date originally scheduled. On the following Tuesday, the 21st, the Bridge Committee, their ladies, their numerous distinguished guests and their engineer, sat down to a formal public breakfast hosted at the Bath Hotel in Clifton by the Bristol Chamber of Commerce. Then, with Sir Abraham and Lady Elton – the most socially influential couple of the Clifton community – in the van, all made their way to a specially prepared spot on the downs not far from the cliff edge. In brilliant sunshine they formed a circle round a largish mound of newly excavated earth and stone, the labourers there promptly downing tools to watch.

At a given signal the dapper, boyish-looking engineer entered the circle at whose centre was positioned the principal pair, picked up a fairly substantial chunk of cream-coloured rock which had of course been selected and prepared in advance and presented it, with a carefully rehearsed bow and appropriate observation, also rehearsed, to Lady Elton. Accepting the offering with equal, though in her case entirely unrehearsed, formality, her fashionably and immaculately attired ladyship somehow contrived to retain a graceful grip on the roughly hewn oolite with neither appreciable sacrifice of dignity nor detectable detriment to elegance. This action prompted a sudden, generally unexpected and therefore somewhat alarming artillery discharge from a battery of cannon positioned close by, but out of sight. As the reverberating echoes of those deafening explosions slowly faded the faint strains of the 'National Anthem' could be heard from the depths of the gorge, the band of the Dragoon Guards having been strategically placed beforehand on the bank of the river at the base of the cliff. At the same time the Union Jack and divers more colourful, if less familiar, banners were ceremonially run up a specially erected array of temporary flagstaffs.

The scene having been set, Sir Abraham Elton solemnly stepped forward to deliver the sort of lengthy, hopefully evocative oration without which no important public occasion could ever be considered wholly complete. It was a pity that Sir Abraham was an incredibly dull speaker who suffered, furthermore, from a curious inability to stress meaning with co-ordinated movement. But when at length he launched into his peroration he nevertheless endeavoured, and not entirely unsuccessfully, to achieve a degree of quite creditable theatrical emphasis by pointing dramatically, if a trifle vaguely, in Isambard's direction.

'The time will come,' he declaimed in hoarse but measured and, for once, reasonably modulated tones, 'the time will surely come, I say, when, as that gentleman,' pointing towards Brunel, 'walks along the street, or as he passes from city to city, the cry will be raised "There goes the man who reared that stupendous work – truly, the Ornament of Bristol – the Wonder of the Age!" '

Chapter Eleven

'THE Wonder of the Age!' That far from original phrase of Sir Abraham Elton's seemed to fall somewhat flat when the flags and the finery had finally disappeared and the site was once more a simple field of fresh-turned earth. Gone were the cheers and the sound of salutes and the stirring strains of martial music. Instead the gorge now echoed with the clash of metal on metal, of metal on stone, and the raucous choruses of labourers' ribald work-songs. And in place of the heady delight of a champagne-fuelled celebration was the stark realisation that, after all, nothing had yet been achieved. All was still to be gained – fame, fortune, fulfilment. Brunel had won the competition, the bridge he had designed might indeed be all its admirers had so lavishly declared it to be, but until that bridge was actually built, until it stood for all to see, it was nothing. This he knew from painful experience. Had he not been involved in a 'Wonder of the Age' before? And had not that experience taught him that everything now, as then, would depend almost entirely on money?

The lowest estimate for the total cost of construction was £45,000. Available funds at the time of the announcement of the second competition had totalled just short of £30,000. Subscriptions since had amounted to no more than a paltry £500, barely sufficient to defray Isambard's personal expenses. The budgeted expenditure on stone and ironwork alone was, to date, already in excess of the actual cash in hand, and to this must be added not only the cost of labour but the inevitable incidental expenses which could only be vaguely forecast. So he was at pains to warn the committee every time they met that unless something was done about raising more cash, and done quickly, the possibility of the whole project having to be abandoned could not, even at this stage, be entirely ruled out.

Committees, however, no matter how constituted or for what purpose, tend to be the same the world over, and the summer was long past before a decision was made to open a new public appeal for funds on 1 November. But in so planning their affairs the members of the Bristol Bridge Building Committee, and their engineer, failed to reckon with the heavy hand of fate. The political situation was again deteriorating rapidly, and this time even more alarmingly.

In the teeth of desperate Tory opposition Grey's second Reform Bill had indeed, as expected, sailed through all its stages in the Commons with resounding majorities, and appropriate celebration. But when at the beginning of October the Upper House had begun its deliberations, an air of hushed expectancy had settled over the land. So far, it suddenly seemed to be realised, the Reformers had won only a battle. The People's Bill, as it had come to be called, like any other bill, could only become law after it had been passed by the House of Lords where the Tories, of course, traditionally commanded an overwhelming majority. The burning question now was, would they dare to block the Commons' legislation. The war was far from over!

A ding-dong debate lasted five days. As its climactic end drew near, packed crowds in Palace Yard and all the approach roads to Westminster waited expectantly for the moment of truth. But Friday midnight came and went without word or even intimation of a conclusion one way or the other. Shortly afterwards the heavens suddenly opened and the crowds hurriedly dispersed to seek shelter from the drenching rain. When the vital division finally took place just before dawn it was still pouring and the streets, fortunately, had been long deserted. Had they been otherwise – and but for the rain they most certainly would have been – their gutters might well have run with blood not water for their lordships, in their folly, had voted out the People's Bill.

Riot and outrage spread like wildfire. Within hours the whole country had erupted in a horrifying preview of the sort of bloody revolution that could so easily follow. Never before had there been such an upheaval. In every county, city, town, village and hamlet chaos, for a time, reigned supreme. All known Tories and Tory sympathisers, both peers and commoners, were stoned in the streets. Public buildings and private houses were attacked by howling rampageous mobs. In London an angry multitude gathered outside St James's Palace, and for a time there were fears for the safety of the king and his family. Nottingham's ancient castle was stormed and razed simply because it had once belonged to the Duke of Newcastle. Property of all kinds, everywhere, was wantonly destroyed.

If at that moment the prime minister had chosen to resign it is doubtful if the country would have been able to pull back from the dreadful abyss into which it seemed intent on hurling itself. But a resounding vote of confidence in the Commons following the Lords' defeat ensured the survival of Earl Grey's government for the time being at least. It was wisely decided, however, to bring that parliamentary session to an early close, in the hope that some measure of calm might be restored. But, declared the chastened monarch in his prorogation speech, the question of constitutional reform in the Commons House of Parliament would be submitted again at the opening of the ensuing session, one month hence. Thereafter wherever men gathered, the recently uttered words of Lord John Russell 'it is no longer possible that the whisper of faction should prevail against the voice of a nation', were oft and fervently quoted.

Isambard had spent the whole of Saturday, 29 October, in Bath as the guest of William Beckford, the famous art connoisseur, whose house in Lansdowne Crescent had once been described as a concentration of elegant splendour rendered agreeable and unostentatious by its purity of taste and well-studied luxury. It was not until he returned in the early hours of Sunday morning that he learned of what had happened in Bristol during his absence.

Since the recent outbreak of violence, which had been curiously brief, the city had been strangely quiet. An ominous build-up of tension, however, had soon made it apparent the disaffected populace was reserving the full force of its fury for the opening of the Autumn Assize – and Sir Charles Wetherall. Then, if rumour was to be believed, and there seemed no reason for it to be doubted, all hell was likely to break loose.

Had the recorder of Bristol been possessed of even a modicum of reason he might, perhaps, have learned a lesson from the demonstrations of extreme disapproval his past parliamentary indiscretions had provoked at the time of the April Assize. Though he in no way represented the people of Bristol – the city had two MPs of its own – he persisted in speaking for them in the House, thus exacerbating an already sorely strained relationship.

Anxious to avert by whatever means possible any sort of

confrontation which must inevitably lead to the worsening of an already near desperate situation, the Mayor, Charles Pinney – neither the most authoritative nor, alas, the most intelligent of civic officials – had sought either to have the Assize postponed, which could be done only with the concurrence of the recorder himself, or dissuade him from attending. But, being the sort of man he was, Sir Charles Wetherall would have nothing whatever to do with what he termed weak-kneed shilly-shallying. His only response to Pinney's appeal had been the reiteration of his determination to enter Bristol with all the pomp and ceremony it was the recorder's prerogative to demand. And, as was customary, he expected to drive in procession, accompanied by the mayor and the magistrates, to the cathedral to attend divine service the following day.

Panicked by the prospect of what such recklessness would be bound to lead to, the mayor hurriedly forwarded an official request to the Home Secretary, Lord Melbourne, for military aid. The Common Council, at the mayor's bidding, approved directives to the chief constables of all wards to recruit as specials as many respectable citizens as they could. But almost the only response came from young, upper-class anti-Reformers who contemptuously regarded all members of the lower orders, irrespective of political affiliations, as rebellious trouble makers, and saw this as a heaven-sent opportunity to teach those they considered rabble a much needed and long overdue lesson.

A belated and impassioned approach was made to William Herepath, president of Bristol's Political Union. Knowing nothing of the arrangements to bring in the military, Herepath at first readily pledged full support. Organised demonstrations were one thing; uncontrolled violence however was to be deplored by all decent folk and – Bristol, like the rest of the country, already having had a taste of it – something to be avoided at all costs. But when he discovered that a troop of 3rd Dragoons and another of 14th Hussars under the command of Lieutenant Colonel Brereton, Resident Inspecting Field Officer of the Bristol recruiting districts, were already in the city, Herepath angrily withdrew his promise. And though he and his colleagues issued a private appeal to all Union members to assist individually in the preservation of public peace, they refused point-blank to cooperate in any way with the civic power.

The day had dawned ominously. Even before sun-up the city's

streets were crowded and the tension at fever pitch. The recorder arrived at Totterdown, where the state coach of the sheriffs and a company of specials were waiting, at ten in the morning instead of the customary two in the afternoon, Wetherall having grudgingly agreed to the last-minute change of time. He'd travelled from Bath in a private carriage, indeed Isambard had passed him on his way to Lansdowne Crescent. All the same there was a large and ugly-looking crowd waiting for him and he was greeted with hisses, boos, shouted abuse and loud dismal groans. For nearly an hour the sheriffs had tried to reason with him. But, deaf to all argument, he'd stubbornly insisted that under no circumstances was he, one of His Majesty's judges, going to be put off by a rabble of noisy louts – which loudly expressed sentiment brought forth a lusty cheer from the specials who had swung their truncheons in eager anticipation of putting them to use.

At last the state coach set off for the Guildhall, the specials following close behind. And with it went a noisy escort, already hundreds strong, swelling in number almost at every step and chanting blood-chilling obscenities. Soon the narrow twisting street seemed to be choked with a milling mass of cursing, yelling humanity, the harassed coachman having to use all his skill to control his terrified horses and guide the heavy vehicle while shrieking ragged women pelted him with sticky slimy cakes of reeking mud. A huge crowd was massed on Bristol Bridge. As the coach lumbered into Temple Street the already frightful din doubled both in volume and in fury. Outside the Guildhall the crush of people was so great the constables were scarce able to get their charges into the building unscathed.

The sheriffs, to a man, were completely unnerved, and even the pugnacious recorder looked shaken. Once installed in his courtroom, however, he quickly regained his stolid composure, in blustering tones reducing the occupants of the public gallery from noisy insolence to sullen silence by threatening to commit forthwith any and all disturbers of the peace. But the traditional call for cheers for the king at the conclusion of the preliminary proceedings was answered in a way that poured the utmost scorn on the bewigged and robed administrator of his justice.

Between the Guildhall and the Mansion House where the mayor was waiting to receive the recorder, the usual civic reception at the

Guildhall having been cancelled in spite of Wetherall's indignant protests, the crowds seemed even more dense and more vocal. Twice the coach was stoned – as it turned into Queen Square, again as it entered the grounds of the Mansion House.

Formalities were studiously observed by the colourfully robed but grey-faced mayor and council, though they and their guests, of whom Nicholas was one, could hardly hear themselves speak such was the nerve-shattering racket that penetrated even the innermost regions of the building. Had there been a single municipal officer outside with sufficient presence of mind or strength of character to use his authority to its full effect, in all probability the crowd, having voiced its protest, would in time have dispersed relatively peacefully. A large number had already departed, and many more were actually leaving the square when, without warning, the fifty-strong company of specials suddenly charged. Shouting 'we'll give you Reform!' and swinging their truncheons indiscriminately, they attacked any and all in their way. In the running fight that followed, they stood no chance. Driven back, first to the walls, then into the no longer secure grounds of the Mansion House, they broke ranks and fled for their lives.

The mob was now completely out of control. In a courageous attempt to plead for restraint and reason, the mayor appeared in the portico. He was howled down. It was far too late for appeals. He started to read the Riot Act but was forced to retreat before a lethal volley of stones. Within minutes every window in the Mansion House had been shattered, its hurriedly barred doors all but battered down.

Also among the civic guests was a Major Mackworth, aide-de-camp to Lord Hill the Commander-in-Chief, who took charge. Having recently completed a tour of duty in the Forest of Dean, where some of the most serious disturbances in the country had occurred, he knew better than to try and stand against the fury of such a mob. He ordered the ground floor to be immediately evacuated and all staircases barricaded. No sooner was this done than the screaming horde stormed in, by now completely berserk and, the reason for the riot forgotten, abandoning itself to a frenzy of looting and wanton destruction. Everything that could be moved was carried away – everything that could not was smashed. Then, having made prisoners of the mayor, every single member of the council and the prime target of their hatred, Sir Charles Wetherall, they began deliberate and systematic preparations to burn the place down.

By this time Nicholas, speaking for the majority, had managed to convince Wetherall that as his presence in Bristol was so obviously the principal cause of all the trouble, the sooner he was as far away from the Mansion House and the city as possible, the better it would be for all concerned. Blustering to the last, the recorder had finally agreed to make his escape through an attic window at the rear of the building from which, by clambering over the roof out of sight of the crowd below, fairly easy access could be gained to the adjacent and as yet unbesieged Custom House. Mackworth had prevailed on Nicholas to accompany him, and once he'd seen Wetherall safely on the road to Bath, he'd gone straight home. Hours later he'd been joined there by Alderman James Hilhouse, also a Clifton resident and his host for the day at the Mansion House. Over a late supper Hilhouse had continued the story.

The arrival of the military had prevented the firing of the Mansion House but had otherwise done little to ease the situation, one of the dragoons unfortunately having fatally injured an innocent bystander during a scuffle en route from their barracks. By walking his men round the square and talking personally with as many of the rioters' leaders as he could, Colonel Brereton, a well known and respected local man, had eventually managed to convince them that Wetherall was no longer in the city and that there was little point in continuing the siege. He'd even gone as far as ordering Captain Gage and his dragoons to withdraw to Keynsham, some distance outside the city. In the opinion of Hilhouse and others, this had been a most unwise concession, though the mayor and most of the council had approved. But Captain Gage had obeyed his superior's order only with the utmost reluctance, Hilhouse said.

Brereton's appeal to Herepath had gone unanswered. And such was now the universal unpopularity of both military and civic authority, that no assistance could be expected from the ordinary law-abiding citizenry of Bristol either. Regardless of the potentially devastating dangers of the situation, they seemed to be completely apathetic.

Just before midnight the crowd had suddenly decided it had had enough. By the time Hilhouse had been able to get away, Queen Square, apart from the hussars, a number of constables and a few stragglers, was deserted. The Mansion House windows had been boarded up, its doors made secure. The mayor was still in residence with three loyal servants – his family had been evacuated, and Major Mackworth was also remaining overnight.

'And is the trouble all over then?' Margaret Roch asked when Hilhouse finally came to the end of his sorry tale.

'Well,' the alderman answered tentatively, but with a distinct lack of conviction, 'as far as anyone can judge at the moment, it would appear so.'

From his perch on the arm of an easy chair by the fire, Isambard grunted.

'What are your plans now, James?' inquired Roch.

'I promised the mayor I'd join him first thing tomorrow – I mean, this morning,' Hilhouse corrected himself after glancing ruefully at the clock in the corner. It was nearly three o'clock.

'In which case I suggest we all retire and try and get as much rest as we can.' Isambard rose and tossed the stub of his cigar into the grate causing a shower of sparks to fly among the cinders.

'We?' queried Hilhouse, also getting to his feet.

'We,' Brunel confirmed with quiet emphasis.

'But there's no reason why you . . .' Margaret started to say.

'We shall need an early and substantial breakfast, if you would be kind enough to arrange it please, Margaret,' he interrupted her, his eyes already alight with the excitement of anticipation.

'But if, as James says, it's all over . . .'

'That, Nicholas, I would personally rather doubt. And I think the alderman here agrees with me?'

'I think I must, Mr Brunel,' sighed Hilhouse.

'Then it's settled.' Though the youngest by some years, it seemed entirely natural to the others that Brunel should take command in this way. 'We leave for Queen Square at dawn.'

Chapter Twelve

THAT the trouble was not over was obvious as soon as they entered the city. In fact, though no one fully realised it at the time, it was soon after first light on that grey Sunday morning that all hell did break loose in Bristol. During the night the criminal elements had been far from idle. By sun-up an army of down-and-outs and ne'er-do-wells was poised to take instant advantage of whatever the new day might bring, for by then it was common knowledge that the civic authority was incapable of maintaining any sort of order, the military force had been halved, and its commanding officer was 'soft'.

When Roch drove Brunel and Hilhouse into Queen Square in an open carriage and pair it was just in time to witness the departure of the soldiers. In spite of the presence of an already considerable and ever increasing number of hooligans obviously bent on mischief, Colonel Brereton was stubbornly insistent on his diminished force returning at once to barracks. Brunel and Roch watched in tight-lipped silence as forty fully equipped and well-mounted men passed them at a jingling trot while Hilhouse tried to reason with their commanding officer. But Brereton, his face already betraying the strain of a command he was in no way fitted to assume, refused even to consider the suggestion that instead of taking his men to the far side of the city, he bivouac them in the grounds of the Mansion House and by so doing maintain at least a presence in what would undoubtedly be the starting point of any further trouble.

Appalled by such incredibly blind and incomprehensible stupidity, Hilhouse fumed with futile indignation. No sooner had the troops moved out of the square than more and more hooligans began to move in.

'Make for the Mansion House, Nicholas,' Brunel rapped out the words sharply. Familiar with the ways of labourers and the like, his experienced eye had marked the threatening demeanour of some of the toughs who had started to close in on them. 'Take it steady to begin with. But be ready to go like the devil as soon as I give the word.'

Under Roch's firm hand the team went forward at an even pace for about a hundred yards. The rush Isambard had anticipated came just as they went into the corner. Whip in hand, he was ready for it.

'Now!' he yelled, at the same time lashing the horses mercilessly. Snorting with terror, they lunged forward.

Fortunately the speed of Roch's reaction and his expertise were sufficient to control that sudden mad career across the square. Caught off balance, however, poor Hilhouse was very nearly thrown from the violently jolting vehicle and for the next few hectic minutes was fully occupied in saving himself from disaster. Isambard meanwhile, somehow managing to maintain his balance without impeding Roch's efforts, was using his whip with devastating effect on the more daring and agile of their attackers who were trying to get a grip on the reeling vehicle. At least one ruffian went under their wheels. Bumping and bouncing crazily over the debris-strewn cobbles, it seemed they must surely come to grief. But with superb calm Roch guided the bolting animals into the grounds of the Mansion House and managed somehow to bring them to a rearing, plunging halt within yards of its door.

Less than a dozen rather surprised-looking men stood between them and the seemingly deserted building, for there was no sign of the constables they had supposed would still have been on duty, notwithstanding the military's dereliction. Nor was there any sign of life within. But many more were thundering in close pursuit and shouting to their friends ahead to stop the three from getting away. There was no doubt they were now after blood, and the thought flashed across Isambard's mind that if the Mansion House was deserted, or they found its doors barricaded against them, they were well and truly trapped and their chances of survival slim indeed. All they could do was keep going, and hope.

'Jump!' he roared, 'then run for your lives.' Hurling his whip stock first into the face of the nearest of the hooligans who had managed to keep clear of the horses' flailing hooves, he leapt from the carriage. As he hit the ground he dropped to his knees, snatched up the broken back of a chair, and was on his feet again in a single flowing movement. Wielding his fortuitous find as a most effective weapon, he raced for the main entrance with Hilhouse and Roch pounding along behind. As they gained the portico the doors swung open and, with heartfelt gasps of relief, they flung themselves inside.

'My congratulations, gentlemen,' cried a grinning Major Mackworth, slamming the doors and barring them once more. 'A remarkably well-executed manoeuvre, if I may say so.' Hilhouse and Roch he already knew, of course, and to Brunel he was hurriedly introduced while the door trembled alarmingly as pursuers hurled themselves furiously against its already weakened timbers.

'That damn thing will be down in a jiffy,' warned Mackworth. 'With a bit of luck this bunch of bastards will make for the mayor's grog before they tackle the upper floors. All the same, we'd best be off.' And so saying he led the way up the grand staircase and through the barricade at its head. Scarcely had this been secured once more than the doors gave way and a swarm of hard-faced ruffians burst in, viciously intent on all manner of villainy, but most of all on pillage. The municipal cellars, long famous for the quantity and quality of their contents, had for reasons unknown been overlooked the previous day and word of this had obviously got round. The invaders, as Mackworth had predicted, made straight for them.

'Give us a bit of breathing space if nothing else,' he observed with grim satisfaction as, with the mayor, the three loyal servants and the newcomers, he watched a laughing shouting human chain tramping back and forth through the battered ground-floor ruins laden with barrels of sherry, madeira and port; bottles of champagne, rhenish, burgundy, beaune, sauterne and such, and cask upon cask of brandy. 'Not an edifying sight, is it? We were just about to decamp ourselves when we spotted your bit of fun outside,' he remarked.

'Thank God you did!' Roch murmured fervently.

'Hear hear!' added Hilhouse, no less so.

'What's happened to the constables, major?' Brunel asked.

'Pah! Rabbits, the lot of them! They ran even before Brereton. And once he'd pushed off we'd no alternative but to run for it ourselves damit!'

'In hell's name, what does Brereton think he's playing at?' Nicholas wanted to know.

'God alone can answer that,' said Mackworth, 'I certainly can't.'

'I have every faith in Colonel Brereton's judgement,' the mayor, a trembling ashen-faced wreck of his former pompous self, interposed in a defensive bleat.

'You're entitled to your opinion, of course,' Mackworth snapped back dismissively.

'And what's your opinion, major?'

'Not my place to say anything really, Mr Brunel. Neither one way nor t'other. My position here is as unofficial as yours.'

'Then I insist it be made official forthwith,' declared Alderman Hilhouse. 'Yours too, Mr Brunel. And you, Nicholas. Our poor city is in desperate need of all the help we can give her. What say you, Charles?'

'Of course, of course,' stammered the mayor. 'I've already sworn in my servants here.'

'Well, gentlemen?' There could be but one answer for, like it or not, the three were already inextricably involved.

'Then, Charles,' Hilhouse prompted impatiently, 'by the power in you invested, come on man! "as Chief Magistrate of the City of Bristol . . ." '

'I hereby appoint you special constables, responsible for the protection of life and property for the duration of this emergency, however long it may last.' The mayor gabbled the words automatically. But then he added, in a tone of fervent, almost tearful sincerity, 'I thank you, gentlemen, all of you,' and, to the servants, 'thank you.'

'Time we were going, I think, Mr Mayor,' said Major Mackworth with a significant nod towards the suddenly increased clamour below. Feeble with fatigue and the burden of strain his now unenviable office had so far exacted, Charles Pinney had to be helped up to the attic room from where they could still escape by the same route Wetherall had used. Just to make sure, Isambard climbed out onto the leads. The ground was still shrouded in morning mist, the slates wet and slippery, but the pitch of the roof was not acute. So it was by no means difficult for a fairly agile man to keep his footing, and the distance to the Custom House was no more than seventy feet or so.

'Presumably the Custom House is still secure?'

Mackworth nodded. 'Built like a fortress. Not like this place. From what I've seen of it, I'd reckon it could hold out indefinitely. And it'll be well manned by now. It's a sovereign to a sixpence that's where all those other fine fellows have taken themselves. And, by

God, am I going to roast them when I catch up with them.'

'Then you three and the mayor go ahead. If these lads,' Brunel indicated the three servants, 'are willing to lend a hand, I'm for doing those blackguards below out of all the loot we can.'

'Good man,' cried Mackworth, slapping him on the shoulder.

'Five can do better,' exclaimed Nicholas. 'We'll shift a deal of stuff across that roof before they even realise what's happening. I'm staying.'

'And I,' chimed in Hilhouse.

'Us too, Sir,' from the servants.

'In that case, Mr Mayor, Major – we shall see you anon.'

Mackworth answered Isambard with an informal salute and a wide grin before turning to assist the tottering mayor to climb through the window.

'For God's sake, don't slip, Mr Mayor,' he whispered hoarsely as they set off. 'If you fall you'll give the game away and spoil everything.'

The rooftop route proved easy enough to negotiate, even when carrying a fairly substantial load. So for several hours the six laboured undisturbed, under Brunel's direction, ferrying to safety pictures, plate and other municipal valuables, small items of furniture, even carpets and a dismantled chandelier, from the untouched upper rooms of the Mansion House.

As the murky October morning slowly wore on the scene in Queen Square became one of bacchanalian orgy. By ten o'clock men, women, boys and girls, all madly intoxicated from guzzling looted wines and spirits, were staggering about screaming, singing, swearing and bellowing obscenities at the tops of their voices. Others, already too drunk even to stand, could only roll on the ground shrieking and shouting a raucous descant. Slatternly women and brazen girls in varying degrees of exposure coupled openly with brutish men before an audience of voyeurs of both sexes and all ages, some of whom bawled advice and encouragement while others howled with derisive laughter.

Such was the close concentration of unwashed humanity in the immediate vicinity of the Mansion House, and so incontinent their behaviour, that the stink they made soon rose through the damp autumnal air to offend the olfactory sensibilities of the still undetected toilers above. But the more enterprising among the motley collection of the very dregs of the city's gutters soon began to tire of mere senseless debauchery. Arming themselves with vicious looking bludgeons, hatchets, hammers, even pieces of ornamental Mansion House railings to use as pikes, and roused to a frenzy of bloodthirsty lust by the inflammatory harangues of their self-appointed leaders, those who were still able trooped off to wreak what havoc they would elsewhere. Those left behind, newly inspired, began to think once more of the sacking of the Mansion House. Which necessarily brought to an abrupt end the activities of Brunel and his stalwart companions.

The wandering gang's first destination was the Bridewell. Its buildings were fired and the inmates freed – most of whom wisely fled. But not so those of the new gaol, a hundred and fifty strong and all long-serving hardened criminals; they promptly usurped the leadership of the mob, urging more and even greater excesses.

It was not until the governor's house was being sacked that Colonel Brereton and the hussars at last put in an appearance. All during the morning, despite frantically repeated pleas and summonses to act, he had done precisely nothing. But now the mob instantly drew back, and had Brereton then used his men decisively and effectively, it might well have dispersed and the riot would have been at an end. But no order for action was forthcoming. So the hussars did nothing, and the precious moment was gone. Soon the rioters had regained their nerve, and once it became known that Brereton was deliberately holding back because, it was rumoured, he had specific orders from the Government not to interfere, the hussars were given a mighty cheer then insolently presented with a cask of looted brandy. Then with renewed vigour, the mob turned again to its wholesale and ruthless depredations.

The Toll House and Lawford's Gate Bridewell were attacked and burned. And still the hussars did nothing. Then it was the turn of the Bishop's Palace. Audaciously outspoken and always controversial, especially on the subject of politics, the Right Reverend Lord Bishop of Bristol had long been particularly unpopular with the Reformers. He had that very day, during morning service in his cathedral when the trouble had still been confined to Queen Square, seen fit to discourse yet again on the issue. It was a powerful sermon preached, as it turned out, not wisely but far too well, and his remarkably ill-chosen words had quickly been circulated round the city.

'Drive the despoilers from our midst,' he had thundered. 'Let the righteous stand shoulder to shoulder before this monstrous onslaught of evil, that it may then dash itself to pieces against the rock of rectitude whereon our cherished probity is justly founded. Let no one among you be weighed in the balance and found wanting.' Thus, from the sanctuary of his pulpit, had His Lordship challenged Reformers and rioters alike, demanding of them, and in the name of the Trinity no less, the immediate surcease of strife.

In so far, therefore, as an excuse was needed to attack the Bishop's Palace, this was as good as any – though the rioters' concern for what he had said was as minimal as their interest in anything even remotely connected with the subject of Parliamentary Reform. But, as the 'despoilers' advanced, the bishop, suddenly as it were beset by second thoughts in spite of his resolute militancy of the morning, decided that in his case anyway, discretion was perhaps after all the better part of valour, and he departed in what could only be described even charitably as undignified haste.

By the simple expedient of placing his men between the gates of the Palace grounds and the rioters, Brereton was again able to keep them at bay. Reckless as they had become, they were still unwilling to face armed cavalry. So when Major Mackworth arrived on the scene with a company of constables, among whom were Brunel, Roch and a number of other newly sworn specials, again it looked as if the trouble could be contained. But, as before, Brereton made no move. His men were ready, eager, anxious to open fire. But the Colonel refused to issue any such order except on the authority of the mayor, and only if the mayor instructed him personally there and then, and before witnesses, to do so. But Pinney had refused either to leave the safety of the Custom House or to put anything in writing.

Meanwhile, although the Bishop's Palace remained untouched, many neighbouring properties had been sacked and were now burning fiercely, while from Queen Square smoke was also rising ominously. As the long minutes ticked agonisingly by, the outlook was growing ever more serious.

'If something isn't done soon, it'll be too damn late to do anything,' Isambard remarked after he and his companions had been standing in line behind the military for what seemed like hours.

'But if the military won't move, there's damn all we can do,' Roch said bitterly.

At that moment Mackworth suddenly turned his back on Brereton and stalked towards them, his face a livid mask of rage.

'Colonel Brereton is pulling out,' he snarled as soon as he was within earshot. So astounding was this statement that his audience, for the moment, could only gape at him in open-mouthed disbelief.

'The man must be mad,' gasped Brunel, finding his voice at last.

'He is,' agreed the major savagely. 'If you ask me, he's as mad as a flaming mad March hare.'

'But, damn his soul!' Roch swore, his eyes wild with anger, 'he can't. He can't pull out now.'

'Oh yes he can,' said Mackworth, suddenly weary, 'and he is – listen.'

As Brereton gave the order for the hussars to form column of twos and prepare to move off, a ripple of anticipation both audible and visible ran through the ranks of massed rioters. Then, deaf to loud murmurs of protest, not only from the deserted constables but from among his own men as well, and ignoring the ironic cheers of the rabble, he calmly left the doomed Bishop's Palace to its fate, just as he had left the Mansion House that morning.

'Order your men out too, please Major Mackworth.' Hilhouse had joined his dismayed comrades as soon as the soldiers had started to move. No longer a young man, the strain of the last few hours was beginning to make its mark. But what he might lack in physical strength the alderman more than made up in spirit. All the same, at that moment, he looked utterly weary. Patiently he quelled the outbreak of protest with which his order was received.

'I know, gentlemen. I fully appreciate how you must feel. Heaven knows, I share your sentiments. But we must be practical. We can do nothing here alone. Our most sensible course of action now is to return at once to the Custom House.'

'Is that where Brereton is heading?'

'The hussars are returning to barracks, Mr Brunel,' Hilhouse answered grimly. 'And as far as I am aware, the colonel is going with them. Carry on please, Major Mackworth.'

Twenty minutes later the Bishop's Palace and the neighbouring Chapter House, with its priceless library of more than six thousand volumes, was in flames.

Chapter Thirteen

A S darkness began to fall, the rioters returned to their starting point. Those who remained in Queen Square, however, had been remarkably unenterprising. Disheartened by their disappointing harvest in the Mansion House – their screams of rage at finding themselves so deprived of loot having been clearly audible in the adjoining Custom House, much to the satisfaction of Brunel and his friends – they had consumed yet more liquor, then wallowed in an undisturbed stupor of semi-insensibility for most of the hours of daylight remaining.

In the late afternoon, however, the Mansion House had been accidentally set on fire. A pimp with a keen eye for profit had installed his prostitutes in the upper rooms of the building. His novel brothel had been doing a roaring trade until one of his drunken clients knocked a lighted candle onto the brandy-soaked skirts of the doxy he was pawing. Instantly the woman became a human torch. In the ensuing panic no attempt was made either to contain or control the fire, which had spread rapidly, or to save those incapable of realising what was happening from being trapped by the flames. Seven men and four women had been burnt to death in that conflagration alone.

No one not immediately involved in the incident, however, seemed to care. But it had served as a terrible inspiration to the hitherto dull-witted drunks who then began breaking into and setting light to other buildings in the square. And with the return of the wandering gang it at once turned into a highly organised and frighteningly efficient operation. One after the other houses were burgled, their looted contents carted away by a never-ending procession of waggons, horses and barrows or simply on the backs of men, women and children. Then the looters moved on, and the incendiaries moved in, not a few of the latter perishing in the fires they themselves had started, their pitiful screams clearly heard above the roar of the flames and the almost incessant crash of falling masonry. But still no one seemed to care, and the horror continued unabated.

By midnight the north and west sides of Queen Square were burning furiously. Two hours later several warehouses in neighbouring King Street and Princes Street were also ablaze, one a bonded store containing over fifty puncheons of rum – the glare of that conflagration so great it was later reported that it had been possible to read a newspaper in the streets of Chepstow, twenty miles distant.

Indeed, from as far away as Gloucester it had seemed as if all Bristol must be burning. In fact, it was only a matter of time before it could be. Only the width of a narrow street from the south side of Queen Square was the Floating Harbour, densely packed with vessels which could not possibly be moved out of harm's way in time should the fire continue to spread. And if they went up there would be literally nothing to prevent the holocaust engulfing the whole city.

From the Custom House, still secure from the mob despite its dangerous proximity to the Mansion House, message after message had been despatched to Leigh Barracks asking, pleading, begging, for military assistance. But because not one had been in the form of a direct written order from the mayor to Brereton, all had gone unheeded, even unacknowledged. Desperate though the situation now was, Charles Pinney still refused to believe that he was dealing not with bona fide militant if extremist supporters of the Reform movement to which he himself belonged, as did so many others, but with ruthless, bloodthirsty criminals.

Throughout that terrible, seemingly endless night Alderman James Hilhouse, whose voice seemed to be the only sane authority still to be heard, did all he could to disillusion him. But his repeated entreaties and demands, both to the mayor and to his fellow members of council who had taken refuge in the Custom House, that Brereton be given unequivocal orders to recall the dragoons from Keynsham and forthwith employ every possible means to restore order and protect the city, even if that meant a declaration of martial law, were either ignored or shouted down.

Eventually, when all else had failed, Hilhouse drafted the order himself. Then, with the willing assistance of Major Mackworth and Nicholas Roch, he forced the mayor, whose nerves by that time were

106

completely shot, to sign it. At last something positive might be done. But there was not an instant to be lost.

It was decided Brunel should carry the order to Brereton at Leigh Barracks, while Roch rode out to Keynsham to fetch Captain Gage and the dragoons. In the meantime Mackworth was to muster as many constables as he could. Their concerted attack on Queen Square, still the focal point of the riot, was timed for one hour before dawn. Without being told, every man knew this would be the last chance of saving the city from utter destruction. The eleventh hour had already come – and gone.

Beyond the immediate vicinity of that main trouble spot the roads, though crowded, were passable and, as the night was fine, a fast horse got Isambard to Leigh Barracks in less than half an hour. There he was received by the commander of 'A' Troop, 14th Hussars.

Captain Peter Claybourne Warrington was young, in his way well meaning, but arrogant, hopelessly inexperienced and consequently inclined to pigheadedness. Far too full of his own importance, his principal talent as an officer was an ability to intimidate his subordinates and impress superiors by his outstanding physique – he stood almost six foot four and was broad in proportion – and the power of his bull-like voice. Opposition from outsiders he simply ignored. Had he had the good fortune to have been born twenty years earlier he might have distinguished himself as a gallant and probably much decorated soldier, his almost total lack of imagination and initiative notwithstanding. To Peter Claybourne Warrington duty was duty, and whatever its demands he could at all times be depended upon to perform it, or die in the attempt. An order, especially if direct from his commanding officer, was an order, to be obeyed without question come what may. And he needed no carping, canting civilian to tell him what his duty was, or where his loyalty should lie. He therefore wasted no time in putting this latest mayoral emissary firmly in his place by telling him so, just as he had told all the others who had similarly pestered him.

'Damn it, Sir!' the exasperated captain exclaimed angrily after Brunel, having totally ignored his outburst, had quietly repeated his demand that Colonel Brereton, who was presumed to be asleep, be summoned immediately. 'Are you perhaps deaf? Can you not hear properly? I've just told you, he has retired for the night.'

107

'Then wake him.'

'That I will not. The colonel left strict orders he is not to be disturbed before sun-up. You may wait outside if you wish.'

Isambard's reply to this fatuous insolence was forestalled by the sudden entry of a breathless captain of militia.

'And who the devil might you be?' demanded the hussar.

'Codrington, Sir,' the newcomer announced with a salute of parade ground precision, completely ignoring the civilian in the room.

'Yes, yes, yes – all right,' snapped the other, infuriated by the unexpected interruption and rudely leaving the formality unacknowledged. 'But what the hell are you doing here? What do you want?'

'I have a troop of Dodington yeomanry under my command, with orders to place myself and them at your, at Colonel Brereton's, immediate disposal.'

Dodington was a village some ten miles out of Bristol on the Chipping Sodbury road. It seemed that the militia captain and whoever his superiors might be had acted on their own initiative, and Isambard's hopes for the safety of the city soared. Even if he should fail to budge Brereton, there was now Codrington and his yeomanry. And where they had led, others must surely follow.

'Yeomanry!' Warrington's tone was derogatory to a degree, and the militiaman's expression was more than sufficient proof that the insult had been taken very much to heart. 'Be advised, Captain Whatever-you-said-your-name-was,' he continued loftily and with positively caustic civility, 'Colonel Brereton has no need of your assistance. Therefore, kindly remove yourself, and your men, from this vicinity immediately.'

Codrington looked at him as if unable to believe his ears. 'Remove my men,' he stuttered. 'With respect, Sir, are you aware of what is happening in Bristol at this very moment?'

'With respect, Sir, that is an order, blast you!' the hussar exploded, his face, already nearly the colour of his tunic, now beginning to turn purple with rage.

'I demand to see the colonel.'

'Are you and your men armed and ready for action?' Isambard cut in quickly before Warrington could reply.

'Fully armed.' Codrington seemed to notice him for the first time and eyed him curiously. 'And ready for action. But may I ask, Sir, what business that is of yours?'

'No bloody business at all,' Warrington bellowed. 'Confound you, Mr Brunel, I'll thank you to keep your nose out of military affairs.'

'And I'll thank you to keep a civil tongue in your head and summon your colonel this instant,' Isambard snapped back in a tone that stopped the burly hussar dead in his tracks. He stared in astonishment at the diminutive figure he literally towered over.

'I said this instant, Captain.' The words were repeated in a voice barely audible. But Warrington heard, and he obeyed with alacrity.

Isambard barely had time to prove his identity to a wide-eyed Codrington and make known to him the purpose of his mission before Colonel Brereton hurried into the room with Warrington at his heels.

The colonel's appearance came as a shock to Brunel. His features were a ravaged mask of fevered torment. Like Josiah Corby, he had been driven to the very limit of mental endurance, and he was obviously not very far from breaking point. Privately Isambard could well appreciate the all but intolerable strain the man was under and the agonies of mind he must have suffered. Bristol born and bred, he had found himself from the start faced with the near certainty that he would be called upon to order his troops to fire on his fellow citizens, many of whom he must have known all his life. They would be neighbours, close friends, relatives even. And, like Charles Pinney, Robert Brereton who was also at one with the Reformers had somehow failed utterly to comprehend that what might have started as a sincere demonstration, albeit a violent one, of legitimate political protest, had long since degenerated into a civil riot of the very worst kind.

But Brunel also knew that at this stage he dare not allow personal sympathies to cloud the issue. As commander of military forces in Bristol, Colonel Brereton had palpably been guilty of what could only be described as gross dereliction of duty. He would be eventually called upon to account for his conduct and to defend himself as best he might. For the moment, however, all that was required of him was that he now perform his duty to the full, and before it was too late.

He was therefore given no chance. Hardly was he through the doorway than he was assailed by a spate of blistering invective the like of which he had never before experienced. The years underground with his Durham miners had broadened far more than Brunel's knowledge of human nature. Could Sam Ball have been there to witness his performance he would surely have been proud of his protégé, for by the sheer power and fluency of his verbal onslaught he forced the bewildered colonel to issue the orders he should have given at least eight hours before, while the two captains could only goggle in open-mouthed amazement.

Within a quarter of an hour Warrington and his hussars, with Brunel and Brereton stirrup to stirrup at their head, and with Codrington and his yeomanry following, were on the road at full gallop. Mackworth already had his constables deployed when they got to the square and within minutes of their arrival Nicholas Roch brought in Captain Gage and the dragoons.

The scene before them was nothing less than sickening. Vast quantities of smouldering debris and piles of rubbish that had once been prized possessions, littered the road. A screaming mob of looters was even now disembowelling a building as tongues of lurid flame began to roar from the sightless windows of another. Two-thirds of the once beautiful Queen Square, Georgian centrepiece of Bristol's municipal pride, was already a crumbling ruin and the remainder well on the way to becoming so. The air was thick with fumes and acrid smoke, and the stench overwhelming.

The major greeted his superior officer formally, but with terse deference. He then informed him that, as of that moment, he, Mackworth, was assuming command of all troops in the Bristol area. To which surprisingly, the colonel at once agreed, and without question. Indeed, he seemed like a man from whose shoulders an intolerable burden had been suddenly and mercifully removed. But when requested to surrender his horse to Mackworth, who was not mounted, he refused indignantly.

'You have my command, Major. And you may lead the charge with my blessing. But, by God, Sir,' he added resolutely, 'you shall not deny me the satisfaction of riding with you.'

So taken aback was Mackworth by this totally unexpected reaction, that it was Brereton and not he who gave the order to draw sabres. With a ringing clash of steel on steel, first the hussars, then the dragoons, then the yeomanry, obeyed the order as it was repeated by respective troop commanders. Finally Colonel Brereton drew his sword and saluted his junior in rank as gravely as if he had been the Duke of Wellington himself.

'Come, Major, we are wasting time.'

'Thank you, Colonel,' Mackworth returned the salute with equal gravity. But then, still afoot, he stepped back. 'Your command, Sir, if you please.'

The charge took the mob by surprise. So accustomed were the rioters to being completely unmolested, they had ceased to concern themselves with even the possibility of interference. Many therefore were cut down where they stood. In blind panic, others fled back into the burning buildings from which they had just emerged, and perished in the flames. The rest bolted for their lives. About a dozen, men and women, all helplessly drunk, were trapped on the top storey of the house they had been ransacking. To escape the ruthlessly vengeful blades of the soldiers they jumped, one after the other, from a window overlooking a flat-roofed annexe of the building next door. Too late did they discover that the heat of the fire raging in the room below had melted the thick layer of lead covering the roof. Held fast in the viscous metal, every one of the wretches was slowly roasted alive.

This hideous spectacle alone was enough to clear any lingering rioters from the square and its neighbouring streets. Thereafter the fires were quickly brought under control. The riot was over. Bristol had been saved.

The new day, the day on which the Bridge Committee was to have launched its new appeal for funds, revealed for the first time the truly appalling extent of the city's wreck and ruin. The cost of restoration must surely run into millions. So what chance could there be for the Clifton bridge now, or even in the foreseeable future? The realistic answer could only be none at all!

The site was deserted. Less than a week had passed since the last spadeful of earth had been turned, but already it appeared derelict. Where before there had been noisy activity there was now only the chill November breeze to rustle leaves that were beginning to fall thickly.

With a half-smoked cigar clamped firmly between his teeth and hands thrust deep into his greatcoat pockets, a small figure in a tall hat walked slowly to the very edge of the cliff. He stood for a long time gazing into the gorge. Through the evening mist wisping upwards from the water's surface, the gaunt masts of a sea-going merchantman moved steadily across his line of vision. But his ear only half consciously registered the echoing shouts of the hobblers urging their plodding horse teams. And though he seemed to watch intently, he saw nothing. Even in his mind's eye he saw nothing. For where there should have been at least the beginnings of a span of a bridge, there was nothing.

PART TWO

December 1831 – January 1839

Chapter One

THERE being nothing to keep him in Bristol once the bridge site had been closed, Isambard had returned almost immediately to London. A few days later he'd learned through a friend of his father's of the proposal for a major dock complex at Monkwearmouth, a minor County Durham port, and promptly left post-haste for the north. It had taken him just fourteen days to complete a survey, commit his ideas to paper and convince the resident dock surveyor and the Dock Building Committee that what he had produced was exactly what they wanted, and even deliver a full set of drawings personally to the appropriate authority in Durham. But he'd carefully kept to himself the conclusion reached before he'd even half completed the survey – that an insignificant fishing hamlet on the opposite bank of the river Wear would be likely to prove a far superior site for the sort of development envisaged. The hamlet was called Sunderland.

He'd visited, inspected, and had been dreadfully disappointed by the Stockton & Darlington rail road, operational now for nearly eight years. Despite a recently completed modernisation programme, both extensive and expensive, the ride was said to be still painfully slow and extremely uncomfortable. So he'd decided he would make his first railway journey on the Liverpool & Manchester instead.

In the fourteen months since its opening, an event marred by both tragedy and farce, and culminating in the worst riots seen in the north since the so-called Peterloo Massacre, the Lancashire enterprise had prospered. In addition to the vast quantity of freight, for which purpose it had been specifically intended, it had carried without mishap more than half a million fare-paying passengers. It had done for railways and the Stephensons what stupendous road works and bridge building had done for Thomas Telford so many years before. In the eyes of the seemingly all-powerful Liverpool merchants and bankers – those wealthy men of vision who had assumed the mantle of Edward Pease, the original promoter of the Stockton & Darlington – neither father nor son could now do wrong. It was primarily Liverpool money that was behind the proposed London to Birmingham line, and already it was rumoured that Robert Stephenson, though not yet thirty years of age, was to be appointed engineer.

Though he in no way begrudged his contemporary what must surely be the greatest of all prizes, Isambard Brunel at times found it difficult to contain his frustration when he compared Stephenson's immense good fortune with his own miserable lot. For such an opportunity he sometimes felt he would willingly sell his soul to the Devil himself, if only he could somehow devise a way of making the Devil take notice of him. And so he'd come to Manchester, and Ellen Hulme.

It had been far from easy for him to swallow the bitter disappointment of Bristol. Nor did he now find it any less hard deliberately to cut himself off from the one person who, despite their differences, had for very nearly five years meant just as much to him as the fulfilment of any cherished ambition. But for far too long he had been making and breaking far too many promises, something he simply could not go on doing. He was still deeply in love with Ellen. He suspected he always would be; insofar, that is, that he judged himself capable of loving anybody. But, he now knew, if ever he was to achieve anything worthwhile, he had to be free. Success, the sort of success he courted, was too demanding, too jealous, a mistress. Their parting was amicable. They remained good friends; but they were never to meet again.

As he had expected, his first train ride was indeed memorable, a most exhilarating experience, an adventure, no less. But not by the widest stretch of imagination could it ever be described as comfortable. For one thing the wheels made the very devil of a din on the rails – a monotonously rhythmic but ragged alternation of clattering crescendo and rattling diminuendo against an incessant obbligato of creaks and squeaks and grinding and groaning. A persistent lateral swaying motion combined with a completely unrelated longitudinal pitching, intermittently and quite unpredictably punctuated by a series of sudden jolts and jerks, threatened to catapult the unwary in all directions at once whenever a reasonably substantial turn of speed was attained.

But despite moments of quite appalling physical discomfort, not one syllable of complaint or even gasp of dismay did he hear from any of his fellow passengers during the whole of the run from Manchester to Liverpool. Just over a year before the same journey could have taken anything up to half a day, more if the weather chose to be inclement, a hazard for which Lancashire in general and Manchester in particular was noted. In any case, abysmal roads, which in rural areas still abounded, had long accustomed coach travellers to conditions very nearly as trying if never before quite as noisy. So, if nothing else, the time saved on that five and thirty mile journey made the fumes and cinders and smoke, the shaking and swaying and jolting, even the occasional bouts of travel sickness to which many a first-time train traveller found himself prone, endurable if not exactly enjoyable.

Wedged firmly into the corner seat of a first-class carriage that was distinctly reminiscent of a French diligence, Brunel smiled broadly. With pencil poised erratically above a blank page of the pocket notebook he habitually carried, he had been trying during the few intermittent moments of less violent movement to inscribe thereon a recognisable circle. Having repeatedly failed even to effect productive contact betwixt pencil and paper, he removed his beaver and set it as firmly as he could upon his knees. Then, resting his notebook on its crown, he tried again.

By a happy coincidence he had arrived at the Manchester terminus just as Robert Stephenson had stepped off a train from Liverpool. They had been introduced and had spent an hour or more in conversation and comparing notes. Stephenson had, in fact, done most of the talking, Isambard being content merely to prompt him with a question or two here and there and then sit back and listen.

Before he was twenty, Robert Stephenson had been in charge of the locomotive works his father had established at Newcastle. Then, in 1824, he'd gone to South America where he'd managed to rescue from penury the man who, in perfecting the world's first double-acting high-pressure steam engine, had at last made possible the much dreamed about but long despaired of locomotive. Richard Trevethick's steam road carriage had appeared on the streets of London in 1803. The following year Samuel Homfray, of the Pen-y-Daren ironworks in the Rhondda, had won that famous 500-guinea wager from Antony Hill, the Taff Vale ironmaster, when a locomotive built by Trevethick had hauled a load of 25 tons from Pen-y-Daren to Abercynon, 9½ miles, non-stop, at a speed of 4 miles an hour. True it was the only trip the cumbersome 5-ton monster ever made, its massive weight having all but ruined the fragile plateway. But it had proved beyond all further doubt the feasibility of the locomotive.

From the moment Brunel set eyes on the railway and the train he had been indefatigable in his searching examination of every aspect of function and detail of construction. He had all but filled his notebook with sketches and jottings, indeed the page before him was the last completely clear one left. He had clambered like an inquisitive monkey all over the locomotive which, as luck would have it, turned out to be *Rocket*. He had even ridden the footplate as far as Eccles and, though the speed had never exceeded a sedate seventeen miles an hour, for the first time he could appreciate to the full Fanny Kemble's colourful and much publicised account of her first ride on the footplate of *Northumbrian* with George Stephenson just prior to the grand opening of the line.

The footplate, however, had seemed relatively stable compared with the carriage. Half a dozen more attempts having produced nothing but a scrawled confusion of wavering lines and grotesquely distorted shapes, he at last gave up, returned notebook and pencil to their customary places about his person, then contented himself with watching the passing snow-blanketed scene through the carriage window.

They were crossing Chat Moss, that four-mile width of treacherous quagmire which had for so long defied all attempts to conquer it. Indeed, during the passage of the Liverpool & Manchester Rail Road Bill the Commons Investigating Committee had been told quite categorically by Francis Giles, a canal engineer of some standing and the opposition's chief witness, that to cross Chat Moss was an impossibility only to be overcome by the expenditure of at least a quarter of a million pounds. But magnificent survey work coupled with George Stephenson's inspired innovation of literally floating the line on a raft of brushwood had achieved the 'impossible' at a cost of less than £40,000. So much for the opinions of the so-called experts. With this in mind Isambard found the thought that this same Francis Giles had since been selected in preference to himself as engineer to the Newcastle & Carlisle – at sixty-one miles one of the longest railway lines yet to be projected – far from comforting.

Now that Chat Moss had been tamed, who could say what the future of what had always been regarded as wasteland might not be. True, the terrain here was level, almost as far as the eye could see. But elsewhere there had been hills to get over, valleys and rivers to span. More then 3 million cubic yards of rock and earth had been excavated by thousands of navvies using nothing but picks and shovels. Only at Rainhill, at Sutton and at Edgehill was there a gradient greater than 1 in 880 – a rise or fall of only 6 feet in a mile. The thirty-five miles of twin, cast-iron roads – each with stone-block mounted or 'chaired' rails exactly 4 feet 8½ inches apart – was carried over no less than 63 bridges, the greatest of which, the 9-arched Sankey Viaduct, was a structure Thomas Telford at the height of his career would not have been ashamed to claim his own. And beneath John Foster's grand Moorish Arch that spanned the line at Edgehill just before it plunged into the tunnel taking it into the very heart of the ever-growing and increasingly prosperous city of Liverpool, those same rails were just 46 feet higher than at the Manchester terminus – an impressive achievement indeed.

But for all that, it would pale to insignificance compared to the task soon to face Robert Stephenson on the London to Birmingham. Three times the length of the Liverpool & Manchester, it would run through tunnels and cuttings and over viaducts such as few had ever imagined. It had already been calculated that not since the building of the pyramids had man embarked on such a gigantic undertaking.

On arrival in Liverpool, he paid a hurried visit to the docks then, after inspecting the new Custom House, a building that impressed him not at all, he went by coach to Chester to view the nearly completed Grosvenor Bridge over the Dee, on the design of which Marc Brunel had been one of the chief advisers. From Chester he went to Shrewsbury, travelled from there to Birmingham on the famous *Shrewsbury Wonder*, and then home to London on the *Hirondelle*, or *Iron Devil* as she was more popularly known. Benton, regarded by many as the finest coachman in the British Isles, was the whip, and Isambard, who had the good fortune to occupy the seat beside him on the box, was spellbound by the man's incredible handling of both coach and horses. Each stage was completed well within the time allowed and, with the exception of just two twenty-minute stops, each change of horses effected in less than two minutes. The 110-mile journey took less than nine hours – ample proof, if proof be needed, that for speed and reliability England's booming long-distance coaching business was second to none. 'Better that with your iron monsters,' Benton challenged him triumphantly as he pulled his sweat-lathered team to a final halt in front of the huge and hideously carved wood emblem of the Bull in Mouth.

Exhausted by his marathon trip – in just over ninety-six hours of actual travelling he'd covered more than five hundred miles – and utterly drained both by the frenetic pace at which he'd driven himself and the emotional reaction to his parting from Ellen, Brunel reached the Barge House to find he had received yet another savage blow. That very day the Exchequer Loan Commissioners had announced their rejection of the long-outstanding request for financial assistance from the Thames Tunnel Company. Though it had seemed that the project might well be moribund, hope had never faded entirely. But now, it seemed, it was indeed dead and was to be buried at last.

'The tunnel will never be finished now,' Sophia Hawes concluded her mournful tidings with an uncharacteristically despairing sigh. Ageing rapidly and ailing once more, Marc Brunel had appeared to have accepted the news stoically enough, his sister told Isambard. But, she confessed, she suspected that the shock to their father might have been little short of fatal.

Somehow, even to Sophia, Isambard managed to appear unaffected and, apart from sympathising with his father, unconcerned. In the privacy of his room, however, the anguish that very nearly overwhelmed him was not to be described. For the first time since his childhood he found himself having to fight back a pent-up flood of bitter tears. Worn out though he was, he found it impossible to sleep, even to rest. So he spent the night methodically going through his notes and from them writing up his journal. It was nearly dawn before he came to the page of meaningless shapes and squiggles. He read what he had later pencilled in a Liverpool coffee house: 'Drawn on the L & M Railway – 5/12/31. I record this specimen of shaking on the Manchester Railway. But the time is not far off when we shall be able to take our coffee, and write, while going noiselessly and smoothly at 45 miles per hour.'

Forty-five miles per hour! A slow smile contorted his fatigue-grey features, lining his face cruelly in the yellow light of the solitary candle on his writing desk. He ran his fingers wearily through his tousled hair. Forty-five miles per hour was an unheard of speed. But then, he suddenly thought, nobody had believed a train to be capable of thirty-six miles per hour until George Stephenson had proved otherwise by his historic run in *Northumbrian* when he'd taken the dying Huskisson – the railway's first passenger fatality – from Parkside to Eccles.

He savoured the thought for some time before once again taking up his pen to write the words 'Let me try!' Then, very deliberately, he underlined them.

Chapter Two

'NEVER seen so many bad hats together under one roof!' was how the die-hard Duke of Wellington described the newly elected House of Commons. After a threat from the King to create sufficient Whig peers to ensure its passage through the Lords, the Tories had climbed down and a third version of the People's Bill had finally become law on 7 June 1832. One of the 'bad hats', returned for Lambeth, was Ben Hawes. Mainly as a means of distraction, for by then he'd been positively desperate for something to do, Isambard had played an active part in his brother-in-law's campaign and, he had to confess, thoroughly enjoyed himself. But he remained as totally disinterested in politics as such as he had always been, once the excitement of the hustings was over.

As far as he was concerned, 1832 might just as well not have happened. Apart from the election, there had been but one other event even worthy of note. In the early spring he'd twice been summoned to Bristol – first, to give evidence in the trial of Charles Pinney concerning the part he had played in the suppression of the riots. The ex-mayor had been acquitted of all charges. The subsequent court-martial of Colonel Brereton had lasted but a single day. During the night the accused had shot himself. It was a tragic end for a gallant if sorely misguided soldier, and his death was genuinely mourned by many.

The dying hours of that miserable 'nothing' year, Brunel had spent alone in his room at the Barge House idly mulling over his situation. He had irons enough in the fire, surely. If nothing else, there was the Thames Tunnel still, for despite the decision of the Exchequer Loan Commissioners twelve months before, there yet remained at least a glimmer of hope. But the Monkwearmouth Dock scheme, which from the start he'd suspected would probably run into some sort of trouble, was 'temporarily' in abeyance, as was a survey for extensive improvements to the Woolwich Dockyard which had been accepted by the Admiralty, then shelved. And there was the Bristol bridge, still starved of funds, still stagnating. Yes, there were irons in plenty; but not one was anywhere near showing signs of becoming hot enough to be worked.

Then, out of the blue had come salvation. For five long fruitless years, Captain Christopher Claxton RN (rtd), distinguished veteran of the French wars and now quay warden of the Bristol Docks, had sought to convince his board of directors of the urgent need for improvements to the Floating Harbour. Finally, and with the indefatigable assistance of Nicholas Roch, he had succeeded. As a result, Isambard had received a somewhat peremptory summons to Bristol which, needless to say, he had answered with alacrity and without question, thankful, by then, to accept any sort of challenge that might open the floodgates for his far too long pent-up energies.

In characteristically whirlwind fashion he had completed a comprehensive survey and submitted proposals which Claxton was convinced could at last solve most of the many problems that had so long plagued the port of Bristol. The Dock Board, too, though not unanimously – for there were many in Bristol who cared neither for Brunel personally nor for what they considered his extravagant style – miraculously made an almost instant decision and gave the go-ahead.

But no sooner had he started work in the new year with Claxton, whom he'd been delighted to discover was a man of his own kidney, than he'd received a second, even more peremptory summons – this time from the lawyer, Osborne.

'A fine wine, Nicholas!' The little ferret-faced man poured himself another glass of prime port, his fourth since dinner, from the exquisitely cut crystal decanter which meticulously he pushed across the table with his left hand, to his solitary guest. Then he drank deeply and noisily, and smacked his lips in loud appreciation.

'One of the first pipes I ever put down,' he mused with inebriate deliberation. 'And, I fear, there's precious little of it left – God damn it!'

'In which case I acknowledge myself most highly honoured.' Nicholas Roch raised his newly replenished glass in salutation to his host. His voice grave, he enunciated with conscious clarity for he, too, had imbibed rather more lavishly than wisely. It really was an exceedingly fine port, one of the best he had ever tasted, and he too savoured it, though with slightly less audible fervour.

'A wine for the occasion, m' dear fella,' declared the little man expansively, his wide toothy grin for the moment softening the stark lines of his harshly drawn features and making his feverish button-black eyes positively light up. Although he had consumed far more port than he should, the ebullience of his mood stemmed not entirely from the influence of the wine. Without it he would probably have been equally euphoric, for Thomas Richard Guppy was this night a supremely, a sublimely, happy man.

Practically all his adult life he had been consumed by a passionate determination to convince his fellow Bristolians of the need for a rail link with London – not as some future possibility that might or might not eventually see the light of day, but as a necessity to be pursued with all the vigour, and backed by the financial power and organisation, essential to success. To this end he had argued, agitated, campaigned and schemed. In the year prior to the opening of the Stockton & Darlington he had tried to promote the London & Bristol Road Company with the object of constructing both a new turnpike and railway on the same route, the one to complement the other. John Loudon McAdam no less, at that time surveyor to the Bristol Turnpike Trust, had been responsible for the preliminary survey work. But support for the venture had never been sufficient to justify an application for parliamentary approval.

A similar fate had in turn overtaken all subsequent promotions, among them the General Junction Rail Road from London to Bristol, a Proposed Rail Road from Bristol to Bath, the Bristol and North Western Railway – a rather grandiose scheme for a line not only to London but to Birmingham as well, and the Taunton Grand Western Rail Road. In 1828, however, he had disdainfully dissociated himself from the Bristol & Gloucestershire Railway – an impressive title for what was nothing more than a horse-drawn waggonway serving the local collieries.

Then the mid-twenties bubble of railway speculation had collapsed, though the success of the Liverpool & Manchester had engendered a resurgence of West Country interest abruptly snuffed out by the riots. But once it became clear the Reform Bill would, after all, become law, the London to Bristol idea was revived – not, however, by Tom Guppy. In May 1832 a circular bearing the title 'The Bristol and London Railway' had been published in London giving tantalisingly brief details of a route – jointly surveyed by William Brunton, a London-based engineer of some repute, and an unknown Bristol man, Henry Habberley-Price – through Bath to Trowbridge, thence to Datchet, Colnbrook and Southall, terminating on a vacant site near the Edgware Road bounded by Oxford Street and the Paddington & City Road Turnpike. From there, it was suggested, a short branch line could unite with the London & Birmingham Railway. A bill for this project was shortly to be presented to parliament and all subscribers were guaranteed a return of no less than 15 per cent on an estimated investment of £2,500,000.

Notwithstanding this promised profit, however, few of the many who openly expressed enthusiastic approval seemed inclined to back their professed interest with hard cash. Nor did there seem to exist any sort of effective organisation. This was little short of calamitous because a recent proposal for what was to be called the Grand Junction Railway linking the Liverpool & Manchester with the London & Birmingham had started what was already proving an even bigger railway boom than that which had swept the country six years before. It was the ideal time for the London to Bristol venture.

So, seriously failing health notwithstanding, Tom Guppy had once more entered the fray. He persuaded George Jones, John Harford and William Tothill, three of Bristol's wealthiest and most influential businessmen, to attend preliminary discussions. These, however, were initially far from amicable, Guppy having alienated their goodwill through his past, and in their opinion hare-brained, promotions. It was only his innate stubbornness and at times astonishing ability to argue his case against the most extreme opposition that kept negotiations going until, inspired at last by his persistently boundless energy, they in turn began to preach what eventually came to be called 'Guppy's Gospel'. By the end of the year the Bristol Corporation, the Bristol Society of Merchant Venturers, the Bristol Dock Company, the Chamber of Commerce, and the much ridiculed but surprisingly successful Bristol & Gloucestershire Railway Company had formed a fifteen-man-strong Railway Investigatory Committee.

Tom Guppy, not unnaturally, had been invited to serve as

chairman but, worn out by months of frantic activity, he had suffered a near-fatal collapse. Such was his determination to see the realisation of his cherished dream, however, that he had confounded his doctors by somehow managing to fight his way back to life, literally, they said, from the very edge of the grave.

The new committee – its members including Nicholas Roch for the Dock Company and George Gibbs representing the Society of Merchant Venturers – met for its first working session on 21 January 1833. It took a month of bargaining and discussion to agree financial and other arrangements pertaining to the preliminary stage, but once this had been achieved things began to move swiftly and become more complicated. Brunton and Habberley-Price, in the belief that their personal ends would be far better served by deserting the rival venture, offered their already supposedly surveyed route and themselves as joint engineers. They were immediately championed by the Bristol Corporation and Society of Merchant Venturers, but not by the Bristol & Gloucestershire Railway Company who were looking to an alternative from their man Townsend. Though he'd built the successful, if modest, horse waggonway between Cuckold's Pill on the Floating Harbour and the collieries at Coalpit Heath and Mangotsfield, W. H. Townsend was not an engineer at all, but a surveyor and land valuer. It was nevertheless strongly felt in quarters represented by the Chamber of Commerce that, as a local man who had so proved himself, he had a legitimate and justifiable claim for consideration. It was therefore up to the Bristol Dock Company to decide the issue. Judging the moment admirably, Nicholas Roch had waited until the ensuing argument had threatened to gravitate to an acrimoniously irreconcilable level before suggesting, as a matter of urgency, another engineer be invited to prepare a third survey.

This, then, was what he and an as yet only partially recovered Tom Guppy were celebrating. Though his doctors had ranted and wrung their hands in horror when told of his intention of consuming at least one bottle of one of his most prized possessions in honour of the occasion, the patient had insisted. He was by no means a drunkard, but to Tom Guppy, in health or in sickness, life without the pleasure and solace of good wine was no life at all, especially in those all too rare moments when a genuine celebration was not only called for but obligatory. He was fully aware of the price he would have to pay for his excess, but the knowledge in no way diminished the measure of his enjoyment, or curbed his indulgence. To live to see the fulfilment of his life's dream, Thomas Richard Guppy, visionary, entrepreneur and engineer – for in his youth he had served a full apprenticeship with none other than Messrs Maudslay, Son & Field – was prepared to make any reasonable or even unreasonable sacrifice. Short, that is, of signing the Pledge.

Looking exactly as he had at their last meeting, Osborne greeted Brunel with his customary flow of flowery phrases. Then he was ushered into the inner sanctum where Nicholas Roch, looking unusually pale, was waiting.

'Well now, gentlemen,' said Brunel as he settled easily into the same armchair he had occupied on his first visit, 'suppose you tell me exactly what this is all about.'

Suffering visibly from the combined effects of pent-up excitement and the previous evening's surfeit of port, Roch launched forth. While he was speaking the shrewd old lawyer scarcely took his eyes from the listener's half-profiled countenance, making use of all the skill gained from his long experience of dealing with men and the affairs of men, to try and assess the reaction to what was being said. But the face so scrutinised remained an impassive, almost an expressionless, mask; though behind the mask a quicksilver mind was racing far ahead, absorbing, analysing, deciding. The mask, however, gave nothing away; though Osborne was certain that at one point at least he detected a distinct glint in those always magnetic brown eyes.

'So, there you have it, my friend.' Having carefully covered every relevant detail he could think of, Nicholas was now summing up. 'Once your recommendations had been accepted by the Dock Board I felt I was fully justified, even without your permission, in putting your name forward to the Railway Investigatory Committee. And, as I've explained, they've agreed to consider Brunton and Price, Townsend and yourself, purely on the merit of the surveys submitted.' He paused for a moment. Then he said, 'My God, Isambard, it's the opportunity you've always wanted. The chance you've been waiting for, the chance of a lifetime!'

As if to mark the conclusion of that hour-long dissertation, the clock on the mantelshelf, the same clock that Nicholas had once so

127

ruthlessly assaulted, struck one. Brunel made no move. He continued to give nothing away. And even though he realised full well that both the others were waiting impatiently for him to speak, he remained silent.

'One question, Nicholas,' Osborne's mellifluously measured tones came as a pleasing contrast to the strident note of strain that had made Roch's voice increasingly harsh. For the first time since he'd sat down Isambard looked directly at the speaker, though he had been conscious all the time of those eyes on him. 'Is it the committee's intention to be guided solely by the element of cost in making its selection of what it considers the most acceptable survey?'

'Not necessarily solely, no,' Roch replied guardedly, 'but I would imagine that the cost factor must essentially be one of the prime bases for judgement.'

'Quite so.' His gaze focussed once more on Brunel. 'In other words, he who submits the lowest estimate . . .' Osborne said no more but the implication was clear.

Unable to contain his impatience Nicholas confronted the still silent figure in the armchair. 'Well?' he demanded.

Isambard exhaled a long slow breath, and dropped his eyes for a moment as if to examine with no particular interest the well-worn leather of the chair arm before looking up at Roch. Slowly, almost sadly, he shook his head.

'I'm sorry, Nicholas,' he said quietly, but firmly. 'I'm afraid it's not on.'

Osborne sighed audibly, and grunted. But whether with disappointment or in satisfaction of a confirmed anticipation, it was impossible to say.

Roch appeared completely staggered, for the moment struck dumb. When at length he regained the power of speech he could only mumble semi-coherently, 'I don't understand. Not on? What's not on? What does that mean?'

'It means, I'm simply not interested.'

Chapter Three

BRUNEL was playing with fire, about to plunge headlong into possibly the greatest gamble he would ever take. He was deliberately hazarding not only his precious hard-won reputation which, if lost, would be forever irretrievable, but also his whole future career. He was going to risk everything he valued, his life even, on one single throw of the dice. And if past experience of the perversity of that most capricious of all inconstant jades was anything to go by, he would be betting against impossible odds. Never before had Dame Fortune chosen to favour him, quite the reverse in fact.

All the same he was determined. Never again would he have such a chance of gaining such a prize. From the moment Nicholas had started talking he had known what his course of action was going to be, and that nothing anyone could say or do would make him change his mind. He was going to build this railway. And he was going to do it alone.

Impressive as Nicholas had made it all sound, all he was really being offered was the chance of a slice – possibly an exceedingly generous slice, but only a slice for all that – of a fabulously rich cake that, by all accounts, had already been mixed and was at least partially baked. But no matter how generous that slice might in the long run prove to be, he knew in his heart that it could never be enough. He wanted not just a slice, he wanted the whole of that cake for himself. He could never be satisfied with less.

It was not greed that engendered the desire which so passionately possessed him. If he was being guided, or perhaps misled, by any vice at all it was that of ambition, not avarice. He was consumed with an overwhelming conviction that he and he alone was capable of creating this railway – that he was the only engineer in the world who could build it.

In his mind's eye he had already done so. Even now he could see

129

practically every single detail of its construction – its cuttings, embankments, its bridges and viaducts; its great iron road, rails glinting in the sun, now running straight, now curving gently to right or to left, plunging deep into the beechwood-forested Chilterns, sweeping majestically across open rolling Berkshire sheeplands, piercing the great grey limestone hills of the southern Cotswolds. He could see it all, as clearly as he could see the contents of that room. It was as if it had always been there, but he had only just become aware of its existence.

He even knew its name. Nicholas had referred to it as the Bristol Railway. Others he had heard speak of it called it the Bristol & London Railway, or the London & Bristol Railway. But they were wrong. All of them were wrong. It was none of these things. It was the Western, no, the Great Western Railway. And come what may, it was going to be his railway. Brunel's railway!

'I'm simply not interested,' he'd said. God, what a lie! Rarely could a man have stated a greater, a more deliberate falsehood. And rarely could any statement, either true or false, have produced a more dramatic effect.

Nicholas was still staring at him in what could only be described as utter disbelief. Osborne had not moved from his high-backed chair behind his huge desk. The lawyer looked composed, but the fingers of his right hand drumming noiselessly on the polished black oak betrayed him. With his own nerves tightly held under an iron control, Brunel inwardly braced himself to weather the storm he knew must surely break.

But instead of going purple with rage, Roch's already pallidly anguished features seemed to turn several shades paler. Instead of the expected explosion of colourful oaths, delivered full throated and tight mouthed, and a demonstration of fist-crashing anger, something like a sigh of despair fell from his flaccid lips, while his shoulders drooped despondently. For perhaps the first time in his life Nicholas was confused. He had engineered everything so well, or so he had thought. He had been so confident that Brunel's response to his proposals would have been one of exultation at having what must surely be a perfect plum of opportunity literally dropped into his lap, that he now felt crushed and completely drained.

'I just don't understand,' he muttered dully for the second time. Then he sank heavily into the other armchair and just sat there shaking his head.

'I think,' Osborne pronounced in his most judiciously pompous manner after what seemed an interminable pause, 'I think we must ask Mr Brunel for an explanation.'

'Indeed.' By now Roch, who had managed at last to collect his scattered wits, was beginning to bridle visibly. 'Indeed yes. I think we must!'

'If you please, young Sir,' Osborne's invitation was solemn, formal, cold, his face impassive, his eyes expressionless.

Now that Nicholas was looking and sounding more like his old self, Isambard was confident of his ability to handle the situation. But the inscrutable lawyer was a completely unknown quantity. Though the coming argument was entirely between himself and Roch, as had been the case over the bridge, in this instance it was going to be Osborne's attitude which would ultimately decide the issue.

'First of all,' he began carefully and quietly, 'I'd like it clearly understood that I appreciate everything you've both tried to do on my behalf.'

'Then all I can say is you've a damn curious way of showing it!' Roch flared at him.

'Now we'll get nowhere at all on that tack,' the lawyer remonstrated with considerable asperity, and Roch immediately subsided, but with obvious ill grace. 'Kindly proceed, Mr Brunel.' Even in moments of extreme stress Osborne never let slip his mannered old-fashioned charm.

'Don't you see, Nicholas, all that committee is doing is holding an unofficial competition?'

'Rubbish!'

'. . . and, as I've made it abundantly clear to you in the past,' he chose to ignore the interruption, 'I will have no part in any more competitions, official or otherwise.'

'We are proposing to ask for what will amount to tenders from four specifically nominated individuals,' Nicholas ground out the words ominously.

Brunel's eyes flashed with mounting anger in spite of his control and Osborne watched both men closely, ready to intervene the instant he judged it necessary.

'That's a perfectly normal and acceptable procedure, is it not?'

The challenge was just a little too churlishly sarcastic, but Brunel refused to rise to the bait and merely shrugged.

'Well you can put it that way if you want to, but it amounts to the same thing doesn't it? Even under those terms it must ultimately come down to, as Osborne puts it, he who submits the lowest estimate.'

'I've already told you, not necessarily.'

'It would still lead to the sort of situation in which I have no intention of ever getting involved again!' snapped Brunel, his tautly strung nerves just for an instant beginning to give way.

'In which case there's nothing more to be said then is there?' And, his temper now fully roused, Roch stood up with the intention of putting an end to the argument there and then by leaving.

'Gentlemen, please!' Osborne called both to order by rapping imperiously on the desk with his knuckles. 'This is surely far too important a matter to be dismissed so pettily. Pray have the goodness to resume your seat, Nicholas.'

Reluctantly Roch did as he was asked.

'And if you can,' Osborne's rebuke was acid, 'do try and listen without further interruption.'

Sheepishly acknowledging himself to be in the wrong, Nicholas nodded a grudging apology in Isambard's direction.

'All right, I'll listen. Say your piece. I've already said mine.'

'Brunton, Habberley-Price, Townsend,' Brunel ticked off the names against the fingers of his left hand. 'Let's just consider them individually for a moment. Who are they? What are their backgrounds, their capabilities? Exactly what do they have to offer? William Brunton I've met and he is of course known by reputation. Incidentally, he must be well over sixty now. He's a competent enough engineer, in some respects an extremely good one. But in all honesty I simply cannot see him, or any man of his age for that matter, taking on a project of this magnitude. And most certainly not if he intends to continue working in partnership with Habberley-Price. Who is Henry Habberley-Price? I'd never even heard of him, and neither had anyone else I've spoken to, until his name appeared with Brunton's on that so-called survey they published last year. What's more I still don't know anything about the gentleman, and I've yet to meet someone who does. So that leaves Townsend, who, as I'm sure you well know, isn't even an engineer. Now, in all seriousness, in all humility, I ask you – are these the men you are expecting me to compete with?'

It was a point of view Nicholas was forced to admit he had not considered. While he savoured the thought in silence Brunel, without stopping to think, produced his cigar case and selected one of its contents. Then he suddenly recalled his host's well known aversion to tobacco. Rather belatedly he asked, 'With your permission, Osborne?'

'Please do,' said the lawyer with polite resignation, stifling with not inconsiderable effort his ingrained abhorrence of the infinitely offensive weed youngsters nowadays seemed to indulge more and more indiscriminately. But he just failed to keep his distaste from registering in his expression as he watched Brunel light up by striking into an evil-looking yellow flame one of those wretched new-fangled sulphur-tipped wooden matches – Lucifers as they were so aptly called – of which he also most strongly disapproved.

'What you are doing,' Brunel resumed to a now quietly attentive Nicholas, 'is holding out a premium to the one who is going to make the most flattering promises. And it must surely be obvious that the man who has the least reputation at stake, who has the most to gain from any measure of success, no matter how small that measure might be, or how transient, and therefore who has the least to lose as a consequence of disappointment, is the one who, in the circumstances, must be the committee's choice. Believe me, I would not stand a chance.'

A second meaningful grunt from Osborne confirmed that the first had most definitely not been an expression of disappointment. Realising that the astute old lawyer, by somehow arranging for this confrontation to take place in his office, had, as it were, come to his rescue yet again, Isambard quickly communicated his appreciation of the fact with a faint nod and a smile of gratitude.

Calm once more, Nicholas Roch could only acknowledge that everything Brunel had said was true. Compared to him the other three were nonentities. And the possibilitiy of any of them rising much above the level of mediocrity was, to say the least, remote.

'I, er, I presume you are interested in the survey then,' he asked at last with a rueful half-grin which indicated that whatever ill-feeling there might have been between them was completely gone. His eyes having been opened, so to speak, inwardly he was roundly cursing what he now considered to have been his blind stupidity and, with the benefit of hindsight, his far too timid approach to the committee. But he had honestly felt that to have gone on openly fostering Brunel's cause as he had over the Clifton bridge and then with the Bristol Dock Board, could have been a fatal mistake.

'Yes Nicholas,' Isambard answered him gravely. 'I am interested, and not only in the survey!'

'Then obviously something will have to be done to ensure a favourable decision,' said Osborne looking pointedly at Nicholas.

'Believe me,' said Roch fervently, 'if it was mine alone to make there would be no question. And I know I speak for Tom Guppy, too, when I say that. But with a committee to deal with – well, that's something else.'

At Osborne's suggestion Brunel agreed to prepare immediately a paper putting forward all his views and an outline of his proposals for the project which Roch could then present to the committee at its next meeting, which was scheduled for 6 March.

'All I want you to do, Nicholas, is get me before that committee. The rest will be up to me. If I can't sell my own ideas, well I'd better give up having them.'

'I'll do everything I can, you know that,' Nicholas told him as they shook hands. 'But it must be clearly understood – the committee's decision, whatever it may be, will have to be final and binding.'

'So be it,' Isambard agreed.

The gamble was on. Win or lose, there could be no going back now.

By the morning of 6 March Brunel had worked himself out and smoked himself nearly sick. The paper had taken ten days of full-time non-stop toil before he'd been completely satisfied with it. But once prepared, he was confident that the arguments he'd put forward were sound. Whether or not they would be accepted however, was another matter. That would depend on the intelligence of the individual committee members, and Nicholas Roch's powers of persuasion. In order to concentrate on the task he'd had to neglect his work at the docks. But he and Claxton had worked so closely together that the quay warden had been able to carry on quite satisfactorily.

Once he'd completed the paper, Roch had insisted on a meeting with Tom Guppy. The three of them had discussed it far into the night even though the invalid was again bedridden and far from well. As with Claxton, Isambard had taken to the little man from the start and, recognising in him yet another kindred spirit, he hoped his eventual recovery would not be too long delayed. If only he were on the committee with Nicholas!

After that Isambard had found it quite impossible to settle to anything. On the spur of the moment he therefore went up to London for the Annual General Meeting of the Thames Tunnel Company, which took place on the 5th and was really no more than a meaningless formality, and travelled back to Bristol overnight. He breakfasted at the White Lion on three cups of strong black coffee and two cigars, forced himself to take a leisurely bath and change at his lodgings, and then spent an hour at the docks with Claxton before going along to Osborne's office at noon where it had been arranged Nicholas would contact him.

The committee had convened at ten o'clock that morning; but Osborne's clerk did not get back with Roch's note until well after two, by which time his long-suffering but ever politely uncomplaining employer had been practically overwhelmed by thick clouds of tobacco smoke, and was very nearly at his wits' end. By but a single vote, Nicholas reported briefly, the committee had finally agreed to Brunel's appointment as surveyor, providing he was willing to accept Townsend as his assistant. If so, he was to present himself at the Council House, where the committee was still in session, at half past three o'clock that afternoon.

Isambard received the news and accepted the congratulations of Osborne and his staff with all the nonchalance he could muster. He had never really doubted he would be successful, though there was no use denying he had found the last few hours of waiting all but unendurable. But excellent though the outcome was, even if that single vote did represent too fine a margin to be considered entirely comfortable, Osborne could not resist a rather deprecating sniff. He, for one, made no secret of the fact he had never held Brunel's newly designated assistant in particularly high esteem.

'You probably have no need of my advice my dear young Sir,' he said as Isambard prepared to take himself and his cigars off to the Council House, 'but I'm going to presume to give you some just the same. That fellow Townsend is a messer. Never mind what the committee says, you take over the whole of the management of this survey. If you must, leave him a bit to play with. But make him your assistant in name only. Otherwise I doubt if you will be able to get the job done.'

When Brunel tried to thank him for all his help and kindness the old lawyer merely waved him away. 'Now don't you be too premature in your gratitude my young friend,' he said with a broad smile. 'All I've really done is land you with an expensive task that is bound to put you very much out of pocket, to begin with anyway. And, you could still be the loser!'

The Bristol Railway Investigatory Committee proved to be a far more formidable body of men than either the Bridge Building Committee or the Dock Board had been. Of the eight members who had voted in favour of Isambard's appointment only George Gibbs, William Tothill – one of Tom Guppy's original 'disciples' – and Nicholas Roch appeared to be more than lukewarm in their support, though the others were prepared to give him a chance. The rest, including the chairman, John Cave, who represented the Bristol Corporation, were openly hostile. For an hour or more they bombarded him with questions to which there were as yet no known answers, and he had to use all his guile and wit to avoid the many traps they tried to set for him. Finally John Cave played what he and his colleagues obviously considered their trump card.

'There still remains the question of the alternative routes,' he stated with a sly sideways smile at Nicholas Roch. 'It must surely be quite beyond the capability of one man – even Mr Brunel here,' he added with thinly veiled sarcasm, 'if only from the point of view of time.'

Isambard waited patiently until he was certain he had the undivided attention of everyone present. Then he said very deliberately, without arrogance, but as a quiet statement of fact, 'There will be no necessity to consider any alternative route, gentlemen. I will give you a survey of but one road from Bristol to London. That road will not be the cheapest, but it will be the best!'

And with that the interview was over.

Chapter Four

WORK on the 'great adventure', as Isambard described it in a letter to his father, began immediately. But it was a far from happy start. As Osborne had warned, Townsend was the trouble.

The first leg of any London bound railway line or road would obviously have to pass through the city of Bath. From there it could then strike out north-east towards Chippenham, or east to Melksham, or south-east to Bradford-on-Avon and Trowbridge, then east to Devizes. McAdam had been the first to survey any sort of line, and he had favoured going south-east. Of those who followed, none had as yet considered going north.

The most direct route for the Bristol/Bath section was along the south bank of the river Avon through the villages of Keynsham, Saltford and Twerton – a distance of between fourteen and fifteen miles. Even though this would necessitate bridging the river in two places, plus some very substantial excavations through high ground at Hanham, just outside Bristol, the levels were ideal. There was everything to recommend it.

As engineer to the Bristol & Gloucester Railway, W. C. Townsend had already built his waggonway as far as Mangotsfield – eleven miles from Bristol, but in a north-easterly direction. To complete a connection with Bath, he argued, all that was necessary was to extend this line for only eight miles instead of building a completely new one, a duplicate, nearly twice that length. Townsend also contended that the Bristol & Gloucestershire's depot at Cuckold's Pill on the Floating Harbour should be developed as the new railway's terminus. Naturally his company, desperately anxious to gain as much control as they could and as quickly as possible, backed him. They in turn were strongly supported by the Bristol Dock Company whose directors, including Nicholas Roch, had an eye to their future interests. They not only controlled The Float, but all the land adjacent to it.

But Townsend's waggonway had been built to be worked solely by horses. Furthermore, the terrain over which it was laid was exceptionally hilly and exceedingly difficult. Nor was the route of his proposed extension from Mangotsfield to Bath, by way of the village of Wick and the Langridge Valley, very much better. Demonstrating considerable engineering skill, the Bristol surveyor had quite correctly made intelligent use of a number of inclined planes in routing the waggonway. All of them were biased in favour of an east–west traffic flow, in other words from the collieries to the staithes at Cuckold's Pill. Horse teams had no difficulty dragging trains of empty or lightly loaded waggons up to the pit-heads, while for the return journey gravity provided most of the motive power, the horses being trained to ride in dandy-carts.

All in all it had been no mean achievement for a man with no engineering background, and Townsend had every right to take the pride in it that he did. But what he either could not or would not get into his head, in spite of all efforts to enlighten him, was that laying out a line which was to be worked by locomotives was a vastly different proposition to laying out one worked by horses. One was a railway; the other wasn't. There was simply no way that a locomotive could negotiate a steep gradient. A railway had to be level, or as near level as possible. On any inclined plane greater than 1 in 100, auxiliary power, either in the form of a second locomotive or a stationary engine permanently installed at its head, would be required. For this reason alone the Bristol–Mangotsfield–Bath proposal was hopelessly impractical, as indeed was any idea of developing the Cuckold's Pill site. Sufficient land on which to build a terminus and adequate depot facilities simply was not available.

Such was the impasse caused by Townsend's stubbornness and the stupidity of the two companies concerned, that the whole of the enterprise appeared for a time to be in jeopardy. It was only broken after Brunel had hurriedly drawn up a new plan which sited the terminus on a stretch of open ground known as Temple Meads. This was to the east of the Floating Harbour, on the north bank of the Avon where the Bath road already crossed the river. And the only feasible approach to Temple Meads from Bath was from the south. Though the Bristol & Gloucestershire and the Dock Company raised every possible objection, their representatives on the committee now lost all their support and were easily outvoted. A much disgruntled

Townsend was then put to work on an exhaustive survey of the Avon route while Brunel, having thus secured his rear so to speak, promptly left Bristol for Bath, and London.

The only thing to recommend the route William Brunton and Henry Habberley-Price had mapped through Bradford-on-Avon, Devizes, the Vale of Pewsey and Newbury to Reading was the fact that it was direct. But, like Townsend, they seemed not to have been particularly concerned about the nature of the terrain. In places the levels were quite atrocious. Neither did they, or any of their predecessors, appear to have considered the prime reason for linking Bristol with the capital by rail.

Brunel had given this matter very careful thought indeed. It seemed to him that the best interests of the city and port of Bristol were likely to be better and far more immediately served if a trunk line to London was to follow a northern rather than a southerly course. From a northern route access to the populous centres of Gloucester, Cheltenham and Oxford – not forgetting the many wealthy estates located in the vicinities of all three cities – could eventually be achieved with comparative ease when the need arose, as it most surely would. In this respect alone, if in no other, the London to Bristol rail link was going to be unique.

The Stockton & Darlington, the Liverpool & Manchester, the Newcastle & Carlisle, the London & Birmingham, in fact all the lines so far built or projected be they railways proper or merely tramways, could be classified into one of two categories. The majority would carry the bulk of their traffic, both goods and passenger, from terminus to terminus. Only a few – of which the Grand Junction was to date the prime example – would, in addition to terminal towns, designedly serve the needs of the major townships through which they passed. In the case of the Grand Junction these would be the great industrial centres of Wednesbury and Wolverhampton. In addition, all these railways were located in mining or manufacturing districts and intended primarily for the economic transportation of minerals, raw materials and manufactured goods.

Now, though the London to Bristol link would indeed furnish the port of Bristol with sorely needed facilities for the speedy passage of materials and merchandise to and from its immediate hinterland, and between it and the metropolis, the prime function of this railway was going to be to provide a fast first-class means of passenger transport which, furthermore, would be of an almost wholly intermediate nature. Speed, therefore, and above all, comfort, were going to be the basic foundations on which this railway would have to be built if it was ever to make anything at all of its vast potential.

In Bath, Isambard hired a horse and set off to map the route that was going to be 'the Finest Work in England'. Through Bathford his way was clear as far as the straggling village of Box where the famous Bath stone quarries honeycombed the hill which, from his study of the map, would appear to be the only really major obstacle that would have to be negotiated. To get to Corsham, just over two and a half miles distant on the far side of Box Hill, would necessitate an annoying detour either to the north or to the south. The Roman road from Bath lay to the south. The alternative was to drive the line straight through the hill itself. But that would mean a tunnel almost two miles long – an unheard of distance. Like the Romans, he chose to go south.

From Corsham he continued in the same north-easterly direction through the ancient market town of Chippenham to Wootton Bassett and so to Shrivenham. Then he turned almost due east through the Vale of the White Horse to Didcot, which brought him to within a dozen miles of Oxford. He was forced to cross the river Thames twice – first at Cholsey, just south of the historic town of Wallingford, and again at Pangbourne, some two miles or so down river. And so to Reading, Maidenhead and Slough.

The railway committee had purposely delayed a final decision regarding a choice of site for the London terminus, so he recommended two possible lines of approach to the capital from Slough – one running due east from Ealing, which would facilitate the still considered possibility of a junction with the London & Birmingham, and another to the south-east, to cross the Thames once more at Kingston in Surrey, and then terminate in the vicinity of Vauxhall Bridge.

On the map the route looked to be ideal in every way. Its level appeared to be as near perfect as could be wished. It could meet nearly every foreseeable future demand for suitable development that might be made on it. But no matter how perfect it might appear on paper, only the most comprehensive survey that was feasible could prove it to be so.

Meanwhile Messrs Brunton and Habberley-Price, two

disappointed and extremely bitter men, had been far from idle. From the moment they had first made their approach to the Bristol committee, it had seemed to them a foregone conclusion that the route they had mapped must be accepted without question for, in spite of the support he received, they had never regarded Townsend as a serious rival. But then had come the eleventh-hour intrusion by Brunel, and that scarcely to be credited single-vote decision of the committee in his favour, even though he'd nothing to offer except vague if grandiose promises. Understandably therefore Brunton and Price had unhesitatingly turned their backs on Bristol, and made contact with the promoters of the currently projected London & Southampton Railway.

It was the manifold difficulties, not to mention the crippling expense, of the transportation of merchandise from the Continent to London via the English Channel, the Straits of Dover and the river Thames that had first prompted the idea of a rail link between London and the south-coast port of Southampton. That was in 1825. But in common with so many similar plans put forward at that time it had come to nothing. A perfectly timed revival of the same scheme six years later however had attracted popular interest and financial support in plenty. It was proposed that the line should run from a terminus to be sited at Nine Elms near Vauxhall Bridge in Battersea through Wandsworth, Wimbledon, Esher, Walton-on-Thames, Weybridge, Woking and Farnborough to Basingstoke; then, by way of Micheldever and Winchester, to the docks on Southampton Water – in all a distance of about seventy-seven miles.

William Brunton's suggestion that this already extensive route now be augmented by a major branch line from Basingstoke to Bath via Newbury and Bradford-on-Avon, and thence to Bristol, was readily agreed to by the enterprising London & Southampton committee. It was too late for such an addition to be included in the bill which was already well advanced in preparation for submission to the House of Commons in the forthcoming Parliamentary session. But there was nothing to prevent the immediate drafting of a future amendment to that bill which would authorise the construction of what was to be named the 'Basing and Bath Railway'. So the Bristol committee suddenly found itself faced with a far more formidable rival than the now defunct London & Bristol Railway Company could ever have been.

141

When Isambard eventually got to London he found a communication from Bristol waiting for him. In it he was not asked by the committee to complete his preliminary survey no later than the end of May, he was directed to do so. He was at first aghast at the prospect. Nearly 120 miles in length, the longest undertaking of its kind yet to be contemplated, it was surely asking the impossible to have it surveyed in less than nine weeks. He nevertheless accepted the mammoth task, the most formidable he, or possibly anyone else for that matter, had ever undertaken.

His first requirement was a dependable field assistent. Though not yet out of his teens, John Hughes, a pupil of Marc's, was exactly the type of young man Isambard had hoped to find. He was clever, quick to learn, possessed of a thorough theoretical knowledge of the type of surveying with which he was to be concerned, but with virtually no practical experience. Already his new master had had more than enough of working with so-called experts.

Next he needed a secretary to be based permanently in London, and an office in which he could work. For the moment this would have to be his old room at the Barge House, for Sophia, who willingly took on the rather daunting task of finding him suitable chambers in Westminster, soon found that with the fast-growing railway boom such accommodation was at a premium and far from easy to find. Isambard engaged William Bennett for the post, a man of indeterminate age – he was in fact just turned forty – whose unkempt appearance and slow manner disconcertingly belied his intelligence and acuity. Long experienced in the ways of both the engineering and the financial worlds, Bennett was to prove himself well worthy of the glowing references he was able to produce. Marc, once more restored to health, also put himself at his son's disposal.

As engineer to a great railway company, even if that company had yet to come into existence and his appointment confirmed, Isambard felt he was justified not only in acquiring an office of his own, but also his personal carriage. For one thing, he was already fed up with hacking round the countryside on hired nags. And though travelling as an outside passenger – for even the thought of being cooped up for hours on end in the draughty, often malodorous and always dismally uncomfortable interior of a long-distance stage or mail coach he found unbearable – was rightly held to be an experience no true Englishman should ever deny himself, it was one which began to pall when too often repeated. An exhaustive examination of available vehicles having produced nothing even remotely suitable to his requirements, he designed his own and placed an order for it with the finest coach builder in London.

He modelled his design on the britzska, an open four-wheeled carriage with a calash top, a style which only the year before had been imported from Poland. In it he installed a built-in unit to accommodate his maps, plans, and paperwork generally, his engineering instruments and a fully equipped drawing table. A similar unit would contain essential creature comforts, including an enormous humidor for his precious cigars, while the seat was so arranged that it could be readily converted into a passably comfortable couch. It would, however, be some months before the vehicle could be ready for the road. So for the time being he was going to have to travel as before.

Just a week after his arrival in London he was off again. He and Hughes travelled down to Bath overnight, and outside. It was the new assistant's first experience of long-distance coaching.

'And I wish to God it could be my last,' he said fervently as they breakfasted at Sally Lunn's in Old Lilliput Alley, and when he had at last managed to control his chattering teeth. 'Honestly, Mr Brunel, I cannot imagine a more telling argument in favour of your railway.'

'Then the sooner we get down to it the better,' was the uncompromising reply.

Isambard spent a week in the field with Hughes, tirelessly schooling him to his method of working, at every opportunity impressing on the youngster the essential basic need for thoroughness, accuracy and speed. He found him a willing and apt enough pupil. So quickly and well did he learn that at the end of the week, during which Brunel had set his usual killing pace, he'd earned more than one word of praise. It was an achievement of which the young man would have been more than justified in feeling proud – had he been given time.

Once satisfied that Hughes could be safely left to carry on alone working eastwards from Chippenham, Brunel went to Slough from where he surveyed both alternative routes into London. But at their next meeting at a prearranged rendezvous there were no words of praise for John Hughes. By then his latest benchmark should have advanced as far as Shrivenham. It was still many miles to the west.

'Make haste, man!' Brunel hammered the message home mercilessly, all the while turning a deaf ear to the other's quite genuine, and perfectly legitimate, excuses. 'You hear me? You must make haste!'

'Dammit, Sir,' Hughes was at last driven to protest, 'I'm already doing the best I can.'

But Brunel quickly smothered the spark of petulance before it could flare into open resentment at what he was fully aware was his unfair bullying. In truth Hughes had done wonderfully well. But more was yet needed from him, and Isambard was confident he had judged his man correctly.

'I want you on the far bank of the Thames no later than mid May. Now you see to it. Be there!'

A dozen and more outraged protests whirled in poor Hughes's tired brain. But not a single one of them did he voice. Hard as he was working, he knew that his employer was doing three, four times as much. Also there was that indefinable something about Brunel, in his expression, in the way he spoke, which convinced Hughes that, impossible as the goal he had been set might seem at that precise moment, he would indeed be on the far bank of the Thames as directed, come what may.

After leaving Hughes, Brunel was forced to spend some time in Bristol on both railway and dock work. 'Between ourselves,' he confided rather ruefully to Claxton who came to see him off on the midnight mail for London at the conclusion of his visit, 'it is harder work than I like. I am at it rarely less than twenty hours out of every twenty-four.'

His days were spent in coaches, or on horseback; his nights in writing reports, working out endless calculations, compiling estimates, planning and replanning the coming day's activities. He slept and ate only if and when he could find time. And if he could not, he simply went without both rest and food and smoked another cigar or two instead. He was driving himself almost to the limits of physical endurance, and he knew he could not maintain his pace much longer. But he was enjoying himself enormously.

Through the almost totally unpredictable permutation of change for which the English climate, especially in spring, is so justly notorious, the work went on. One day would be as perfect as any that could mark the climax of high summer. The next would plunge again into the lowest depths of winter, to bring frost, or fog, or rain, or sleet, or sometimes even snow. But the white blanket would soon yield before drenching downpours which swept in from western seas like fugitive marauders, though driven by winds so icy they seemed to penetrate with ease the thickest of protective clothing. Then would come the sun once more to shine warm and comforting, and with an eye-searing glare, out of a cloudless, newly washed, azure sky. But, regardless of the weather, the labour never ceased. Benchmarks were set; theodolites lined up on distant levelling staffs; azimuths and elevations recorded; gradients marked, and chain links checked then double checked, tally by tally.

As the thin blue line which marked the progress of the survey gradually inched its way across the map, so the excitement of anticipation in the city of Bristol steadily mounted, for the projected railway had at long last caught the public's imagination. On 6 May both the London & Birmingham and the Grand Junction had been incorporated by Acts of Parliament. Soon it would be Bristol's turn. On 31 May the committee accepted Brunel's survey.

Then came anticlimax. But eventually, after weeks of endless discussion and debate and much toing and froing between London and Bristol, came the announcement of a public meeting to be held in the Guildhall, Bristol, on 30 July at which one of the principal speakers was to be Mr I. K. Brunel. It was not a prospect he relished. He had an intense dislike of speaking in public. He was, he maintained, an engineer, not an orator. He proved, nevertheless, an outstanding success, receiving for his effort an all but overwhelming ovation. It was a moment of personal triumph, a just and memorable reward for his labours, a recognition far too long denied him. And he enjoyed every single minute of it. All the same, he was glad when it was all over.

'I hate having anything to do with the general public,' he later confided to Osborne. 'I always feel it's like playing with a tiger. All one can hope is that one may not get scratched, or worse.'

The Guildhall meeting resolved that a company, yet to be named, be formed without further delay with the object of establishing railway communication between Bristol and London. Twenty-four directors – twelve from each city – were to form a General Board of Management, their initial task to secure subscriptions necessary to obtain an Act of Parliament. A prospectus was compiled detailing capital as £3,000,000 issued in £100 shares, deposit £5 per share; estimated expenditure £2,805,330; anticipated revenue per annum £747,752. It also contained a map of the proposed route as surveyed, with the two alternative entries into London and three probable branch lines – Didcot to Oxford, Swindon to Gloucester, Chippenham to Bradford-on-Avon. The prospectus was issued over the signature of Charles Alexander Saunders.

Though still only in his mid-thirties, Saunders – a sometime academic and ex-civil servant of quite phenomenal administrative talent who, in ten short years, had made a considerable fortune as a shipping agent in Mauritius – was seriously contemplating retirement. He'd been back in England but a few days when he'd quite by chance run into an old business acquaintance, George Gibbs, the first of Tom Guppy's 'disciples'. Gibbs was in London to persuade his cousin Henry, managing director of Antony Gibbs & Sons, to join the Bristol Railway venture as chairman of the London section of the new management board. Much intrigued, Saunders, to whom because of his years abroad railways were a complete and intriguing novelty, promptly put aside all thought of retirement when Gibbs suggested he offer his services as company secretary.

Brunel, meanwhile, had at last acquired an office at 53 Parliament Street, Westminster, where he now lived when in London and in which Bennett had been installed. For the time being young Hughes, who in the end had acquitted himself admirably, was to work from there as well. Brunel had also hired, at his own expense, five more assistants, Hudson, Stokes, Clark, Hammond and Frere.

Number 47 Lime Street was one of the finest examples of the work of the celebrated Jacobean architect John Thorpe to have survived the Great Fire of London. And it was in the singularly beautiful first-floor room that had once been the principal library and now served as boardroom for Messrs Antony Gibbs & Sons that the Great Western was born. At precisely one o'clock in the afternoon of Thursday , 22 August 1833, the General Board of Management convened for its inaugural session – the grand culmination of those seemingly endless weeks of complicated consultations and preliminary arrangements. The formalities, elaborate and prolonged, were finally concluded with the unanimous adoption of Isambard's suggested title the 'Great Western Railway Company' and the official confirmation of I. K. Brunel as engineer.

The gamble had been won.

Chapter Five

THROUGHOUT the summer the weather had been dreadfully disappointing. But as the season approached its end, blue skies and blazing sunshine finally displaced the almost permanent overcast of dismal grey which had shrouded London and the Home Counties seemingly since spring, and a drab world suddenly found itself basking in a veritable bounty of brilliance. Never before had grass seemed greener, nor flowers more colourful, especially the roses. Everywhere, as if revived overnight from a rain-sodden stupor, they blossomed in a fragrant riot of red and yellow and pink and white, and nowhere did they bloom more beautifully than in Mr and Mrs Horsley's garden at 1 High Row in the village of Kensington Gravel Pits. So, at least, did it appear to Isambard Brunel as that idyllic September Sunday, the last he would spend in London for some time, drew rapidly to an all too early end.

His acquaintance with the family had been renewed but a few days previously when he had unexpectedly visited the Barge House to find the three Horsley girls being entertained to luncheon. Sophy was now a very grown-up and outspoken fourteen-year-old; Fanny, as quiet as her younger sister was noisy, was seventeen, and Mary, looking even more beautiful than he remembered her, nineteen. He hoped he'd not imagined it, but she had seemed particularly pleased to see him again. After a most pleasant afternoon – he had naturally accepted his sister's invitation to join them – during which he had endeavoured not to make his attraction to Mary too blatantly obvious, he had driven the girls home in his britzska. He had taken delivery of the vehicle and its superbly matched pair of coal-black high-stepping thoroughbreds that morning, and to show them off had been the reason for his calling on Ben and Sophia. Mary had sat beside him and long after she had gone he'd remained acutely conscious of the touch of perfection her elegant presence had given the sleek lines of the carriage, and of the lingering aroma of her perfume.

147

When he had mentioned to Mrs Horsley that he would be leaving London the following Monday for an indefinite period all three girls had insisted he come to the party arranged for the day before to welcome Felix Mendelssohn Bartholdy – a day he had planned to devote to the host of last-minute loose ends of final preparation for the start of the great detailed survey. But for once he allowed pleasure to take precedence over business and accepted. Mary he'd thought seemed delighted, and it was from that moment he'd begun to notice the roses.

After lunching en famille with the Horsleys, and being made to feel he had always been one of them, he joined in the welcome to the guest of honour who arrived with Karl Klingemann and Professor Rosen shortly after half-past two. Tall, dark and slimly built, with sharp but delicately cut features and strong long-fingered hands that were later to cavort over the keyboard of William Horsley's grand piano, the Jewish musician's greeting to Mary was familiar enough to make the engineer catch his breath.

'*Ach, meine liebe,*' the accent was thick but beguiling, and he held her hand tightly after kissing it with undisguised and unabashed passion, 'to be with you again is to know it is not by chance those dear flowers you gave me, which I wore in my button-hole – you remember? – and which I pressed as soon as I got home in Hamburg, still smell as sweet as they did when I last saw you.'

He had, so Isambard learned from Sophy, stayed at High Row for two months the year before. His music had enchanted her and her father and her younger brother Charles, rather bored Fanny and her other brother John, and he had fallen head over heels in love with Mary. But her eldest sister, Sophy had assured him, though she had apparently enjoyed what at times had been rather more than a mild flirtation, had evinced no further interest after the departure of the family's guest, in spite of the ensuing cascade of correspondence. All the same, Brunel felt much more at ease once the German's attention had been diverted by Sophy's inquiry regarding her autograph album.

'Sophy, child, have patience,' her mother admonished. 'Let poor Felix at least sit down before you start to pester him.'

But whatever Felix's feelings towards Mary might be, his first love was obviously music. Soon he was seated on the piano bench between Charles and Sophy with their father, John, Fanny, the Professor and Klingemann peering over their shoulders as they eagerly examined the album's newly inscribed pages. There was no room for either Mary or Isambard.

'Perhaps Mr Brunel would care to see the garden, Mary,' Mrs Horsley suggested.

'Indeed I should, Ma'am. Thank you,' he said, only just remembering that it would not do to sound too eager to be alone, even if only for a few minutes, with her beautiful daughter.

It was during the next half hour as he and Mary strolled together in the hot sunshine that he discovered just exactly how much more magnificent than any others he'd seen, the Horsley roses really were. Decorum alone dictated their return to the cosy back parlour which served as William Horsley's music room – at least, as far as Isambard was concerned. To what, if any, extent Mary reciprocated his feelings he was as yet unable to judge; she seemed relaxed and attentive in his company, but of what was actually going on inside her beautiful head he had to admit total ignorance.

Of the group they had left round the piano only Felix, Mr Horsley, young Charles and Sophy remained. Fanny and John had taken Klingemann and Rosen off to look at their latest paintings while Mrs Horsley had retired temporarily to the kitchen to supervise preparations for Sunday tea – always an event in the Horsley household. So, while the two composers talked shop, irregularly punctuating their discussion with illustrative chords or curious combinations of chromatics and arpeggios on the piano, Sophy, with Charles's eager assistance, proudly showed off the album which Felix had taken away with him the previous year. It was a tiny leather-bound booklet, measuring no more than two by one and a quarter inches and about one inch thick. Earlier autographs included those of Felix and of his father who had been with him on an earlier visit, Karl Klingemann who had written a short verse in German, and Professor Rosen who had added a sentence in Sanskrit beneath his signature. Then came the harvest Felix had reaped during his travels round Europe. There were the internationally famous names of Maria Felicia Halibran, the greatest of all operatic contraltos; Giudetta Pasta, the soprano for whom Vincenzo Bellini had written both *La Sonnambula* and *Norma*; Bellini himself with a couple of bars from another of his most popular operas, *Il Pirata*; Frederic Chopin with a complete song plus a signed dedication; and Nicolo Paganini, whose short phrase of music terminated in two impressive blots.

149

Mary suggested that Mr Brunel who, she explained, was now in his way very nearly as famous as any of the other signatories, should be asked to add his name to the collection. Sophy, however, politely refused, explaining that her book was to contain the autographs only of musicians, authors and artists, whereas Mr Brunel was an engineer. And, Charles added gravely and much to Isambard's if not Mary's amusement, an engineer was, after all, only an engineer.

After tea they all returned to the music room to hear Felix play several of his latest compositions. He accompanied Mary lovingly once she had been persuaded to sing her song – a rather sad melody which Isambard did not care for and with German words he could only imperfectly understand. Felix then played duets with Sophy, duets with Charles, and finished up with a frenetic trio with both which became so high spirited it left all three breathless, everyone helpless with laughter and the piano sounding somewhat the worse for wear. Isambard kept the merriment from flagging by performing a few conjuring tricks while they rested before climaxing the entertainment with some adventurously harmonised renderings of a selection of Mr Horsley's most popular glees.

In the cool of the evening the young people adjourned to the garden, there to romp in a noisy and hilariously exhausting game of 'ghost' in the course of which Mary's hair, normally always faultlessly coiffured, came down, and her squeals of near hysterical delight were as loud as any of her sisters'.

A final intimate stroll in the dusky and sweetly scented rose arbour was finally brought to an end by the sudden appearance of a lighted lamp in an upstairs window – a tactful but definite signal for them to go back indoors.

'That's Mama's domestic moon,' Mary explained with a smile.

'And time, I'm afraid, for me to go,' said Isambard regretfully.

The evening was still comparatively young, so it was with considerable reluctance that he bade goodnight to his fellow guests before taking leave of his host and hostess. When Mrs Horsley politely told him he must come again he swore inwardly that he fully intended to, and at the very earliest opportunity.

As he said good-night to Mary it was only with the greatest difficulty that he managed to resist the insane temptation to indulge in a display of Gallic gallantry that would have put the German composer's earlier performance to shame.

Chapter Six

DURING the next two months the black britzska and its black team became such a familiar sight to the inhabitants of the various villages and hamlets near which the new railway was to pass that they irreverently dubbed it the 'flying hearse'. Day after day, in all weathers it could be seen bearing its solitary occupant along lonely roads, through narrow lanes, over remote sheep tracks, even where there were no tracks at all – from sunrise to sunset following the line of staves marking the route.

At night the horses rested comfortably either in the stables of a convenient inn or in the barn of some hospitable farm. Not so their master. He spent most of the hours of darkness compiling reports, drafting directives, redrawing maps or plans, revising estimates, always writing, writing, writing. Often he did not go to bed at all. But, whether he slept or not, every morning without fail he was ready for the road again before dawn and on his way by sun-up.

He soon lost count of the number of times he traversed that one hundred and twenty-odd miles of mostly open country, for this was an exercise vastly different from the relatively simple operation the preliminary survey had been. In addition to the direct superintendence of his field assistants, he now had to try and conciliate landowners and farmers on whose property he had perforce to trespass. It was an unenviable task, more often than not repetitiously long-winded, rarely agreeable, never easy.

Because he was by nature outspokenly forthright, it was labour to which he was totally unsuited. Always he had to discipline himself rigorously in order to cultivate the essential ability to dissimulate. But he quickly learned when to bend before the force of an irresistible argument, no matter how ridiculous or illogical; when to shatter with his own immobility a legitimate objection though it be one with which, in different circumstances, he might well have found himself in complete accord; when to be glib; and, most

151

important of all, when to hold his tongue.

The prejudices he encountered were very nearly as numerous, and at times quite as ludicrous, as any that had hindered the progress of George Stephenson and his assistants in the building of the Liverpool & Manchester. Otherwise intelligent and reasonable men somehow had to be convinced not once, but again and again, that among other things smoke from a locomotive would not kill birds which happened to fly over it; that sparks from its chimney would not set fire to crops or grass or woodland; that cattle and sheep would not stampede at its approach; that cows would not cease to give milk, horses would not throw their riders, bolt uncontrollably, even become extinct; that oats and hay would not become unmarketable produce; that pheasants and foxes would not cease to exist in the vicinity of the railway line; that women would not be made barren, would not suffer miscarriages; that babies would not be born dead or deformed; or that anyone foolish enough to be persuaded to travel by such an infernal contraption would not be risking life or limb or sanity. All such objections and many more besides had to be answered satisfactorily, and the superstitious fears of ignorant yokels, whose mode of existence seemed to have changed but little since the days of the Crusades, assuaged.

It all took valuable time. Voraciously it consumed essential and irreplaceable reserves of energy. It required a pertinacity of which few could be capable, plus an instinctive ability to differentiate immediately between the sincere protestations of a genuine objector and the empty cavilling of a mere opportunist rogue with an eye to the main chance. It called for a willingness to negotiate on equal terms with the highest and the lowest. It demanded infinite patience.

While Brunel was busy thus persuading and placating, Saunders too was travelling the country tirelessly wooing support and soliciting vital subscriptions for shares. Already he had succeeded in winning to the cause an impressive number of Members of Parliament and peers. But in spite of all attempts to spur the general public, results remained disappointing. Parliamentary standing orders required at least half the capital investment be guaranteed by subscription before a bill to secure the necessary act could be submitted. But by the end of October, less than a quarter of the stated number of shares had been taken up, and the closing date for submission to the coming session was fast approaching.

But not only was time running desperately short, there were disturbing rumours of the probable intentions of the London & Southampton Railway Company. Once again the General Management Board met at 47 Lime Street. Specially summoned from their duties, Saunders and Brunel made their respective reports. As a result it was decided, after hours of intense deliberation, temporarily to suspend field operations between Reading and Bath, and to concentrate on the London to Reading and Bristol to Bath surveys and submit an application for authority to construct only those two sections, with a branch line to Windsor. For this the number of shares required would be only 12,500 of which one-fifth could be reserved for the proprietors of the land. A considerable proportion of the remainder having already been taken up, once the balance had been subscribed no further applications need be entertained for the immediate future. This, it was hoped, would spike the guns of the London & Southampton.

So, while Saunders set about obtaining the necessary balance of subscriptions, Brunel concentrated on preparing revised plans. It proved no easy task for either. But by the beginning of December all was ready.

The second reading of the Great Western Railway Bill in the House of Commons was moved by Lord Granville Somerset on 10 March 1834. Seconded by the Earl of Kerry, the motion was easily carried at the conclusion of an encouragingly short debate. It was then referred to committee under the chairmanship of Lord Granville Somerset.

'Well, that was mercifully brief,' commented Saunders afterwards to Sir George Burke KC, who had been retained as the company's parliamentary agent. Burke's chambers were located exactly opposite Brunel's offices in Parliament Street and it was thither the three were walking after leaving the public gallery of the House.

'Ah, the worst is yet to come, I fear,' Burke said. He was a big man with a voice to match his stature. Though exceptionally well modulated it could, when its somewhat theatrical owner chose, boom as effectively as any popular barnstormer's. 'I've no desire to sound unduly pessimistic,' he went on, 'but I suspect there's likely to be some devilish heavy weather ahead.'

'And some rough seas too, I shouldn't wonder,' added Brunel. The barrister, he knew, was not exaggerating. He had no illusions about the magnitude of the task confronting them. He also knew it would be on his shoulders, almost entirely, that responsibility for ultimate success would rest.

'Think you'll be able to keep your sea legs all right?' Saunders asked with a sly good-natured grin.

'I shall do my humble best to steer you clear of the rocks,' put in Burke, whose sense of humour matched his professional acumen.

'Frankly, I'm not particularly concerned how pleasant or otherwise the voyage might be,' Isambard carried the nautical metaphor to its logical conclusion, 'as long as it proves prosperous.'

The hearing before the Commons committee, which began on 16 April, lasted fifty-seven days. Burke's case was an excellent one and he used his skill to make the best of it, submitting near incontrovertible evidence to prove the advantages the general public would derive from the operation of the Great Western Railway.

Between Bristol and London goods were carried mostly by water – on the river Avon as far as Bath, thence, since its opening nearly a quarter of a century earlier, via the Kennet & Avon Canal to the river Kennet and so to the river Thames. By this means, one barge-load of goods took a whole day to travel just the dozen or so miles from Bristol to Bath. By rail, up to ten barge-loads at a time could be transported the same distance in considerably less than sixty minutes. Just four hours later that same cargo could be unloaded in London.

As things were at present, frost and winter floods commonly caused delays which could run into weeks, as not infrequently could droughts during the summer months. Then all shipments of merchandise were halted, save for that fraction which could be moved by road and only then at enormous expense. In addition to such seasonal delays there was an almost permanent bottleneck at Reading where the tributary Kennet joined the Thames. Moreover, the water route from there to the centre of London was over eighty miles longer than that the proposed railway line would follow. Even under ideal conditions, which were all too rare, it was a journey that seldom took less than three days. By rail it would be accomplished in as many hours.

Small wonder then that the promoters had been assured they could count on the whole-hearted support of a large number of merchants and manufacturers in both Bristol and London and the intervening towns, as well as a majority of farmers and stock-breeders save those whose holdings were in the immediate vicinity of the capital. As far as the transport of passengers was concerned, little proof of the benefits that would accrue to them was either needed or offered.

But despite this mass of favourable evidence and Sir George Burke's persuasive eloquence there was, as he had predicted, opposition to the Bill in plenty. And it came from a variety of sources.

The majority of landowners, great and small, rich and poor, aristocratic and otherwise, of the counties of Middlesex, Buckinghamshire and Berkshire, raised a mighty storm of angry protest. It mattered not that most of them would be in no way affected, directly or indirectly, by the new railway. They opposed in principal and en masse.

The Provost of Eton opposed because the intended proximity of the line to his college would undermine the discipline of that hallowed institution. It would, he claimed, result in the wholesale moral degradation of his charges by providing the more enterprising among them with too easy a means of access to the corruptive influences of the sinful metropolis. But the more practically minded citizens of Windsor opposed because they thought the line would not come as near to their town as it should and could, and that they would therefore fail to benefit from the railway as much as they felt they ought to. On the other hand, the corporation of Maidenhead, through which town the line would pass, opposed because they feared the loss of revenue they would suffer in consequence of a possible reduction in tolls from the Thames road bridge.

Farmers near London opposed because the produce the railway would bring to the city's fruit, vegetable and meat markets from outlying districts would end their time-honoured monopoly. Proprietors of stage-coaches, canals, canal barges and river craft opposed, as did turnpike trusts and innumerable road hauliers – all for predictable and obvious reasons. And last, but by no means least, the promoters of the London & Southampton Railway Company joined forces with that polyglot army of opposers. They too were seeking an Act of Incorporation, although their bill contained no provision for the now openly mooted Basing & Bath Railway. Nevertheless they went out of their way to attack the Great Western Bill with a well-prepared and, on the face of it, convincing contention that the needs of Bristol and the West Country as a whole could be equally well served by the simple addition of a branch line to their own proposed system.

Eventually, as the Great Western's principal engineering witness, Brunel was called to give evidence. He had to face an exhaustive cross examination lasting no less than eleven days. One after the other, seven learned counsels, each representing an independent opposition faction and each an expert practitioner of his subtle art, challenged him. Each attempted to break down his impenetrably calm defence of his testimony, to undermine his quiet but authoritative confidence, to trap him into some contradictory statement which might then be exploited to their clients' advantage.

Not once did any of the seven succeed. His knowledge of his subject and of the ground he had surveyed was positively encyclopaedic. Master of himself as well as of his adversaries, he simply refused to be rattled. Rapid in thought, infallible in his pronouncements and always careful to be as clear and concise as possible in the language he used, he punctiliously answered every question put to him and contested every argument posed, no matter how nonsensical or how provocative. He never said too much; he never left any loose ends; and he never lost either patience or presence of mind.

It was a tour de force of unparalleled brilliance. For the full eleven days the committee room was packed to capacity by an audience that thrilled to every single nuance of a fascinating duel of words and intellect in which one man held at bay seven of the best minds in the legal profession. It was a duel in which quarter was neither asked nor given.

When at last all was over he was cheered to the echo, and openly acclaimed by the muster of eminent railway engineers present as the latest addition to their select number. They were there to add the weight of their own expert opinions to the argument, both for and against, and one of the first to shake the triumphant protagonist by the hand was none other than the great George Stephenson himself.

'I can imagine a better line than the one you've surveyed, young man,' rang out those distinctive Geordie tones for all to hear as their owner pumped Isambard's arm until it ached, 'but I'll be damned if I know of one!'

Chapter Seven

'IT is not GREAT! Neither is it WESTERN! Nor is it even a railway! It is nought but a gross deception. A trick. A fraud on the public – in name, in title and in substance.' These were the words with which, on Saturday, 26 July 1834, one of London's leading newspapers ended its report of the previous day's calamitous event in the House of Lords.

Having survived that marathon investigation in committee, the Great Western Railway Bill had been voted through the Commons' third reading by a comfortable majority. Lord Wharncliffe's motion for its second reading in the Upper House, however, had been voted out. The Bill was lost, completely and irretrievably lost, and with it perished all the company's carefully laid plans – much to the delight of its foes.

It was a bitter disappointment for all concerned but, once the initial shock had dulled, one from which everyone seemed to recover remarkably quickly. As Sir George Burke was quick to point out, because of the unprecedentedly prolonged procedure in the Commons, it was far too late in the current parliamentary session anyway for there to have been much hope of getting the Bill through all its stages in the Upper House. But that time in the Commons had not been wasted. Despite persistent antagonism in the press, public opinion seemed to have swung very much in favour of the lost Bill. In fact, practically the only criticism now being levelled against it was that its proposals had been incomplete. The General Management Board therefore decided that once the balance of required subscriptions had been secured, a new Great Western Bill, this time for the whole of the line, would be presented next year. The public had woken up at long last.

Before the summer was over a new prospectus had been issued; unlike its predecessor it was extremely well received, and by the end of February 1835 Saunders was able to announce that the subscription list was complete.

At a total cost now estimated at exactly £2,500,000 – the engineer's calculations this time being based on the more accurate detailed survey – the overall length of the line was to be 114 miles. This was six miles less than at first stated, for, instead of diverting to the south between Bath and Corsham, Brunel now intended driving that two-mile-long tunnel under Box Hill. It would be the greatest feat of its kind ever to be attempted, the greatest challenge of the whole enterprise.

Since receiving their Act of Incorporation, ironically on the very day the Great Western Bill had been lost, the promoters of the London & Southampton had diligently canvassed support for their contentious Basing & Bath Railway. Even though, at a public meeting in Bath, Brunel had so demolished and ridiculed their argument that a resolution in favour of the Great Western was carried so enthusiastically that the pro-London & Southampton organisers of the meeting had been forced to beat a hasty and ignominious retreat from their own platform, the directors declared their intention of again challenging the Great Western before the parliamentary committees. And, mindful of Brunel's performance, they announced that this time they too would have an expert spokesman who would, in similar but superior fashion, champion their cause.

It was the publication, in 1823, of a major treatise on algebraic geometry that had first rocketed the name Dionysius Lardner into prominence. This had been followed by another weighty work dealing with the intricacies of the calculus. A graduate of Trinity College, Dublin, Lardner's original inclination had been towards the Church. He had, in fact, been ordained. But he had chosen to channel his energies and not inconsiderable talents into much more remunerative scientific – and later literary – activities. He was the newly founded London University's first professor of Natural Philosophy and Astronomy.

With a voice that would undoubtedly have been heard to its best advantage impressively complementing the echoing Gothic splendour of some ancient cathedral, and possessed of a platform manner and technique of delivery which were the envy of many a rising Thespian, he was much in demand as a lecturer. Willing to expound, for a suitable fee, on practically any subject from theoretical mathematics to theosophy, he had established himself in the eyes of the public as an eminent scientific sage. So much so, indeed, that what the learned Doctor Lardner considered acceptable was invariably judged to be so, while that which he chose to condemn, for whatever reason, was liable to be dismissed out of hand. There were many who considered him the greatest scientific theorist since Isaac Newton, and his forthcoming battle of wits with Isambard Brunel was most eagerly anticipated.

Initially, however, the expectant public appeared to be doomed to disappointment. The second reading of the second Great Western Bill in the House of Commons was unopposed. The report of the previous session's proceedings was thereupon adopted and referred to committee, this time with Charles Russell, the member for Reading, taking the chair. No sooner had the committee convened than Russell declared that, inasmuch as the public advantages of a railway between London and Bristol by the route proposed had already been sufficiently established, no further evidence would be required nor would additional argument need to be considered on that particular point. He therefore instructed counsel to confine their case either to proving or disproving the merits of the line as surveyed.

This caught all the objectors very much on the hop, not least Doctor Lardner, for his so carefully prepared brief would now go unheard. Unfortunately, extemporisation not being one of his foremost talents, he failed dismally to create the profound impression so confidently expected of him. Nor did he gain ground when, during a sharp exchange with his quicker-witted adversary, he allowed himself to be panicked into the fatuous observation that while the gradients of Brunton and Price's survey were indeed individually steeper than those of Brunel's line, they were so balanced that the rises and falls could be said to be mutually compensatory and thus rendered the Basing & Bath route overall practically level. Which prompted the rather wry observation from Russell that assuming such a principle to be correct, the Highlands of Scotland might therefore be considered as ideal a district as any in which to construct a railway.

At this juncture the discomfited doctor, though he still had much to say particularly with regard to the proposed Box Tunnel, wisely decided to concede the Commons contest. But on grounds of his own choosing, he contended, he would still put young Brunel well and truly in his place. Of that, he hastened to assure his somewhat more than slightly anxious supporters, there could be no doubt whatever.

The only opposition to the Bill's third reading after its return to the Commons came from an earnest but eccentric Sabbatarian who demanded that on the Lord's Day the railway not only be closed to the public, but between the hours of midnight and midnight no engine or carriage be so much as moved, under penalty of a £20 fine. The proposal was defeated.

The following day, Wednesday, 27 May, the Bill was introduced in the House of Lords for its formal first reading. Then, on 10 June came the all-important second reading, the motion this time carried by a reasonably comfortable majority and referred to a committee presided over by Lord Wharncliffe. The moment everyone had been waiting for had finally arrived.

Lardner's attack was nothing if not full-blooded, and was concentrated on what he chose to describe as 'that most monstrous and extraordinary, that most dangerous, impracticable, unprecedented two-mile-long tunnel Brunel blithely intended driving beneath Box Hill.' Quickly warming to his subject, the loquacious doctor asserted that the inevitable consequence of the perpetration of an act of such arrogant and arrant foolishness could not possibly be other than the eventual wholesale destruction of human life on a scale never before imagined.

His voice now vibrant with emotion and positively sensual in its tone of righteous verisimilitude, he warned that no amount of care, no foresight, indeed no means at all with which he or anyone else was acquainted, could in any way prevent the occurrence of some future catastrophe should the tunnel ever be constructed; that if it was, no person would desire to be shut away from the light of day for as long as it would take to travel from one end of the wretched excavation to the other with the awful consciousness of such a superjacent weight of earth which could not fail to crush him into oblivion or, possibly worse, entomb him alive should there be a serious or even a minor mishap; that the noise of two trains passing within the tunnel's depth would be of a magnitude no normal human ear could endure without putting at serious risk its owner's sense of hearing, or his sanity, or both; and that, in any case, no passenger, assuming by some miracle he survived his ordeal, would ever wish to suffer a second time the

160

ghastly experience of a journey through such a monstrously hellish place by train, or by any other means.

To this denunciation their lordships listened with patient attentiveness and when the speaker paused to acknowledge the adulation of his followers – at the conclusion of what turned out to be, to the dismay of many, merely his introductory remarks – the committee as a whole seemed duly impressed. The great pundit then proceeded, with the aid of numerous detailed diagrams and a whole series of complicated mathematical calculations already carefully copperplated onto an enormous blackboard, to prove conclusively that if its brakes were to fail a train would run down the tunnel's incline, which was admittedly acute, with a constantly increasing velocity that would cause it to emerge at a speed in excess of 120 miles per hour. 'And at such a speed,' Doctor Lardner thundered in sepulchral tones deliberately calculated to send a shiver down the most sceptical of spines, 'at such a velocity my Lords and gentlemen, it is to be doubted if even the most stalwart among a train-load of passengers could possibly survive the dire effects of inevitable asphyxiation!'

It was the climax of his dénouement and he made the most of the moment by garnishing it with all the panache his long years of experience at the lectern had taught him. He even managed an ironic bow in the direction of Brunel who was seated at a small table between Saunders and Sir George Burke on the far side of the room. Then he sat down and with a smile of triumphant superiority revelled in the protracted buzz of appalled consternation his doom-laden pronouncement had engendered.

'My God!' muttered Saunders, aghast. 'He's not right, is he?'

Brunel, who was scribbling frantically, ignored the question.

'Is he?' Saunders demanded uneasily of Burke.

'No idea,' grunted the barrister, shaking his head and looking far from confident. 'The damn fellow lost me completely before he was half-way through his first blasted equation.'

'There's your answer,' said Isambard calmly, handing Burke the sheet of paper on which he had been so busily writing. 'You can put it in your own words.'

Mystified, and watched by a worried-looking Saunders, Burke hurriedly scanned it. 'Well, I'll be damned,' he said in a very loud voice, and guffawed so heartily he saved the committee chairman the trouble of calling the still noisy room to order.

'You have something to say, Sir?' Lord Wharncliffe, notorious for his insistence on correct and formal procedure even in the most extreme circumstances, questioned icily.

Burke lumbered to his feet. 'Indeed I have, m'Lud. I categorically reject everything the last witness has just said.'

The sudden hush could almost be heard. 'And I call upon the members of this illustrious committee,' and here Burke had to raise his voice as the hush became a howl of outraged protest, ' I call upon this committee to do likewise.'

'Order! Order!' But Wharncliffe had to wield his gavel with all his strength before he was able to make himself heard. 'On what grounds, pray, Sir George?' he managed at last to ask.

'On the grounds that our valuable time has been utterly wasted by a dissertation of the most absolute drivel, m'Lud,' Burke replied blandly, his heavily jowled countenance a picture of pained innocence.

For the better part of a full minute the outburst was quite uncontrollable. Again Wharncliffe had to hammer with his gavel until the uproar subsided.

'An explanation!' His normally benign features contorted into a mask of near-demonic fury, Lardner's mellifluous tones were rage strangled into a shrill squeak. 'I demand an explanation!'

'I shall be most happy to give you one, Sir,' Burke boomed expansively.

'And an apology,' yapped the purple-visaged doctor.

'Ah, now that I fear I can't promise.'

'Gentlemen, you will both have the goodness to address the Chair,' commanded its irate occupant, once more busy with his gavel.

Panting for breath, his mouth working horribly, Lardner literally spluttered with rage as he did his best to point a trembling finger at Sir George Burke. But words failed him and he very nearly choked. 'I demand an explanation, my Lord,' was all he could manage.

'Well Sir,' Wharncliffe, not at all amused by this astounding turn of events, addressed the Great Western's parliamentary agent with some asperity.

'M'Lud, if the learned gentleman could be persuaded to sit down and shut up I should be only too delighted.'

'Please be seated, Doctor Lardner,' Wharncliffe soothed, 'and pray, do your best to compose yourself.' When Lardner had reluctantly obeyed, he once more turned his gaze on Burke's impassively towering bulk. 'Proceed, Sir George.'

'Thank you, m'Lud.' The barrister assumed his very best courtroom manner. 'M'Lud, Doctor Lardner has just demonstrated and, if I may be permitted to say so, most ably demonstrated, the truly terrifying possibilities that could apparently eventuate should a train fully laden with freight and crammed with passengers have the misfortune, due to a failure of its braking system, to run out of control down this incline through the proposed Box Tunnel with whose merits or otherwise, I hasten to point out, I am not, at this particular juncture, specifically concerned. The doctor has shown, and proved to his own satisfaction at least, that such a train in such a situation would, as a direct result of uncontrolled and uncontrollable acceleration, achieve a potentially fatal velocity of 120 miles per hour.'

'Not potential, Sir,' snapped Lardner acidly, 'fatal, absolutely fatal!'

'Chair,' murmured Wharncliffe with a reproachful bang of his gavel. 'Continue, Sir George.'

'Thank you, m'Lud. Being myself but an humble practitioner of the law, m'Lud, and therefore lacking the good doctor's wealth of scientific knowledge and justly famed wisdom, I must, of course, without the benefit of medical evidence to the contrary, accept his opinion that such an extreme velocity might well have the deleterious effect on life he has today so graphically described. That is to say, m'Lud, I would accept his esteemed opinion if – and I repeat "if", such a velocity were to be obtained.'

The barrister, as wily and as skilled as the professional lecturer in manipulating and exploiting to the full the rapt attention of his audience, paused just long enough to allow the full portent of what he had just said to sink in. Then, judging the moment to perfection, he went on, 'But I suggest – no, m'Lud, I will go farther, I will affirm categorically and without equivocation on the best possible authority,' and here Burke picked up and brandished the paper Brunel had handed him, 'that Doctor Lardner has been talking through his hat!'

Never had such a statement been made before a Lords' committee. It was, not surprisingly, received with the sort of astonished silence during which the proverbial pin might well have been heard to drop.

'If I may make so bold, m'Lud,' Burke continued with suave equanimity, 'I would advise that the witness for the opposition be instructed to go home and do his sums again. And that this time he takes the trouble to include the twin factors of friction and air resistance in his calculations.'

During the silence it had seemed the doctor had been about to explode with indignation. Clutching the back of his chair and the edge of the table before him for support, and with his features once more alarmingly convulsed, he'd forced himself to his feet. But at the mention of 'friction' and 'air resistance' he suddenly appeared to stagger, almost as if he had sustained a physical blow. His jaw dropped. Colour drained from his face. Then, muttering incoherently, he sank back into his chair to scrabble frantically among his scattered papers as a growing babble of voices finally burst into a discordant chorus of derisive laughter and agonised groans of disbelief.

'Order! Order! Order!' This time, however, things had gone far beyond the control of even the redoubtable Lord Wharncliffe. There was only one voice powerful enough to be heard above that extraordinary hullabaloo, and that belonged to Sir George Burke.

'Incidentally, m'Lud,' he bellowed, 'for the record and Doctor Lardner's enlightenment, I am informed by Mr Brunel here that a runaway train in such circumstances could not possibly exceed a velocity of six and fifty miles per hour.'

But whether or not Doctor Lardner was grateful for the information thus gratuitously offered was never minuted, for Wharncliffe wisely decided to adjourn the day's business there and then, and the doctor never again appeared to give evidence.

Chapter Eight

THE Great Western Railway Bill received the Royal Assent on 31 August 1835. Within hours Brunel had installed Hammond as resident engineer in London and sent Frere off to Bristol to take charge there, Townsend having already resigned. Because of the massive undertaking at Box, once the Bristol to Bath section had been completed all progress would have to be westward. But Brunel, wise in the ways of mankind, had no wish that Bristol should feel itself left behind. So work on the line was to start from both termini simultaneously.

'We shall have our flags flying over the Brent Valley tomorrow,' he told Frere lightheartedly just prior to the latter's departure for Bristol by the night mail, 'so you'd best waste no time when you get there.'

Immediately to the west of London the valley of the river Brent was to be crossed by a 300-yard, brick-built, stone-capped viaduct, 65 feet in height with each of its 8 arches spanning 70 feet. It would be the largest and by far the most important piece of constructional work between London and Maidenhead and already Bennett, with the help of a new assistant, Seymour Clark, was preparing contracts for tender.

Then, not content with the truly magnificent prize he had won, Isambard Brunel promptly hazarded everything on a second single throw of the dice.

The distance between the rails of the Killingworth Colliery waggonway for which young George Stephenson had built his first locomotive twenty years before, just happened to be 4 feet 8½ inches – other waggonways had gauges, the technical term for that distance, which varied as much as a foot or more either way. It was therefore understandable, yet at the same time no more than pure chance, that he should have constructed the Stockton & Darlington and the Liverpool & Manchester to the gauge he had worked with all his life;

and simply because they were to connect with the Liverpool & Manchester and had been designed by the Stephensons, both the London & Birmingham and the Grand Junction railways were to have the same gauge.

Thus 4 feet 8½ inches had in effect become the so-called standard for English railways and been so specified in Acts of Incorporation, with the notable exception of the London & Southampton Bill. Undetected until after the Bill had been passed, it had been a genuine error of omission. But, citing it as precedent, Isambard had persuaded those responsible for the final draft of the Great Western Bill to exclude from its provisions any reference to gauge.

As he had progressed with his survey he had realised the truly tremendous potential of the extraordinary straight and level road he was preparing to build. The more he had studied it the more he had been convinced that, having regard to the speeds which in future would be attainable and to the masses eventually to be moved by more powerful locomotives, the machinery he had examined so diligently on the Liverpool & Manchester and on other lines since was on much too small a scale. In his opinion, great though the achievements so far had undoubtedly been, the Stephensons, Hackworths and all the other designers had merely proved the potential of the locomotive, rather as Trevithick had proved the possibility. Their machines were all under-powered. They were too small. Increase the overall size of the locomotive, he reasoned, and its power could likewise be increased – perhaps even doubled. And what more obvious way of increasing its size, also the carrying capacity of both waggons and carriages, than by widening the distance between the rails on which it ran.

'Brilliant!' was Tom Guppy's unequivocal assessment of the engineer's proposal to the management board. But George Gibbs solemnly pooh-poohed the whole idea. He also declared his intention of withdrawing from the project altogether. He regarded the sudden fantastic rise in all railway shares – Great Western was already being quoted at a premium of £40 and was going up daily – as an unmistakable sign that a crash must come soon. 'Too much money chasing too little security,' he warned lugubriously. 'You mark my words; it's a classic formula for disaster.' Nor was he alone in holding that view. Even Nicholas Roch, despite his personal loyalty to both Brunel and Guppy, was beginning to sound reticent.

But the ever ebulliently persuasive Tom Guppy was not to be so easily denied. 'Damn all this blasted belly-aching about shares,' he told Isambard, clapping him heartily on the shoulder, 'I for one intend backing you to the hilt.'

The first full General Meeting of the Great Western Railway Company in the London Tavern on 29 October 1835 was a noisy, mostly light-hearted affair lasting several hours. There were formal votes of thanks to Lord Wharncliffe, Lord Granville Somerset and Charles Russell for their efforts in Parliament on the company's behalf, to Brunel, to Sir George Burke, to Saunders and a host of others. Then came the question of the gauge of the new railway.

It is to be doubted if more than one person in ten among those present really understood the technicalities involved when Brunel spoke of friction factors as measured in terms of pounds per ton weight and the like. In order, therefore, to ensure a more general comprehension, Tom Guppy by prearrangement posed a series of questions which could be answered in simple but informative non-technical terms. Thus was Isambard enabled to convince the majority of proprietors of the enormous advantages to be gained by adopting a 7-foot gauge rather than building the Great Western line to what Guppy scornfully dubbed 'the coal-waggon gauge'.

There existed, however, a 'Liverpool Party' – so called because its leaders were Henry Boyle, James Crossthwaite and Benjamin Raskell, three of that city's most prominent and powerful merchants – which, though small and without representation on the board, was able to command considerable attention. Not unnaturally they championed the Stephensons, and looked on Brunel's advocacy of a broad gauge as little short of heretical.

But the only practical obstacle was the proposed junction of the Great Western with the London & Birmingham. From the engineering point of view the addition of a third rail to both lines would present no great difficulty. But should the London & Birmingham refuse any such modification then the broad gauge would have to be abandoned unless, and here Brunel openly challenged both directors and proprietors, the Great Western company was prepared to make alternative arrangements for entry into the capital.

As things turned out, the issue was resolved well before the end of the year. The London & Birmingham board, seemingly dominated by its secretary, Captain Mark Huish, refused to countenance any reasonable arrangement; and at a special meeting held in Radley's Hotel, Blackfriars, by an overwhelming majority – the Liverpool Party's vote being the only one against – the adoption of Brunel's broad gauge was sanctioned.

'Give him his head and this young fellow will end up taking us to the moon,' grumbled Henry Boyle, the Liverpool Party's self-appointed spokesman, to his cronies over dinner afterwards. Though it was not intended that he should, Brunel, seated at the next table with Guppy, heard. 'Why stop at Bristol?' he could not resist challenging Boyle. 'Why not have a steamboat go from Bristol to New York and call it Great Western too?'

'Why not indeed!' murmured Tom Guppy, his eyes suddenly shining.

The simple salutation offered by Mary Horsley meant more to Isambard than any of the countless toasts and similar expressions of congratulation, both formal and informal, proposed in celebration of his triumph. The house at High Row on the December Sunday when he was guest of honour had been crowded. It was not every day a friend of the family could be so fêted, and Mr and Mrs Horsley and all their children had done their best to make the most of the occasion. So only for one precious, all too fleeting, moment had he found himself alone with Mary by the punch bowl in the drawing room. 'With all my heart, I wish you every success,' she'd murmured softly, her beautiful hazel eyes holding his as she raised her glass to her lovely lips.

Her voice was a caress that seemed to stir him to the very core of his being. But he who had so impressively defied and defeated all his adversaries in that recent war of words and wit now found himself as tongue-tied and as helpless as any lovesick swain. Did she suspect, he wondered, how he felt about her? And even if she did, could she possibly imagine just how much he yearned to possess her? In those long months since the evening when they had strolled in the moonlit rose garden his mind had been concentrated to the exclusion of all else on the many different aspects of his work. But never once had

Mary Horsley been absent from his heart.

The time to tell her he decided was not yet, however, and until he judged it to be so he was determined to hold his peace. It was a struggle, but somehow he managed to resist the temptation to gather her into his arms and smother her with passionate kisses.

'With all my heart, I thank you,' was all he had been able to trust himself to say in reply.

And now, as on New Year's Eve three years previously, he sat alone and quietly took stock of his situation. The contrast between the two occasions was scarcely credible. Not in his wildest dreams had he ever imagined he could have achieved so much in just six and thirty months. His 'Castles in Spain' had indeed become virtual realities. Not all of them – not yet; but certainly as many as were necessary to guarantee that never again would their architect be forced to fight his way through that seemingly endless wilderness of obscurity from which he had so triumphantly emerged. No longer the self-despised near-penniless nonentity whose only claim to distinction was his father's name, he was now, to his peers, the undisputed master of his own proud and rapidly expanding estate, already the envy of many – soon, possibly, to be the wonder of all.

With a salary of £2,000 a year from the Great Western Railway Company and the prospect of as much again as engineer to the Bristol & Exeter with its already proposed extension to Plymouth, plus more besides from a line to be called the Cheltenham & Great Western Union Railway, he could consider himself a successful man of substantial means. He had, therefore, purchased the leasehold of 18 Duke Street, once the Earl of Devon's town house and long considered one of the most desirable of London residences. In addition to his now famous britzska he kept a fine travelling coach, his own fly for getting about London, and a stable of a dozen excellent horses. He employed a staff of domestics as well as a full-time private secretary who in turn had two assistants. In future he would work from Duke Street.

The office in Parliament Street, apart from being now far too small, was quite the wrong setting for the future he envisaged. But he would miss the familiar atmosphere of the place, and more particularly the friendly proximity of his neighbour Sir George Burke. Since the first parliamentary proceedings more than two years before, scarcely a day had gone by without their meeting. The barrister's chambers were directly opposite on the same level as his and he had, much to Burke's amusement and the outraged astonishment of the occupants of their respective buildings and those adjacent, carried a cord across Parliament Street, thereby establishing a novel but effective means of direct communication. When, as was often the case, the permutation of signals on the bells to which the ends of the cord were attached failed to convey their more complicated messages, the two were frequently to be seen by wondering passers-by leaning precariously from their office windows energetically waving flags in Brunel's ingenious adaptation of the recently introduced semaphore code.

In addition to the Great Western, the Bristol & Exeter, and the Cheltenham & Great Western Union he was to be engineer to a new Bristol & Gloucester Railway and to the Taff Vale Railway. The Monkwearmouth Dock Scheme was to go ahead, the Bristol Dock Company were considering development at Portishead as well as further improvements to the Floating Harbour and, wonder of wonders, the Thames Tunnel Company was again in business. But, most gratifying of all, work on the Clifton bridge – his favourite child, his 'firstborn' – was soon to be resumed.

He calculated the capital likely to pass through his hands in the foreseeable future to be just short of £6,000,000. Not bad for a man not yet thirty! Everything he'd touched had been suddenly bathed in golden sunshine. It was almost too good to be true. He was only too well aware that things could not continue so indefinitely; sooner or later, bad weather must surely overtake him. For the time being, however, he would make the most of it. He would run before this wind of fortune under a full spread of canvas for as long as it chose to favour him and hope, when it changed, he would be able to gather in his sails in time.

Of one thing only, he told himself, could he really be certain. Before the next twelve months had passed he was going to be a married man.

Chapter Nine

WHEN Mary Horsley accepted his proposal she had set her heart on a wedding and a reception befitting the marriage of the 'Duchess of Kensington' to the man she and many others regarded as one of England's most famous and eligible bachelors. She had also looked forward with eager anticipation to a luxuriously memorable honeymoon of, at the very least, a month's duration in Paris or Rome or Vienna or Venice, plus perhaps a visit to Greece or Egypt, or both. Alas! it was not to be.

Instead, bravely managing to look as desirable and beautiful as ever in her bridal white, she was quietly married in Kensington Church on 5 July 1836. Afterwards, at Isambard's side, she presided with charming dignity over a simple wedding breakfast at her parents' home to which only family and a few favoured friends were invited. She then endured eight days of typical Snowdonian weather at Capel Curig. And even that fleeting interval was really more than her frenetically busy husband could spare from his time-consuming labours.

By arrangement Saunders met them at Cheltenham with two enormous bags crammed with papers requiring Isambard's urgent attention. Then, after he'd been closeted with Saunders the whole day, they went on to Bristol where he was immediately caught up in what seemed to Mary a raging whirlwind of work, leaving her to savour her first, but soon to be only too familiar, experience of grass widowhood.

In many respects she was as happy as any young bride should be. Never once did she fail to respond as she should, or in any way neglect her newly assumed wifely duties. Nor did she say or do anything to betray her disappointment. But secretly, and despite her happiness, its bitterness at times made her feel quite ill.

For the first six months of that year the Great Western Railway Company, instead of building and consolidating the firm foundation

171

on which its future fortunes would depend, had reeled drunkenly from one crisis to another. There had been trouble with the levels between Hanwell and Paddington; trouble over the purchase from the Bishop of London of land required for the Paddington terminus; and a threat from the London & Birmingham to build an extension to Tring which would have robbed the Great Western of its proposed Cheltenham branch had had to be contained, then countered. Decisions had been made regarding the designs of locomotives and rolling stock in the face of totally irreconcilable uncertainties; and decisions had been taken to commence operations on the Paddington approach before final parliamentary approval had been obtained. Also there had been a constant fluctuation in the value of the company's shares which one day would plummet to a near-disastrous low and the next soar to an equally worrying high.

That the infant company had survived at all was regarded by many as nothing short of a miracle. But survive it had, thanks mainly to the efforts of Saunders and Henry Gibbs, and Brunel and his devoted, not to say dedicated, staff. But to her dismay Mary Brunel found there was far more in Bristol than just the Great Western Railway to keep her husband from her. Isambard's casual gibe at Boyle in the dining room at Radley's had proved an inspiration to Tom Guppy. A born speculator as well as a visionary, he'd found the idea of a transatlantic steamship quite irresistible. After dinner he and Brunel had retired to a private sitting room where, sustained by good wine and excellent tobacco, they had talked far into the night.

Fifteen years before, the American *Savannah*, a tiny vessel equipped with only a ninety-horsepower single-cylinder auxiliary engine, and far from being a true steamship, had crossed from her home port to Liverpool in twenty-seven days. But for a total of eighty-five hours only, had she progressed entirely under steam. Though there had been subsequent impressive transoceanic voyages by various steamers – notably the British-built *Rising Star* round Cape Horn to Chile in 1821 and the *Enterprise* from Falmouth to Calcutta four years later – no vessel had yet completed an extended ocean passage without having to rely substantially on the elemental power of wind for at least half the time at sea.

An unassisted and commercially successful transatlantic crossing was regarded as the golden goal of marine engineering, but was generally believed, by those who were supposed to know, to be quite beyond the bounds of possibility. The insoluble problem, it was said, was fuel. No ship could ever be capable of carrying sufficient coal for the duration of any lengthy voyage. And though some had tried, none as yet had proved this accepted theory to be false.

'I used to make model boats when I was at school,' Brunel remarked as they smoked and drank. 'And though I can well remember my father telling me that steam would never do for distant navigation, for years afterwards I dreamed of one day building a fleet of powered ships that could sail anywhere in the world – around the world, if you like.'

'Now that would be impossible,' his companion scoffed.

'Not at all. You'd only have to build a vessel big enough.'

At which Tom Guppy had looked long and hard at Isambard Brunel, his eyes narrowed against the sting of pungent tobacco fumes. Then he asked 'Are you sober?' They had been talking for some considerable time and had consumed several bottles of the best port Radley's could provide.

'Perfectly sober.'

'And serious?'

'Perfectly serious.'

But Guppy's grounding in the elements of engineering were not to be so easily denied. 'My dear Brunel, I would not presume to contradict you, of all people; but I was always taught that size was simply no solution. Double the size of any hull and you merely double the power requirement to shove the thing through the water. And to double the power you've got to double the amount of fuel you carry.'

'Yes, I know,' Isambard sighed and lit a fresh cigar. 'We were all taught the same thing, weren't we? And it's still being taught. But it's wrong.'

'Wrong?'

'I always suspected it was. But it was some time before I managed to put my finger on the basic flaw in the logic.'

'Flaw!'

'I'll explain. You see, when you're dealing with a vessel's tonnage you're talking in terms of volume.'

'Right.'

'But when you're dealing with the power required to move that vessel you've got to think, not in terms of volume, but of resistance.

173

And resistance is determined solely by the surface area of the hull which is in contact with the water.' He took a pencil from his pocket and jotted figures to illustrate his argument. 'Now take a vessel any size you like, the carrying capacity of its hull increases as the cube of its dimension. But, and this is the crux of the matter, the resistance of that same hull increases as the square of its dimension.'

Open mouthed, Guppy studied the illustration before him for some considerable time before he looked again at a broadly smiling Isambard and said 'Do you mean to tell me it's as simple as that?'

'As simple as that.'

'My God!' Another prolonged pause. Then, 'Who else knows about this?'

Brunel shrugged. 'I've no idea. It's there for anyone to work it out for himself.'

'But no one else has.'

'Presumably not.'

The little man, his pale deeply lined face frozen into a frowning mask of fierce concentration, was silent. 'A transatlantic steamer,' he murmured at last, 'Bristol to New York, the *Great Western.*' Another silence, and then, 'Can you do it?'

'Yes! I can do it.' Isambard answered with a nonchalance that totally belied his sudden surge of excitement. He had not set out to push the Bristol businessman into anything. They had merely intended to discuss generalities. But having come this far he saw no reason to say anything which might prevent such a decision being made. 'Once the correct proportions have been established,' he went on easily, 'it would be possible to design a ship for any length of voyage.'

'Then, by God!' said Tom Guppy, 'do it we will!'

Within a month the Great Western Steamship Company had been formed in Bristol – its object, to engage in passenger transport by steamship across the Atlantic ocean. Peter Maze, a close friend of Guppy's and a Great Western Railway director, was chairman, Captain Christopher Claxton managing director, and Isambard Brunel the engineer.

Managing somehow to accomplish the task on top of all his railway and other work, he'd had the designs for both hull and engines ready by Easter. On 28 July 1836 the sternpost was set up in William Patterson's yard in Bristol, an event Tom Guppy insisted on celebrating in a manner that was very nearly the despair of his still worried doctors. But it was indeed an occasion worthy of some sort of commemoration for *Great Western* was to be the largest steamship ever conceived, with engines of unprecedented size. She would be constructed of the finest oak, according to traditional methods, but on an improved principle recently evolved by Sir Robert Sepping, Surveyor to the Royal Navy, and with ribs as massive as those of a ship of the line. Sheathed in copper, her hull would be the strongest ever to challenge the wayward wrath of the wild Atlantic wastes. When finished, her luxury would be second to none. Her maiden voyage, however, would be under canvas, for her engines, already under construction at Maudslay, Son & Fields in Blackwall, were to be fitted on the Thames. Then would come the conquest of the ocean – or would it?

It so happened that during the first week in August the British Association, founded by Charles Babbage and others in 1831 for the promotion among laymen of a general interest in the sciences, was meeting in Bristol. One of the principal speakers was Doctor Dionysius Lardner, now happily recovered from his unfortunate experience of the previous year, the subject of whose main address was to be 'Trans-Atlantic Steam Navigation'.

Sorely pressed though he was, as always, for time, Isambard made a point of attending, though in a purely private capacity. The hall was packed, the audience not so much interested in the subject of the lecture as in the possibility of witnessing another dramatic exchange between Lardner and Brunel. The doctor, as was his way, came equipped with his wealth of complicated calculations – all, this time, very carefully checked indeed – and a mass of illustrations, his intention, predictably, to prove the impossibility of any steamship being able to complete a transoceanic voyage. To this end he delivered, with his customary mastery, a most impressive lecture which was received with long and ecstatic applause.

Then came the anticipated clash with his old adversary. But, try as he might, Isambard found it quite impossible this time to shake the pundit from his perch, or his following from their faith. On this occasion it was Doctor Lardner who had the last word.

'Consider, for example, a vessel of 1,600 tons burthen,' he finally urged his audience to visualise, 'provided with engines of, let us say, 400 horsepower.' The number of those listening actually capable of doing this was quite immaterial, for the speaker ploughed on without pause, intoning like a pontiff proclaiming Holy Writ. 'You must take 2⅓ tons of fuel for each horsepower, so our vessel must have 1,348 tons of coal. To that you must then add 400 tons. So our vessel must carry a total burthen of 1,748 tons.' To this, the flock, as unimpressed as its single-minded self-opinionated shepherd with the cogent argument of the true prophet in their midst who sought to enlighten them, responded with what almost amounted to a Grand Amen.

'Under the circumstances, therefore,' the exultant sage concluded, favouring his apparently humbled opponent with a smile of perceptible pity, 'I think it would be a waste of time to endeavour to convince you further of the inexpediency of attempting any direct voyage from Bristol, or from any other British port, to New York.'

It was.

Chapter Ten

THOUGH it was some time before Brunel would admit it, even to himself, it was young Daniel Gooch who saved him from an embarrassment that could well have finished his career.

The two first met in August 1837, in the Manchester office of Tom Gooch, Daniel's elder brother who was then engineer to the Manchester & Leeds Railway. Daniel's first love was locomotives and when it became known that Brunel was looking for a locomotive engineer he had applied for the job – much to the disgust of his brother who, like the Stephensons, already regarded the broad-gauge idea with considerable scorn. He had served his time under Homfray at Tredegar and at the Vulcan and Dundee foundries before going to work for Robert Stephenson & Company. There he had been very much involved in designing and building a couple of six-foot-gauge locomotives originally intended for Russia. A lucrative offer from Sir Robert Hawks had wooed him away from the Stephensons, but when six months later Hawks's plans to open a new engine works at Gateshead had been abandoned, Daniel had joined his brother Tom on the Manchester & Leeds.

He was tall, well built but angular, with long arms, large feet and enormous clumsy-looking hands which he habitually clasped loosely together in front of him as if never quite sure what else he could do with them. His sun-browned, slightly pockmarked features were gaunt and big boned with a high broad forehead across which an unruly cowlick of black hair persisted in falling no matter how many times or how carefully he brushed it back. Quietly and deliberately spoken, with a rich Geordie accent, he had about him an air of reassuring confidence and maturity that, coupled with his physical appearance, completely belied his years. He looked and conducted himself like a man of at least forty. He was, in fact, barely half that age.

But despite his youth, he immediately struck Brunel as being the ideal man for the job, and at the conclusion of that single short interview Daniel Gooch was appointed locomotive engineer of the Great Western Railway. He moved to London, took lodgings in Paddington, and began work.

For the first few weeks he found himself almost completely on his own, Brunel by then being deeply involved in Bristol with *Great Western*. So, on his own initiative, he embarked on a tour of inspection of the various manufacturers with whom orders had been placed for locomotives. A total of nineteen had been ordered – six from the Vulcan Foundry; six from Mather, Dixon & Company of Liverpool; three from Sharp, Roberts & Company, Manchester; and two each from Hawthornes of Newcastle and the Haigh Foundry. It appeared a most impressive start.

But the almost impossible conditions Brunel's characteristically explicit specifications had imposed on the designers immediately caused the greatest concern to the amazed and horrified young man. Almost before the ink on his contract was dry, Daniel had discovered that his new master, for whom he had enormous and sincere respect and with whom he had already established a most satisfactory working relationship, had committed a truly monumental blunder. Narrow-gauge locomotives in excess of ten tons, the weight limit Brunel had imposed, were already being designed, and piston speeds very nearly twice that of Brunel's stipulation were becoming commonplace. So what on earth, Gooch asked himself, could be the reason for such a crippling limitation on the broad gauge. Its designer seemed to be deliberately denying himself the opportunity to exploit the advantages his genius had created. In order to stay within those quite ridiculously unnecessary limitations, the engines' boilers would have to be skimped and the driving wheels enlarged almost to grotesque proportions.

Daniel very nearly wept when he saw what had been done. With the exception of the two Hawthorne engines, all of them had pitifully small boilers, hopelessly inadequate cylinders and outsize driving wheels. Tom Harrison of Hawthornes had ingeniously endeavoured to get round the weight limitation by mounting separate engine and boiler units on entirely independent carriages coupled together by ball and socket steam pipes. The result was a pair of impressively immense, but far from efficient, monsters.

When, finally, he returned to London, Gooch made no mention of his doubts that any of these mechanical freaks could ever be capable of producing the results Brunel so confidently expected of them. But he did persuade his superior to purchase from Stephenson the two six-foot-gauge locomotives that were still in Newcastle. In his unassuming way young Daniel Gooch had just as much confidence in his own specialised ability as Isambard Brunel had in his many talents.

On the very day Gooch took up his duties, *Great Western* sailed for her fitting-out berth in London's river. She had been launched exactly one month earlier. She was the biggest vessel ever built in Bristol or anywhere else, and in celebration of such an historic event a company numbering three hundred had consumed a sumptuous banquet in her main saloon – itself a source of wonder to all who had the good fortune to behold it.

The elegant lines of her huge hull, of unrelieved black save for the elaborately carved and gilded figures of Neptune and his attendant dolphins that glittered above the graceful prow, looked sleek and sure under a crowning spread of snowy canvas. Triumphantly she braved the Bristol Channel, rounded Lands End and in stately progress made her way along the south coast and into the Thames in company with the tug *Lion* and steamers *Herald* and *Benledi*. The moment she moored at Blackwall sightseers from near and far flocked to stare at her, to wonder at her size, to marvel at the stupendous machinery that was to be installed in her. Of a conventional side-lever design, the engine would have a pair of cylinders each capable of driving both paddle wheels should the need arise, steam being supplied by four independent boilers each weighing no less than twenty-five tons. Stupendous indeed was the word for it!

'God Save the Queen!' the always enterprising mudlarks screeched as they scurried about capitalising as hard as they could on the still novel idea of a queen-regnant on England's ancient throne for only the fourth time in over a thousand years; for eighteen-year-old Victoria now sat in her Uncle Silly Billy's place. 'God bless the Queen of the Ocean!' echoed *Great Western*'s countless admirers who had come to regard her as a timely and tangible manifestation of what had already been popularly hailed as the dawning of a new age. As England had flourished under Elizabeth, they said, so would she now under Victoria.

But the 'Queen of the Ocean' was not without her rivals. Alarmed by the bid the sometime Metropolis of the West was making to regain her lost supremacy, the formation of the Great Western Steamship Company had been closely followed by that of the Liverpool Trans-Atlantic Steamship Company whose directors included Great Western Railway Company shareholders Boyle, Raskell and Crossthwaite. With a vessel built by Humble & Milcrest to the order of Sir John Tobin, they confidently expected to win what had rapidly developed into a race. Then had come a third contestant, the British & American Steam Navigation Company of London, their ship *British Queen* to be built by Curling & Young of Limehouse.

When it began to look as if *Great Western* would be ready much earlier than either of her challengers, the Liverpool Company chartered the City of Dublin Steam Packet Company's *Royal William*. Then it was announced that *British Queen*'s place would be taken by *Sirius*. Both ships, recently launched, had been designed specifically for the Anglo-Irish service and modifications for a trans-atlantic voyage, though considerable, were relatively simple.

Sirius, fitted out in record time, sailed on Wednesday, 28 March 1838. The trim little two-master – she was less than half the size of Brunel's ship – with her dazzling white figurehead of a hound holding the dog star twixt its paws, was given a tremendous send-off. Captained by Lieutenant Roberts RN, her crew numbered thirty-five and she carried forty passengers, all of them booked to New York. She was followed down river by the clipper *Quebec* also bound for New York, and the wagers laid as to which would arrive first, or even whether the gallant, many said foolhardy, *Sirius* would get there at all, were many and great. Just three days later, and to the cheers of an even bigger crowd, *Great Western* followed – aboard her Claxton, Guppy and Brunel.

'The ship has performed splendidly, gentlemen,' declared her delighted master, Lieutenant James Hoskens RN, for perhaps the twentieth time since the completion of her final trials, while normally dour chief engineer George Pearne grinned a happy if slightly self-conscious grin as he appreciatively sipped his champagne. Early though it was, Tom Guppy had insisted that Brunel, Claxton, Hoskens and Pearne share the magnum he had brought along for the occasion. So, gathered on the quarter-deck and deliberately in full sight of the watchers on both banks of the river, the five toasted the ship, her future, and each other as, with engines pounding a steady rhythm and her huge paddle wheels swishing and splashing through the water, *Great Western* steamed sedately seawards.

'Even though *Sirius* did get a three-day start on us, we should still catch her, eh Captain?' said Claxton.

'I regard that as rather more than an even possibility Sir, yes,' Hoskens smiled his agreement.

'Besides,' put in Tom Guppy, 'she's got to coal at Cork, remember.'

'I've calculated you should gain on her at a rate of about two knots an hour once you're away from Bristol,' Isambard quoted from his notebook. Unlike Guppy and Claxton, he would be leaving the ship at Bristol where she was to take on cargo and embark most of her passengers. Already he had spent far too much time away from London, where he knew there must be a mountain of work awaiting him.

By introducing what he always insisted on calling 'a few improvements' he had involved himself in an ever-increasing volume of detail. It was like having suddenly adopted an entirely new language was how he had described it once to Saunders in a rare moment of depression, a language known only to himself, every word of which had to be translated before even the most rudimentary communication with others was possible. Inadvertently he had cut himself off from the help he might otherwise have had, and was obliged therefore to do everything himself. The quantity of writing involved in merely drafting instructions alone occupied him for a minimum of five hours a day – every day of every week of every month of every year.

'And you know, Saunders,' he'd ruefully concluded, 'invention is rather like a spring of water, it tends to be limited. I've sometimes found I've pumped myself so dry that I've remained for an hour or two afterwards utterly stupid.'

But such moods were few and fleeting, and despite the merciless demands he'd made on them, his reserves of energy seemed as endless as ever. And on a day such as this he was on top of the world.

The forenoon watch was but fifteen minutes gone when the fire broke out. Without warning, flames and smoke began to belch from the fore stoke-hole. There was no panic, but every man aboard was instantly alive to the deadly peril of fire in a wooden ship. Closely followed by Claxton and Guppy, Pearne made a dash for the engine room, while Hoskens ordered an immediate alteration of course which, if the worst should happen, would enable him to ground the ship on the Chapman Sands just off Canvey Island.

Brunel, meanwhile, hastened to discover the cause of the conflagration. It was immediately apparent that the felt and red-lead boiler lagging beneath the base of the funnel had been carried too close to the furnace flues. Once the lagging had reached a critical temperature it had ignited spontaneously, setting light to the deckbeams and the underside of the deck planking. The fire was fierce, but far from fatal. Nor had anyone been hurt.

Filled with smoke and with its upper part already blazing furiously, the engine room had been evacuated by the time Pearne got for'ard. But intent on saving his precious boilers, the chief engineer did not hesitate. Heedless of the heat and fumes, he groped his way to the boiler feed-cocks and opened them after putting on a feed-plunger to make the engines pump more water before the steam, which was generating much too quickly with the heat of the fire, could reach too high a pressure to be contained.

Beneath the boiler-room hatchway, in a barely penetrable fog of smoke and escaping steam, Claxton and Guppy had taken charge of a fire hose which they were directing onto the burning deckbeams. A sound of splintering wood above his head, barely audible in the general din, caused Guppy to look directly upwards. The impression rather than the actual sight of something falling caused him to jump to one side.

'Look out!' he warned his companion.

But Claxton could not move quickly enough, and the falling object caught him a glancing blow which sent him sprawling. Shaken but unhurt, he scrambled to his feet. When he and Guppy went to retrieve their hose they found it pinned beneath a body lying face downwards in a foot of water.

As Isambard had started down the ladder from the deck to the engine room, a partially burned-through rung had given way under his weight. It was an eighteen-foot drop. Had not Claxton been there to break his fall he must have been killed. He was surely hurt though how badly, for the moment, it was impossible to say.

'We must get him out of here,' muttered Guppy thickly, his chest wheezing alarmingly from the effects of the smoke.

'The pair of you,' Claxton croaked, still breathless from the blow he had sustained. 'Deck there – ahoy!' he managed to shout, and almost immediately he was answered. 'Two men injured below here. Heave a line and stand by to haul them clear.'

Once the still-inert Brunel and weakly protesting Guppy had been pulled to safety, Claxton returned to his fire-fighting, refusing to be relieved of his hose until there was no further use for it. By which time Guppy had recovered and Brunel, though in great pain and unable to move, was conscious and seemed otherwise all right.

With the falling tide the ship had grounded, and she would now have to stay on the Chapman Sands for the next twelve hours or so. But apart from considerable charring of her deck round the base of the funnel she had suffered no damage, whilst George Pearne's prompt and heroic action had saved the boilers. Once Guppy, the master and the chief engineer had made a detailed inspection for him, Brunel could see no reason why *Great Western* should not proceed as planned.

Though in urgent need of medical attention he refused to be taken ashore until, again with Guppy's help, he had specified the modifications which would prevent a repetition of the accident, and for which a lot of the preparatory work could be done whilst at sea. If Patterson was forewarned he could have everything ready to make good the damage to the deck and relag the flues as soon as the ship docked at Bristol. With any luck at all they should be ready to sail for New York no later than 7 April.

Having failed to destroy either herself or her creator, *Great Western* floated easily on the tide, and with her paddle wheels once more driving her forward she resumed her interrupted voyage. She rounded the Longships at record speed and anchored at Kingroad just after midday on 2 April laying, once and for all, the wild rumours that Bristol's beautiful ship had burned and foundered in the Thames.

She was indeed ready for sea again by the seventh, as Brunel had predicted, but bad weather delayed her departure for another twenty-four hours. So it was not until ten o'clock on the morning of Sunday, 8 April 1838 that *Great Western*, cheered on her way by a huge crowd of proud Bristolians, made history by spurning the help of hobblers as she made her majestic way through the Avon Gorge.

The goodwill of the whole city went with her. But alas! she carried only seven fare-paying passengers, over fifty having cancelled their passages because of the fire. A commercial flop though the voyage must be, the race might still be on, for *Sirius* had apparently sailed from Cork only four days before.

And race it certainly turned out to be. The master of *Sirius* was a seaman of remarkable brilliance and iron determination. Only such a man could have brought his tiny seven hundred ton vessel across the Atlantic in just nineteen days under the constant threat of equinoctial storms and with a hair's-breadth margin of safety measured by no more than fifteen remaining tons of coal. Soon rumour and fatuous journalism were to mislead the public into believing that only by burning her cabin panelling, her furniture, even a child's wooden doll, was that epoch-making voyage brought to its triumphant conclusion. Had this been the case, it would, of course, have served to add weight to Doctor Dionysius Lardner's gloomy prognostications. Even so, it was only great good fortune that had enabled Lieutenant Roberts to prove him wrong.

But conclusive proof came with Brunel's brainchild, even though she was forced to concede the honour of being first, if only by a mere sixteen hours. Amazed New Yorkers barely had time to realise that history had been made when, at two o'clock in the afternoon of St George's Day, 1838, *Great Western* was spotted from Governor's Island, fifteen days and five hours out from Bristol. She had indeed overhauled *Sirius* at a rate of two knots per hour. And she still had two hundred tons of coal in her bunkers.

James Gordon Bennett in the *Morning Herald* described her as looking black and blackguard, rakish, cool, reckless, fierce and forbidding as she swept over the broad blue waters to circle the anchored *Sirius* before turning towards Staten Island, then shot up the East River at an extraordinary speed with smoke pouring from her funnel and curling about her four tall masts. But as she ran alongside the Pike Street wharf her moment of glory was marred by tragedy. While blowing down the boilers, George Pearne, who had so gallantly saved her from certain destruction just three weeks before, was fatally scalded.

Great Western was back in her home port by 22 May. In spite of having one engine out of action because of a broken connecting rod, the crossing took only fifteen days. She carried a full cargo and sixty passengers. On arrival she was fêted as no other ship had been fêted, and her captain was given a hero's welcome – as were Kit Claxton and Tom Guppy.

But the man who made it all possible was not there. He was in London. Already he was talking about building an even bigger and better ship. Just for the moment, however, he had a railway to think about.

Chapter Eleven

FOR a variety of reasons, not least of which had been the quite appalling weather, the Grand Formal Opening of the first section of the Great Western Railway – Paddington to Maidenhead – had had to be postponed for six months. It would now take place, it was announced, on Thursday, 31 May.

By 21 April Isambard had recovered sufficiently from his fall to go to Paddington where he found preparations for the forthcoming event well in hand; which was heartening for latterly there had been even more problems than had long since come to be accepted as usual. It had all started when the Liverpool Party had demanded that Boyle, Raskell and Crossthwaite be nominated directors. This both London and Bristol had vehemently opposed, on the grounds that the addition of a non-residential or purely sectional faction to the board was not desirable. Whereupon the Liverpool Party had turned on Brunel – all three of their nominees being so closely associated with the Great Western Steamship Company's deadly rival was not without significance. Taking their cue from some rather derogatory remarks about the broad gauge made by George Stephenson at the March Annual General Meeting of the Manchester & Leeds Railway Company, they launched a virulent campaign which quickly escalated to what amounted to open vilification.

Nor was the broad gauge their only target for censure. Scorn was freely poured on his work generally, but most of all on the bridge over the Thames at Maidenhead. Subsequent to having agreed the bridging site, the Thames Commissioners had stipulated there must be no obstruction either to the navigable channel or the paths on the river's banks. It meant that a solitary central pier, of minimal height if the essential level of the line was to be preserved, would now have to support the 300-foot-long bridge. Brunel had tackled the very ticklish problem this posed with typical audacity by designing a bridge whose two arches would be the longest and flattest ever to be built in brickwork, each 128-foot span having a rise to its crown of only 24 feet 3 inches.

From the moment the plan for the Maidenhead bridge had been made public, it had been condemned as a glaring example of Brunel folly. The collapse of the whole structure was confidently predicted as inevitable, even before a train could get anywhere near it. When, on 1 May, the centrings were prematurely eased without the sanction of the engineer, and the eastern arch showed signs of minor distortion, his enemies were jubilant. The fact that the western arch was firm and perfect in all respects seemed to impress them not at all. Nor would they heed Chadwick, the contractor, who freely accepted full responsibility for the mishap. They were out to get Brunel at all costs.

As the May days sped by, so the momentum of work on the line increased. Like ants, navvies swarmed over the twenty-two and a half mile road from Paddington to Taplow, the station for Maidenhead, the surrounding countryside echoing round the clock to the sounds of seemingly frantic but in fact highly organised activity, while Gooch's motley collection of locomotives puffed and bustled back and forth. Brunel, as tireless as always, his famous britzska now forsaken in favour of a locomotive's footplate, seemed to be everywhere at once while, in the midst of it all, newly recruited company servants learned and practised their multifarious duties.

On 28 May commemorative tickets were issued to the two hundred guests invited by the directors to attend the private opening. On the 29th the apparent chaos at Paddington and all along the line made it seem scarcely possible the railway could ever be in a fit state to open at all. But by dusk on the 30th, after nothing less than a minor miracle had somehow been wrought, a recognisable semblance of order gave hope at last for the morrow, though no one in any way concerned with the event was to get any sleep or even much relaxation that night.

Just before eleven the next morning, which had dawned dull and wet, the directors welcomed their guests to Paddington. And a most impressive gathering it was, the ladies' fashionable attire and their animated admiration of everything they saw at once bringing a hitherto rather dismal scene to noisy colourful life. Precisely at half-past eleven all took their allotted places in the carriages. Then, with Gooch driving and Brunel beside him on the footplate, *North*

Star, one of the two Stephenson locomotives Gooch had helped to design and the only one of ten so far delivered on which he dare place any reliance, steamed out of the temporary terminus at Paddington bound for the temporary station at Taplow. The bands played, the crowds cheered, the passengers waved, while the rain, which at first had threatened to spoil everything, obligingly stopped. But somehow it was not nearly so grand or impressive as everyone, including Brunel, had expected it would be.

Travelling at an average of twenty-eight miles per hour, which was perhaps somewhat sedate after all that had been said and written about speed and the broad gauge, the train reached Taplow in forty-five minutes. A conducted tour of the works there was followed by a banquet concluded, of course, with the inevitable welter of words and complement of toasts. The return journey – at a slightly less sedate average of thirty-two and a half miles per hour – was made memorable by Tom Guppy exuberantly walking the full length of the train over the tops of the carriages.

On 2 June a full-page insertion in *The Times* announced that as from eight o'clock on the morning of Monday, 4 June 1838, eight trains per day each weekday and six on Sundays would carry passengers only between London, West Drayton, Slough and Maidenhead at fares ranging from 3s 6d by second-class open carriages to 5s 6d by first-class passenger coach for the maximum journey. And that on and after Monday, 11 June 1838, carriages and horses would be conveyed on the railway as well as passengers and parcels booked for conveyance by coaches in connection with the railway company to the West of England including Stroud, Cheltenham and Gloucester, and to Oxford, Newbury, Reading, Henley, Marlow, Windsor, Uxbridge and other contiguous places.

With Gibbs and Saunders, Isambard travelled to Maidenhead on the first train that morning, returning to London by the third. Both trips were extremely disappointing – the one taking, including stops, one hour and twenty minutes; the other one hour and five minutes. Nor was the ride particularly smooth in either direction.

The fourteenth of June was Gold Cup Day at Ascot. It was also the new queen's first visit to the races. As *The Times* later reported, thousands came trooping from the neighbouring termini of the Great Western and London & Southampton Railways – the latter having opened as far as Woking on 21 May – and the Great Western duly carried its share of the 'thousands' without accident, undue delay, or even minor mishap. But that most successful day of operation was sadly marred. A manoeuvre on the Stock Exchange, obviously the work of the pro-Stephenson faction, brought about such a serious fall in the value of the company's shares that the danger of a panic among the proprietors rapidly became acute. By the 20th the Great Western board had a full-blown crisis on its hands. Less than one month later Brunel's instant dismissal was being openly demanded.

As he had known it must, the wind had changed, and changed with a vengeance. Nor could it have done so at a worse moment. By now in the latter stages of her first pregnancy, Mary's health was suddenly giving grave cause for concern; neither had he himself really been at all well since the accident aboard *Great Western*. And now, far from being the 'finest work in England', his railway seemed much more likely to turn out to be the greatest failure.

Though premature and prolonged, and more than justifying the attendance of eminent physician and surgeon Sir Benjamin Brodie as well as the most highly recommended accoucheuse in London, Mary's confinement proved in the end to be irksome rather than dangerous. Safely delivered of a six and a half pound boy, she was soon on the road to a complete recovery. The child's left foot, however, showed distinct signs of a deformity diagnosed by Brodie as *talipes equinovarus*. The condition could be rectified, he assured both parents, by a relatively simple operation; but one, he warned Isambard, not to be too long postponed.

That worry apart, Brunel found the easing of his domestic situation a timely relief enabling him to concentrate on what had in fact developed into a threat to his very livelihood. No longer content with merely discrediting him, the more extreme elements of the Liverpool Party now seemed set on nothing less than his complete professional annihilation, a fact made abundantly clear at the company's half yearly meeting in Bristol. This time the tiger did far more than scratch.

The *Bristol Mercury* which had championed Telford in the Clifton bridge affair and had never since let slip an opportunity to snipe at Brunel, detailed the events of that meeting, which had gone on non-stop for an exhausting seven hours, in a special and impressively biased supplement. Revelling in verbatim reports of the Liverpool Party's attack, it dismissed disparagingly the desperate defence of their engineer by what had become a sadly dwindling number of loyal directors. Finally it puzzled, as had everyone else, over the mysterious failure of the Liverpool men, who from the start had seemed in a position to carry the meeting by an overwhelming majority, to put their intended resolution calling for the appointment of a consulting engineer to the vote there and then. Had they done so they would have forced Brunel's resignation, for he had already made plain that under no circumstances would he countenance any such appointment. Instead they had temporised by blocking acceptance of the directors' Half Yearly Report and proposing an adjournment until 10 October.

Shortly afterwards, however, the board had had to agree to their nominee, John Hawkshaw, engineer to the Manchester & Leeds Railway, being invited to make an impartial assessment of the working of the broad gauge. This was to be in addition to and independent of a similar survey already in progress conducted, at Brunel's suggestion, by Nicholas Wood, one of the judges of the Rainhill Trials nine years before.

But, strongly entrenched in the Stephenson camp – he had been trained by Fowler and Alexander Nimmo – Hawkshaw was anything but impartial. The results of his thirty-four-day examination made known on 6 October were, predictably, hailed by the Liverpool Party as conclusive. In essence, however, they fell considerably short of what was urgently required, for Hawkshaw had merely theorised at great length on the desirability of adopting the Stephenson gauge as standard, ignoring almost completely the problem plaguing the Great Western – his suggested solution being to tear up Brunel's road and start again. And for this he had collected a handsome fee in addition to substantial expenses.

'Dammit all!' complained Henry Gibbs on the eve of the adjourned meeting, 'the wretched man could have written the blasted thing without coming anywhere near our line.'

Gibbs was one of the few London directors still loyal to Brunel; with the exception of Tom Guppy nearly all the Bristol men had already deserted him, while even Saunders appeared to be wavering. Brunel, however, defended himself brilliantly at the resumed meeting on the tenth. Taking full advantage of the board's perfectly legitimate decision to withhold formal presentation of Hawkshaw's report until the one being prepared by Wood was ready, he virtually tricked the disconcerted opposition, who had expected an easy victory, into withdrawing their August amendment and agreeing to the adoption of the directors' original Half Yearly Report. The meeting was then adjourned again until 20 December.

But it was to prove no more than a reprieve, a breathing space, a lull before the full fury of the storm. During the lull it seemed for a time that the wheel of fortune might once more be turning in Isambard's favour. One by one problems began to be solved, mistakes realised, rectified, and the lessons thus learned applied. Even the design errors which had so inhibited performances of all the locomotives, with the exception of *North Star* and her recently delivered sister, *Evening Star*, had been largely overcome thanks to the now fully recognised ingenuity and expertise of the locomotive engineer. Indeed, Gooch had been given a free hand in planning a second generation of engines. All in all, until 10 December, when Nicholas Wood's much delayed report finally appeared, things were going very well indeed. Trains were running regularly and, even if not yet as swiftly as promised, at least on time. In fact each day had brought improvements in some aspect of the railway's function.

Wood's report however came as, perhaps, the bitterest blow of all. As long winded as it had been long awaited, it was a perfect model of inconclusive sophistry. Its timorous author managed on practically every one of its eighty-six closely printed octavo pages to avoid committing himself either to a recommendation or a rejection of any aspect of the broad gauge. What faults he did find, and all were trivial to a degree, had long since been put to rights. But an appendix briefly summarising performance tests and various experiments on the Great Western locomotives, carried out at Wood's request by none other than Doctor Dionysius Lardner – whose own report was still being prepared and promised to be of even greater length – presented the Liverpool Party with just the evidence they needed to decide the issue.

North Star, Gooch's crack locomotive, under test conditions had hauled 82 tons at 33 miles per hour, 33 tons at 37 miles per hour, barely 16 tons at 41 miles per hour. Furthermore, to produce that 4 miles per hour of extra speed, coke consumption had doubled – from 1.25 to 2.76lb per ton per mile. This, Doctor Lardner contended, was due entirely to increased atmospheric resistance occasioned by the extreme width of the locomotive's frontage. The wider the gauge, the greater the resistance, therefore the more limited the speed. It was arrant nonsense, but it was this statement alone that had forced from Wood his single outright condemnation of Brunel's broad gauge. 'As it has been proved by experiment to be inadvisable to attempt any extreme rate of speed,' he had written, 'then 35 miles per hour may be considered the absolute limit of practical economic velocity for all broad-gauge trains.'

'A-way!' said Daniel Gooch disgustedly after he had studied Lardner's figures and read Wood's summing-up. He was with Brunel at Duke Street. For some time now Isambard had suffered almost constant migraines, a legacy from the accident aggravated by constant worry and unceasing overwork. To get some relief from the nagging pain he had taken to wearing a velvet skullcap in the privacy of his home. The fact that he had not bothered to remove it when Daniel had been shown up was highly significant. Normally he would never have permitted an outsider to see him other than as the familiar black-clad figure, seemingly immune to either fatigue or fear, whose very presence was normally sufficient to inspire all with whom he came in contact. But the events of the last few days seemed to have changed him alarmingly and Daniel eyed his superior, who was indeed looking desperately tired and ill, with scarcely veiled concern.

That same afternoon Isambard had been summoned to the Princes Street office to be informed by Saunders that in view of Wood's report the board was to seek authorisation at the meeting in ten days' time for the appointment of a consulting engineer. In other words, they were going to surrender to the Liverpool Party. Which meant, of course, he was through. He had not been dismissed, nor was there any suggestion by the board that he should be. But, he had reiterated to Saunders, under no circumstances would he agree to being associated in any way with any other engineer.

'So,' he finished explaining to Gooch, who could hardly believe what he had just heard, 'unless Lardner and Wood can be proved wrong about *North Star*, and that before the 20th, I shall resign.'

'Then, by God! so shall I!' cried Gooch passionately in a rare outburst of youthful recklessness.

'Now that you will not!' Isambard told him sternly. 'But I

appreciate your loyalty. Thank you, most sincerely, for the thought.'
And from that moment the bond between them was sealed. Then, as
if taking on a new lease of life, he pulled the cap from his head, and
with it the depression that had all but destroyed him. 'Daniel, we
have one week in which to make the learned Lardner eat his words
for the third time. Do you think we can do it?'

'We can that, Mr Brunel!' His normally dour features suddenly
creaking into a boney grin, Daniel brought his huge palms together
in a resounding clap that made Isambard's hypersensitive ears ring
painfully. 'Aye, man, there's a canny lot can happen in the space of
seven days.'

A canny lot did happen, though it took a little longer than seven
days. But by the eighteenth they had convinced Saunders and the
board that Lardner was again talking through his hat. The adjourned
meeting, at Brunel's suggestion and with the ready agreement of the
opposition who were busy splitting shares and gathering proxies just
as hard as they could in order to muster as many votes as possible for
the final battle, was postponed yet again. It would now take place at
the London Tavern in Bishopsgate on Wednesday, 9 January 1839.
They had discovered the cause of *North Star*'s poor performance to
be nothing more than a simple design fault.

'So much for Doctor Dionysius Lardner and his fancy bloody
twaddle,' whooped Daniel Gooch delightedly as *North Star*, with a
load of eighty tons plus behind her, roared along the rails near West
Drayton at a truly breathtaking speed on her final secret test run.

Isambard, who was acting as fireman, paused in his labours and
grinned like an impish schoolboy at his excited companion. 'Not a
word about this to anyone, mind,' he cautioned, 'not until the time is
right.'

'By the Christ, no!' Daniel agreed, his white teeth startlingly
luminous in the black mask of his face. Then, shouting above the
combined din of rushing wind and clattering machinery, he
unexpectedly quoted ' "but we shall delve one yard below their
mines, and blow them to the moon!" '

'Well said, Daniel,' Brunel chuckled in approval of this sudden
disclosure of the other's hidden depths, adding ' "For 'tis the sport
to have the engineer . . ." '

' ". . . hoist with his own petard!" ' they chorused happily.

They came from the capital and the home counties, from towns and villages throughout the West Country, from Bristol, from Gloucester, from Cheltenham, from Oxford and Worcester, from south Wales and from north Wales, from Birmingham and Manchester and, not least of all, from Liverpool. They arrived by private carriage, by hired hackney, by fly, by the newfangled low-slung two-seater one-horse cabriolets on which the driver perched above and behind his passengers and with whom he communicated through a small trap-door in the carriage roof. They came on horseback and they came on foot. By eleven o'clock they were over a thousand strong. And still they kept on coming to crowd noisily into the ballroom of the London Tavern in Bishopsgate, furnished as adequately as possible for the occasion with a motley selection of chairs and benches and stools.

Brunel, who walked in with Saunders, was greeted with a subdued but reassuring murmur of welcome, quickly countered by a growl of unmistakable enmity.

'Sounds as if the blighters are after your head as well as your resignation,' Saunders observed, receiving in reply a slightly rueful but far from cheerless grin.

On the precise stroke of noon, chairman William Unwin Sims declared the Adjourned Special Meeting of the Great Western Railway Company's proprietary duly open. First came the minutes of the meeting held on 20 December. Then followed the directors' Second Half Yearly Report, containing what Brunel had gleefully dubbed 'Daniel's mine'. It could not have been more effectively sprung, Isambard's only disappointment being that, as he was not a Great Western proprietor, Doctor Lardner was not present. It produced immediate consternation in the opposition's ranks. But Henry Boyle, a waspish man well able to make use of his sting, managed to save the Liverpool situation by literally bullying Sims, who sadly possessed neither the authority of a Wharncliffe nor the perspicacity of a Russell, into accepting an amendment calling for consideration of both Hawkshaw's and Wood's reports before the vote for the adoption of the Second Half Yearly Report be taken – despite Guppy's proposal that it be so having already been seconded from the floor. Which meant yet another adjournment, there being,

194

by this time, more than twelve thousand proxies to be recorded, checked and counted.

The ballot was finally completed by noon the following day. But it was three in the afternoon before Saunders was able to declare the result, by which time speculation as to the outcome was at fever pitch. On a straight show of hands the Liverpool Party and their adherents would be outnumbered by at least ten to one, but it was the proxies they commanded that would count and, according to Boyle and his far from modest colleagues, they had more than enough to carry the day.

'I shall deal with the proxy vote first,' Saunders announced to his tensely expectant audience, his voice calm and matter-of-fact, his face expressionless. 'Total in favour of the amendment – 5,969.'

There was a stunned silence. The Liverpool men stared in disbelief. They had expected more, far more than that. As realisation dawned on the rest of the proprietors that Boyle's amendment must be lost, their initially startled expressions slowly gave way to smiles of relief and happiness. Brunel, who from the start had been quietly confident of victory – 'We shall win,' he had maintained all along, 'it may be only by a whisker, but we shall win' – alone seemed entirely unmoved.

The battle for the broad gauge had been won.

PART THREE

July 1843 – June 1848

Chapter One

HIS Royal Highness The Prince Albert, accompanied by the Marquis of Exeter and others, left Buckingham Palace shortly before seven o'clock in the morning on Wednesday, 19 July 1843, destination Bristol – the occasion, the launching of Brunel's *Great Britain*. And, naturally, the royal party were to travel by Brunel's Great Western Railway, 'God's Wonderful Railway' as some of its more exuberant admirers were now wont to describe it.

Since the opening of the Paddington to Maidenhead section five years before – the Bristol to Bath stretch had come into service on 31 August the same year – the line had reached Reading by April 1840 and Faringdon Road, some sixty-three and a half miles from Paddington, four months later. By May 1841 the last link had been forged – that two-mile-long tunnel under Box Hill. Consuming more than 100 tons of gunpowder, 150 tons of candles and with the aid of up to 300 horses, 4,000 men had excavated 250,000 cubic yards of soil and laid 30 million bricks in just over 5 years.

Tragically, 100 lives had been lost. But when the east and west galleries eventually met, the line was true – so true, in fact, than on 9 April the following year it was discovered that an observer at the western mouth of the tunnel could see the sun rise before it topped the hill. That 9 April was Isambard's birthday was purely coincidental. But it was immediately rumoured to have been deliberately planned, and from then on his apparent genius for showmanship had been firmly established and further enhanced. Of all the modern so-called miracle workers, he had become, in the eyes of the multitude, the mightiest.

Two months to the day after the triumphant opening of the tunnel at Box, Marc Brunel had been able to announce the completion of the Thames Tunnel, for which achievement he had subsequently been honoured with a knighthood. The following spring Sir Marc had proudly carried his grandson, Isambard III, from Rotherhithe to

199

Wapping and back without the child once seeing the light of day. Had he had the full use of both legs the otherwise healthy four-year-old might well have walked beside the grandfather he so adored. But Mary Brunel had steadfastly refused to give her consent for the operation Brodie wished to perform. No kith or kin of hers she'd sworn, would ever be subjected to the barbarous torment of a surgeon's scalpel; and she had remained deaf to all succeeding arguments, an attitude which had in the end sorely strained her relationship with her husband.

So instead of running freely as he might have done, young Isambard had stumbled and walked awkwardly from infancy to childhood. Nor had he shown any sign whatever of the brilliant precocity that had so characterised the formative years of both his sire and grandsire. He had been loved no less because of his apparent intellectual lack. But he was a bitter disappointment to his father.

Young Henry, however, though not yet three, could wield a pencil with recognisable expertise and even recite a couple of simple Euclidean theorems more convincingly than his brother could yet stammer through his repertoire of nursery rhymes. Then there was baby Florence, at nine months already showing signs of having inherited both her mother's good looks and her Aunt Sophia's commonsense.

Already known to all who mattered as the most beautiful woman ever to be presented at Court, the prospect of eventually being Lady Brunel would have been to the sometime 'Duchess of Kensington', who had become the 'Empress of Duke Street', the ultimate in social achievement. Mary had always been one of nature's *grandes dames* and she had revelled in the way Isambard's success had enabled him to show her off before an admiring world. To her, appearances were all-important – the best in clothes and jewellery, the most exotic and expensive perfumes. She had not one but two carriages for her private use. During the day she rode in one lined with cream moire silk, another lined with the same material in green was for evenings. She entertained in one of the most luxuriously appointed drawing rooms in all London – its furnishings Louis Quinze, a grand piano occupying pride of place at one end, an organ installed at the other. Always she was accompanied by a liveried footman who followed at a respectful distance even should she choose merely to stroll in the park beneath her own windows, while on Sundays he carried her ivory and gilt-clasped prayer book to and from church like an item of royal regalia. Wherever she went all eyes would follow her, and an overheard remark of 'There goes the wife of Isambard Brunel', however often repeated, never failed to make her eyes flash with satisfaction and her bosom swell with pride.

An already fairly serious marital estrangement had therefore been further exacerbated by Mary's bitter disappointment in her father-in-law having been created only a knight-bachelor and not, as she had expected and fervently hoped, a baronet. Nor had it been improved when Isambard had declared that not only did he not give tuppence for being unable to inherit his father's title, but, should he be offered a similar honour, and generally this was assumed to be far from an improbability, he would unhesitatingly decline it. To him, he'd told her, his work was everything and more than adequate reward in itself.

So far that reward had been tremendous. At thirty-seven – though he had to admit to looking and sometimes feeling nearly twenty years older – he was internationally acknowledged as responsible for not only the finest and fastest railway in the world and the most successful steamship afloat, but also the largest and most advanced vessel ever conceived and about to be launched. Nor was that all. His plans for the South Devon Railway, the proposed continuation of the nearly completed Bristol & Exeter to carry the broad gauge into Cornwall and rumoured to be audaciously revolutionary, were yet to be disclosed.

But, for the present, the royal journey was the important matter in hand. Formally received at Paddington by a select representation of Great Western Railway and Great Western Steamship directors, the prince's party boarded a special train. As on the occasion of the first royal railway journey thirteen months before when the queen and the prince had travelled from Slough to Paddington, the engine, of the Firefly class, the successors to the Stephenson Stars, was driven by Daniel Gooch, with Brunel on the footplate beside him.

Clear of the Paddington complex – a temporary establishment still although plans for its development were well advanced – the train covered the twenty-two and a half miles to Maidenhead in well under the half hour and, as Brunel had predicted, the ride was smooth enough for passengers to take their coffee, relax, converse in perfect comfort, even write if they so desired while travelling at speeds in excess of fifty miles per hour. Once over the Thames, by that now world famous bridge, the train thundered westward as the drab grey London brick with its dressing of Bramley Fall stone of which the railway works were constructed gradually gave way to the more colourful combination of deep-red Berkshire brick and Bath Oolite, while the terrain changed from gravel beds and alluvial mud to flint-strewn chalk and sand and marl.

Through a series of minor cuttings alternating with modest embankments, it sped past Ruscomb station and Twyford before plunging through the great Sonning cutting – two miles in length and in places more than sixty feet deep. Then on again from Reading to rush through stations serving Pangbourne, Wallingford, Moulsford, Cholsey and Moreton to Didcot, the junction for Oxford, and to Steventon. With a magnificent view to the south of the huge and mysterious White Horse on Uffington Hill, from which the beautiful Berkshire vale takes its name, it passed through Shrivenham, and so to Swindon, the company's main depot and engineering works.

Though much nearer Bristol than Paddington, Swindon made the ideal half-way station for the main trunk line – Brunel's near dead-level road to the east enabling Gooch to show off the fantastic speeds of which his seven-foot singles were now capable. Here all trains stopped, primarily to change engines, the slightly steeper western gradients, especially those at Wootton Bassett and Box, requiring a smaller-wheeled and slower but more powerful locomotive.

From the old Georgian market town perched on the summit of a hill about a mile distant, the view was superb. To the south was the great chalk ridge from Hackpen to the Chilterns; eastward lay the prehistoric camps of Banbury and Liddington, the woods of Wayland's Smithy, the White Horse, Uffington Castle, Dragon Hill and a line of ancient barrows – the site, it was believed, of the earliest Celtic settlements, of King Arthur's struggles with Saxon invaders, of later battles for survival between the descendants of those same Saxons and the Danes – all clearly visible on a fine day. As was the new railway, snaking east and west as far as the eye could see, while the Cheltenham & Great Western Union line disappeared north-westwards into the gently rising foothills of the Cotswolds. To the south was Avebury with its sarsen stone circles, the bleak immensity of Salisbury Plain, the once notorious 'rotten borough' of Old Sarum, and Stonehenge.

New Swindon, the railway town, had been laid out in a well-planned geometric pattern. Where, from time immemorial, cows and sheep and goats and pigs had grazed in open pastures, there now stood street upon street of neat terraced houses. The church, newly completed, had been generously endowed from the estate of the late Henry Gibbs who had died in Venice just one year before. Nearly five hundred feet long and over seventy wide, the engine shed housed forty-eight locomotives and their tenders, all ready for instant service. For running repairs and routine maintenance there was an adjacent, slightly smaller engine house; a third comparable and communicating building, the erecting house, was where all major repairs were carried out.

There were two three-storeyed station houses, one on either side of the line, their elaborately decorated ground-floor refreshment rooms scenes of frantic activity during every compulsory ten-minute stop. But alas! it was generally agreed the fare available justified neither the arrangements made by the caterers – the Queen's Hotel of Cheltenham – to provide it, nor the sometimes frantic efforts of all too often sorely harassed passengers to obtain it.

The prince having inspected the Box Tunnel on a previous excursion from Bristol, the penultimate stop was Bath. Brunel had taken the line through the city at a considerable elevation, thus affording the railway traveller one of the finest views possible of that exquisite creation of the eighteenth century so popularised by Beau Nash.

Bristol was *en fête*, had been so since dawn, and by the time the royal train drew to a final halt in Temple Meads station at precisely ten o'clock, those who could remember were ready to swear that not since the glorious victories of Trafalgar and Waterloo had the city indulged in such a celebration. As well as the crowds thronging the handsomely decorated streets between Temple Meads and the Floating Harbour, more than thirty thousand souls were said to be massed on Clifton Heights with a similar number on Brandon Hill. An official holiday had been declared; all shops and factories were shut, all offices closed. Gaily coloured bunting festooned the façade of every public building and many a private house as well. A flag of some sort flew from every available flag pole, while church bells pealed non-stop their endless changes of welcome and ovation. Ships in the Float, the New Cut, the Cumberland Basin and the river Avon cannonaded incessant salutes which reverberated above a continuous cacophony of martial music assailing the ear mercilessly from, it appeared, every direction at once.

The Queen's Consort, his sombre black attire relieved by snowy neatness of shirt front and cuffs and the sky-blue riband of the Garter, was formally welcomed by the mayor, a host of civic dignitaries, numerous representatives of the city's commercial and industrial communities and no less than sixty prominent clergymen of all denominations. After being presented with the freedom of the Bristol Society of Merchant Venturers, contained in a gold casket, he belatedly and briefly breakfasted in Brunel's Elizabethan-styled station house. Then came a lengthy and circuitous drive by open carriage to the Great Western Steamship Company's works at Wapping, the prince graciously acknowledging the ecstatic greetings of the crowds by repeatedly removing his hat.

Crammed into her dry dock like some monstrous unborn infant that had outgrown its brick-lined womb, *Great Britain* looked enormous, and magnificent. Above red-leaded bilges her hull gleamed black with, to pick out her rectangular ports, a single line of dazzling white from elegant clipper bow to stylish gold-decorated square-cut counter. Dressed over-all, she flew her House Flag and those of the United States of America, Russia, France and Belgium at five of her six mastheads, with the Union Jack fluttering from her jackstaff and a huge White Ensign billowing over her stern. Her figurehead, in gold on a white background, was an ornately carved representation of the Royal Arms with trailboards either side on which were depicted, also in gold on white, a beehive, two cog-wheels, a dove, a set square, a Jovean thunderbolt and a winged staff – the caduceus of Mercury.

Excluding her thrusting bowsprit, her length stem to stern was 322 feet, her beam 51 and her burthen an unbelievable 3,443 tons. She would have a crew of 130, accommodate 252 first- and second-class passengers in 26 single and 113 double-berth cabins, plus another 100 travelling steerage, and carry 1,200 tons of cargo. Colossal in every respect, she was even equipped with five huge iron lifeboats, said to be unsinkable.

The hull was constructed entirely of wrought-iron plates, measuring on average 6 by 2½ feet, some up to an inch thick, overlapped and close riveted to reinforced iron frames. Five transverse and two longitudinal bulkheads gave additional strength to this already tremendously robust structure as well as dividing the ship into separate compartments individually sealed with watertight doors.

The largest and the most powerful ever built, based on a design patented by Marc Brunel in 1822, her engines comprised two pairs of giant cylinders, each 88 inches in diameter and situated deep in the bowels of the ship. Four gigantic pistons, inclined inwards thirty degrees from the vertical and with a ponderous 6-foot stroke, drove an overhead crankshaft centred in a huge 18-foot diameter drum whose upward arc rose some 4 feet above deck level in the engine-room deckhouse just abaft the towering 8-foot wide funnel. By means of massive endless toothed chains the 3-foot wide drum in turn drove a geared wheel on the propeller shaft, a thin-walled 30-inch diameter tube with shorter solid shafts revolving in bearings at either end of its 60-foot length. The propeller, 6 bladed and weighing 4 tons, stood very nearly three times the height of an average man.

Power for the engines came from three huge boilers each served by four separate furnaces fired from the forward stokehold, another four fired from the after stokehold – twenty-four in all. The combined weight of engines and boilers alone, a staggering 520 tons, exceeded by a considerable margin the total burthen of any of the fast American sailing packets which, despite the challenge of British steam, still maintained their thirty-year monopoly of the North Atlantic passenger trade.

In the late summer of 1838, when the Great Western Steamship Company had announced plans for a second vessel – to be named, for obvious reasons, *City of New York* – it had been Brunel's intention merely to build a sister ship to *Great Western*. Indeed, a cargo of prime African oak, sufficient for a third ship as well, had actually been purchased. But a subsequent evaluation of the relative merits of building in iron, which was yearly becoming ever more plentiful and cheap whereas wood was already scarce and increasing in cost at an alarming rate, prompted him to suggest to the board that Claxton and William Patterson – who had built *Great Western* and was to be responsible for her consort – should investigate at first hand an iron vessel actually at sea.

Much progress had been made in the maritime use of iron since

Aaron Manby had built the first successful iron steamer, mainly due to the pioneering efforts of such as John Grantham, a leading naval architect; Charles Williams, the enterprising managing director of the City of Dublin Packet Company; and William Fairburn, better known latterly for his railway and bridge work. In 1834, John Laird of Birkenhead had launched *Garry Owen*, the largest iron paddle steamer so far built and currently in service on the lower reaches of the river Shannon.

It was the performance of Laird's most recent vessel *Rainbow*, of 407 tons, on which Claxton and Patterson had taken passage from Bristol to Antwerp and back, that decided Brunel not only to build in iron but to increase the already massive burthen of *City of New York* to an unimaginable 3,500 tons. Opposition from the board was quickly swept aside once it had been made clear that the cost would, in fact, be fractional compared to that of building the much smaller wooden ship. Also an iron ship, because of totally different construction techniques, would carry up to twenty per cent more cargo. In any case, *Great Western*, with only half the capacity of the new vessel which had been aptly renamed *Mammoth*, was the optimum size for which wood was suitable. So, on 19 July 1839, in the brand-new dry dock at Wapping specially equipped at a cost of £50,000, the keel that was to herald a new era in marine engineering had been laid.

But that was by no means the end of the story. Before the year was out, Isambard was beginning to have serious second thoughts regarding methods of propulsion. Joseph Bramah had considered the screw propeller as an alternative to paddles as long ago as 1785. Though a number of engineers had since conducted innumerable experiments, only one, Bennett Woodroft in 1832, had achieved any sort of practical success, and then only on a minor scale. Because the difficulties were considered far too great to be surmounted, the screw propeller, it was believed, could never be more than an experimental toy, perhaps ultimately for use on small craft but never for an ocean-going vessel.

Experience with *Great Western*, however, had highlighted the many major drawbacks which could seriously impair the efficiency of paddle-wheel propulsion, not least heavy weather. On more than one occasion her engines had sustained damage when one or other paddle wheel had suddenly started racing clear of the water.

Then, in May 1840, a 240-ton topsail schooner powered by a Rennie Brothers engine and driven, not by paddles but an entirely new type of propeller, the recent invention of Sir Francis Petit Smith, had suddenly appeared in the port of Bristol. *Archimedes* was the first sea-going vessel in the world to be screw propelled, and for the next six months she was under private charter to Isambard Brunel.

Mammoth's paddle engines, meanwhile, were already under construction, work on them having commenced before the keel had been laid. Such was their magnitude, no established firm had been prepared even to tender for the contract. The Great Western Steamship Company had therefore been forced to build an engine works at Gas Wharf, on the opposite side of the Floating Harbour to Wapping, and had invited Francis Humphrys to adapt the marine trunk engine he had invented, to serve as the new vessel's power unit.

Humphrys had soon discovered he had taken on a truly daunting task, if not a wholly impossible one, for the intermediate paddle shaft would be of such dimension that it could not be forged. There simply was no tilt-hammer in existence big enough. Nor could one be made that would not be gagged by the size of the billet laid across its anvil. Driven to desperation, Humphrys for a time had even toyed with the risky alternative of using cast iron for the shaft. But then he discovered not even this would be possible. The thing was just too big.

Eventually James Nasmyth, a former pupil of Henry Maudslay and now a partner in Nasmyth, Wilson & Company, had come to Humphrys' rescue by inventing, literally to order, the world's first steam hammer, soon acknowledged to be the most important contribution to engineering progress since the screw-cutting lathe.

But the problem of the shaft had no sooner been solved than Humphrys had been told to build instead a unit to drive a screw propeller. Tragically the shock was too much for him. Outstandingly gifted though he undoubtedly was, he lacked that spring-steel resilience of temperament which Isambard Brunel had discovered from bitter experience could alone bring greatness even to the most brilliant engineer. The poor fellow collapsed on the spot with a brainstorm and died a few days later. Tom Guppy had then taken over, and he and Isambard together evolved their successful adaptation of the elder Brunel's original engine design.

Prince Albert was received at Wapping Dock by the Great Western Steamship Company chairman who introduced the numerous officials carefully singled out beforehand to be so honoured. As he stepped aboard *Great Britain*, the Royal Standard was run up to the main masthead while a military band on the poop played the 'National Anthem'. For the next two hours the prince, in company with the ambassadors of the United States of America, Prussia and Sardinia, inspected the vessel with Tom Guppy as their guide, Isambard, as was his wont on such occasions, being content to remain in the background.

A grand luncheon for five hundred with the prince as guest of honour, was served in one of the dock's workshops suitably converted for the occasion. But for once the toasts and speeches which followed were commendably brief, for by three o'clock all had taken their places on the launching platform.

It was, in fact, to be a ceremonial floating out into the harbour. While lunch was being served the dock had been flooded and its gates swung open. With a line from the steam packet *Avon* (which was standing by to tow her free) already aboard, *Great Britain* was ready to move.

Having delivered a short address in his still heavily accented but not unpleasing tenor, the prince invited Mrs John Miles, who had named *Great Western* six years before, to perform that happy duty once again. The lady's voice was powerful enough to be heard by nearly all who watched her take a firm grip on the cradled champagne bottle preparatory to releasing it against the soaring bow. But *Avon*'s captain had been a trifle premature taking up the slack of his towline. Already her target was out of range and the horrified spectators gasped with dismay as the bottle swung wildly to the limit of its attached cord, which then parted, depositing the bottle with an impotent plop into the ever-widening gap between ship and shore. To a seafaring fraternity such a mishap, coming as it did on top of a ship already courting disaster by having had her name changed, not once, but twice, could be considered nothing less than an omen of unmitigated catastrophe. Happily, the quick-thinking prince was more than equal to the occasion. Grabbing the extra bottle some thoughtful official had had the foresight to provide, he hurled it with all his might at the now rapidly receding bows.

The crowd seemed to hold its collective breath. Then, as the bottle shattered and its foaming contents seemed almost to soak into the iron, the people of Bristol cheered as they had rarely cheered before. The band on the poop struck up 'Rule Britannia', the bells of the cathedral and all the city's churches rang out anew, while the guns of the ships in the harbour, the Cut, the Basin and the river, again thundered their deafening salutes. *Great Britain* had been launched.

Chapter Two

IN latter years an indulgence of his talent for performing sleight-of-hand and magic tricks had in general been the only form of relaxation Isambard had allowed himself from the pressure of work. Every day, Sundays included, his offices which occupied the whole ground floor at Duke Street would be thronged with an endless procession of contractors' representatives, surveyors, land agents, consultants from practically every branch of the engineering industry, locomotive and field engineers and an army of railway officials from the Bristol & Exeter, the South Devon, the Cornwall, the Bristol & Gloucester, the Cheltenham & Great Western Union and others to which, in addition to the Great Western, he was engineer. They even came from as far afield as Italy where he had already surveyed two railway routes – from Florence to Pistoja, and between Genoa and Allassandria – and from India.

To his many other talents Bennett had added that of virtuoso in the art of shielding his master from all but absolutely essential confrontations, at times being inspired to wonders of organisation and diplomacy. But not even he had been able to devise a means of coping with a work-load that was forever on the increase. In consequence a working day was seldom less than eighteen hours in length, which left little or no time at all for socialising – a fact that never failed to infuriate Mary, resigned though she had perforce become. She entertained lavishly, mostly in the afternoons, and her husband, more to mollify her than anything else, invariably made a point of looking in on her guests gathered in the first-floor drawing room to take a quick cup of tea and perhaps exchange a word or two with a favoured few, after his daily half-hour romp with the children in the nursery. But that was all.

On the very rare occasions he did fulfil the function of host, however, it was never difficult to persuade him to demonstrate his prowess as a parlour magician. His favourite performance was a spoof séance in which he took a mischievous delight in exposing the ingenious illusions with which many a charlatan masquerading as a medium had been known to swindle gullible, and sometimes not so gullible, clients. Such was now his fame as an entertainer, that no social gathering of consequence at Duke Street could ever be deemed complete without at least a sample of his talent.

Though pressed for time as sorely as ever, Papa had promised to be free for young Isambard's sixth birthday party, to which had been invited Grandpère and Grandmère Brunel, Aunt Sophia and Uncle Benjamin, cousins Ben and Sophy, now grown-up of course, Grandpapa and Grandmama Horsley and Aunt Sophy. Unlike her sisters and brothers, Sophy had not married. Nor had she become the concert pianist she could and should have been, had she not foolishly allowed herself to be persuaded by Mary that it would be most unseemly for the sister of the wife of Isambard Brunel to be known as a professional musician.

It was a splendid party, enjoyed by all. But unfortunately it was to end in near tragedy. With a fast sequence of intriguing tricks Isambard soon had everyone gasping in wonder and the children clapping their hands in delight. But as he was about to pass a half-sovereign 'magically' from his ear to his mouth, where it had of course already been surreptitiously secreted, he suddenly choked and swallowed it. To the growing consternation of his audience his increasingly frantic efforts to prevent it slipping deeper into his throat proved vain.

Hurriedly the children were whisked away to the nursery. Half an hour later, and by then in extremis as a result both of the mishap and the series of well-intentioned but quite unhelpful, if not positively harmful, ministrations to which he had been subjected, he had to be carried to his bed. 'You must send for Brodie at once,' Ben Hawes commanded Mary, having at last managed to take charge of the situation and in so doing probably saving his brother-in-law's life.

Naturally Mary was distraught as was everyone else, but she had managed thus far to remain creditably calm. At the mention of that dread name, however, she at once began to give way to hysteria. For the moment it seemed her ingrained terror of surgeons might almost prove greater than her concern for her husband's life.

'Oh, dear God! Ben, no! Not that, not Brodie!' She clutched convulsively at her own throat as if in horrified anticipation of what such a summons must mean.

'Mary, you must,' Sophia urged, quietly but sternly. 'If he doesn't come at once Isambard must surely die.' She was deathly pale, and with scarcely contained fear of the worst she too shuddered, haunted by the memory of her brother's face contorted into a purple mask of agony as he'd fought for breath through paroxysms of uncontrollable coughing.

By the time Brodie got to Duke Street – fortunately he'd been quickly located – Isambard had, by dint of painful but persistent experiment, ascertained that the coin, stuck somewhere in the upper region of his right lung, could be dislodged with relative ease by his bending forwards and downwards. But, try as he might, he could move it only so far before it began to choke him so severely he was forced to desist and it fell back to its resting place, where sensitive membranes were beginning to protest most emphatically. Now every breath was torment, his throat felt as if it had been flayed and his chest ached abominably.

'Aye, it seems to be lodged in the right bronchus,' Brodie confirmed at the conclusion of his examination. 'Unfortunately, the extent of its movement appears to be limited to a position somewhere just short of the glottis.'

But diagnosis was one thing, prognosis something else and England's most eminent surgeon made no secret of the fact that he was baffled. 'If only there was some way to entice the thing to shift just a fraction of an inch further,' he mused helplessly.

There was a way, Isambard told him, having given much serious thought to the problem whilst awaiting the surgeon's arrival. Forbidden to speak – he was in any case unable to without bringing on another fit of coughing – he had to communicate with scribbled notes and hurriedly drafted sketches. He need only be suspended head downwards, he explained, and, with a little coaxing, gravity might be persuaded to do the rest.

But Brodie was doubtful. The simplistic approach was all well and good in its way, of course. There were, however, complexities of which its advocate was totally ignorant. Indeed not even he, Brodie, could claim as yet to have recognised or to be prepared for all the potential hazards involved, or even to be aware of their existence. There could be many a slip – and so on and so forth. This was no engineering experiment. A life, not to mention a professional

212

reputation, was at stake.

'More likely you'll choke yourself,' he commented dourly. In his opinion the only way for the coin to be removed was surgically. That would mean a tracheotomy, a simple but risky operation normally resorted to only in extreme cases of which this, without doubt, was one. But even should Brunel survive that initial hazard, the coin would be hardly more accessible. There just wasn't an instrument in the surgeon's bag with which the cursed thing could possibly be reached.

'Then, dammit, I'll design one,' Isambard croaked impatiently, and promptly paid for his incontinent outburst with a fit of coughing so violent it made those attending him almost despair. After it had subsided he was so exhausted that it was some time before they were convinced that his demise was not imminent.

Under careful sedation, however, he survived the night. Despite the acute discomfort in his chest, when he woke he found the restorative effects of his enforced rest quite amazing. Within forty-eight hours he was up and, deaf to Brodie's protests, able to work at his drawing table, though he remained confined to his room and obliged to limit all physical exertion to a minimum. Also, he was forbidden to smoke, a constraint he accepted with the worst possible grace. That apart, however, he was amazingly cheerful.

In this philosophical attitude he was admirably and nobly supported by Mary, whose courage now seemed equal to anything the situation might demand of her. She was, in fact, almost out of her mind with worry. But having at least bridled her genuine terror of any form of surgery (never would she be able to conquer it) not once did she allow Isambard or the children to suspect the turmoil of emotion that was always just behind her truly superb façade of calm.

For the operation Isambard designed a horrific surgical instrument – a pair of finely balanced forceps, made of the best stainless steel with blades no less than two feet in length. Through the incision in his throat, these tapered blades would have to enter his windpipe, be gradually eased down to the bronchus, manipulated first to find the coin, then seize and hold it fast and lift it with infinite care back to the incision from whence it could be withdrawn. And while Brodie was doing all this he was going to have to endure as best he might the acute and prolonged discomfort, not to mention the pain. It would be an all but intolerable ordeal for both of them. Well, if Brodie was willing to try, so was he. Indeed, it seemed he had no alternative. But he could not help having very serious doubts of his ability to remain sufficiently passive for long enough to allow the surgeon to complete his almost impossibly delicate and onerous task.

Brodie having examined, advised on and finally approved the drawings for the mammoth forceps eventually to bear his name, they were immediately dispatched to the surgical-instrument makers for a prototype to be produced as quickly as possible. After that there was nothing more to do but wait.

By no means relishing the prospect, Isambard diverted himself by designing an apparatus on which he could be safely up-ended. It was like a door frame anchored to a substantial base, with a stout board pivoted between the uprights to move freely through 360 degrees. Secured to the horizontal board, he would first of all be raised to the perpendicular, then swung upside-down and back. Then, if he could somehow manage to synchronise the coughing this would induce with a critical moment of movement, the weight of the coin plus the centrifugal force thus generated should, with any luck at all, be sufficient to achieve ejection. Such was the theory anyway.

The apparatus was ready long before the efficiency of the forceps could be proved to the surgeon's complete satisfaction. With the greatest reluctance Brodie agreed to letting the patient have his way on condition that it be under the supervision of a selected panel of the most prominent medical men available. But there was nothing any of them could do as they watched Isambard being swung about on his contraption frantically hacking and hawking. For days he persisted. All he succeeded in doing was wearing himself out. Again and again he was advised to stop, and again and again he ignored the advice. Only when it became obvious he was literally killing himself did he finally give in. Brodie's operation was his last hope.

Another fortnight now had to pass before he was in a fit enough state to face the appalling ordeal. Meanwhile all London, the whole country even, informed by daily bulletins waited anxiously for news, be it good or bad, as a stream of well-wishers from all walks of life called regularly at Duke Street and messages of goodwill and hope and condolence poured in.

Strapped to an operating table in the room adjacent to his own, fully conscious and only too well aware of all that was happening, he bore with incredible fortitude the sharp agony of the surgeon's blade first slicing deep into his throat then penetrating with sickening force the surprisingly tough wall of his windpipe. He was allowed ample time to recover and to brace himself once more before facing the glittering, menacingly curved blades of those horrendous forceps.

But for all his skill and patience, Sir Benjamin could progress no more than a fraction of that frightful distance to his goal. The obstruction in his windpipe so inhibited his breathing that within minutes Isambard had fainted, and long before the forceps could be withdrawn without themselves inflicting fatal damage he was deeply unconscious.

Such disappointing and near-tragic failure did not bode well for the future. Brodie, however, was anxious to try again and, once he had recovered, Brunel stoically agreed to the incision in his throat being kept open for a second operation. But that, too, and for the same reason, had to be abandoned.

Her nerves ravaged by the unbearable strain of what had now dragged into a six-week ordeal, Mary Brunel, a pathetically haggard shadow of her former beautiful self, clung to Sophia Hawes as they listened with fast fading hope at the door of her husband's bedchamber. Swinging desperately up and down once more on his pivoted board, Isambard was making one final savagely heroic effort to survive.

Time passed as attempt succeeded attempt, the ghastly sounds of choking each produced getting steadily worse and generally weaker. Then there was silence – an ominous, all-pervading, frightening, seemingly endless silence. Fearing the worst, Mary broke down at last and began to sob quietly, while her sister-in-law, usually the most phlegmatic of women, found she too was unable to hold back her tears.

The bedroom door slowly creaked open, Sir Benjamin Brodie appeared, his face pale and drawn, but expressionless. From inside the room there came no sound. 'I think, ladies, you had better come in now,' was all he said in a voice thick with emotion and faint from fatigue.

Less than two hours later Thomas Babington Macaulay, Her Majesty's sometime Secretary at War, raced through the colonnaded entrance porch of the Athenaeum like an excited schoolboy bellowing 'It's out! It's out!' Every member and every club servant knew exactly what he meant and every single one, from the Duke of

Wellington to the humblest bootboy, cheered the tidings at the top of his voice.

As had been his daily habit, Macaulay had called at Duke Street late that afternoon for news of the sufferer's condition. 'At half-past four precisely I was safely delivered of my little coin,' an exhausted but jubilant Isambard had told him. What he'd said in response, Macaulay could not recall. Neither could the illustrious parliamentarian add to the simple eloquence of the engineer's own words when afterwards he related the detail of his visit again and again for the benefit of all who wished to hear.

'It simply dropped out,' Brunel had said, with disarming nonchalance, 'just as so many like it have in the past, and doubtless will in the future, drop through my fingers. I shall be myself again by the end of the week, have no fear.' And he was.

The final word on his unique misfortune eventually came from the pen of the Reverend R. H. Barham, Reader of Divinity at St Paul's, but better known as the popular author and wit, Thomas Ingoldsby. As part of the moral in *The Housewarming* he wrote:

> All conjuring's bad – they may get in a scrape
> Before they're aware, and whatever its shape
> They may find it no easy affair to escape.
> It's not everybody that comes off so well
> From '*leger-de-main*' tricks as Mister Brunel!

Chapter Three

B RUNEL'S survey, in 1836, of a route from Exeter to Plymouth had recommended bridging the estuary of the Teign, following the line of the coast as far as Torquay, then proceeding over the river Dart and down through the South Hams country, all ideal levels for the broad gauge. Subsequently, however, and mainly because of cost, this route had been abandoned in favour of a much shorter line along the north bank of the Teign inland to Newton Abbot, bridging the Dart at Totnes, then on to Plymouth by way of South Brent, Ivybridge and Plympton.

Monetary savings, though substantial, would unfortunately be at the cost of speed. Gradients beyond Newton Abbot, particularly in the vicinity of Dainton, Rattery and Hemerdon, were such that not even Daniel Gooch's immensely powerful locomotives could reasonably be expected to maintain an acceptable level of economic operation. But with an alternative power source, one that could in addition make single-line working feasible, even greater economies might be effected without detriment to performance.

The idea of using atmospheric pressure had been the subject of much debate, a deal of experiment and not a little controversy ever since first mooted by an enthusiastic optimist some thirty years earlier. The theory was simple enough; and so, at first sight, appeared the practicality. Between the rails was laid an airtight pipe into which a piston depending from the underside of the leading coach of a train was introduced. A pump, located at the next station along the line, evacuated the pipe. The pressure behind the piston, being now greater, drove it forward. Thus would the train progress from station to station, smoothly, safely, silently – no noise, no smuts, no smoke.

As with all things seemingly simple, however, there was one major difficulty; how was the connecting arm 'twixt piston and train to travel freely through the continuous slot, which must be let into the pipe, without impairing the essential integrity of the seal? Many attempts to achieve this had been made, but all had failed miserably. The problem had seemed unsolvable until, in 1839, Joseph and Jacob Samuda had registered a patent for an ingeniously devised and cleverly engineered valve.

The following year, on just over a mile of roughly laid line in London, they had demonstrated that a hinged leather flap backed with iron, opened and closed by special rollers attached to the piston arm, effectively preserved the seal in the slot of a nine-inch pipe. Results from a series of test runs appeared quite phenomenal, and all subsequent experiments witnessed by an impressive number of railway engineers seemed to prove the Samuda Brothers' system worthy of a commercial trial. Not all agreed. George Stephenson for one dismissed the system outright as so much humbug as, predictably, did both his son and his sometime star pupil, Joseph Locke. But William Cubitt, engineer to the South Eastern Railway, gave it his blessing; while Charles Vignoles, who had built Ireland's first railway, the Dublin & Kingstown, had decided there and then to install the Samuda system on the proposed Dalkey branch line.

By the end of August 1843, over a distance of 2,590 yards, on a gradient of 1 in 128, trains between Kingstown and Dalkey were running regularly and, so far, without even minor mishap. The method of operation was that five minutes before departure from Kingstown the engineer at Dalkey started his pump, which was powered by an enormous Fairburn engine with a thirty-six foot flywheel. At the same time the train was pushed forward until its piston entered the fifteen-inch pipe through a treadle-operated valve. Held on its brakes until all the air had been pumped out of the pipe, it accelerated rapidly as soon as they were released. Deceleration was automatic when the piston emerged from the pipe about a hundred yards short of Dalkey terminus. No power was necessary for the return journey, the gradient being sufficiently acute and so contrived at the Kingstown end as to allow a train, no matter how laden, to coast relatively speedily and come to rest alongside the station platform.

Operational speed up the incline was an average thirty miles per hour. But some very impressive results indeed had been recorded before the line had opened to the public. The most spectacular run, which had taken just one and a quarter minutes – a speed of eighty-four miles per hour – had in reality been an accident that might well have ended in tragedy. The leading coach had been improperly coupled to the rest of the train. Even so, the fact that young Frank Ebrington, the engineering student son of a Regius professor of Dublin University who could now claim distinction as the fastest man on earth, not only survived his at the time hair-raising experience but once he'd recovered from the initial shock swore he had actually enjoyed it, gave rise to confident predictions of speeds in excess of one hundred miles per hour or more. Even allowing for the remaining problems which, it had to be admitted by its most ardent advocates were neither few nor simple, the future of the atmospheric system seemed assured.

Chief among these problems was that the train itself was virtually remotely controlled. When the atmospheric pipe had been evacuated the 'driver' had to hold his train more or less stationary on far from efficient brakes against the almost irresistible pressure behind the piston. Once in motion he had no way at all of stopping. All he and his passengers could do then was hang on and hope. An immediate improvement in braking systems was therefore imperative, both before and during the run and to bring the train to a controlled halt at the end of its atmospheric journey instead of just letting it coast for the last hundred yards. Also there was need for an effective means of direct communication between stations. Here, it was thought, the hitherto much neglected electric telegraph might well prove ideal.

Some months prior to the opening of the London to Maidenhead section of the Great Western, Brunel had persuaded the board to agree to a trial of Wheatstone and Cooke's invention between Paddington and West Drayton. The installation had consisted of five wires, individually insulated with cotton thread and gutta-percha, contained in a continuous iron pipe fixed above ground at the side of the rails. Powered by voltaic batteries, a display of five magnetic needles on dials at either end of the line could be moved through a series of prearranged permutations to transmit and receive all the letters of the alphabet, plus numbers one to ten. The procedure was complicated and laborious, but in the hands of competent operators brief messages could be passed with reasonable efficiency.

Unfortunately, due to rapid deterioration of the insulating material it had ceased to be functional long before its potential could be properly evaluated. But an improved version was shortly to be installed requiring only two wires suspended from a series of cast-iron standards varying in height from ten to twenty feet, sometimes as much as a hundred and fifty feet apart and placed parallel to the line. But for conventional railways, instant communication generally was still regarded as an impressive but scarcely necessary novelty.

As a result of the Dalkey trials and without waiting for publication of the Board of Trade findings, William Cubitt had made known his intention of installing an atmospheric system on the London & Croydon. Following this lead, Monsieur Mallet of the French Public Works Department recommended its widespread use on all French railways, while others talked prophetically of the eventual abandonment of all conventional locomotive traction. Finally, when Sir Frederick Smith the Government Inspector General of Railways and Peter Barlow of the Woolwich Academy in their joint report on the exhaustive Board of Trade inquiry both declared in favour of the system, the matter appeared to be settled.

The Stephensons, however, still refused to accept that the Samuda Brothers' system would be far more economic than comparable locomotive working. Nor would they agree that as much two-way traffic could be accommodated on a single atmospheric line as on any existing conventional double line, which was one of the fundamentals in the pro-atmospheric argument, the installation costs of a double line being prohibitive. Even when two of Robert Stephenson's most trusted assistants advocated the adoption of the atmospheric system forthwith on the infamous Camden Incline – the exit from the Euston terminus of the London & Birmingham up which trains still had to be hauled by cable – he remained obdurate.

'Quite apart from anything else,' he persisted, 'wear and tear of the longitudinal valve and the consequent constant attention it will need are factors about which we know absolutely nothing.'

But Brunel categorically disagreed. 'The mere mechanical difficulties can and will be overcome. The atmospheric system has been proved and will operate,' he told Daniel Gooch, 'with far less incidence of interruption than can be guaranteed with locomotives.'

Gooch wisely kept his own counsel. Inwardly, however, he merely snorted in disgust.

Chapter Four

NOT until January 1845 did London get its first view of the new 'Queen of the Ocean'. Too wide to pass through the lock gates of the Cumberland Basin, the dilatory Dock Company having still not widened the entrance as had been recommended in Brunel's survey eleven years before, *Great Britain* had remained a helpless prisoner in the Floating Harbour for eighteen months, likened by the *Bristol Mirror* to a weasel in a farmer's granary grown too fat to escape. The argument between the Great Western Steamship Company and the Dock Board as to whose was the responsibility had become so acrimonious that the Board of Trade had eventually been called upon to arbitrate. Its decision, unjust and unhelpful in the opinion of the company, that it was entirely up to the owners to get their vessel to the open sea and furthermore to pay for whatever might be necessary to achieve this, was final. Six weeks later, the alterations to the gates having been accomplished in record time under Brunel's supervision, *Great Britain* was on her way to the Thames.

The company, however, was now in dire financial straits. In 1839 *Great Western*, its one source of income, had had no rivals worthy of note. The Trans-Atlantic Steamship Company had ceased to exist – yet another slap in the face for Brunel's still vociferous Liverpool based detractors; while the British & American Steam Navigation Company, following the loss of its vessel *President*, was teetering on the verge of extinction. But a year later Samuel Cunard, a Canadian shipowner who had founded the Liverpool based British & American Royal Mail Steam Packet Company later to be known more simply as the Cunard Steamship Company, having secured an extremely lucrative contract from the Admiralty for the carriage of all transatlantic mails, mounted a challenge that could only be met by massive reductions in passenger fares and cargo rates and hence the profit *Great Western* was capable of producing. With a passenger and cargo capacity at least four times that of any other ship afloat, *Great Britain* would of course change all that. To do so, however, she had to be fully operational.

But so desperate was the company for cash that she was kept moored in the Thames for another six months, a quarter of a million people paying no less than £25,000 for the privilege of seeing her. While there she received her second royal inspection, this time by the queen. Eventually on 26 July she embarked on her first transatlantic voyage. Ironically, she sailed not from Bristol but from Liverpool, to New York. Never again was *Great Britain* to visit her home port.

It was by no means the success so confidently anticipated. The crossing took fifteen days, she carried a mere fifty passengers, with cargo holds only half full. In New York she was put on show again for nearly three weeks, a thousand sightseers a day willingly paying 25 cents each to gaze wide-eyed and open-mouthed at the marvel most could scarce believe was actually before them. Her second voyage, however, was a near disaster. This time she carried 102 passengers but took eighteen days, and arrived in New York with her propeller so seriously damaged she had to return to Liverpool under sail to go straight into dry dock, there to remain until the following May. It was not an auspicious start to her career.

Almost as he reached his fortieth birthday, Isambard discovered to his dismay that the long years of abuse to which he had so ruthlessly subjected his small frame were beginning to take their toll. Mentally he was stronger than ever. But physically there could be no doubt he was beginning to fail. He had foolishly ignored Brodie's oft-repeated insistence that he give himself plenty of time to recover from those two abortive operations. Instead, as so often before, he had stretched his credit to the very limit, recklessly mortgaging the future for the moment. Now, it seemed, his credit had at last run out. Nature was demanding payment, and with interest.

The terrible plague of headaches which had so tortured him seven years before suddenly returned. One evening he collapsed. The diagnosis was exhaustion. But next morning his ankles were so painfully swollen he could not walk; scarcely was he able to rise from his bed. Thereafter, recurrent raging fevers racked his tormented body without warning, leaving him weak and listless and unable to work for days at a time even after they had subsided.

Desperately he sought to keep the seriousness of his suffering secret, partially succeeded, and in so doing of course denied himself the full benefit of the help and support he needed and which could have been his for the asking. As a consequence Mary, though she worried constantly about her obviously ailing but increasingly distant husband, did so behind a façade of apparently indifferent calm and unblemished beauty which, however, fooled no one but him.

The harrowing experience of the coin had had a profound and far-reaching effect on Mary Brunel. The near tragedy had awakened in her a memory of her original premarital feelings for Isambard, feelings she had subconsciously stifled since her acute shock of disappointment over their honeymoon, or rather its lack, and her ever-growing resentment since of what she had unreasoningly considered his blatant and callous neglect of her. Only belatedly had come a full realisation that this was no ordinary man she had married, that a man of such unique genius could be so very different in so many ways from those who, in comparison, were just mortals, and that her past expectation of any sort of conventional existence with him had, from the start, been totally unreasonable. Suddenly she found herself haunted with a fear of having betrayed his trust in her, that she had failed him miserably; that it was all her fault young Isambard should have turned out such a disappointment; that Henry, bright though he might be in comparison with the elder boy, still fell so far short of his father's expectation; that even baby Florence, despite early indications to the contrary, might be blessed eventually with her mother's looks and nothing else.

Plagued with this imagined guilt, she had sought desperately for some way to make amends. Though she had never actually neglected her children in favour of her friends, they had always taken second place to the latter in their demands on her. Never had she, as had Isambard, made a point of setting aside time each day specifically for them. But once the Brunel household had returned to some semblance of normality, she too had joined in and enjoyed the daily nursery romp. It had been an essential part of her deliberate endeavour to re-establish some sort of rapport with her estranged husband. Nor had her efforts been entirely without success – until, that is, the breakdown in Isambard's health. Then, suddenly, it seemed to Mary, they were as far apart as they had ever been.

Desperately she appealed to her brother John who had always been close to Isambard, to his sister Sophia, to Lady Brunel and Sir Marc. 'Please,' she secretly begged them, 'try to stop Issy,' the pet name she had not used since before their marriage, 'for mercy's sake, help me to stop him working himself to death.' For that was precisely what he was now doing.

Only Sir Marc was able to exercise any influence, and for a time it seemed the son might well take heed of the father. Appreciably he slowed his suicide-inducing pace. He began to talk of leaving London, of building the house he had always dreamed of designing, even of retirement. Already he had won more glory than many a predecessor and most contemporaries. He was wealthy enough. He was, he said, more than satisfied. And Mary's heart heaved with renewed hope.

But after Sir Marc had suffered a stroke which left him confined to a wheelchair partially paralysed, there was no more talk of retirement. Mary choked back her tears of disappointment and quelled as best she could her fears for the future, for it seemed to her now it could only be a matter of time before Issy too must become a permanent invalid like his father.

But it wasn't only the volume of work that, physical weakness apart, so sapped Isambard's strength. As much as he had in the past, he revelled in any challenge to his powers of ingenuity and invention. It was more the climate of the times. Each day he grew ever more disgusted and disillusioned by the orgy of speculation in which, no matter how he might seek to escape, he could not help but become involved. A new railway was no longer the great adventure it had been barely two years earlier. There was no place now for that quintessential exercise of individual talent that had created such pioneering masterworks as George Stephenson's Stockton & Darlington, the Liverpool & Manchester, the Grand Junction, Robert Stephenson's London & Birmingham, his own Great Western. No one cared a fig for technical achievement any more; now it was all money, money, money. Anything would do so long as it was cheap to build and profitable to run. The bankers, the businessmen, the manipulators of the Stock Market – that mad menagerie of bulls, bears and stags – the promoters who merely exploited the greediness of the gullible, the professional plungers, the profiteers posing as public benefactors, and the blatant out-and-out swindlers who were probably far more honest in their way than any of the others, these were the ones who now paid the piper, called the tune, then set the whole world a-dancing to a tempo of their choosing. This was progress!

If he could have turned his back on the whole sordid scene he would gladly have done so. He could not. It just wasn't possible. There was simply too much at stake, too much capital, too many people depending on him alone. And there was always so little time.

The prime cause of it all was what the press had long since dubbed 'the gauge war'. If only Brunel had built his Great Western five years sooner things might have been so very different. There could be little doubt that by now the broad gauge would have been the country's, nay the world's, standard. Fast and dependable, it was far more efficient and comfortable, luxurious even, compared to the very best to which the narrow gauge could ever hope to aspire. In short, it was all the things the narrow gauge would like to be but, if only because of its smaller scale, never could.

Nevertheless, the broad gauge still had far more enemies than friends. As the first in the field George Stephenson had chosen his disciples-to-be with the utmost care, indoctrinating them so thoroughly that few had ever thought even to question his creed. In addition the 'grand old man' had sired, as had his contemporary Sir Marc Brunel, an entirely independent but steadfastly loyal genius. In his prime now, Robert Stephenson was proving an even greater power to be reckoned with than his father.

There was also the matter of money. Superior the broad gauge might be, but there was still only just over 250 miles of track at present in existence compared to 1,000 or more of narrow gauge, plus the hundreds currently under construction, already authorised, being promoted or yet to be proposed, and nearly all the result of senseless speculation. A recent estimate of total current investment in this 'railway mania' had put the figure considerably in excess of one hundred million sterling. Judging by the current mood of the market there seemed no reason to doubt it would be doubled within the year, probably doubled again thereafter. That a crash must be inevitable was obvious. It was a bubble that would surely burst, just as so many similar bubbles had done. But no one could tell when that might be, and no one seemed to care.

225

Bedevilled by this savage dog-eat-dog situation, successive governments had shrunk from grasping the nettle of standardisation. But a choice between the broad and narrow gauge would have to be made sooner rather than later, and when it was who would be liable for the cost of conversion? Who, in fact, could even begin to contemplate what that cost might be? In order to survive therefore – for, as long as the game lasted, there would be everything to play for and little to lose – both factions could only continue to expand and in the process do their best to ensure that wherever possible it would be somehow to their own benefit and the other side's detriment.

On 9 July 1845, a Royal Commission was at last appointed to make an extensive examination of the vexatious gauge question and by its findings settle the issue once and for all. When called on, Isambard gave his testimony in characteristic manner. But in conclusion he could not resist the observation that the merits of the two gauges, insofar as the performance of locomotives was concerned, should forthwith be put to a decisive comparison under strict test conditions.

It was nothing more or less than a direct challenge which, surprisingly contrary to past reactions, the Narrow-gauge Party lost no time in accepting. Whereupon Brunel mischievously suggested the 194-mile Paddington to Exeter run – which Gooch's engines, since the opening of the Bristol & Exeter the previous year, had been regularly covering in less than five hours – as the broad-gauge trial, well knowing there was nothing remotely resembling it anywhere on the narrow-gauge network. Needless to say, the proposal was turned down flat. After much haggling, the modest fifty-three-mile stretch from Paddington to Didcot and even more modest forty-mile narrow-gauge run from Darlington to York were finally agreed.

Though he was by no means averse to such a trial, indeed for years he had been agitating for one, Daniel Gooch was more than a little put out at being given no time to build a new engine for it. It was known that the narrow-gauge people had several new locomotives of considerably increased power – which was why in this instance they had picked up Brunel's gauntlet with such uncharacteristic alacrity – while the most recent addition to the broad-gauge stable, *Ixion*, was over three years old.

'Oh come now, Daniel,' Brunel had playfully chided his somewhat peevish locomotive engineer. 'I'm surprised at you. After all, it wouldn't be fair if we didn't give these fellows odds.'

That December *Ixion* performed quite magnificently, producing a maximum of 60 miles per hour drawing an 80-ton train and averaging well over 50 miles per hour with 60 tons. There having been no precondition to prohibit the practice, Gooch, who had insisted on driving the engine, had preheated the feed water in the tender. But even allowing for this perhaps questionable ploy, the results were better than even the most optimistic could have hoped. His earlier pique and foreboding completely forgotten, Daniel was jubilant. 'New locomotive or no new locomotive,' he reported to the once more seriously ailing Brunel, 'the narrow gaugers are going to have to work a miracle now to beat us!'

But the narrow-gauge trial a few weeks later did not produce a miracle. Indeed, it did not achieve even a satisfactory result in spite of Bidder, Gooch's opposite number, preheating the feed water in his tenders almost to boiling point and secretly installing a portable boiler at Darlington to give his fires a blast of superheated air before starting the return run to York. Gooch, when he found out, was furious. But this desperately elaborate stratagem had been to no avail whatever. Even with their new Stephenson-designed locomotive, cryptically identified merely as *Engine 'A'*, the best Bidder had been able to manage was a top speed of 53¾ miles per hour with a train of only 50 tons. His second locomotive – the Narrow-gauge Party had insisted on two even though Gooch had relied solely on the ageing *Ixion* – was also brand new and called *Stephenson*, and it was on her, following the disappointing performance of *Engine 'A'*, that all remaining narrow-gauge hopes were pinned. But *Stephenson* had run for only twenty-two miles before her recklessly enthusiastic driver put her off the rails. The Broad-gauge Party went wild with delight. What more proof was needed? they asked.

But the commission's findings not only recommended adoption of the narrow gauge as the future standard for the country, but the immediate conversion of all broad-gauge lines to narrow. It was, the report took infinite pains to point out, all basically a question of cost. Brunel's response was in the form of a pamphlet, one of many to be published. Its persuasive technical content and the lucid logic of its uncomplicated argument so undermined the commission's conclusions that it left the Government with no choice but to remove any teeth a Gauge Act might and should have had. In other words, the war was by no means even nearing its end.

Gooch was now ordered to produce a new locomotive, bigger and more powerful even than the proposed successors to the Fireflies, to be fully tested and ready for service no later than mid-May 1846. It was then the middle of February. It was an outrageous, an impossible, demand. A project of such complex magnitude normally took months if not years to plan. Nevertheless Daniel Gooch took himself off to Swindon where, in just thirteen weeks, he and Archibald Sturrock the newly appointed works manager, working shoulder to shoulder and round the clock, first at the drawing board, then at the bench, and finally on the workshop floor, produced what their crew predictably nicknamed 'Lightning'.

The railway world was soon agog with expectation for, while she'd been a-building, seeds of rumour regarding her size and expected performance had been deliberately and diligently sown. Named officially *Great Western*, the new locomotive was truly enormous, her eight-foot driving wheels powered by a huge boiler capable of working to unprecedentedly high pressures. Her like had never been seen before. For once rumour had neither lied nor exaggerated. She was to the railway what *Great Britain* was to the sea, and narrow-gauge sympathisers, whether they'd seen the monster for themselves or not, positively quailed at the very thought of her.

On 1 June 1846, *Great Western* arrived in Exeter just 3 hours and 28 minutes after leaving London, taking but 3 minutes longer for the return trip the same day, an average speed in excess of 55 miles per hour for a journey of nearly 400 miles. Less than a fortnight later she had shattered her own record by hauling a 100-ton train the 76 miles from Paddington to Swindon in just 78 minutes – an average this time of 59 miles per hour.

Cost or no cost, it was said, the broad-gauge must surely prevail now!

Chapter Five

A S suddenly as it had begun to deteriorate, Isambard's health started to improve, and as his strength returned so the melancholia he had consciously had to fight off for so long had gradually released its hold on him. Since the Thames Tunnel disaster an underlying tendency to acute depression had become an integral element of his complex character. Possibly it had always been there lurking unrecognised beneath the brilliant gloss of gaiety, wit and high spirits he had always shown to the world in his younger days, an intrusive weed of self doubt that could so easily sully an otherwise faultlessly tended garden unless kept constantly under ruthless control. In later life he had identified this as his 'stamp of one defect' and realised that he could, in time, as Shakespeare's ill-fated Dane had put it, 'take corruption from that particular fault'.

But cursed with this defect though he might be, the blessings of talent, acute intelligence and, not least of all, tenacity, had been his to command at will and in full. They had enabled him to turn that potentially fatal weakness into an anvil of creativity on which, with the tools of his genius, he had been able to forge such amazing realities from those romantic fantasies he still called his 'Castles in Spain'.

So often had he flown furiously in the face of tradition, of basic technological theory, supposed fact and current thinking, yet been proved right against all apparent odds, that there was always the danger he might fall victim to the delusion of infallibility. Here, however, his weakness had again served him well, for he had always forced himself to be constantly aware of this fatal pitfall. Never, he had sworn, would he back himself into a cul-de-sac of complacency or a blind alley of bloody mindedness, as had so many before him. Not for him the role of a Telford. Always would he seek to picture the route ahead, and to anticipate what might be round every corner, hidden from view by the bends in the road. Always would he be alive to, though rarely heedful of, the 'informed public'; he was now too experienced a public figure to attach more importance than was warranted to mere popularity. The tiger, to him, was still a creature of totally unpredictable temperament of which but one fact was certain – never would it change its stripes.

Not even the launching of the *Great Britain* had fired the public imagination as had those truly fantastic record-shattering performances of Gooch's *Great Western*. As a result the newspapers had conferred on Brunel the rather obvious though fitting title 'Father of the broad gauge'. In their eyes, for the moment at least, he could do no wrong. Eagerly they, and his ever increasing army of ecstatic admirers, looked to the next marvel with which he was going to astound them, and the world.

'I'm sure some of these people think I produce what they choose to call miracles simply by waving some sort of magic wand,' he observed one evening after reading a particularly outlandish panegyric.

'And I sometimes wish you really did have such a thing,' Mary answered with rueful vehemence, fully aware that once fully recovered there would be nothing she or anyone else would be able to do to dissuade him from resuming the murderous pace that had so very nearly killed him.

The miracle so eagerly anticipated was the South Devon Atmospheric Railway, about which Mary had long since felt rather as her mother-in-law had felt about the Thames Tunnel nearly twenty years earlier. A month before *Great Western* had made her triumphant debut, the first stretch of the new line had come into service. It had been a sore disappointment in that for some time to come trains were to be hauled by conventional locomotives, installation of the actual atmospheric system having proved far more difficult than anyone could ever have imagined. This, of course, had delighted the project's many critics; but few of the still aggressively loyal pro-atmospheric faction entertained any really serious doubts that the problems, immense and manifold though they might be, could not and would not, in time, be solved.

Brunel, quietly confident of success, was as usual an inspiration to everyone else. But not even he was able to disguise the fact that he was more than a little depressed by the dismal rate of progress so far. Each day, it seemed, the difficulties haunting him mounted and multiplied. Only after months of tedious experiment had Tom Guppy managed to perfect a casting technique to produce the atmospheric pipe. Then followed endless delays in finding suitable caulking material for the joints. Manufacture of the longitudinal valve, from the finest oxhide leather, had also been fraught with difficulties, while the process of fitting it into the pipe had turned out to be an operation so tricky that only one or two of those entrusted with the task had yet been able to acquire the necessary skill.

Then there was the complicated arrangement of valves at every station and engine house. Entrance valves, exit valves, separating valves, control valves, isolating valves, all to be constructed with meticulous precision, installed and tested, the perfect operation of each vital to success. Not least of the countless causes of infuriating delay were the complex contrivances at every level crossing to protect the atmospheric pipe and its vulnerable longitudinal valve from the hooves of animals and the wheels of vehicles.

Eight engine houses, at three-mile intervals along the line – at Exeter, Countess Weir, Turf, Starcross, Dawlish, Teignmouth, Summer House and Newton Abbot – had been completed on time. The pumping engines made by Boulton & Watt, Maudslay Son & Field and the Rennie Brothers had all been installed, though as yet only the first three had been fully tested and were actually working satisfactorily.

But if everything else had appeared to conspire to hamper progress, the weather for once had been ideal. With a will born of physical contentment, the navvies had toiled tirelessly from dawn to dusk under clear skies and in brilliant sunshine, and often through the hours of darkness by the light of flares. The black britszka, the famous 'flying hearse,' had become as familiar a sight on the roads between Plymouth and Exeter as it had been on the Buckinghamshire, Berkshire, Wiltshire and Gloucestershire highways and byways ten and more years before.

Because Isambard was having to spend so much time on the South Devon, Mary had insisted on their renting a furnished house for the summer and autumn at Torquay, the new seaside resort which since the advent of the railway had been yearly increasing in popularity. It was the first time she had ever accompanied her husband in the field, as it were, and she took infinite pains not to interfere in any way with his work. But whenever she could she would persuade him to devote a little of his time to her, and on such occasions insisted they explore together that beautiful stretch of Devon coast. So it was they had discovered Watcombe, a tiny village perched high above Babbacombe Bay from which the views of both sea and landscape were breathtakingly beautiful.

'If ever you do build that house you've always dreamed of,' Mary remarked as they picnicked near the village one balmy Sunday afternoon in September, 'this would make the perfect setting.'

'I do believe you're right,' Isambard agreed. Until that moment his mind had been occupied exclusively with the latest atmospheric problem, but at Mary's words he deliberately put all thought of work from him and looked anew at his surroundings. Then he looked at his wife. In a plain but exquisitely cut gown of white muslin, hatless so that the sunlight glinted lustrously on her thick casually dressed russet-coloured hair, she could have stepped out of a Watteau painting. Never had she seemed more beautiful, and he was aware of a sudden resurgence of the passion he had once felt for her. Memories, either long forgotten or sadly forsaken, began to crowd his brain. He recalled their first meeting just before the Bristol riots; the day he had driven her and her sisters home to Kensington Gravel Pits in his new britszka; the rose garden at High Row with its wonderfully fragrant blooms on that September Sunday and his quite unfounded jealousy of Felix Mendelssohn-Bartholdy whose latest composition 'Elijah' had been given but a few months before at the Birmingham Festival. He remembered it was as he had walked back to his rooms in Parliament Street that same night, that he had decided life without Mary Horsley would be unimaginable. Then, with an acute twinge of conscience, he thought of what their life together had been.

Though he had always provided for her every want and whim without question or quibble or even a word of criticism, he knew he had failed her as a husband. Perhaps in many ways she had failed him as a wife, though he had to admit she had always been there when he'd needed her. The trouble was, he had seldom needed her. So he had ignored her. He thought then of his father and his mother. Always Marc and Sophia had been together, devoted to each other, needing each other – he adoring her, she worshipping him. They were now both approaching their eighties, but still they could sit alone for hours in utter contentment with their hands clasped, smiling secretly like two young lovers.

That he and Mary could ever be so close, or indeed would ever wish to be, was doubtful. But they could surely be so much more to each other than they had been hitherto. Perhaps a house here at Watcombe was what they needed. If they could get away from Duke Street and all that it meant, right away from London and all London stood for, who could tell how their future relationship might not develop.

Nothing further was said on the subject; but the next day Isambard contacted an agent in Torquay and, on being informed the owners were open to offer, immediately began negotiations for that very piece of rich red land with which they had both fallen so much in love. Within a few days a price had been agreed and a contract of sale drawn up. When he told her what he had done, Mary's beauty became positively radiant, such was her sheer joy.

'Oh, my darling!' she cried ecstatically. 'I hoped, oh, if only you knew how I hoped! But I never thought you really would.'

'And I never thought you would want to leave Duke Street.'

'Yes,' she agreed, grave for a moment at the thought of her past foolishness, 'there was a time . . . but that's all over. I've learned there are other things far more important than social position and fashionable style.'

'Oh, Mary,' he took her in his arms, 'I too have learned a great deal over these past years.'

That night their new found happiness brought them together for the first time in many months; and afterwards they talked excitedly till dawn like a pair of starry-eyed newlyweds about the house he would build for her and about their future together.

But the idyll was rudely shattered the very next day when Bennett, Isambard's personal secretary who should have been holding the fort at Duke Street, arrived unexpectedly. He had come down on the morning train to Exeter then ridden posthaste the twenty-two miles to Torquay.

'Forgive the intrusion, Ma'am,' he gasped hoarsely as he burst into Mary's sitting room without waiting to be announced or even doff his dust-covered hat. 'Mr Brunel, where is Mr Brunel? I must see him as soon as possible. They told me in Exeter I'd find him here.'

'Mr Bennett! Whatever's happened? What's the matter?' Mary

asked in alarm, for the look on the secretary's deathly pale face frightened her.

'I've news for the master, Ma'am. Terrible news! If he's not here tell me at once where he can be found. I must get to him without delay.'

No longer a young man, he was close to total exhaustion and could hardly stand. Mary seized him by the arm, led him protesting to a chair and forced him to sit down.

'My husband will be at the Turf engine house. Please rest, Mr Bennett, and compose yourself. He shall be sent for immediately. And I shall order some tea which you,' she pushed him back into the chair as he shook his head and made to rise 'shall take and without argument. But first, can you not tell me this terrible news?'

'Aye Ma'am,' the secretary's voice was weary and choked with emotion. 'It's *Great Britain*, she's lost, and with all hands . . . wrecked on the coast of Ireland!'

Chapter Six

THE news was not quite as bad as Bennett had reported. But it was bad enough. Following her extensive refit in the Liverpool dry dock, *Great Britain* had been in service again since May and, apart from some minor problems, had steadily consolidated her position as the new Atlantic Queen. On 22 September she had left Liverpool for her fifth crossing with no less than one hundred and eighty passengers aboard – not as many as she could accommodate, it was true, but the greatest number ever carried by a transatlantic steamer nevertheless. The fervent hopes of her now sorely pressed owners that she was at last the immensely profitable investment they had for so long dreamed she could be, seemed about to be fulfilled.

The weather when she sailed had not been good and was rapidly deteriorating. But bad weather held no terrors for *Great Britain*; already in her short career she had encountered the very worst even the Atlantic was thought capable of producing. None on board had suffered any undue inconvenience or indeed excessive discomfort, even though by midnight a truly terrifying storm had been raging. Then, in the small hours of the morning, the ship had been driven hard onto the treacherous rock-strewn sands of Dundrum Bay.

Any other vessel must indeed have been lost, more than likely with all hands in so fierce a tempest, and the ill tidings Bennett had carried to Torquay in all good faith had been based on that assumption. But all aboard *Great Britain* had survived, and the ship, though sorely hurt, was far from lost. However, stranded on that storm-torn shore her days must surely be numbered.

How she came to be there was a mystery. Just before she'd gone aground Captain Hosken and his navigating officer had been convinced they were about to round the southern tip of the Isle of Man. When dawn broke they had been flabbergasted to find themselves confronted, not as they had expected with the familiar contours of the Calf, but with the unforgettable sight of the

Mountains of Mourne, looking at that moment anything but beautiful, sweeping menacingly down to a still ferociously white-capped sea. With the dawn had also come rescue for the passengers; the ship, however, helplessly marooned with stern and port quarter dangerously exposed to once more worsening weather sweeping in from the south-west, was already badly holed in at least two places. It was imperative she too be rescued just as quickly as humanly possible.

'But you can't go to Ireland,' a near desperate Mary Brunel remonstrated with her husband following the emergency meeting of the Great Western Steamship board hurriedly convened in Bristol the day after Bennett's appearance at Torquay, by which time a dispatch from Hosken had been received.

'I most certainly can't,' he agreed, but not, she knew, from any consideration either for her or for himself. The situation on the South Devon was such that Isambard dare not risk an absence of more than twenty-four hours at any one time. He was, in fact, intending to return to Exeter, where his britzska would be waiting for him, first thing the following morning by special train. 'No, Claxton will have to go. And, I'm very sorry my dear,' he gave her a wry smile, 'but I'm afraid I'm going to spend most of the night briefing him.'

Oh, damn the ship! And damn the South Devon Railway! And damn Tom Guppy too for choosing this of all times, to go abroad, Mary thought bitterly, realising that all her efforts to nurse Issy back to health could now so easily come to nothing. No sooner had she managed to persuade him to a relatively normal existence than something like this had to happen to put him back on the murderous treadmill. But instead of making a scene as she might once have done, she merely smiled her understanding and encouragement.

By the time Claxton got to Dundrum Bay, Hosken, having lightened the ship as much as possible, had already made several attempts to refloat her. No tide had yet been high enough, but the spring tide due on the 28th should produce sufficient depth. It was the last chance they would get that year. The tide was even higher than forecast, but just before it reached full flood a southerly gale of quite malevolent fury sprang up, piling the incoming water into huge waves that pounded the ship like monstrous battering rams. Any attempt to float her free in such dreadful conditions would have been nothing less than completely disastrous. Claxton therefore ordered sail to be set so that the gale could drive her further up the beach and out of the reach of the destructive water, for not even *Great Britain* could have long survived such punishment.

The problem now became one of preservation. Hurriedly Claxton secured the services of James Bremner, the shipbuilder and salvage expert whose reputation for toughness and unorthodox invention when faced with apparent impossibilities was second to none, while from Bristol was summoned William Patterson who, having built her, knew more about *Great Britain* than anyone. The combination of Bremner's experience and Patterson's knowledge, Claxton reasoned, should at least achieve something. It did not.

Not until December did Isambard manage to get away from the mounting worries of the South Devon only to find his beautiful creation a rusting and all but abandoned hulk kicking about on the most exposed shore it was possible to imagine, as if she was of no greater value than a broken saucepan carelessly thrown away on Brighton beach. It was poor Hosken who quite undeservedly took the full brunt of his fury as he made a thorough survey of both ship and situation. That night, in the local tavern which served them as temporary headquarters, it was the turn of Claxton, Patterson and Bremner.

'Does the ship still belong to the company?' he demanded scathingly of a dispirited and utterly weary Claxton after scornfully dismissing as futile all the efforts of the last three heartbreaking months.

'Indeed, she does,' Claxton sighed, wishing at that precise moment she did not.

'And for protection, if not for removal, is the company still free to act without the underwriters?' Brunel persisted. Time was rapidly running out. Negotiations, the result of Bremner's last report to the effect that nothing more could be done to save the ship, were already in progress in Bristol – hence his flying visit to Ireland. But the answer, for the moment, was 'yes'.

'Very well. Then if we have no more than ordinary luck and comparative freedom from storms for the next three weeks, I have little or no anxiety about the ship.' All three stared at him in silent amazement, scarcely able to believe they had heard aright.

'But, my dear Brunel . . .' Claxton started to protest.

'I tell you, she is as straight and virtually as sound as she ever was,' eyes blazing, the engineer angrily interrupted. 'The very first glimpse I had of her was enough to satisfy me that above her five- or six-foot waterline she is as true as ever. Indeed, she is still beautiful to look at. How can she be talked of the way she has been,' here he glared at Bremner, 'as a wreck, a write-off, a valueless hulk?'

Red of face and breathing heavily, Bremner opened his mouth to say something, but was given no chance to put his outraged thoughts into words.

'And by you, of all people,' Brunel rounded on Claxton. 'It's positively cruel, like taking away the character of a young woman without any grounds whatever.'

'Now come! That's easy enough to say, but . . .'

'But, nothing. I tell you, apart from being much bruised and holed in several places, that ship is perfect. Even within three feet of the largest rupture, there is no evidence at all of strain or other injury.'

'She's taken considerable punishment to her stern,' William Patterson, who till that moment had wisely maintained the most diplomatic of silences, ventured tentatively.

'I grant you that!' Brunel glared again at Bremner. 'And largely because of the failure of the quack remedies tried so far.' Again he gave the red-faced Scot no time to speak. 'But that's not important except to point to the necessity for extra precaution if she is to be saved. Do you not agree?' But given his chance at last, the most Bremner could manage was an eloquent snort and a brief nod.

'I say "if", gentlemen,' continued Brunel passionately, his fury once more beginning to flare, 'because when I saw her lying unprotected and abandoned by those who ought to know her value, the finest ship in the world and in such condition when four or five thousand pounds would be more than enough to repair all the damage done to her, I felt you all intended from the start she should die where she lay.'

'Never!' cried Patterson.

'Not so, by God!' Claxton swore. 'And what's more, you know it!'

'Aye, Kit,' Isambard's anger was spent at last and he gripped Claxton by the shoulder in apology, 'I know it. But the question still remains, why are we wasting time? Dammit, the steed is being quietly stolen from under our very noses while we sit here discussing the relative merits of a Bramah or Chubb lock that should have been put on the stable door.'

'Then I take it you have a solution to the problem of how to protect your ship?' Bremner asked, still seething at having been taken so unceremoniously to task, but nonetheless ready and willing to co-operate to the best of his ability. As usual Isambard's keen perception had immediately enabled him to grasp the significance of detail the others had overlooked. To build a breakwater, as Bremner had valiantly but vainly attempted, was to him an obvious impossibility.

'Yes Bremner, I have. I should lash faggots together in bundles, skewer these bundles together with iron rods and weight them down with iron, sandbags or whatever, then wrap the mass round her with chains like a huge poultice, under her stern and half way up her length on her sea side.'

Claxton seemed far from convinced that this would prove any more successful. But the frowning Scot, after taking a moment or two to conjure a full mental picture, signified his agreement with another curt nod.

'It sounds feasible to me,' Patterson answered Isambard's questioning look.

'Very well,' Claxton gave in, 'we can but try.'

'Good,' said Brunel, well satisfied with even that grudging agreement. Then, typically, he added, 'I went with Hosken to Lord Roden's agent this afternoon. They will start delivering the faggots first thing tomorrow morning. I'll leave the procuring of the rest of the material you'll need to you, Bremner.'

During December, locomotive operation on the South Devon had been extended as far as Newton Abbot. Then, early in January 1847 came the moment everyone had been waiting for; the first atmospheric trains were put into service between Exeter and Turf.

It was a modest start, but all things considered a reasonably impressive one which, inevitably, had to be suitably commemorated.

To the layman it seemed indeed a miracle. The ride was everything people had been led to believe it would be – smooth and eerily silent even at speeds of over sixty miles per hour. Crowds flocked to Exeter daily to throng the South Devon railway station, vying with each other to travel back and forth and then again, just to be able to say they had.

When the trains ran, they ran very well indeed. But, alas, after only a few days' operation the incidence of breakdowns was such as to render any semblance of a reliable service out of the question. The atmospheric trains were withdrawn. The consequent return to locomotive operation, it was emphasised, would only be temporary. But as the crowds, disappointed and not a little disillusioned, dispersed, Brunel and his equally disappointed team grimly applied themselves to what a growing number of hitherto passionate supporters of the atmospheric system were beginning to suspect might, after all, prove an impossible task.

Nor did that new year at first bring good news from Ireland. Despite all efforts to lash the bundles of faggots together and weight them down, the fast-running sea had scoured the ground beneath so quickly that all had been swept away before they could be effectively secured.

'If anything,' Claxton concluded his sorry tale of frustrating failure, 'we've progressed even less than when trying to build Bremner's breakwater.'

Isambard dismissed this reference with a shake of his head. 'This is a practical solution,' he declared.

'Perhaps in theory. But that's all, I can assure you. I've seen the results for myself, or rather the lack of same. You haven't.'

But Brunel remained adamant. 'I'm sorry to have to put it like this,' he said quietly, 'but the real fact is that you have failed so far for the simple reason you have not done enough to succeed.' Silencing what would have been Claxton's indignant denial that this could be so, he went on, 'And that, my friend, is what causes nine-tenths of all failure in this world. The one principle that can be relied on, is to formulate one plan and stick to it.'

'Even when the plan is wrong?' Claxton's tone was harshly sarcastic, but seemingly it went unnoticed.

'No, when it is proved to be wrong, I change it . . . but not until then. And until I change it I concentrate everything on that one plan. Similarly, I stick to one single method to make that plan work, before I allow myself to be diverted in any way.'

'Yes, yes, yes,' Claxton was in no mood for a lecture, 'that's all very fine, but this situation. . . .'

'. . . is no different from any other. Believe me, you have only to stick to that one point of attack and keep on attacking. If the force at first is not sufficient then use ten times as much, then ten times as much again. If a six-bundle faggot won't reach out of the water, try a twenty-bundle one; and if hundredweights won't hold the thing down, use tons.'

It worked . . . just as he had said it would. Once the foundation had been established, the protective screen – Brunel's 'poultice' – was quickly raised. The result was immediate and astonishing, the relentless force of the pounding seas far more effectually broken than ever it could have been by Bremner's breakwater. But even with the poultice in place, *Great Britain*'s ordeal was far from over.

Heedless of the fact he might well be using up those last reserves of strength which had so recently been all that had saved him from the grave, Isambard was again working round the clock and daily driving himself mercilessly to the very limit. Mary, in turn worried sick about his health, or furious because of his stubborn refusal to listen to reason, had long since returned to London, her continued presence at Torquay, in the circumstances, pointless. On tenterhooks she waited for news of the railway, news of the ship. Each day without word from south Devon was an endless torment, while every letter delivered to Duke Street became, until opened, an unbearable agony of anticipation.

Even though involved with the children once more – young Isambard was eight, Henry nearly seven and Florence five – and with her now onerous social duties to perform, as always with the utmost punctilio, she found she still had insufficient to keep her from worrying. With the perfection of her looks seemingly unimpaired either by age or circumstances, she appeared unaffected by, almost indifferent to, the ebb or flow of her husband's fortunes. But now more truly the wife of Isambard Brunel than ever she had been before, Mary's love for Issy and her concern for him mounted daily.

When, towards the end of spring, the time came to commence preparations for the long awaited attempt to refloat *Great Britain*, it was discovered that the foundations of her protective poultice had become so firmly consolidated in the surrounding sand that only with the greatest difficulty could they be broken up and removed. It was, Claxton reported, a rock-like mass quite as stubborn as the hardest granite.

Once the poultice had been removed, the ship's bows had to be raised by the infinitely laborious process of driving wedges of timber under her on the full flood of every tide. As soon as they became accessible, the holes in her bottom were patched to reduce the inflow of water to a rate that hopefully could be controlled by hand pumps, her engines and steam auxiliaries having been dismantled and removed. When judged sufficiently seaworthy she was to be warped from her resting place on the beach, floated on a spring tide over the reef on which she had originally foundered, then towed to Liverpool and dry dock to undergo a second and even more costly refit.

Many dreary weeks of bitter disappointment, however, were to drag by before nature obliged with an adequately high tide, and even then the huge, helplessly wallowing and scarcely controllable mass cleared the terrifying obstacle of those rocks with just inches to spare.

HMS Victory and *HMS Birkenhead* were standing by to take her in tow, but she was leaking so badly that Claxton wisely decided to beach her again so that she could be pumped as clear as possible before attempting a crossing of the always potentially treacherous Irish Sea. Though the hard-worked pump gangs were only just able to hold their own, the voyage proved uneventful. But the convoy reached its destination just in time, for no sooner had the ship been manoeuvred into position than she sank like a stone onto the gridiron the instant the pumps were stopped. *Great Britain* had been saved, hopefully to sail the Atlantic again. When that might be, however, no one could say.

Good news from Ireland was matched by good news from the West Country. From the beginning of September, four atmospheric trains a day in each direction again began to operate between Exeter and Teignmouth with reasonable regularity. Four months later the service was extended to Newton Abbot. Again to the general public it seemed success was just around the corner, and again hopes rose.

'Notwithstanding numerous difficulties, I think we are in a fair way of shortly overcoming the mechanical defects with which we have been so plagued and bringing the whole apparatus into regular and efficient working,' was how Brunel prefaced his report to the South Devon board that February. He went on, 'As soon as it is possible to guarantee good and efficient communication between the engine houses and thus ensure a proper regularity in the working of the engines, we shall be in a position to test accurately the overall economy of the system.' The new Wheatstone & Cooke telegraph, installed now throughout the length of the line, had been subject to almost as many infuriating delays as had the railway itself.

The report continued: 'At present this is not possible owing to the want of the telegraph compelling us to keep the engines almost constantly at work, and for this the boiler power is not really sufficient. The consequence is that we are not only working the engines nearly double the time required, the boiler fires must be constantly forced which, of course, means an irregular and excessive consumption of fuel. There is, however, every prospect this evil will be removed. When it is, then and only then will the atmospheric become the subject of actual experiment and its value practically tested. Until it is I shall refrain from offering any further observations on it.'

The report was accepted almost without question, even by those who made no secret of the fact they suspected its author of having astutely side-stepped the question now paramount in all minds – was the atmospheric 'caper', as Devon had dubbed it, really a viable proposition? Or, despite all its most illustrious champion had achieved, was it in the end going to turn out to be only the nine days' wonder its critics had damned from the start? The answers, most definitely, lay not in that report.

It had long been accepted that all such official reports of progress tended to err on the side of optimism. There were in any engineering undertaking subtleties of technicality the average lay mind was incapable of comprehending and of which it was best, therefore, left in ignorance. Neither was it unknown for a less than scrupulous engineer, finding himself in a temporary tight corner, blatantly to make use of outrageously sophistical explanations of facts and events in order to bluff his way out of trouble.

Isambard had always frowned on such questionable tactics. Throughout his career he had taken justifiable pride in leaving facts to speak for themselves, his comments serving a purely interpretative function. This was the first time he had been forced to indulge in what he inwardly scorned as vague ambiguities and deliberate evasions. That he had done so in a desperate attempt to buy time, and for no other reason, in no wise eased his feelings of guilt and self-betrayal or, for that matter, altered the fact that the atmospheric service could only just be maintained.

Before a rising flood of trouble that was rapidly assuming the proportion of a tidal wave, a less determined man would probably have long ago given up the struggle. But the word 'defeat' never had nor ever would find a place in Isambard's vocabulary.

'There comes a time in every man's life when, no matter what the price may be to his pride, discretion really is the better part of valour,' Sir Marc, frail in body but still remarkably strong in mind, tried vainly to reason with his son. But Isambard had made his decision, and nothing could persuade him to change it. In the same way that *Great Britain* had been saved against all odds, he argued stubbornly, so would the South Devon Atmospheric Railway be brought to eventual success. All he needed to do was to follow his own advice as faithfully as Claxton had done in Ireland and he could not fail.

Regardless of the force applied this time, however, the troubles only multiplied. The auxiliary piston device used to start the trains continued to cause mishaps without number; the valves in the atmospheric pipe played havoc with the piston-cup leathers; water accumulated in the pipe from excessive condensation with disastrous results; and lack of communication between stations wasn't the primary reason for having to overload the pumping engines so uneconomically, it was the totally unpredictable failures of the longitudinal valve – a gap of but a thousandth of an inch being equivalent to no less than the fifteen-inch diameter of the pipe itself over the distance of one mile.

Indeed, as Robert Stephenson had predicted, it was that continuous valve, its efficiency dependent on a constant airtight seal, that was the crux of the whole system. It was seated in a shallow trough filled with a special sealing compound, originally a mixture of beeswax and tallow which had proved so unsatisfactory during hot weather that it had been replaced with a lime-soap based composition. On exposure to light and air, however, this had formed a hard skin and so had been replaced by a less viscous compound of cod-oil and soap, which in turn had proved unsatisfactory because it tended to be sucked into the pipe every time the valve opened and had therefore to be continually replenished. Then, to top all, rats had started to eat the leather.

But there was even worse to come. The winter had been unusually mild. Not until the last days of February was there even a hint of frost. But at its very first touch the longitudinal valve froze. Only then was it realised that the repeated action of the vacuum had gradually robbed it of so much natural oil content that the leather had become pervious to water. It took no expert to realise that, far from being the semi-permanent installation around which the whole system was planned and constructed, the valve had a useful life at the most to be measured in months rather than in years. Once it had begun to absorb moisture, the leather became virtually useless. Already there were signs of it beginning to tear and it was only a matter of time before the whole length would rot away. Before the line could even be finished a complete replacement would have to be installed. And that, at a cost of £25,000, made the whole thing impossible.

The party at 18 Duke Street to celebrate the ignominious demise of the Chartists following the April fiasco of 1848 was but one of many held in nearly every house, great and small, in fashionable London. But this one was unique in that it also marked the recent award of a KCB to Ben Hawes, who appeared to be approaching the zenith of a distinguished career.

'It is an honour thoroughly deserved and of which we are all infinitely proud,' Mary Brunel told her husband's brother-in-law perhaps a trifle primly as they danced together in the ballroom Isambard had built after acquiring the house next door and substantially extending No 18 a couple of years before. She spoke with genuine sincerity. In no way did she actually begrudge Ben his fine reward. But at the same time she could not stifle completely the feeling that Issy's far more substantial achievements were more worthy of such recognition. Nor could she put from her mind entirely the thought that, but for his recent appalling reversal of fortune with the now accepted failure of the South Devon Atmospheric Railway capped only days later by the doom-laden announcement that the Great Western Steamship Company had at last been forced into liquidation, she too might have been able to call herself 'Lady Brunel'. Truly she had tried so very hard not to be jealous of Sophia Hawes; but she had not altogether succeeded.

'What will you do now?' Sophia asked her brother as the two couples sat talking quietly after the last of the evening's guests had departed.

'I'm not sure,' Isambard replied, though he had, of course, given the matter a great deal of thought. There was the distinct possibility that the two catastrophes, coming as they had so quickly one after the other, could despite all that had gone before ruin him professionally. Who could tell?

Mary was beside him on the sofa. On a sudden impulse he reached for her hand and grasped it tightly. Never had he done such a thing before. She looked at him quickly, her expression startled, for the moment quite disconcerted. Then slowly her features softened into a smile that answered his.

'I think,' he went on quietly, 'I'm not by any means certain, mind, but I think there is a strong possibility that I may retire.'

PART FOUR

February 1856 – September 1859

Chapter One

'YOU may possibly have heard of a project on which I am at present engaged,' Isambard Brunel declared testily, his words bitter with uncharacteristic sarcasm, 'the construction of a rather large steamboat?'

Sir Benjamin Brodie, in no wise intimidated, merely grunted noncommittally, peered over his spectacles at the small figure furiously pacing the carpet of his Wimpole Street consulting room and quietly repeated, 'You have, as usual, been working far too hard for far too long,' a pause, 'you're not getting any younger, you know.'

'I am not yet fifty.'

'No, but from the look of you you'd be lucky to pass for an ageing sixty-five.' A longer pause this time, the silence broken only by the regular creak of a loose floorboard beneath the restless pacer's feet.

'Man, I beg you to listen to reason,' Brodie said at last. 'What you need is rest, urgently – desperately! You hear me? And by rest I mean a complete break. A holiday abroad somewhere, a long holiday!'

Brunel ignored him and continued pacing, his left hand, tightly clenched, pressed hard into the small of his back beneath his coat tails, his right clutching a half-smoked cigar that had long ago gone out. Shoulders hunched, chin sunk deep in the cleft of his high-winged collar and with features grimly set, he sought vainly to ignore the dull but persistent discomfort of his aching body. He had come to Brodie that afternoon in a last desperate bid for at least some relief from his misery, only to be told there was nothing more to be done for him unless he was prepared to vegetate somewhere in the sun for at least three months, something he could not even begin to contemplate.

'Furthermore,' Brodie went on ominously, 'if you continue to ignore my advice I cannot and will not, either as your physician or your friend, be responsible for the consequences.'

249

Stiffly, awkwardly, his movements those of a tired old man, Isambard lowered himself into the chair which now stood fully in the shaft of pale winter sunlight that had advanced from the window during that long, at times acrimonious and now seemingly pointless, consultation. He tossed his dead cigar impatiently into the ashtray – a strict non-smoker, the surgeon always made certain of having several strategically placed whenever Brunel visited him – selected another from a waistcoat pocket and, with hands that trembled, struck a match.

Brodie's keen gaze never wavered from those unhealthily puffy features which by the light of the match seemed paler than ever. The man was obviously ailing, had been for months; and could only get worse. By now his kidneys must be in a shocking state. There was, after all, a limit to what could be done with medicines, and that limit had long been passed. Prolonged and absolute rest was his last, his only, hope.

Brunel, cigar satisfactorily alight, caught Brodie's eye and, smiling wearily, he slowly shook his head.

'It's no good, Ben. I simply can't afford to be out of touch with this business, not even for three days, never mind three months.'

'You're a damn fool. You know that, don't you. You do realise the risk you're running?'

'After all you've said this afternoon, how could I possibly be in any doubt?'

'Hmm,' Brodie grunted again, accepting at last what he had really known all along was inevitable. The Brunel mind, once made up, was unchangeable. 'Well, I can't force you to be sensible, you must do as you think fit. But I give you this solemn and final warning – if you wish to continue in this life the time is fast approaching when you'll have no choice but to damn well do as you're told. And when you do I can only pray to God, my friend, you won't have left it too late.'

Needless to say Isambard had not retired, though for some time following the disasters of 1848 he had indeed toyed with the idea of doing so once his crossing of the river Tamar, the last link in the broad gauge to Cornwall, had been achieved. But the near catastrophic financial crash the very next year, which abruptly brought to an end the era of railway mania and deservedly beggared many of its ruthless proponents, so radically changed the climate he had had very serious second thoughts. Then had come involvement in preparations for the Great Exhibition, in which the broad gauge, and in particular Gooch's *Great Western*, was prominently featured. One thing inevitably leading to another, this in turn sparked a new interest which culminated in what he had sarcastically described to Brodie as 'a rather large steamboat'.

In 1851 gold was discovered in Kalgoorlie. Before the year was out the rush was on. Hitherto little thought of despite the closure of the penal settlements, suddenly no one could get to Australia quickly enough. Sailing ships took months, and even steamers like *Great Britain* successfully flying the flag of her new owners Gibbs, Bright & Company of Liverpool were severely handicapped by having to bunker at innumerable coaling stations en route. Though by then fully involved with the Saltash project, as well as the building of the grand terminus and hotel at Paddington to provide the broad gauge with a gateway to the capital to surpass Hardwicke's undeniably splendid narrow-gauge citadel in Euston Square, when consulted by the Australian Mail Company Isambard was unable to resist the temptation. For that dauntingly long haul round the Cape of Good Hope he recommended a vessel nearly twice the size of *Great Britain*. It was, he'd endeavoured to explain to his horrified clients, merely a question of horses for courses. *Great Britain*, like *Great Western* – now, alas, no more; her useful life at an end, she had recently been broken up – had been specifically designed for the transatlantic service. For the Australian run she was simply too small.

Twelve months passed before this 'most impractical proposition' had even been seriously considered by the timid board of the Australian Mail Company, by which time Brunel had progressed to the concept of a vessel not twice, but a staggering six times the size of *Great Britain* – a vessel big enough to carry fuel for a voyage from England to Australia and back. She would, he reasoned, be cheaper to construct than two smaller ships, would be faster and more economical to operate, having eliminated entirely the crippling expense of establishing, manning, supplying and maintaining overseas bunkering facilities.

For the Australian Mail Company this had been just too much. Nor had he entertained really serious expectation that any established shipping line could be persuaded to commit itself to such a project. But at the suggestion of John Scott Russell, a London shipbuilder, in the late spring of 1852 an approach was made to the Eastern Steam Navigation Company. Formed only the previous year with the aim of establishing steamer routes to India, China and Australia, Eastern Steam Navigation, having lost the vital government mail contract to the arch rival Peninsular & Oriental Steam Navigation Company, was already in desperate straits. Nor did its decision to back the 'great ship venture,' as it had come to be called, save it from eventual extinction. At the end of a series of bitter boardroom battles that raged for two interminable years, only the name of the company remained. A new board consisted mostly of Brunel's nominees while its far from adequate capital had had to be bolstered by the bulk of his personal fortune. Never before had he been so heavily committed financially, never so deeply involved with the day to day administration, and never so alone.

Sir Marc had died in December 1849, a keen loss to the son he had so ably assisted for so long. That same year Tom Guppy had decided to live permanently abroad and shortly afterwards Kit Claxton, by then nearing seventy, had retired. This was when young Isambard, nearly sixteen now, should have been ready to serve his father as his father had served Sir Marc. But the boy, totally and tragically denied the talents of sire and grandsire by the inexplicable caprice of fate, was quite unfitted to do so, while Henry, though more fortunately blessed, was still too young.

To replace his lost stalwarts, Isambard had turned to John Scott Russell, a graduate of both Glasgow and Edinburgh universities and a co-founder of the Great Exhibition. Secretary to the Society of Arts, vice-President of the Institution of Civil Engineers and of the Institute of Naval Architects, of which he was also a co-founder, in the late forties he had acquired William Fairburn's old shipyard on the Isle of Dogs and had since enhanced an already wide reputation. His had been the tender Eastern Steam had eventually accepted to build *Leviathan*, as she was to be called.

But brilliant though the rather unctuous Glaswegian undoubtedly was, Mary Brunel could neither tolerate nor trust him. For her husband's sake she fought hard to conquer her antipathy; but she simply could not rid herself of an oppressive foreboding that for once Issy's hitherto near-infallible judgement of human nature had

252

somehow failed him. All too soon was she to be proved right.

The *Leviathan* contract, which was signed on 22 December 1853, provided for the construction, launch, trial and delivery of an iron ship of the general dimensions of 680 feet between perpendiculars, 83-foot beam (excluding paddle boxes) and 58 feet deep, according to the drawings of I. K. Brunel, the engineer, who was to have entire control at all times over all proceedings and workmanship.

Russell's yard being far too small, Eastern Steam acquired the lease of an adjoining frontage and built a railway to connect the two, the keel to be laid on the leased frontage leaving the Russell premises free for all manufacturing works. The ship would be launched sideways, which immediately prompted a sneering clamour from the press; since the South Devon débâcle few of the fourth estate had been able to resist any opportunity to ridicule what they delighted in describing as Brunel's madcap schemes. But there was no other way a ship of such size could be launched in that confined waterway. In any case, to have built on a conventional slipway, even with a maximum incline of only 1 in 12, would have sent the vessel's forefoot towering to the unmanageable height of forty feet or more. But, the predatory doubters persisted, once built, how was the ship to be moved over three hundred feet to the water's edge before she could be launched? By means of a mechanical slipway, was the answer. This Brunel would design, to be afterwards dismantled, removed to the vessel's home port and there re-erected for the purpose of carrying out all future maintenance and repairs, there being no dry dock in existence big enough.

Towards the end of June 1854, all preliminaries having been completed in record time, construction began. For the next two years, to the never ceasing clang of iron hammers on iron plate, the gigantic structure at Millwall gradually clawed its way upward until it dominated, to the exclusion of practically everything else, not only London's skyline but nearly every aspect of the capital's, nay the country's, life. Brunel's latest miracle was in the making.

The public had immediately dubbed her *Great Eastern* and soon seemingly endless varieties of souvenirs were being sold, including hopelessly inaccurate lithographs, elaborately framed and gaudily coloured. *Great Eastern* songs, waltzes, galops, polkas and marches were being churned out by Charing Cross Road hacks, while there was even a 'Great Eastern ABC' to teach children how to read.

A lengthy newspaper article which appeared towards the end of November, was the first intimation that all was perhaps not as it should be. Already there had been published a deal of wordy nonsense about the ship, of how, were she to be placed adjacent to this or that London landmark she would, in length and breadth, reach from here to there and top the height by so much of such-and-such a familiar edifice – the customary meaningless comparisons so beloved of popular journalism and so haphazardly indulged. But this particular article was markedly different, its author obviously well briefed, though pointedly omitting to name or even hint at his source. Curiously, Brunel's name was mentioned but once, and then only almost in passing. Mr John Scott Russell, on the other hand, merited considerably more attention, being somewhat effusively described as the gallant engineer who had taken on the onerous task of executing the design and so on, the inference being that Brunel as 'consulting engineer' of Eastern Steam Navigation had merely sanctioned the adoption of plans suggested and brought to fruition by others. But who those 'others' might be was not disclosed.

Content to suffer rather than seek publicity, Isambard had always resisted the temptation to rise to the bait of provocative newspaper articles; in the past there had never been need to do other than ignore them. But none, as far as he could remember, had ever been characterised by such grossly deliberate misstatements or stamp of apparent authority as this article exhibited, and which could well result, as Mary had been quick to point out, in the piece acquiring the status of authorised statement and in time being accepted as such.

It was all very disturbing. And at the thought of the weary hours of mental and physical labour Issy had for three long years lavished on what he lovingly called his 'Great Babe,' not to mention the many sacrifices she had been called upon to make, Mary Brunel's eyes had positively flashed with fury. She had her suspicions of who might have been responsible for what was really nothing less than an outrage. But she chose, for the time being anyway, to keep them to herself.

Three months passed, during which a series of discreet inquiries produced no clue as to the identity of the article's instigator, but progress in the ship's building programme appeared to be continuing most satisfactorily. Then, suddenly, there came a glimmer of light that had made Mary's eyes flash once more.

Discussing in the drawing room at Duke Street the visit of the prince consort to Millwall during Brunel's absence in Birmingham for the casting in Watts' famous Soho Foundry of the first screw-engine cylinder, John Scott Russell, quite out of the blue, had remarked: 'I took the opportunity of explaining to his Royal Highness what I supposed he and everyone else knew – to wit that you, Mr Brunel, are the father of our great ship, not I.'

So startled had Isambard been by this curious observation, that before he could make a reply the other had continued: 'And while on the subject allow me to assure you, my dear Sir, I already have as much reputation as I desire.'

'And deserve, Mr Scott Russell,' Mary could not resist adding silkily.

'And, as you say, deserve, Ma'am.' But the slight bow he had affected as if in acceptance of a compliment, failed to mask from Mary the glint of eye which immediately convinced her that her suspicions had not been ill-founded.

At first, aware of her antipathy, Isambard refused to believe she could be right. But in spite of subsequent similar protestations it soon became all too apparent that Russell was, and always had been, almost insanely jealous. But what was even more disturbing was a sudden revelation of the truly chaotic state of his finances. Martin's Bank, it appeared, for the previous three months had been refusing him all credit facilities. Nor, apparently, had he taken any steps at all to stave off what must now be inevitable bankruptcy. Amazed by the discovery, Isambard could only wonder at the man's scarcely credible duplicity, and at his own past gullibility. But his Great Babe was his first and main concern. Mary, however, was already worrying about the additional strain this must now put on him.

Knowing her husband possibly even better than he knew himself, though once more bitterly disappointed she had been neither surprised nor dismayed by his decision not to retire. And despite the traumatic strain of those closing years of the preceding decade, his health had since held up remarkably well. Indeed, thanks probably to the stimulus of work, particularly the Paddington project, it seemed to have improved considerably. Initially, even this great ship venture, notwithstanding the fact that his unprecedented financial involvement had robbed her almost at the eleventh hour of any immediate hope of a fulfilment of their Watcombe plans, had provided that element of added zest on which Isambard thrived. To start with, therefore, Mary had been content once more to play second fiddle. But that was before the present spate of troubles had begun to mount and multiply, and exact their inevitable toll. The decline, once started, had been swift and frightening and, as before, it had opened a gap between them – a gap which Mary, no matter how hard she tried, was this time quite unable to bridge.

Besotted with his Great Babe, Isambard had callously cut himself off from both her and the children concealing, or at least attempting to conceal from them, the seriousness of his condition both physical and financial, deliberately keeping from his wife all knowledge of his repeated consultations with Brodie and other doctors, forbidding her to interfere in any way. Deeply hurt though she was by this wholly unreasoning and unreasonable attitude, she had persisted in her struggle to maintain at least the pretence of a domestic harmony that no longer existed. Such was the measure of her loyalty she never gave up, or admitted defeat; the price she paid, however, was her love.

The obvious course of action following such a gross betrayal would have been for Isambard to have sent Russell packing there and then. Most certainly that is what he would have done in the past. But to Mary's astonishment he temporised, arguing there could be no question of terminating Russell's contract to build *Leviathan*, that things had gone much too far for this to be feasible. True, the half-completed hull stood entirely on leased adjacent river frontage, but all the essential manufacturing equipment was in Russell's yard. Moreover, he and his senior shipwright and manager, Hepworth, were in possession of all working drawings. There were copies to be sure, but there could be no duplication of Hepworth's experience and intimate knowledge of the vessel – and Hepworth was Russell's creature.

So Eastern Steam were left with no option but to go bail, as it were, for Russell, and in order to do so immediately institute the strictest economies, for neither the company's nor Brunel's personal financial resources were anywhere near limitless. One of the first casualties was the planned mechanical slipway for the launch. 'Just let *Leviathan* slide into the river' was John Scott Russell's advice, which the Eastern Steam board seemed prepared, indeed anxious, to follow; for near bankrupt though he might be his reputation as a shipbuilding expert remained untarnished. Were the ship to be so launched there would indeed be a substantial saving, and one devoutly to be wished for it could ultimately represent a difference between make or break.

Brunel was horrified, and quite beside himself with rage. It was, he fumed, unthinkable. It would be nothing less than criminal if such an immense mass were permitted uncontrolled movement for any distance at all, let alone to slide freely down a 1 in 12 three-hundred-foot slope to plunge into a restricted waterway. The possible consequences of such unmitigated folly could not even be imagined. 'Whatever the means employed,' he insisted, 'the launch, from the start and at all times, must be meticulously controlled.'

The last thing he had needed at that particular juncture had been any form of distraction. But when Sir Benjamin Hawes, then Permanent Under-secretary at the War Office, asked his brother-in-law's assistance in alleviating the dreadful sufferings of the sick and wounded from the Crimea, he promptly put everything else to one side. In less than a fortnight he had produced a comprehensive set of plans for a prefabricated, fully equipped, self-contained thousand-bed hospital easily adaptable to a variety of different ground conditions. He had then taken it upon himself to supervise personally, and largely at his own expense, its production, packing and shipment, not to Scutari as had at first been intended, but to Renkioi whither one of his assistants had already been sent.

From first to last the whole operation took less than six months – a miraculous achievement indeed, and one that, but for Brunel's inspired bullying of bemused and bumbling officialdom, would never have been possible. In the end, nearly two thousand men were to owe him their lives.

But dealing with petty-minded muddle-headed minions of a blundering bureaucracy was as nothing compared to the infinitely more ticklish task of trying to maintain any sort of productive relationship with the wily and wilful Russell. No sooner had the terms of his financial rescue by Eastern Steam been agreed, than an increasingly acrimonious war of words and wits between shipbuilder and engineer was being waged against a background of a continuing flood-tide of troubles which, as Mary had feared, from then on remorselessly undermined still further her husband's already seriously failing health.

As the months dragged by and progress steadily faltered, so had things gone inevitably from bad to worse. Then, on 4 February 1856, Martin's Bank, without any warning at all this time, took possession of the Millwall yards, summarily suspended all activities in both, and dismissed the whole of the workforce.

John Scott Russell's business and, it seemed, the affairs of the Eastern Steam Navigation Company, now lay in irretrievable ruin.

Chapter Two

A HURRIEDLY arranged meeting of Russell's creditors took place just one week after Isambard's visit to Brodie. He went accompanied by Yates, company secretary of Eastern Steam, with the intention of proposing arrangements whereby, once liability to each had been determined, a relative precedence might be agreed for all works in hand. Not until after there had been a full examination of all Russell's affairs had it come to light that secretly he had negotiated, quite illegally as far as Eastern Steam were concerned, no less than six additional construction contracts, of which the keels of two had actually been laid and were already obstructing progress on *Leviathan*'s stern. For such casual disregard of basic ethics the man deserved no mercy. But for the sake of his Great Babe, Isambard was prepared to save Russell's skin yet again.

But the carpet was unceremoniously pulled from beneath his feet. First came the shocking revelation of the sum total of liabilities – no less than £130,000 – and that the principal creditor was Samuel Beale & Company of Rotherham, who had supplied all the iron plate for *Leviathan*. Of a total of £300,000 paid to Russell so far by Eastern Steam, a considerable portion simply could not be accounted for. Eastern Steam, therefore, found itself wrong-footed from the start.

There followed an even more disturbing disclosure. The first fully comprehensive survey William Jacomb, Eastern Steam's official observer at Millwall, had been able to complete free from the ever-fussing presence of Russell himself or his two henchmen, Hepworth and Dixon, had disclosed extremely serious discrepancies. Not only had much of the iron plate not been paid for, an alarming amount was also missing. Denied further access to the yard until the day prior to the meeting, Jacomb had worked feverishly through the night to double check the accuracy of his figures. There could be no doubt they were correct, and Isambard could only curse impotently at his own past foolishness. In his anxiety to protect the ship and carry its builder through the crisis of the previous year, he had personally authorised contract payments in no way warranted by now known results.

Finally revealed was the true depths of the scheming Scot's criminal deception. On the evidence of Jacomb's findings, Yates immediately attempted to invoke the default clause in the *Leviathan* contract whereby Eastern Steam reserved the right in the event of any such breach of terms to distrain on the builder's estate – only to be informed that John Scott Russell had no estate. Everything at Millwall, including the machinery installed specifically for the building of Brunel's great ship, was already mortgaged in full to Martin's Bank, and had been for the past twelve months. Furthermore the bank, its representative made clear, was not prepared at this stage even to discuss with Eastern Steam the possibility of future negotiation, on the grounds that they, Martin's Bank, and other creditors, possessed in law a prior claim.

Thereafter Isambard could do nothing but listen helplessly as the very plan he had proposed was adopted, but from which Eastern Steam was to be specifically excluded. It meant, in effect, that Russell had managed legally to repudiate the *Leviathan* contract, his most acute embarrassment. Though, of course, it could not be proved, it was difficult indeed not to suspect this all along had been his intention. Certainly, if the results of that meeting were anything to go by, he appeared from his own point of view to have handled the whole thing quite brilliantly from first to last. As if to confirm this suspicion, once all had been agreed, came the crowning effrontery.

'Although it is no longer possible to continue construction of the *Leviathan* and the contract with Eastern Steam for same is effectively cancelled,' Russell remarked blandly, 'personally I can see no reason, assuming of course successful fulfilment of all other outstanding contracts first, why the ship should not then be completed also. Provided Eastern Steam,' and here he looked directly at Brunel for the very first time, 'would be prepared to guarantee continued future financing at the rate of, shall we say, £15,000 per calendar month.'

A murmur of astonishment greeted this quite outrageous suggestion, for it was nothing less than blackmail. At last the room fell silent as all eyes turned to Brunel. Outwardly unruffled, he held the challenge of Russell's insolent gaze for a full half minute before removing his smouldering cigar from between tightly clenched teeth. He tossed it with casual accuracy into the ashtray on the table in front of him. Then, his voice frigidly calm but vibrant with contempt, he said, 'Not under any circumstances would I or Eastern Steam be prepared to offer Mr Scott Russell any such guarantee. Not now, nor at any time in the future.' He rose: 'Good-day gentlemen.' And, with Yates and Jacomb, he left.

'So where do things stand now?' Mary wanted to know that evening when he'd finished relating the day's events.

'On the face of it our position is quite impossible. We can't even get to the ship.'

'Then somehow Yates is going to have to work out some sort of negotiation with the bankers.'

'Somehow,' he sighed wearily. 'But what's to be done, and how long it will take, I know not.'

But while the mist-shrouded skeleton of *Leviathan* brooded over the unnatural silence that had so suddenly and devastatingly descended on the Thames at Millwall, and the lawyers and the bankers, the accountants and the rest went on arguing volubly but in vain, the banks of another river, the Tamar, became again the bustling scene of exciting activity.

In June 1849, Isambard had assisted Robert Stephenson – though deadly professional rivals the two had been firm friends almost since their first meeting – in the tricky floating-out and raising operations to position the two 400-foot iron tubes for the latter's high-level bridge over the Menai Strait. Just three years later Brunel had announced his intention of bridging the 'Cornish moat' at Saltash – a task less spectacular perhaps but far more difficult technically, for there was no conveniently placed Britannia Island in the middle of tidal Tamar. Here the central spans, exceeding those of the Menai, and in accordance with the Admiralty's still unchanged stipulation to be no less than one hundred feet above the highest spring-tide level, would have to be supported by foundations laid on bedrock beneath treacherous beds of mud and sand, themselves under seventy feet of water.

The 2,200-foot overall length was to be divided into 2 equal spans of 455 feet flanked by 17 side spans, varying from 70 to 90 feet, to carry the sharply curving approaches. All piers of the side spans and the two bearing the land-ends of the trusses would be entirely in masonry. But the masonry of the central pier would terminate 12 feet above the river's high-water mark to provide a platform on which would stand 4 great octagonal cast-iron columns soaring skyward to a height of 120 feet. All three main piers would be topped above the level of the rail platform by 70-foot-high arched stone supports for the huge gracefully curving wrought-iron trusses, each weighing more than 1,000 tons.

It was to be a truly stupendous undertaking in a magnificent and suitably historic setting. Never before had this estuarine eastern boundary of the ancient Celtic kingdom been bridged. Such truly Olympian grandeur, even its harshest critics were at long last beginning to concede, would without doubt immortalise for ever the name and fame of the engineer whose inspired vision and remarkable professional skill had first conceived, then brought it into being – but only if and when it was successfully completed.

At Chepstow, where the broad gauge since 1852 had bridged the river Wye, a similar construction, though on a much smaller scale, had already served to evolve and develop the necessary techniques. But even this had not silenced the doubters. Long thought to be an impossibility because of the lie of the land and the dangerously rapid flow of the river, the Chepstow bridge, they had reluctantly conceded, had indeed been an undeniable triumph. But Saltash – well, that was something else again. And lack of capital, that inescapable and rarely curable malaise, had meant that no appreciable progress on the Tamar had been possible for three years.

This economic impasse had been broken only after Brunel had modified the bridge design to accommodate a single instead of the double line of rails at first proposed. This had made a saving of £100,000. Another major economy had resulted from the acquisition of the tension chains originally intended for the Clifton Suspension Bridge – the ill-fated white hope of Isambard's youth. After more than two decades of struggling to survive the many vicissitudes which, from the very beginning, had threatened its existence, the Bristol Bridge Company had finally gone under. All that now remained of its once golden promise were the half-completed towers, forlorn monuments to a totally undeserved failure. But the suspension chains, those ingeniously simplified innovations which had once been the cause of so much controversy, made years before by the Copperhouse Foundry of Hayle in Cornwall, were there still and could easily be adapted and lengthened.

In a way, therefore, Isambard's deeply felt disappointment that the work he looked on even after all his countless triumphs as his particular favourite, his first love, would now never be completed, was made easier to bear by the knowledge that one of the primary components of his first bridge was to form an integral part of what he was beginning to suspect might well be his last.

To sink the Wapping access shaft for the Thames Tunnel, the Brunels had conceived the idea of using a form of non-pressurised diving bell. Though never actually put into practice, he now considered it as an alternative to the caisson method employed at Chepstow. He reasoned that if a large enough iron cylinder were to be constructed in such a way that its perimeter would function as a temporary coffer dam when the bottom edge had been sunk deep enough into the river bed to make it reasonably watertight, it might then be pumped sufficiently dry to permit the pier to be erected. Thus all the cumbersome and potentially dangerous complexities of a complicated system of airlocks, not to mention the fearful risks of caisson disease to which a workforce would be constantly exposed, would be avoided.

Once made known, this intention was, as usual, much decried. Fortunately, however, before the creeping paralysis of want of cash had had a chance to be fully effective its practicality had not only been demonstrated, a detailed survey of the river bed contours and composition had also provided sufficient information to determine the shape of the bottom edge of the cylinder.

At 85 feet long and 35 in diameter, its construction on site on the Devon bank of the river took a year and a half. It was, in effect, a tube within a tube, the 4-foot annular space rising some 20 feet above the highest point of the obliquely cut base. Here a domed constriction of the inner wall formed the roof of what was to be the diving bell. From the centre of this dome the inner tube, now reduced to a mere 10-foot-wide shaft, continued upwards. The annulus, sealed from above so that eventually it could be pressurised, was divided into 11 compartments, access to which was through a single airlock in a short 6-foot-wide communication shaft.

The cylinder would be lowered into position between two gun-brig hulks and allowed to sink through the mud until its contoured cutting edge rested firmly on bedrock. Water in the annulus and, later, from the main body of the bell, would be expelled pneumatically by powerful steam pumps. Once all the mud in the annular compartments had been cleared, the partitions removed and a ring of masonry erected, the airlock would be broached and the inner cylinder wall dismantled. Work on the pier could then be continued at normal atmospheric pressure within the safe confines of the coffer dam.

Such was the plan, and so, eventually, was it executed, despite all the unforeseen hazards encountered. First the slowly sinking cylinder struck an uncharted bed of oyster shell which had to be cut away by hand. When finally it came to rest it was canted so far from the vertical that an exceptionally strong tide might well have caused it to tilt over completely, and it was necessary to pressurise the annulus prematurely so that the area of irregularity on which the lowest part of the cutting edge had fouled could be removed. Excavation within the annulus then revealed an immensely deep fissure from which erupted a flood so powerful it was for a time almost impossible to contain. Even after the massive ring wall of granite ashlar had, after several failures, been successfully raised to the prescribed height – the inflow from the fissure preventing cement from hardening quickly enough – it was found that the power of the pumps, again because of the volume of the inflow, was not sufficient to effect a complete evacuation.

At first it was thought the whole cylinder would have to be pressurised, a virtual impossibility with it in situ. Whereupon Brunel's critics crowed delightedly in eager anticipation of the imminent collapse of what they had always held to be a foredoomed and utterly foolish enterprise. But, perhaps inspired by Guy Fawkes's dictum that 'a desperate disease requires a dangerous remedy,' Isambard quickly improvised a method of channelling excess water into a temporary reservoir from which it could be pumped separately. Then fully aware that if he failed he was finished, he ordered all pumps to be run at full power. The gamble paid off handsomely, and once again the scoffers were silenced.

Thereafter progress was excellent. The inner wall of the annulus was cut out and the base of the pier, bonded to the ring of the coffer-dam wall, continued to the full height of the dome. The dome itself and the internal shaft were removed, the reservoirs drained and filled in and the remainder of the masonry of the pier completed.

Finally the outer wall of the cylinder, which had been constructed in longitudinal halves, was unbolted and taken away. Simultaneously, work on the land piers for the two main spans had been in progress and now all three stood twelve feet above high water ready to receive the first truss.

Experiment and research prior to building the Chepstow bridge had brought Brunel to the conclusion that to withstand most effectively the enormous compression forces to which the upper member of any bridge girder or truss is constantly subject, the shape of its section should be circular, or nearly so. Instantly recognisable even to the lay eye, this distinctive construction had quickly been labelled the 'Brunel girder'. The lower flange of the Chepstow trusses comprised a series of conventional angular iron girders joined end to end, located just beneath and forming the main support for the double rail-line platform. The upper flange was a straight wrought-iron tube, nine feet in diameter, to the reinforced ends of which were attached the suspension chains.

Not since those flattened brick arches at Maidenhead had his innovations created such a stir, although the ingenious use he had made of timber for the innumerable viaducts to carry the South Devon, Cornwall and West Cornwall broad-gauge lines deep into the rugged terrain of the West Country had for a time come close to doing so. All were now familiar landmarks, while several, which had come to be considered positively classic, had soon become favourite subjects for popular lithograph artists.

For the much larger requirement at Saltash he'd modified the basic Chepstow pattern, first by arching the upper-truss member so that its rise would complement the fall of the suspension chains, then flattening the tube into an oval, 12 foot 3 inches by 16 foot 9 inches broad – the exact width of the single-line rail platform. These modifications, as well as substantially strengthening the trusses, improved both functionally and aesthetically the overall design, for the suspension chains would now fall vertically instead of being inclined as at Chepstow. In all other respects the basic principle of the 'Brunel girder' was the same.

On temporary piers close to the edge of the river bank the Cornwall truss, the first to be completed, had undergone a series of stress tests, the results so satisfactory that by the time the bridge piers were ready the elaborate preparations to float it out were well advanced. Nearby, docks had been excavated, each of sufficient dimension to accommodate a pair of specially constructed iron pontoons, which could be flooded and pumped out at will, and of a depth to permit them to be submerged onto underwater staging. Already in position, each pontoon was equipped with lifting gear of six hundred tons capacity.

To warp the 455-foot-long truss from the bank when the pontoons had been refloated there were to be two main cables, one hauled by one of the gun-brig hulks now moored to the central pier, the other by a barge securely anchored upstream. Secondary manoeuvring cables would go to various other strategically anchored craft, while to control any sudden lateral drift there would be additional lines to both river banks manned by gangs of local labourers. A dozen or more naval vessels of a variety of size, shape and function but all equipped with both manual capstans and steam-powered crabs, had been assembled for an operation in which no fewer than five hundred men would be involved. Personally directed by Brunel from a control platform on the top of the truss it was to be, from first to last, conducted in the unruffled, unhurried calm of absolute quiet.

The weather on the day, 1 September 1857, was perfect – wind practically non-existent, the sun, comfortably warm but never too hot, blazing out of a cloudless sky onto a colourfully crowded scene. From every village, hamlet, farm and smallholding within a twenty-mile radius the gentry and countryfolk had come by whatever means they could to witness a once in a lifetime wonder; and by train from Truro, Penzance, Bristol, Bath and even London came hundreds more.

To assist as he had at the Menai just after the rescue of *Great Britain* from Dundrum Bay, Kit Claxton had emerged from retirement. But regrettably Robert Stephenson, because of failing health, was unable to fulfil a long-standing promise to be there. Preliminaries were supervised jointly by Claxton and Brunel's chief assistant, Robert Brereton, who during the actual operation would be stationed in a signalling tower high above the control platform on the truss. From there he would relay, by means of numbered placards and coloured flags, the engineer's orders. All vessels and their lines were identified by numbers, as were the various teams on the banks, and to each was assigned a signals officer whose job it would be to maintain the two-way flow of relevant information by pre-arranged permutations of numbers, colours and actions. A red flag displayed would order the identified recipient of a signal to 'heave in', a white flag to 'hold on', a blue flag to 'pay out', a flag waved gently would indicate 'go slowly', waved violently 'go quickly'. Somewhat bigger than those used for semaphore signalling, the flags were stiffened with rods and would be displayed in front of large blackboards to make them clearly visible at all times. Every possible move that could be foreseen had been meticulously rehearsed and all boat commanders and haulage-team captains, as well as signals officers, had been issued with specially printed instruction and procedure manuals.

When the engineer set out from his headquarters in the town, the streets of Saltash and the road to the river were deserted. But as he passed the church, a deafening peal of bells warned the waiting crowds on the river bank of his approach. He was greeted with a mighty roar of cheering. It was like the launching of *Great Britain* all over again. The terrible fiasco of the atmospheric railway forgotten – another pointed reminder of just how short memory could be – he was again a hero, once more the worker of miracles. At the thought he smiled to himself a trifle cynically. He acknowledged the ecstatic reception. But his waves and smiles and answers to the numberless platitudes with which he was bombarded from all sides as he was ferried across the river and then made his way to his place on the truss, were made automatically.

'Everything's in order. Exactly as it should be,' Brereton reported cheerfully to his chief. But he had to shout to make himself heard, and he added a shade more sombrely, 'I just hope to Heaven the crowd behaves itself when the time comes.'

As the hands of his watch slowly crept towards noon, Isambard judged the tide high enough to order the pontoons to commence pumping out. The operation had begun.

'Pier's signalling,' reported a naval rating on the platform. Using his influence with the Admiralty, Claxton had arranged for a team of semaphore signallers from *HMS Ajax* to provide additional communication should it be needed. 'Captain Claxton to IKB – personal, Sir,' the rating read the flags with practised efficiency. ' "Good luck!" Message ends.'

'Acknowledge with "Thank you".'

'Aye-aye, Sir.'

The flurry of signals had already warned the crowd something was about to happen so even before Brereton hoisted his black 'stand-by' flag the noise had begun to abate. Isambard breathed a sigh of relief. As he had told his men, silence for this operation was more than golden.

With two crews working alternately to maintain a brisk rate, the pontoons, gaining buoyancy by the minute, rose from their underwater cradles, their progress monitored by observers whose reports were continually relayed to the platform via a co-ordinator on the bank.

A growing dissonance of protesting metal and timber and ropes gradually made itself heard above the din of the clanking pumps as the tackle on the pontoons began to take the strain. Then slowly, oh so slowly, but inexorably, the ends of the truss were forced from their seatings on the support piers. When they were three inches clear, the pumps were stopped. For what seemed long minutes the only sound apart from the now subdued creak and murmur of tackle was that of water slapping lazily against the heavily wallowing but soundly buoyant pontoons. Each was reported in perfect condition. From the awe-struck crowd came a sound like a sigh, a sigh that grew to a reverberating whisper of disbelieving, doubting or still only half-convinced wonder. Then, the evidence of their eyes at last accepted, the whisper burst into a thunderous, rolling roar of triumph.

'She floats! She floats! She floats!' echoed and re-echoed from bank to bank across the glittering, sun-dappled water to be lost in an unintelligible crescendo of cheers and shouts and whistles and clapping, while on the bank and the pontoons and the platform hats were hurled high in the air. But Brunel, deeply involved mentally with the next stage of the operation, merely ordered a widely grinning Brereton to alert the towing crews.

Down came the black flag to be replaced with a white banner, the signal that the actual float-out was to commence. Again the crowd settled obediently. Only to those directly involved did the seemingly random sequence of numbers displayed by Brereton with their curious accompaniment of sometimes waved, sometimes static coloured flags have any meaning. But unintelligible though they were to that silently watching majority, they were regarded with intensely absorbed interest.

Dwarfing all other man-made features and every visible natural phenomenon as well save the river itself, the truss swung majestically across the fast-running tide to be inched by its ant-like handlers towards the waiting western piers, the journey, of no more than a few hundred yards, taking just under three hours. In a silence that could only be described as monumentally impressive the pontoons bore their huge and ungainly burden to its prescribed position where it seemed simply to slide into place. In such a way, commented a sightseer afterwards, one could imagine the legendary Temple of Solomon might have been raised. The ends of the truss were secured to the rams of hydraulic presses already installed on the heads of the piers just as the tide began to turn. As the water level fell, the pontoons, their work now done, dropped clear.

'Pier signalling, Sir,' said the rating at Isambard's elbow. 'Captain Claxton to IKB – personal. "Congratulations. Very well done indeed." Message ends.'

But before the now relaxed and happily smiling engineer was able to dictate a suitable reply, a Royal Marine Band from Plymouth, with which Kit Claxton had partially and secretly crewed the gun-brig hulk, struck up 'See the Conquering Hero Comes!' Immediately the crowd, no longer disciplined, no longer restrained, no longer orderly even, but still well-behaved for all its rowdiness, reacted to the stirring melody and with one voice chorused the refrain 'See the conquering hero comes! Sound the trumpets, beat the drums!'

Chapter Three

BETWEEN them Brunel and Yates had eventually managed to convince Russell's mortgagees that Eastern Steam did possess some rights, both legal and moral. As a result, a grudging agreement had been concluded granting the company occupancy of the yards and use of plant and equipment in order to complete the ship. But that agreement was to terminate on 12 August 1857, just fourteen months from the date it was signed.

Once again smoke from a hundred and more rivet hearths hung heavily over the Isle of Dogs, at times forming a pall so dense the sun could scarcely penetrate. The light from flares almost turned night into day, and day and night without respite the never ceasing, deafening din of riveting hammers rent the air. No sooner had work on the ship restarted than back flocked the sightseers. Within a month Brunel, now personally in charge, much to Mary's alarm, had been compelled to insist on a strict limitation of numbers. Angered by what they considered unnecessarily harsh strictures, the board promptly complained of the consequent loss of income, paltry though it was. But the engineer was adamant. If there was to be any hope at all of the ship being completed within the period specified, he declared, it was imperative all impediments to progress be minimised or, better still, eliminated. Reluctantly the board agreed, but not one of its members had ceased to grumble.

During Brunel's enforced and sometimes prolonged absences, William Jacomb had taken over at Millwall and it was an unhappy partnership indeed that he and John Yates found themselves forced into with Dixon, who was supervising the construction of the paddle engines, and Hepworth, the senior shipwright. Still stubbornly loyal to Russell, both went out of their way to stir up trouble. Following their example the whole workforce repeatedly demanded and got exorbitant rates of pay and never ceased to agitate for more and more. The company had no choice but to give in every time, for these men

270

alone had the special skills essential to finish the job. From the leading craftsmen to the lowliest workboy, all were indispensable, and every one of them knew it.

Once satisfied all was well on the Tamar, Isambard returned to London, back from the sunshine of success to the brooding shadows of uncertainty and possible disaster. On the murky river bank lay his beloved Great Babe. By now she should have been afloat on the high seas and earning her keep. Instead the still inert hull – a huge, cliff-like mass of rust-streaked metal, visible for miles – sprawled 330 feet from the rubbish- and weed-strewn tide mark of her natural life-giving element. But, at last, she was at least ready to be moved.

Impossible though that task might seem it could, he was confident, be accomplished with comparative ease, given time. Time was the key to the problem – time to experiment with and prove the equipment, to test and try every single item to its limit and beyond, time to modify, where necessary to replan, time, if need be, to re-design. Such meticulous attention to the tiniest detail had always been his greatest strength; rarely, if ever, had he left anything to chance. Time, in the past, had always been of the essence, but now it was the one thing he did not have; and it was no exaggeration to say that an engineer without sufficient time at his disposal when faced with a task such as this, could well be as vulnerable as Samson shorn of his hair.

The news awaiting him at Duke Street was, as he had more than half expected, not good. Yates's attempt to persuade Martin's Bank to agree to a substantial extension of Eastern Steam's occupancy of the shipyard, so that adequate arrangements for the launch could be completed with at least some time to spare, had produced nought but a niggardly grant of a bare two months – and that at an additional cost of no less than £2,500, payable in advance.

'It's extortion!' Yates exclaimed bitterly. 'Downright, bloody extortion. But, they've got us at their mercy, and they damn well know it.'

Brunel, however, cared not at all about the money. Time was now his only concern. To vacate the yards by 10 October meant that the launching operation would have to commence no later than the 5th, the day before the essential spring tide. In his heart he knew it could not be done. But, having heard Yates out, he sat at his drawing table, sunk in thought, scribbling endless calculations in a desperate attempt to conjure some workable solution from the latest progress reports with which Bennett had greeted him. But no matter how many different ways he juggled with facts or how much he permutated figures, the answer was always the same. He needed more time. Another three months at the very least, three months he was simply not going to get.

'The fifth of October,' he said at last. 'That gives us just four weeks.' He looked up, staring hard at Yates, his eyes burning feverishly, his face pale beneath the tan he had acquired in the Devon sunshine. 'Supposing,' he asked quietly, 'supposing I'm not ready by the fifth. What then?'

It was the question the secretary had been dreading, the one for which he knew he had no answer. 'It will be impossible for us to remain in the yard any longer,' was all he could say. 'We must launch on the fifth. Otherwise we shall be in the hands of the Philistines.'

'My dear Yates,' Isambard sighed resignedly, 'neither extortionate demands nor Biblical threats will ever move that ship. Only I can do that. And I can only do it if and when I'm ready.'

He was being asked to do the impossible, to commit himself blindly even before all the equipment he would need had been properly assembled. Suddenly it all seemed too much to bear any longer, and for a fleeting moment his iron self-discipline faltered allowing the full ferocity of his frustration to flare into a sudden all-consuming rage. Hot blood pounded in his temples, icy sweat prickled from every pore of his body, he had to clasp his hands tightly together to stop himself shaking uncontrollably. Then, as quickly as it had come, the spasm had passed.

Yates, who at that precise instant had turned away to pick up hat and gloves preparatory to taking his leave, saw none of this.

Alone, Isambard pushed his papers to one side, rose wearily and went to the window to gaze unseeingly into the fast fading light of what had been another perfect autumn day. He was calm once more; but he felt strangely dispirited and dreadfully tired. It was as if he was caught in a trap from which there was no escape, like a moth in a spider's web. Never before had he been plagued by such agonising doubts, haunted by such frightening forebodings. But he must, he knew, keep his fears to himself.

To impart gravitational force equal to an initial propelling power of an estimated one thousand tons, one-twelfth the ship's total mass, two slipways had been constructed on artificially raised gradients of exactly 1 in 12. Each 120 feet wide and 110 feet apart, they were founded on a 2-foot thickness of concrete laid over a total of 1,000 piles driven to a depth of 30 feet. This left the unsupported bow and stern sections projecting 180 and 150 feet respectively beyond the launching cradles on which the hull now rested – at first a rather alarming sight that had not failed to prompt much pseudo-sagacious shaking of heads and clicking of tongues. But, confident of the proven longitudinal strength of the enormous girder-like structure, Brunel knew what he was about. Had not *Great Britain* been built to an almost identical design? And even if the slipways and their cradles were going to have to be used untried, their design too was the result of practical tests on accurately scaled-down models.

A triple-tiered lattice work of foot-square timbers, the slipways were 240 feet long with standard GWR bridge-rails bolted to their top-most baulks. Down these the launching cradles, shod with inch-thick iron bars at right angles to the rails, would carry their 12,000-ton burden. Nine thousand separate points of contact between bars and rails would put the loading on each at less than 1½ tons – well within the limits calculated.

In place of hydraulic equipment originally planned but ruled out by the board as an unnecessary expense, at the head of each slipway there were checking drums, 29 feet long and 9 in diameter, securely mounted on solidly anchored bases of 40-foot piles driven shoulder to shoulder – their function, to hold the ship back should she slide too quickly. On the other hand, if she became stuck on the slipways, huge chains at bow and stern, rigged through sheaves borne on barges anchored in the river then doubled back to steam winches on shore, would start her again, with an additional pull amidships from four 80-ton crabs aboard other barges. Finally a number of hydraulic rams ranged along her landward side would be available to give the ship an extra initial push, should one be needed.

In all it represented a mammoth two thousand tons plus of propelling force, theoretically more than sufficient for the greatest weight man had ever attempted to move. But despite the still almost universal doubt that such a feat was possible and a growing belief that the great ship would remain forever where she lay as a mocking monument to the presumption of human folly, Isambard's paramount worry was how to stop his Great Babe sliding too fast down the slipway. If she did get stuck she could come to little harm. Once out of control when moving, however, no power on earth could avert a complete and utter catastrophe.

The procedures so successfully used for the floating-out operation at Saltash had been adapted for the launch or, as he preferred to put it, the moving of the ship down to the water's edge. Not until safely re-positioned within reach of the tide would she even come into contact with water, and even then she was to be lowered gently, not pushed into the river. But no matter how he tried to make clear there would be no spectacular splash, he could convince neither the press nor the public.

Claxton was again to be in charge of the water-borne part of the operation. At Isambard's side would be Daniel Gooch, who had willingly volunteered his services, and two newly acquired friends and followers as well: the Great Babe's recently appointed captain and chief engineer, William Harrison late of the Cunard line, and Alexander McLellan. Robert Stephenson, recovered now from his illness, had sent word that he too would be at his disposal if needed.

Success, Isambard repeatedly emphasised to his team would, as it had at Saltash, depend entirely on perfect regularity at all times in the conduct of the operation, upon the absence of all haste and its inevitably concomitant confusion. In short, silence again would be golden.

But no amount of preparation, however painstaking, could achieve the impossible. There was simply no substitute for time. As Yates had predicted, Eastern Steam were shown no mercy. Within hours of the expiry of that hard won and cripplingly expensive extension, the Millwall yards were being reoccupied by Russell's mortgagees and the company once more found itself denied access to its property. Overnight an already desperate situation had become much more than merely potentially disastrous. For Brunel's Great Babe it literally was now or never.

Following a series of stormy board meetings, at which the directors made no effort to conceal their increasingly hostile attitude, he was finally forced to agree to Tuesday, 3 November, as the day the ship was to be moved.

'But I must insist on having sole possession of the whole premises,' he warned his angrily unreasoning colleagues. 'And there must be no one, not even our own men, and still less strangers, in any part of the yard, only those who will be there specifically to carry out their assigned duties. Everything, and everybody, must be completely under my control.'

Chapter Four

IT soon became apparent that there was no chance of Brunel's wishes being heeded. The board had already instructed Yates to have printed and sell immediately to the highest bidders, three thousand tickets for what they proposed to advertise as 'The Forthcoming Grand Spectacle of THE LAUNCH'.

Promptly Brunel protested. But his protestations were in vain and, all but worn out by work and worry, in the end he had no option but to accept the fait accompli. Three thousand sightseers willing, in fact only too anxious, to pay hard cash would at least replenish in part the company's fast emptying coffers – was not the launch itself costing an unprecedented £14,000? Three thousand people would, in any case, be lost in the vastness of the yard, Yates soothed as diplomatically as he could, and provided they were well disciplined by the police who were to be specially engaged, what difference could their presence possibly make. All Mr Brunel had to do, the secretary went on, was concentrate on his arrangements. Nothing had really changed. He would still be in absolute control.

But those three thousand officially privileged ticket holders were to be just the minute tip of a monstrous and treacherous iceberg.

Just after dawn on that raw November morning men, women and children, of all classes and conditions and all completely undaunted either by the biting chill of a bitter east wind or the dismal prospect of being slowly but surely soaked to the skin in the constant drizzle of icy rain, began to descend on the Isle of Dogs. In hundreds they came, then in their thousands – more people than the shy but shrewd island folk had ever seen before and, for many a long year to come, would ever see again. Soon, despite the early hour, the gin shops and beer houses, the countless coffee stalls, the scores of itinerant piemen, fish, fruit and sweet sellers, were all doing a roaring trade. So, in their respective ways were the beggars, the buskers, the thimble riggers and three-card men, the raucous-voiced pavement pedlars of all sorts of rubbish and cheap souvenirs, not to mention seemingly endless supplies of 'official' tickets. Less obviously, but equally profitably, lone mountebanks and highly organised gangs of pickpockets ran riot, for the most part undetected either by victim or onlooker.

But the majority of those milling multitudes had come with but one purpose in mind – to see for themselves this much vaunted wonder of wonders, to marvel at the launching of the *Leviathan* or 'Great Eastern' as nearly everyone bar her owners had long persisted in calling her. And whether they possessed tickets to get them into the shipyard or not, nothing on this earth was going to stop them.

Across the narrow Millwall streets flew broad banners, colourfully new and miraculously crisp and clean still despite the wet. Yards of red, white and blue bunting covered the fronts of buildings public and private, large or small, while here and there flapped a frayed and faded flag, flown in the past for all manner of occasions. From every hostelry came atrociously discordant strains of raggedly performed popular music, mostly songs about 'Great Eastern', the singers' voices wailing and keening painfully above a hubbub of shouts, peals of inane laughter, shrill shrieks and the non-stop unintelligible babble of already more than half-inebriated drinkers.

Soon it seemed the Isle must be filled to capacity. But still, from the north, from the south, from the east and from the west, yet more crowded in to converge on the entrance to the shipyard, to add their weight to the already desperate press of people against the gates, until the harassed keepers were at last forced to fling them wide to admit all and sundry, ticket holders or not. By noon the place was no longer recognisable as a well-ordered shipyard. In less than two hours it had been transformed into a fairground, a gigantic circus, a tumultuous clamorous confusion of excited, expectant, jostling, careless and carefree humanity numbering, so one estimate later put it, little short of one hundred thousand souls. It had become a bear garden over which the pitifully inadequate police detachment originally deployed to keep an expected three thousand well-behaved visitors in order had, from the start, no possible chance of exercising any kind of authority or control.

On a platform in front of the towering bows and high above the noisy throng were assembled the directors, their personal guests and a host of distinguished foreign visitors, most prominent among whom was the recently arrived exotically cloth-of-gold-clad Siamese Ambassador to the Court of St James. The company chairman's daughter was to christen the mighty ship in time-honoured fashion; a rather pointless exercise in view of the fact that many hours must elapse before the hull would be actually afloat. Nevertheless Miss Hope, nervous but well rehearsed, champagne bottle within reach, was ready and waiting.

As the appointed hour drew near, all eyes turned expectantly to the spot from which the engineer was to direct operations. The men at the giant windlasses, at the hydraulic rams, at the winches, on the barges and the boats, were all ready. The ways had been cleared, thoroughly greased and inspected for the last time. The signallers had checked their flags and their procedure manuals. All that could be done in preparation had been done, and excitement now soared to fever pitch.

Millwall, London, the World, was agog for, like those hundred thousand expectant watchers, all believed, in spite of everything stated to the contrary, that the greatest man-made craft since Noah's Ark was about to take to the water.

Isambard had been at the yard all night. During the hours of darkness, with Henry Wakefield, his principal assistant, William Jacomb and other key men, he had gone through the whole of the day's carefully planned procedure for the last time. Since sunrise he had been busy inspecting the ship, the ways, the chains and the cables, the boats and the barges, every single item of equipment ashore and afloat that was to be used. He had eaten little, smoked incessantly and slept not at all, in spite of his solemn promise to Mary he would take care not to overtire himself.

But in vain, Daniel Gooch, Claxton, Captain Harrison, chief engineer McLellan and others had done their best to persuade him to sit down and relax for an hour or so in order to recoup his flagging strength. There had been and there still was much that only he and nobody else could do. When his Great Babe was safely in the water, he'd told them, then, and only then, could he relax. So he'd spent the latter part of the morning fighting his way back and forth through the crowd-swamped yard repeatedly seeking out the all but helpless constables, adjuring them again and again to keep everyone clear of the ship, the ways, the machinery and, hopefully, all possible danger. But to no avail.

With his tall slightly battered hat, stuffed as usual with a miscellany of vital memoranda, jammed hard on his head, his boots and trouser bottoms caked with mud and slime, and enveloped in a borrowed greatcoat, shabby and tent-like for it was several sizes too big for him, he ducked under the ship for a final check of the launching ways. Then, summoning from somewhere the will to keep at bay the nausea of exhaustion now constantly threatening to overwhelm him, he climbed the steps of the control tower, situated amidships and on the landward side of the vessel. When he got to the top he was so out of breath it was several minutes before he was even able to speak. Wakefield and the others who had been waiting patiently for him to arrive, tactfully allowed him time to recover. To mask his distress he made much of the business of selecting a cigar from the huge case he habitually carried. But he made no attempt to light it. Daniel Gooch was the first to speak.

'Are you all right, Mr Brunel?' he asked quietly, sidling close, his craggy young-old face lined with concern.

'Sick at the sight of this, Daniel.' With a puffy and very unsteady hand Isambard gestured angrily at the sea of upturned faces that seemed to stretch as far as the eye could see. 'But otherwise hail enough I think, old friend,' he added with a slow grateful smile. Then with a supreme effort, he straightened his aching back and squared his shoulders. 'Come, we've much to do. Time to make a start.'

Wakefield was on the point of releasing the flag to signal the commencement of the long awaited operation when Hope, the company chairman, and Yates appeared on the platform.

'The name, Brunel,' Hope, red faced and breathless, gasped out between huge convulsive wheezing inhalations. 'We have, I fear, a total impasse.'

'Impasse?' Brunel snapped, his still unlit cigar elevating to a dangerous angle.

'On the launching platform,' panted Hope, removing his hat and mopping at brow and bandeau with a multi-coloured silk bandana. But the interruption had so cut across the engineer's train of concentration, that for the moment he could only wonder what the hell Hope was talking about.

'I thought we had definitely settled once and for all on *Leviathan*,' the other was plaintively bumbling. 'And now, if you please, at the very last minute, I am faced with a demand she be christened *Great Eastern* instead.'

'It is, after all, what the public have been calling her all along,' put in Yates heatedly. 'And I for one think we should. . .'

'But a double adjective, Yates! No, no, no – it simply will not do. I consider it most unsuitable. And my poor daughter is now so confused! My dear Brunel, I appeal to you. The name was agreed.'

'Dammit, you may call the cursed thing *Tom Thumb* for all I care!' Isambard exploded at last. 'For God's sake just clear out of my sight. Both of you!' And such was the force of his fury the pair fled without another word.

Miraculously the hitherto deafening noise began to abate appreciably as soon as Wakefield's signal flags were spotted, and for the moment Isambard's hopes rose. Perhaps, after all, he was going to get the silence on which he knew whatever chance they had of success so crucially depended. Perhaps, as at Saltash, all would be well.

'I name this ship *Leviathan*,' rang out the clear soprano of the chairman's apparently no longer confused daughter. The tinkling crash of the champagne bottle smashing against the ship's bow was also clearly audible. 'May God bless her, and all who sail in her!'

'Hurrah,' roared the crowd harmoniously in what might have been a meticulously rehearsed response. 'Hurrah! Hurrah! Hurrah!'

But then there was worse pandemonium than ever as successive choruses of wild cheering shattered the hearing and pulverised the mind. Chewing furiously at the end of his cigar, Isambard waited minutes for the infernal racket to subside. But the longer he waited, the worse it got. Soon the crowd would be out of control and he remembered only too vividly the terrible scenes he had witnessed during the Bristol riot. Impossible though the situation now was, he had, he knew, no choice but to proceed.

To marshal his temporarily scattered thoughts he discarded his now unsmokable cigar, again made much of choosing another from his case, then lit up with seemingly calm deliberation. Not until he was satisfied it was burning to his complete satisfaction did he nod to the anxiously waiting Wakefield – any other mode of communication impossible in that din. The signallers were alert and ready. Beneath the hull gangs of shipyard navvies, in their best buckish turnouts of short trousers and tightly laced boots, swung their forty-five-pound sledge hammers with a will to knock away the giant wooden wedges that secured the cradles, the heavy rhythmic blows felt rather than heard. Next the sixty-ton checking drums at the tops of the ways were warned to stand by, likewise the steam winches carrying the bow and stern cables. Before the last of the wedges had been cleared, all were reported in readiness.

Now poised unrestrained on the ways, held solely by the inertial force of her 12,000-ton weight, the ship seemed as immobile as before, and in every mind but one there was a suspicion she would forever remain so. Brunel alone was confident, supremely confident that she would move, and that once she did she would continue down the ways to the distant water's edge. His prime concern was still how to stop her sliding too swiftly. Owing to the lack of time, neither the checking drums nor their chains had been tested to breaking point. It only needed one of those massive two and a half foot links to fail!

He acknowledged Daniel Gooch's bellowed progress report and immediately indicated to Wakefield that the vessels in the river be now ordered to take the strain; the bow and stern winches were also alerted. Gradually the crowd quietened, aware of a sound that soon began to drown their own infernal racket. It was strange, unearthly, awe inspiring, frightening – a sound the like of which no one had ever heard before. Deep within that massive, naturally resonant, iron structure the slowly increasing pull of chains and cables was building up strains and stresses which in turn were causing innumerable minute movements, the noise of each echoing and re-echoing through the length and breadth of the hull, at first reverberating like an ominously growling drumroll, then blurring into a thunderous spine-chilling devil-inspired diapason. The monster was stirring, *Leviathan* was coming to life, her vibrant voice ringing out like a thousand giant deep-bass-noted bells. Still she had not moved. But the crowd, stunned into breathless silence, watched and waited in wide-eyed wonder.

For what seemed endless enthralling minutes the ship groaned and trembled in a convulsion so stupendous that the ground around her quaked as if in sympathy. And high above, the Great Babe's sire, as fascinated as anyone but calm and unconcerned, judged perfectly the moment to apply pressure from the hydraulic rams. Suddenly, with a nerve-torturing squeal of metal against metal, the bow cradle started to slide.

'She's moving! She's moving!' screamed the crowd. Terror stricken, those nearest tried desperately to push back against serried ranks which were at the same time pressing forward to confirm incredulous disbelief. The fatal seeds of failure, long since sown, already germinated, began to burgeon and bear fruit.

The instant the ship started to move, the crew of the bow cradle checking-drum capstan took up the slack on their chain and were able to control the rate of pay-out. But, as Brunel had feared might happen, the stern crew, distracted by the crowd, were caught completely unprepared. One of them, an Irishman named Donovan, was actually standing on top of the capstan for a better view of what was happening at the bow. Too late the men tried to grab the already whirling windlass handles when, without warning, the stern cradle also started to slide. But the unsecured capstan, suddenly spinning like a huge top, hurled Donovan doll-like high into the air and smashed the legs of four other unfortunates. Whereupon the densely packed crowd became a wildly erupting human volcano of panic.

Had the engineer been able to make himself heard, total disaster might yet have been avoided. Notwithstanding the panic, people were well clear of the launchways; nor was the moving ship anywhere near out of control. But having, perforce, to act on their own initiative, the forward drum crew just failed to pay out sufficient chain quickly enough. The result was inevitably catastrophic. Held by the bows, *Leviathan* slewed slowly sideways, the stern cradle twisting beneath her. Then she lurched sickeningly to a squealing, grinding earth-shaking standstill.

Chapter Five

COMMENTED the *Times* leader with rather more than gentle sarcasm the next morning: 'We seem to have been a little less than fortunate in our grandiose schemes of late. Within the space of but a few short months the Valencia cable has parted, Big Ben has cracked and ceased to chime, and now *Leviathan* refuses to budge!' And the richly detailed accounts of the previous day's proceedings to which the columns of several inside pages were exclusively devoted, all came to the same conclusion – that the whole dismal affair had been, from start to finish, nothing less than a monumental fiasco.

The real fact of the matter was that, apart from the tragic accident which regrettably had claimed the foolish Donovan's life and the immediate aftermath – the result of the violent reactions of an uncontrollable mob that should never have been permitted to enter the yard in the first place – Brunel had meticulously anticipated practically every single occurrence. But of this the various reporters made no mention at all. Instead they vied with one another by indulging in the most lurid descriptions imaginable of what one alliteratively referred to as a mass exodus from the scene of 'disgruntled, duped, dispirited and distinctly damp thousands', all vociferously blaming not the Eastern Steam Navigation Company but their late idol, the engineer. 'Having, not for the first time in his career,' the writer pompously concluded, 'arrogantly presumed too much on his so-called talents and foolishly gone too far, Mr Brunel must bear prime, if not sole, responsibility.'

'Oh, it's not right,' cried Mary in a passion of anguished impotent fury. 'It's all too cruel! It's criminal!' And she flung the paper furiously from her as she recalled once again the ghastly haunted expression in her weary husband's eyes when he had finally returned to Duke Street the night before. It was the closest she had ever seen him to defeat, and she prayed fervently she should never see him so again.

It had taken several hours before sufficient semblance of order could be restored for a thorough inspection of the ship to be made, and even then Brunel and his men had had to fight their way through a screaming mob that would respond neither to reason nor to threats. But the ship seemed none the worse. Even the stern cradle was not nearly as severely damaged as had at first been feared. It had therefore been decided to straighten the vessel and, if successful, renew the attempt to move her. But the failure of the bow winch had eventually brought that dreadful day's efforts to an abrupt and forlorn end. 'By which time everything was in such confusion,' he'd told Mary, 'there was nothing to be done but see the ship secured and wait till morning.' Then, instead of going to bed to rest, to Mary's dismay he'd locked himself in his office and worked through the night.

His principal concern was for the immediate safety of the ship. Though bow and stern cradles had moved no more than a few feet, it meant the weight of the vessel was now partly on the building slip, the foundation of which was absolutely rigid, and partly on the launching ways whose foundations were not, the pilings having been concentrated along their edges to prevent extrusion of ground from beneath the concrete bed. The reason for this was to effect a more even distribution of weight as the ship slid down to the water and thus minimise any unequal settlement; but in her present somewhat precarious position, should these foundations begin to fail, serious distortion of the bottom plates between her bulkheads could well result. So although she could not be floated until the next spring tide, due in a month's time, it was imperative to get her down to the water's edge as quickly as possible.

Already John Scott Russell's mortgagees had informed Yates of their intention to demand rent at the same extortionate rate imposed to 3 November for as long as *Leviathan* remained on their river frontage. Again, it was robbery; but, again, there was nothing Yates could do about it.

First thing next morning Hope stormed down to Millwall. But rant and rave though he might, he could provoke Brunel neither to committing himself to what would have been false and foolish promises, nor to a comparable display of anger, more than justified though it would have been. Isambard's fury, in fact, was still such that he could scarcely contain it. But he was too wise to fritter his precious remaining reserves of energy in pointless recriminations, and too strong of will to allow himself to be distracted from the job in hand. So, angrier than ever, Hope stormed off, leaving him and his assistants in peace.

Not until 19 November was the next attempt to move the ship made, it having taken a fortnight to complete all the necessary modifications to tackle and machinery. The four crabs had been removed from the barges to be mounted instead on specially piled foundations ashore, their chain cables now arranged in similar fashion to those of the bow and stern winches. Another pair of presses had also been installed, making the total hydraulic power the equivalent of 800 tons. But the new press abutments were found to be not strong enough and another nine days were lost while they were being reinforced, by which time hope of catching the next spring tide was already fading.

On Saturday, 28 November, the ship, once satisfactorily straightened, was laboriously moved literally one inch at a time a total distance of fourteen feet, though so much tackle was damaged that the next twenty-four hours had to be devoted to servicing presses and steam winches, general repairs and organising replacements – activities which incurred the wrath of horrified Sabbatarians. But it meant that by noon on Monday a further thirty-six and a half feet had been gained, this time with no serious mishap. They could, perhaps, make the tide in two days' time after all. All hopes, however, were cruelly dashed when a ten-inch press on the forward cradle burst its cylinder; which the now smugly complacent Sabbatarians immediately recognised as just retribution for the insult previously offered the Almighty.

Nor was the situation in any way improved by another angry visit from Hope, this time accompanied by a number of equally angry colleagues. With infinite patience Isambard, puffing quietly at the inevitable cigar, let each have his say. Then it was his turn.

It seemed, he told them without emotion, that every circumstance had conspired to drive him into a situation only to be described as nightmarish. Not only had he suffered the insolent defection of a fellow engineer in whom he had placed absolute trust, he had had to endure a degree of unscrupulous extortion amounting to out and out blackmail. In addition, he'd had to bear the brunt of vicious condemnation from an uninformed press and the hurtful ridicule of an ignorant public – a public, he reminded them, they had sought to exploit, not he. And because of their cheap betrayal he had been forced to attempt the most hazardous of tasks with hopelessly inadequate and untried equipment, in the very worst season of the year.

'You, gentlemen, have sown the wind,' he told them. 'Now I must reap the whirlwind. I shall succeed, never fear. I shall succeed no matter what the cost may be. But until I do, I'll thank you all, henceforth, to leave me in peace!' Silenced, not so much by his words as by the ever more perceptible aura of strength that seemed to flow from and surround this little giant of a man who stood before them, they departed without another word.

The damaged press could not be brought back into service until 3 December – the day of the tide which, ironically, provided what would have been ideal conditions for a launch. But another fourteen feet were gained, the next day thirty. Despite the loss of two more presses and destruction of yet more valuable tackle, all of which had somehow to be replaced, progress of a sort, albeit at a depressingly decreasing rate, was maintained until the 17th, by which time *Leviathan* stood more than half-way down the slips.

But Brunel's troubles were far from over. On the contrary, they were being added to daily, mainly because of the ever increasing concentration of power needed to start the ship moving each time – stoppages being necessary to permit the press abutments to be repositioned.

Though again ailing, Robert Stephenson unhesitatingly left his sick-bed and braved the lethal Millwall mists to assist the friend whom *The Engineer*, in reproof of popular mockery, had recently taken pains to describe as 'this brave man struggling with adversity, a spectacle on which the Gods, according to the ancients, should love to look down'. His advice, to suspend operations until even more press power could be assembled, was sound; and Isambard, grimly ignoring the renewed outcry from Hope and the others, did not hesitate to act on it.

Flourishing like some freshly reincarnated phoenix, John Scott Russell chose this moment to voice far and wide his uncompromising criticism. 'Brunel's biggest blunder of all lies in his utterly senseless determination to launch his monster on rails,' he declared in public and in print. 'It must be obvious, even to the most uninformed in such matters, that the hull can only slide a few feet before the lubricating stuff is rubbed off and the rails begin to bite one another, just as the wheels of a locomotive engine bite into the rails on which it runs. It is indeed nothing less than crass idiocy to expect other than that she will be held firmly and permanently in place.'

Taking their cue from this apparently rehabilitated oracle, the press promptly exploded into a positive orgy of vituperation the like of which had not been known since Sir Marc's early Thames Tunnel days. 'Why do great companies believe in Mr Brunel? Is it really because he is, as has sometimes been supposed, a great engineer?' *The Field* questioned portentously, then went on to pronounce that if great engineering was to be measured in terms of stupendous but useless monuments to folly created by enormous expenditures of shareholders' money and the senseless shedding of labourers' blood, truly I. K. Brunel, like his father before him, must indeed be numbered among the greatest of all.

'The Hero of Millwall may be currently observed every evening gazing hopefully on his *Leviathan* and murmuring like a second Galileo, "E pur si muove!" ' reported *Punch* waggishly.

' "Canst thou draw out *Leviathan* with an hook?" ' quoted the *Morning Advertiser*.

'*Leviathan, Leviathan*, the Leave-'er-'igh-n'dry-athan,' taunted the latest music-hall masterpiece.

But John Scott Russell's calumny was founded on fancy not fact. It was because even the hardest of timbers would almost certainly have become grain bound by such tremendous pressure that Isambard had elected to launch on metal rails. The nub of the problem was not the insurmountable resistance of metal against metal. It was simply that the hydraulic presses could move the ship only in fits and starts. More power was needed. So more power he would get.

During the weeks that followed the scene at Millwall all but beggared description. Never before had such a titanic concentration of mechanical power been assembled. Day after day and in all weathers – rain, sleet, hail, snow, even in the thickest of fogs – singing gangs of labourers toiled non-stop from dawn to dusk and sometimes, by the uncertain light of smoking torches, deep into the night. They hauled on ropes and cables, dragged enormous lengths of massively linked chains backwards and forwards, rolled the huge timber pushing-pieces for the presses up and down the ways, manhandled the presses themselves and seemed to be forever either dismantling or rebuilding their abutments. While all this was going on, other smaller gangs were constantly checking, rechecking, servicing, repairing or replacing various pieces of sorely damaged or totally destroyed machinery.

Brunel seemed to be everywhere at once, constantly enveloped in a thick halo of pungent tobacco smoke, from head to toe caked with mud and smeared with slime and more often than not soaked to the skin. The first to arrive, the last to leave, never, while he was in the yard, did he rest or relax. He alone issued all orders, his words stentoriously relayed by a hand-picked entourage of burly bull-voiced foremen.

First the presses had to be primed to full pressure. Next the bow and stern cables had to be hauled taut, followed by the mid-ship crabs. When all was ready would come the order to let go the chains. Then would follow the agonising wait, seconds as long as minutes, until at last the ship would start to slide and the creaking, groaning, already ear-splitting crescendo of tormented abutments and pushing pieces would be suddenly drowned by the shrill roar of actual movement – the discharge of power making the ground sway as if an earthquake had struck.

For the few privileged to see it, among whom were Prince Albert and the sixteen-year-old Prince of Wales – the public having long since been banned – the sight was never to be forgotten. But even that spectacle was nothing compared to the incredible damage done to the equipment used to make it all possible. The massive iron drum of a windlass, the largest ever to be cast and considered indestructible, was crushed like an overripe nut. Water was forced like thick dew through a solid iron ram-head until its cylinder, with walls half a foot thick, was literally ripped apart. The huge cast-iron slab against which the base of another ram rested was split asunder as if no stronger than a rotten board.

So it went on, with Brunel tirelessly driving, urging, inspiring his flagging assistants and exhausted men until, at long last, his Great Babe was within reach of the tidal water of the Thames.

Chapter Six

'SIR Benjamin Brodie.' Huntley, the Brunels' butler, formally announced Mary's unexpected visitor, then withdrew closing the panelled double doors of the ornate first-floor drawing room behind him.

Looking as beautiful as ever in a high-necked, long-sleeved, simply cut dress of pale-grey silk shot with white – Mary had been one of the first English ladies to adopt the chic yet informal style popularised by the French Empress – she rose to greet the famous surgeon. Her welcoming smile masked her puzzlement, for it was not yet noon and therefore a strange time for anyone to call; and Brodie was no socialite anyway.

But this was far from being a social visit, of that she'd been convinced even before seeing the grim expression that rendered the rather battered Scots countenance even more dour than usual. Formalities were quickly exchanged and, once seated, he came straight to the point.

'Brunel is in danger of killing himself. Did you know that?'

Notwithstanding Brodie's not altogether enviable reputation for refusing to mince words, the savage bluntness of his statement for the moment took her breath away.

'I do not *know* anything, Sir Benjamin, for my husband has not told me anything.' He had not had to, of course; she had eyes and she was no fool. Suspicion and concern, however, could never substitute adequately for facts, and these, she knew, had always been kept from her – until now. 'But,' she went on, 'shocked though I am by what you say, I have to confess I am not altogether surprised.'

Which brought forth an irritable grunt followed by a despairing sigh.

'I take it Issy has consulted you?' she asked tentatively.

'Not recently, no. Not for over a year, in fact.' Briefly he told her of the examination he'd made in February 1856 of which she had known nothing, of the advice he had vainly attempted to give and of his growing concern since, as he had observed the gradual, but all too obviously progressive, decline in the health of his friend.

'My coming to see you in this way, Mrs Brunel, is I realise an unprecedented, not to say an unethical, act on my part as your husband's physician. But, blatant breach of professional faith though it is, I offer no apologies. I have done everything in my power to influence the man, but I have failed. All I can do now is appeal, most humbly, for your help before – and believe me I am not exaggerating, nor am I being melodramatic – before it is too late.'

With both heart and head in a whirling turmoil of emotion at this brutal confirmation of her long-repressed fears, Mary managed to maintain the semblance of dignified composure, though she knew the man watching her, his deep-set, piercingly blue eyes holding hers in an hypnotic vice, was in no way deceived. He had intended to shake her to the very core of her being. And he had succeeded.

'Tell me, Sir Benjamin,' the question was more to gain time to think than anything else, 'exactly what is wrong with my husband?'

'Kidney failure, already chronic. Likely, I suspect, soon to become acute. And when that happens – fatal!'

The words were vicious, stinging, physical blows, each more painful and unbearable than its predecessor. Her senses were reeling. But her composure remained.

'And the cure?' she heard herself asking.

'There is no cure. My colleague Doctor Robert Bright, of whom you may possibly have heard, has made a lifelong study of this disease. He has already confirmed both diagnosis and prognosis. Should the worst happen, I fear not even he, expert though he is, could help.'

'*Should* the worst?' Like the proverbial drowning person Mary clutched desperately at the flimsy hope of the straw-like phrase.

'There is no cure, Ma-am!' Brodie repeated emphatically. 'Pray understand that once and for all. But there can still be containment, even at this late stage, provided action is taken now! It means his having prolonged and absolute rest, a complete change, abroad somewhere, in the sun. Och, I've already told him all this.'

'Rest, for how long?'

'Three, six months, possibly a year.'

'When?'

'Immediately! Woman, at this stage every single day is vital! Delay could, well let's just say, add to the difficulties – compound the problem.'

'It really is as bad as that?'

'Aye, Ma-am,' he said gently, 'I fear it really is as bad as that.'

She was silent for a moment while she took this in, conscious all the while that Brodie's eyes never left her. Then she asked: 'And afterwards, what? Retirement?'

'Semi-retirement, at least. Certainly a vastly different life style to that he has followed hitherto.'

Again she sought for time to think. 'How?' she asked. 'When?'

'All started years ago; the result of a severe blow in an accident when he was a young man. Put him in bed for the better part of a year, I understand, and apparently he was gai lucky to survive then. If only the glaikit hash had had the ken to take more care of himsel' since, he wouldna be in this parlous state now!' Brodie snorted in a sudden flash of anger. Then he composed himself. 'However, there's nought to be gained by if-ing and and-ing about what's past. The plain fact of the matter is that your husband's life is in deadly danger and you, my dear lady, are the only one on God's earth who can possibly save him.'

For some time after Sir Benjamin had taken his leave, Mary, once able to think again coherently, pondered deeply on what he had said. That she was the only one who could save Issy's life might very well be true – if, that is, he would let her, now that the closeness they had found in the aftermath of the terrible crash of 1848, had evaporated.

First, last and always Isambard Kingdom Brunel was the great genius whose overwhelming personality somehow elevated him above all others. Precociously, at times arrogantly, bold, and to the commercial world outrageously extravagant, he possessed – uniquely, according to Daniel Gooch, Claxton, Guppy, and so many others – the greatest originality of thought and the most effective power of execution. Great things, it was rightly said, were never achieved by those who hesitated to count the cost, either to themselves or to others, of every thought and action.

Always the public, this was now also the private, man. And she, both in public and in private, was in reality no more than the wife of I. K. Brunel, the engineer; the wife whose looks could still cause heads to turn, whose presence never failed to captivate and charm. But that, alas, was all.

Fifteen-year-old Henry Brunel travelled down from school on the North London Railway, arriving at Millwall during the early morning of Friday, 29 January 1858. As the final stage of the marathon launching of his father's great ship was to be completed on the morrow, the headmaster of Harrow had readily agreed that, in the absence of young Isambard at school in Switzerland, Brunel's second son should be present at this so long anticipated and undeniably historic event.

It was, of course, far from being Henry's first visit to the shipyard. All the same, as he made his way from the main gate to where the giant hull now lay, a full five and twenty feet beyond the ends of the already partially dismantled launching ways, he marvelled wide eyed at the scene. Gone were the giant Saltash crabs, the huge checking drums with their massive chains, and most of the hydraulic presses which in the end had done their work so well. All that remained seemed to be a gigantic litter of rusting scrap iron – broken chain links, grotesquely twisted bridge rails, shattered ram-heads and ruptured cylinders, and mass upon mass of splintered timber. It was like the debris that might have strewn some unbelievably fantastic battleground. The aftermath of Waterloo, thought Henry, might well have looked something like this.

Gone also were the familiar singing gangs of toiling labourers. In their place forlorn groups of tattered shipyard scavengers were sorting through the mountainous piles of junk and rubbish, some carefully stacking to one side anything considered worthy of salvaging, others feeding various bonfires with useless pieces of wood. Smoke rose lazily to mingle with the winter mist then drift in grey smut-laden wisps over a scene of desolation that only a few days before had been one of constant and, to the casual observer, frantic activity.

But that part of the battle at least was now won. The ship, still firmly on her cradles, was already partially in the water even though the tide was at low ebb. Indeed, for the past eleven days she had had to be ballasted to prevent her floating prematurely. This precaution had been necessary because of sudden worsening of the weather, whose unpredictable vagaries had been the cause of so many of Brunel's most serious problems. Fog, frost, high winds, snow, ice, heavy rain – all had plagued him with malicious persistence. Nor did it appear at all likely the elements were going to be in any way kinder during the next vital thirty hours or so.

To assist in making quick assessments of a constantly changing situation, Isambard had weather observers in Liverpool and Plymouth maintaining almost constant contact with Millwall by telegraph. Also under the closest possible scrutiny was the erratic behaviour of the tides. Quite as perverse as the weather, for the last few days they had been unusually low, certainly inadequate for what was required. So every half hour relays of watchers were recording levels on a specially designed chart pinned to the wall of the tiny clapboard site office close to the ship.

It was there the engineer, looking desperately tired and ill, but still apparently bursting with his customary energy, greeted his son.

'We have a fine problem to solve this time, Henry,' he told the boy. 'Come,' he went on, sweeping a space clear on the cluttered deal table that served him as a desk, 'we'll go through it together and then you can tell me what you think.' The son, unfortunately, was far from being the prodigy the father had been when he was fifteen. Henry, however, was by no means a dunce, and for the next few hours his attentive interest did much to ease the strain Isambard had been under for so long.

'So you can see, in comparison with what we now have to do,' Brunel finally summed up, 'getting her this far down the ways could be considered a fairly straightforward operation in which at least every factor was known beforehand and, relatively speaking, could be reasonably well controlled. And if only we'd had the right tackle and the hydraulic equipment I wanted originally, it could all have been done without any real difficulty at all. Of that I'm certain. But actually getting the ship into the water, now that's something else again.'

His eyes glazed with fatigue and stinging painfully from the clouds of acrid tobacco smoke which by then had made the thick dank-smelling air in the tiny unventilated office scarcely breathable, Henry valiantly stifled a yawn and, somehow managing to still the protesting rumblings of a too long neglected stomach, forced his flagging wits to concentrate. Not for anything would he have

293

offended his respected and much loved sire by allowing him to see that his attention was beginning to wander.

'As you say, Father,' he mumbled, 'we haven't got an inch to spare.'

'Not a single inch,' repeated Isambard, lighting yet another cigar. Henry had already lost count of the number he'd smoked since his arrival. 'There is no margin for error at all. The hull must be so positioned and trimmed to float on a precisely even keel and at an accurately predetermined draught. Above all else, the trim is vital. It must be absolutely perfect. Perfect, Henry. Otherwise. . . .' And a shrug of truly Gallic eloquence conveyed far more meaning than any words.

But instead of the triumphant conclusion of his father's Herculean labour which young Henry Brunel with the blind natural exuberance of inexperienced youth had so eagerly anticipated, the following thirty hours were to be a well-nigh unendurable agony of frustration and disappointment. After a hurriedly gobbled meal of stale and very indifferent sandwiches washed down by hot but poisonously stewed over-sweet tea – of which the first mouthful nearly made him sick – he accompanied his father on a tour of inspection.

In a tiny dory, that seemed to Henry likely to capsize at any moment, they were rowed out first to a fire-float which was standing by to pump out the great ship's water ballast, then in turn to the four newly arrived steam tugs to confer briefly with each captain. When finally afloat, *Victoria* and *Friend To All Nations* were to take *Great Eastern* – the name with which she had been 'christened' now seemed to have been completely forgotten – by the bow and, with *Napoleon* and *Perseverance* steadying her stern, tow her across the river to her fitting-out berth at Deptford. It would be no mean feat of seamanship in the confines of that notoriously treacherous waterway even in the most ideal conditions, and a virtual impossibility any other time.

Last of all they went aboard the great ship herself, where Captain Harrison and chief engineer McLellan with a skeleton crew were already occupying permanent quarters. Then, long after darkness had fallen, the exhausted lad curled himself up on a rug in a corner of the office ashore. Though he had no such intention, he slept soundly until dawn.

He woke to learn that while much had happened during those

intervening hours, nothing at all had been achieved. Weather reports from both Liverpool and Plymouth had been consistently bad and the expectancy from neither source was encouraging, though at first there had seemed at least a promise of improvement. So, even though it had been raining hard at Millwall, Brunel, the worrying possibility that if he should miss this spring tide the launch would have to be yet again delayed paramount in his thoughts, had given orders just before midnight to begin pumping out ballast.

No sooner had this long and tedious operation been started than a fierce south-westerly gale had suddenly sprung up. By half-past three it was blowing full against the ship's starboard beam – the river side – with such force she had had to be hurriedly re-ballasted.

The dim grey light of the new day revealed thick, angry looking, low-hanging, swiftly scudding black smears of storm clouds from which deluged curtains of heavy rain shredded by the wind's fury into a never ending succession of blinding squalls. And there seemed no prospect of any improvement within a foreseeable and now seriously limited future.

Though acutely preoccupied with what could well prove the final catastrophe, Isambard still found time to be concerned for Henry. He should, he suggested, go home to Duke Street. 'In what seems, at present, to be the unlikely event of anything happening, you shall be sent for immediately,' he ruefully promised the boy. But Henry was having none of that. He had come to Millwall to see for himself and record everything step by step in his diary and, true son of his father in that respect if in no other, nothing and no one, he said, was going to stop him, come what may.

All Saturday the storm raged. Remorselessly the rain lanced down and the wind continued to howl furiously, frighteningly. At times it became so violent it was only superb seamanship that kept the four steam tugs and the fire-float on station in that racing rain-battered wind-torn river.

Re-ballasting had been completed only just in time to meet the fast-rising morning tide which, had it not been for the wind, would have been ideal for floating the ship off. Then in the evening the Thames rose even more rapidly, this time to an unprecedented height. As the swirling tidal flood took hold of her hitherto inert and now 15,000-ton mass, the tethered ship became an animate colossus that would indeed have been well named *Leviathan*. Until the tide turned there was nothing anyone could do but pray that the cradles would not disintegrate nor the cables holding her snap like pieces of rotten string.

Miraculously they did not. But as the tide fell it became obvious that neither ship nor cradles nor moorings could possibly survive a second ordeal like that. Whatever the weather, and irrespective of all consequence, on the very next tide she would have to be floated off.

Midnight saw little or no improvement. Still the rain was falling in torrents, still it was being driven by the same south-westerly gale. It must, of course, let up sometime, but when? With a bare seven hours to go before the next high tide, there was precious little time left, and hopes were now fading fast. Curled up once more on his rug, but wide awake and determined to remain so at all costs, Henry silently watched the glowing tip of his father's cigar in the fuggy half light of a smoky turned-down oil lamp.

Isambard had now been without sleep and virtually without rest for nearly sixty consecutive hours. At Mary's insistence a sofa had been placed in the office for him to use. But he'd hardly been anywhere near it. He simply could not relax. His voice was firm, his hand steady and his face, though drawn with fatigue and of the ghastly pallor that betrayed bodily weakness, expressionless. His mind, however, was a scarcely controllable tempest of doubt confused with confidence, a mad mixture of hope and despair. But he could still succeed, if only the weather would let him.

The break finally came just after one o'clock. As suddenly as it had started nearly twenty-four hours earlier, the wind dropped and the rain became a spasmodic drizzle. Minutes later a telegraphed message from Liverpool reported a similar easing of conditions there, adding that all indications pointed to the wind backing to the north east. No sooner had the portent of this been appreciated than a similar message arrived from Plymouth.

'It's the chance we've been waiting for, Mr Brunel,' said Captain Harrison, who had brought the Plymouth telegram to the office himself. 'All we need now is the tide.'

'High water will be at twenty minutes to two tomorrow, I mean this afternoon,' piped Henry who had scrambled up from his rug to consult the chart on the wall.

Isambard flashed the boy a proud and grateful smile. Here, after all, was the son he had always dreamed he would have.

'Call in the fire-float. Tell McLellan to stand by.' Fatigue forgotten, doubt and despair dismissed, weakness banished by a supreme effort of will, it was the old Brunel, the real Brunel, the Brunel who had conceived and built the Great Western Railway, *Great Western*, *Great Britain*, the Saltash bridge and, now, the greatest ship the world had ever known; the Brunel who, for the past thirty years and more, had flown in the face of all adversity and inspired his fellow men to achievements never before imagined, who now snapped into action.

'We start pumping out ballast at,' a quick consultation of his watch, 'precisely half-past three o'clock. And we launch on the afternoon tide – Henry's tide, Captain.'

'Aye-aye, Sir,' chirruped Harrison, who threw the smiling engineer a flamboyant salute then skipped out of the office as excited as a young beau on his way to his first assignation.

'Henry,' commanded Brunel parentally, 'go and lie down again. And this time – go to sleep!'

Henry obeyed with alacrity and without argument.

'What about you, Father?' he asked.

'I, my boy,' said the engineer, stubbing out the remains of his cigar then stretching himself luxuriously on the sofa, 'am going to do exactly the same thing.'

Within five minutes both were sound asleep.

The first thing Henry saw when he looked through the grimy office window were the stars – a myriad of pin-point lights set like diamonds in the black-velvet cushion of a cloudless sky. He had almost forgotten they existed, so long did it seem since he had last seen them. Rubbing sleep from his eyes he hastily chewed on crusty toast, gulped down a mug of shipyard tea – without retching this time – then hurried to the ship to join his father.

By the growing light of a truly splendid sunrise, gangs of men began to move the bolts securing the cradle wedges. Well before they had finished, McLellan reported his pumps sucking air. Harrison then ordered the fire-float to stand off.

'Dismiss her completely, if you please Captain,' Isambard, spruce and clean shaven, called from the bank. 'Signal our thanks, then send her on her way. She'll not be needed again.' His words were greeted by a resounding cheer. The Great Babe was ready at last.

The presses and winches were to have been manned by eleven o'clock. But long before the hour the tide was rising so fast that messengers had hurriedly to be despatched to round up the gangs. As soon as they were at their posts, Isambard brought them into action for the last time. The depth of water surrounding the ship slowly increased and the cradles were eased forward.

Word had been sent to Duke Street. At one o'clock Mary's carriage drove into the yard. She had come via the Barge House in Lambeth and with her were Sir Benjamin and Lady Hawes. Importantly Henry conducted his mother, his uncle and aunt to the vantage point his father had pointed out to him.

But from then on everything went so smoothly, the moment of ultimate triumph, which came at 1.42pm precisely, almost passed unnoticed.

Chapter Seven

CAIRO seemed a curious place to be spending Christmas, and a curious place indeed for Isambard, quite by chance, to run into his old friend and rival, Robert Stephenson. Both were wintering abroad on medical advice and had come to Egypt in the hope of regaining something of their lost health – Stephenson as usual, alone, Brunel with Mary and young Henry who had proved himself an excellent travelling companion. They spent a day together reminiscing, reliving past triumphs and tragedies, comparing notes and exchanging opinions as they had always done when they'd met, talking at great length of practically everything under the sun – everything, that is, except the future.

It was almost as if there existed between them a tacit understanding that, despite their apparent mutual recovery, for both were bronzed and looked remarkably well, the chances were they would not meet again. Then they parted, Stephenson to return to his yacht in Alexandria, the Brunels to embark on a voyage up the Nile as far as Aswan in a chartered dahabiyah.

This was Isambard's second enforced absence from England in just over half a year, his second attempt to repair at least in part the damage he had so recklessly done himself. Seven hours after *Great Eastern* had floated free of her cradles almost eleven months before, he had disembarked at Deptford, his popular reputation at least partially restored but with his own and his company's fortunes decimated and his health in ruins.

For weeks thereafter he had languished in Duke Street, feeble of body and, at times it seemed, of mind. His spirit was as resilient as ever, but long bouts of semi-delirium steadily gnawed away what little strength he had left. He was, as he put it to Ben Hawes – one of his most frequent visitors – regularly floored with a veritable concatenation of evils.

The remedy, the only remedy for his ills, Sir Benjamin Brodie had

299

continued to insist, was a complete change of scene and absolute rest. Eventually he had allowed himself to be persuaded. He and Mary had gone first to Vichy, then on to Switzerland for a month. But his idea of a complete rest proved to be a quite unshakable determination to complete his designs for the Eastern Bengal Railway, a commitment he had been forced to shelve and now long overdue. Equally determined, Mary had managed to limit this labour to just a few hours a day – a far from satisfactory compromise although, so she'd believed at the time, the work did serve to keep his mind free of worry over his accursed great ship. Within days of their return, however, it had been all too painfully apparent that whatever benefit he might have derived from his cure and his 'holiday' would all too soon be dissipated.

Apart from having been spruced up for an official summer visit from the Queen and Prince Albert, *Great Eastern* was as he had left her. She had cost her despairing owners nearly three-quarters of a million, twice the original estimate, and would still need another £170,000 spent on her before she could even begin to be operational. All efforts to raise funds had been abortive; the current trade recession had not helped. So the board of Eastern Steam, led by Hope, had decided almost unanimously – there had been but two dissenting voices – to cut the company's losses by putting the hull to immediate auction just as she stood. It was all Brunel's fault, they had publicly contended, with which canard the press had at once gleefully agreed in a renewed spate of personal attacks on the absent engineer.

But the Little Giant, bloodied and bowed though at present he might be, was not beaten – not yet, not by a long chalk. Persuading the two dissenters, Campbell and Magnus, to join him, he proposed the flotation of a new company which would purchase the hull at a nominal figure from Eastern Steam, recompensing the latter's subscribers with shares in proportion to their original holdings.

The prospectus of the Great Ship Company, issued on 18 November 1858, with Campbell named as chairman, Yates as secretary and Brunel engineer, despite fierce opposition from Hope and his friends was surprisingly well received. One month later Eastern Steam had ceased to exist. The slate, as it were, seemed clean.

With the new slate came a new plan. Acutely mindful of past

disasters and in complete disregard of the strain this would once more place upon his health, Isambard was adamant that he must personally prepare not only overall estimates for the work yet to be done on the ship, but detailed specifications as well. It was yet another lethal treadmill, and the result was inevitable. Within three months he was in a worse state than ever. That he managed to stave off the final collapse until he had finished his mammoth self-imposed task seemed to Doctors Brodie and Bright little less than a miracle. If he was to have even the slightest chance of survival, both categorically declared, he must go to a warmer climate at once.

But with work on the ship about to start at long last, the one thing he did not want to do was leave the country. This time, however, Brodie was adamant.

'God dammit, man, ye've scarce the right to be alive at this moment,' he raved at the now near-helpless invalid. 'It's the Mediterranean for you, and Egypt – from now till the summer at least, or I wash my hands of you. Now, for the last time, either be told, or be damned!'

The news awaiting the Brunels on their return to Cairo was not good. Like some malevolent evil genius, the sinister figure of John Scott Russell had again appeared. It was he, so the faithful Jacomb related in his long and detailed report, that the board of the Great Ship Company had contracted to complete the fitting out of *Great Eastern*. Deeply concerned by the possibility, even probability, that this latest breakdown in Brunel's health would be permanent and marked the end of his active participation in the management of the ship, so wrote Jacomb, the directors, in panic, had turned to the only man who possessed comparably intimate knowledge of her design and construction.

By what means the apparently indestructible shipbuilder had contrived to regain enough credibility to resume control of his business was a mystery. But having done so, and having apparently held his hand until Brunel was safely out of the country, he had somehow managed to convince even the most hostile directors that he and he alone could guarantee the ship being operational by September 1859, the date specified in the company's prospectus.

Jacomb was at pains to reassure his chief that notwithstanding

301

Russell's unwelcome return to the scene, all work was progressing swiftly and satisfactorily. The paddle engines, which had been languishing unfinished and untouched for two years in his workshops, had at last been completed and were being installed. So far at any rate, all, it seemed, was well.

But not even Brereton's lengthy postscript, in which he corroborated everything Jacomb said as well as reporting completion of the Saltash bridge – the second truss having been floated out under his direction the previous July – could altogether allay Isambard's forebodings. His first impulse was to return to England with all possible haste. However, the winter there had been severe, it was not yet spring, and he needed neither his doctor's solemn warning nor Mary's near-frantic pleading to convince him that to do so before the weather was much improved would be nothing less than suicidal.

Chapter Eight

WHEN Brunel stepped aboard *Great Eastern* early in the morning of 18 May 1859, he found a nightmare situation almost identical in every detail to that which had obtained at Millwall from the beginning of 1855 until the ship had finally been launched and towed across the river.

It was a shattering blow, both physically and mentally, which came near to breaking both his heart and his reason. It was unbelievable. It was like a weird caprice of fate that had a place only in the fantastic world of Greek tragedy, the sort of extravagantly contrived twist even a writer of the most outrageous romantic fiction would have spurned as too artificial, too incredible.

But it was not fiction; nor was it Greek tragedy. It was real, it had happened, it had to be accepted, and the cruelly familiar problems posed had somehow to be solved. As Isambard had suspected and feared from the start, Russell, having secured his new contract with the Great Ship Company by the well-tried tactic of bidding low and arguing his way out of trouble later, had been on the lookout for the loophole that would enable him to engage once more in all his familiar and ruinous tricks.

At first it had seemed Jacomb had the measure of the man. But when a major fault in the construction of the paddle engines had belatedly come to light, Russell had contended that as the original contract with the now defunct Eastern Steam Navigation Company was *ipso facto* no longer in existence, the cost, which was considerable, of rectifying the fault should be borne by the present owners of *Great Eastern*, his contracted responsibility having been to Eastern Steam not to the Great Ship Company.

Yates had strenuously refuted this contention, which was, of course, ridiculous, whereupon Russell had ordered his men forthwith to ignore Jacomb and any other Great Ship Company representative and take orders directly and only from himself. The result had been a total stoppage of work, an apparently unbreakable deadlock and an already near-fatal loss of time – once again the crucial element. Scarce three and a half months now remained before the ship was due to sail on her much advertised maiden voyage. Postponement, under any circumstances, simply could not be countenanced. But with the mountain of unfinished work increasing daily, plus the fact that *Great Eastern* still had to be put through all her trials – indeed, she had not yet been to sea – utter and absolute ruin for the Great Ship Company seemed inevitable.

Concern for everything save the fate of his Great Babe driven from his mind, the solemn promises to Mary and to Brodie not to overtax his limited reserves of strength forgotten, Brunel, once more heedless of consequence, threw himself as of old into the task only he could accomplish. That first visit which should have been no more than a quick tour of inspecion, lasted well into the small hours of the following morning. By which time, driven by the implacable force of a personality that brooked no opposition, the men of Deptford, regardless of former partisan allegiances, found themselves back at work, working together, and working with a will.

Yates, peremptorily summoned from the comparative calm of his office to be immediately caught up in this unexpected but by no means unwelcome explosion of renewed activity, had managed to send word to Mary to tell her what had happened. Her first impulse had been to rush to Deptford, if need be to drag Isambard forcibly from that precipice over which he was even now in the process of hurling himself. It was too cruel a return for all the care and the love she had lavished on him. But she knew it would have been useless to do so. She had lost the battle she had up till that moment been convinced she had won. In the end it was the ship, his Great Babe, that had claimed him.

When they finally brought him home, utterly exhausted but still almost diabolically possessed by his newly shouldered burden, she was calm. She had known what to expect and, though still appalled, she was prepared for the worst. Only when they were at last alone did he relax his iron grip on the will which was all that had kept him going. She wanted to summon Brodie, but he would not let her. Helplessly she watched with a curiously detached fascination as the sheer physical weakness of this man whose life was already beginning to ebb came so close to destroying forever his spirit.

Deathly pale, unable to move, breathing only with the greatest difficulty and scarcely capable of speech, he lay on the sofa in her drawing room to which he had had to be carried.

'It's as if the clock has somehow been put back a full three years,' he gasped out the words from a depth of racking despair. 'Oh, great God in Heaven – what am I to do?'

Suddenly blinded by tears, Mary dropped to her knees beside him. She groped for his flaccid hand and, gripping it tightly, pressed it to her heart. For a long time he did not respond. Then at last he turned his head slowly to gaze at her. But only, it seemed, with half-seeing eyes.

Since their return to London a never ending procession of relations, official visitors, close friends, even the most casual of acquaintances had called at Duke Street to welcome the travellers home and wish them good fortune for the future. All had commented on how·much Isambard had obviously benefited from his trip, on how well he looked. Even Sir Benjamin Brodie had seemed impressed.

Apart from *Great Eastern*, two things had brought them back to England: first, to be present at the formal opening of the Saltash bridge to which Prince Albert, who was to perform the ceremony, had graciously consented to give his name; second, for Isambard to accept in person the only honour he had ever coveted and which had been unanimously accorded him in his absence – Presidency of the Institution of Civil Engineers. The intention had been to spend a quiet summer partly in Devon and partly in London perhaps involved, but superficially only, with the ship, see her safely away in September, then winter again abroad. By this time next year, Brodie had conceded, there could be a possibility of Isambard resuming a relatively normal existence, provided he would be prepared to reduce drastically in scope and scale his professional activity. There were to be no more railways, no more Saltash bridges, and certainly no more *Great Easterns*. Those days were gone forever.

To which conditions it seemed he had become wholly reconciled. He was, after all, now fifty-three years old and not entirely unwilling to enjoy a little well-earned leisure. He owed, he confessed, that much at least to Mary – poor, hitherto always neglected Mary whose devotion, despite their differences, had sustained him since even before their marriage. Despite his recent crippling financial losses he could still afford to build for her that long-promised house at Watcombe. The sale of Duke Street would more than cover the cost. He could, he said, end his days quite happily there, in comfort if not in luxury, as George Stephenson had ended his. Besides, there were other men, younger men, talented men, waiting their opportunity to make their mark just as he, as a young man, had waited so impatiently to make his.

The eyes of the man whose hand Mary held slowly came fully back to life and focussed on her as his pulse and grip both gradually strengthened. She smiled her encouragement, willing him to return. Slowly his breathing eased and deepened. His free hand reached out to touch her hair, her head, her neck, then gently to wipe the tear stains from her cheeks, full realisation of the terrible hurt he had done her dawning at last. What am I to do, Mary? What am I to do? he pleaded mutely.

She kissed him lightly on the forehead and wrist, her lips full with a tenderness she had never felt before, comforting, reassuring him, communicating in no other way possible her new found strength.

'My dear,' with an effort she kept her voice calm, strangling an unbearable surge of mixed emotion and dread, 'you know better than anyone else what is at stake. You must make your own choice, your own decision. I can only say that, whatever you decide, I will stand by you. I will be here, always – till the end.'

Without Mary he could have done nothing. She did not wait to be asked to make their excuses to the Palace for being unable to be present at the opening ceremony of the Royal Albert Bridge – an event at one time she would never have considered forgoing. But knowing how much the honour meant to Isambard, she did her best to persuade him not to refuse the Presidency of the Institution of Civil Engineers. When he insisted, she personally delivered his letter of regret. She bullied Sir Benjamin Brodie, in his way the greatest bully of all, into an ultimately compliant and infinitely helpful acceptance of a situation his every instinct rebelled against.

'My calling is to preserve life, not to condone self destruction!' he'd bellowed at her at the height of their violent exchange.

'Sir Benjamin,' she'd answered with calm dignity bred of a certitude impervious to all argument, 'now that I, like you, have failed to save my husband, I must and I shall, whether you approve or not, do everything I can to make what time remains as happy and as fulfilling for him as possible.'

'For such unselfish devotion and courageous determination, Ma-am,' the gruff old surgeon had at last conceded, 'I can only say – I salute you.'

Subtly she insinuated herself into the hectic day to day conduct of the engineer's affairs without ever intruding or giving offence. Rarely was he out of her sight. She was there to soothe and restrain him when he got too excited; to offer encouragement when he tired; to bring him comfort when he became depressed. Her presence at his side was accepted without question or comment. All, even John Scott Russell, were persuaded to refrain from doing or saying anything which might unnecessarily upset Isambard. She became his indispensable if unofficial personal assistant, his mediator, his mentor, his guardian and, most important of all, his doctor and his nurse. To save him the tiresome journey from the West End to Deptford, Mary acquired the lease of a modest but adequate property in Sydenham from which he was able, even on his worst days, to get to the ship and back with comparative ease. She still kept the house open in Duke Street and insisted they both retire there for at least one full day of complete rest every week.

Towards the end of that long, exhausting, and to Mary infinitely depressing summer, she arranged through Daniel Gooch for a special train to take Isambard to see for the first and probably the last time, the finished bridge at Saltash. By then a pathetically wizened shadow of the dynamic genius who had conceived and built this now universally acknowledged masterpiece, he could do no more than gaze at it wistfully from the couch placed for him on an open goods wagon. Gooch himself drove the locomotive of the train that bore the dying engineer back and forth beneath those soaring stone arches supporting the massive trusses. With Mary beside him he examined meticulously through a telescope every detail of the structure, the while dictating notes to the secretary who had accompanied them. The weather all the way from London had been atrocious. But as they'd approached the bridge the skies had cleared, and the sun had shone throughout the whole of their three-hour stay.

'Of all my bridges,' he told Mary as they crossed the Tamar for the last time, 'it is still the one at Clifton by which I would like to have been remembered. But,' he smiled sadly, 'as that was never built, I think this may do just as well.'

Monday, 5 September 1859, dawned bright and clear. For the past week Isambard had been so ill he had been unable to leave the house. But this morning he rose early and, for once defying his nurse, insisted on going to Deptford. In two days' time *Great Eastern* would at last make her majestic way down river to the Nore, first to adjust her compasses, then to sail to Weymouth on the first of her sea trials.

'And I,' he told Mary, 'am going to be with her.' It was necessary, he continued stubbornly, ignoring all her protests, for him to satisfy himself that all was as it should be and to put in hand personally arrangements for his cabin to be made ready.

The ship looked magnificent. In the bright morning sun she was sleek and glossy under a final coat of paint, trim and neat despite her enormous bulk, riding easily at her moorings with her five slim funnels and six tall masts reaching for the sky. Workmen still swarmed about her decks – carpenters and plumbers and their mates, upholsterers, carpet fitters, painters, all kinds of metal workers busily clearing away the clutter of their equipment, putting finishing touches here and there, completing last minute alterations or improvements, while gangs of stevedores tramped up and down gangplanks loading all sorts of ship's stores from coils of hemp to cases of champagne. She had been coaled, and thin plumes of smoke floating from her funnels showed that her boilers were already fully fired.

Again the most popular attraction in London, she had been luring sightseers to Deptford just as she had at Millwall. This morning the crowds were even more numerous. Word had somehow spread that Brunel was coming. Today it was the engineer they had come to see as well as his great ship.

But there were few indeed who recognised him as he limped slowly aboard on the arm of his lady. And those who did were too stunned to see how their once jaunty, cigar-smoking hero-villain had changed in just two short years, to give voice to more than a sigh of sincere sorrow or a quietly muttered expression of genuine pity.

Weak to the point of collapse though he was, he insisted on inspecting the ship from stem to stern. The former maze of starkly echoing iron caverns had been transformed into the gleaming efficiency of boiler and engine rooms, capacious cargo holds, chain

308

stores, rope stores, water tanks, bunker holds and hundreds of wonderfully spacious, superbly appointed and luxuriously furnished cabins. Ornately carved oaken staircases rose regally from deck to deck. There were no less than five separate public saloons, all richly carpeted and brilliantly illuminated by gas-lit chandeliers. The Great Saloon, the grandest of all, measured 63 feet by 47, with a decorated ceiling 14 feet high. It had two full-length balconies supported on elegantly ornamented wrought-iron columns. Its walls were hung with richly patterned cloth of gold. Octagonal panelling covered the funnel casings, four enormous mirrors alternating with elaborately decorated arabesques. Heavy crimson portières, matching the Utrecht velvet-covered sofas and chairs, masked the doors; while the buffets were of the finest carved walnut topped with flawless green marble.

The rusting, useless, helpless hulk, so abused in the past, had, entirely by his genius in handling both men and materials and by his unimaginable courage, been transformed into a floating palace, a creation more fantastic than anyone could have dreamed.

Leaning heavily on his walking stick and supported by Mary's arm, he was busily examining the rigging stays and deck skylights when they came upon John Scott Russell holding court, his audience including a *Times* reporter, whom Isambard recognised, and a photographer accompanied by an assistant laden with camera, tripod and essential paraphernalia.

' "Now, I am not a shipbuilder", were Mr Brunel's very first words to me.' Unaware of the new arrivals, the familiar and as always mellifluously persuasive voice continued in full flow, ' "Nor," he said, "am I an engine builder. So it is for those two very good reasons that I have come to you, Mr Scott Russell, to ask you to devote your mind and your attention to do what I cannot do. In other words, to carry through to a successful conclusion the ideas I have outlined to you." Well, of course I said "yes". How could I possibly have refused such a request. And it was all agreed in principle and in detail between us there and then. "You shall design the ship according to your own lines," Mr Brunel said. "You shall make the engines upon your own plan. And you shall construct the ship according to the best of your experience and your knowledge." Which as you can now see, ladies and gentlemen,' and here Russell, turning slowly as he did so, spread his arms wide in a grand theatrical gesture, 'from the evidence now before you, is exactly what has been done.' Only then did he spot the Brunels.

'Good morning, Mr Scott Russell.' Mary's voice was acidly polite, but her fury was obvious to all. Russell, seemingly quite unabashed by the unexpected confrontation, acknowledged her greeting with a courtly bow. Sensing a story the *Times* reporter immediately stepped between them, pencil poised, his notebook at the ready.

'Have you any comments to make, Mr Brunel, on what Mr Scott Russell has just said?'

Mary's eyes were flashing ferociously and she would have replied on his behalf had he not restrained her.

'I will only say that I know Mr Scott Russell very well.' Isambard spoke softly and slowly for he was finding even the effort of talking now almost too much. 'Oh yes, I know him very well indeed. And have done for a very long time, have I not, Mr Scott Russell?'

At which John Scott Russell, though obviously unrepentant, at least had the grace to look somewhat discomforted.

'May I ask you to pose for a photograph, Mr Brunel?' asked the photographer, who had already had his assistant set up camera and tripod in readiness. 'Just one pose. It will take only a minute or two, I assure you,' he added hastily as Mary showed a reluctance to agree.

'A minute or two will not kill me, my dear,' her husband murmured, patting her arm.

'Very well,' she relented. 'But one only. Then we must go home.'

The photographer knew his business, placing his subject exactly in position against the funnel and explaining succinctly just what he wanted. As he ducked beneath his black cloth to check the focus, Isambard glanced briefly at Mary who was standing behind the camera and slightly to one side. With her eyes and a faint mute movement of her lips she asked her inevitable question – was he all right? He nodded slightly and gave her a slow grateful smile. Dear Mary, she had indeed been to him what his mother had always been to his father. But how can I ever tell her, he thought.

'Look to the camera please, Mr Brunel,' sang out the cloth.

He did so with a start. Then he relaxed once more.

'That's good. That's fine, Sir. Splendid. Now, hold it quite still please, until I say "When".'

It was at that moment the engineer began to lose touch with reality.

Chapter Nine

HE remembered the last time he had posed for a picture. It was at Millwall, in the shipyard, just before that nightmarish attempt to launch *Great Eastern*. He had stood in front of the giant stern checking-drum, next to the windlass on which poor Donovan had shortly afterwards died so unnecessarily. It had only just stopped raining. The light was barely adequate. Everything was wringing wet. The yard was a sea of mud. The mud clung to his boots. It caked his crumpled trouser legs to high above the knees.

He had taken off his borrowed greatcoat. His jacket was damp, his waistcoat rumpled and creased, his cravat a limp rag, his shirt ruined – its front hideously stained by the leather strap of his famous cigar case. Whenever they had written about him there had always been a mention of that cigar case. He could feel again its weight on his hip, feel too the old familiar sharp-soft pressure against his scalp of the edges of rolled up bundles of notes he habitually stuffed into his tall hat, feel the aching drag of his coat weighed down as always by the contents of its bulging pockets. He could actually feel all this.

Yet he could see himself in the picture, while the picture was being taken. There he was, standing as he was standing now, but with hands thrust deep into trouser pockets and a cigar in his mouth; he could even taste the bitter tang of its raggedly chewed end.

But he could also see quite plainly the huge barred links of the great ship's stern checking-chain looped crookedly round the drum behind him. He was standing there, and he was standing somewhere else as well, looking at himself being photographed. It was all very strange. Confusing – totally inexplicable and not a little disturbing. His sense of logic told him that what he was seeing was impossible. But there it was. He could see it all very vividly. Then, suddenly, it was all gone. And he could see nothing. For the moment – there was nothing.

He was unconscious before he fell. He did not feel the bone-jarring

311

impact of his body hitting the deck. He did not feel them lift him and carry him to his carriage. Nor was he aware of the anxious touch of Mary's hands during the journey back to Duke Street. He knew nothing of Sir Benjamin Brodie being urgently summoned, of his being examined, of the dread diagnosis of severe stroke, of being put to bed, of being watched over by Mary day and night for practically every minute of every hour he remained unconscious. He knew nothing of any of this.

He did not move. He made no sound. Though his heart still beat and his lungs still functioned, his body it seemed was dead. Not so his mind, however. His mind was not dead. His mind was very much alive. It was racing, racing, racing, through constantly changing kaleidoscopic patterns of half forgotten memories, a meaningless jumble of distorted shadowy images. But all so real, and all going back, and back, and back.

'What are we going to do about Marchant?'

There'd been an incessant, sometimes deafening, but always maddeningly unintelligible droning of voices – somewhere, ever since – ever since when? He couldn't remember. They were all in his head perhaps, or in his imagination? He did not know. But now he clutched at this particular voice, clung to it desperately as a drowning man might cling to a floating log. He steadied himself with that voice. By concentrating on it he slowly stilled the whirling confusion that seemed to surround him.

'. . . going to do about Marchant?' said the voice again, louder this time, clearer, recognisable and seeming to echo through his brain. It was Charles Saunders – Saunders of the Great Western Railway. But where had he come from? And where on earth was he? And what the devil was he talking about? Marchant – who the hell was Marchant?

Saunders's voice again: 'Unless we get rid of him there isn't a hope in Hades of ever getting the blasted tunnel finished.'

Now he could see him. There, perched on the corner of a desk – not his own desk, he wasn't in his office. This was in Oxford. The offices of the Oxford, Worcester & Wolverhampton Railway Company – 'old Worse & Worse', they'd called it – and not without good reason.

Amazing how young Saunders looked, he thought. He's seven

years older than I am at least, and, dammit, there he is looking a good ten years younger than when I last saw him. Amazing!

'Now,' demanded Saunders impatiently, rapping a heavy ebony straight edge on the desk top then pointing it directly at him, 'what do you propose to do about Marchant?'

Marchant! Of course, the contractor at Mickleton, the tunnel that was to carry the old Worse & Worse under the escarpment of the northern Cotswolds near Chipping Campden. 'The Broad Gauge to the Mersey' had been the war cry of the early fifties.

'But we're not going to get there in a month of blue moons,' snapped Saunders, 'if something drastic isn't done about Marchant. And quickly too!'

He remembered it all perfectly now. The old Worse & Worse, the vital link in the broad gauge's northern advance, and the rock on which the whole campaign could founder. There had already been problems aplenty. And now, on top of everything else Marchant had stopped work and was refusing to vacate the partially excavated tunnel.

'. . . do about Marchant?' Saunders's question hammered hollowly in his head.

'We go in in force,' Brunel heard himself saying.

'No good.' This time it was Varden, the resident engineer at Chipping Campden. They were in his office there, a dusty, makeshift, clapboard affair. 'Marchant's no fool. As soon as he knows we're coming he'll whistle up the magistrates. He's a local man, remember, and they'll not stand by and see him lose, whether he's in the wrong or not.'

Varden was right. The magistrates were there waiting for them with a posse of police armed with cutlasses.

'I told you,' said Varden.

But Marchant, local man or no local man, wasn't going to get away with a manoeuvre like that. He remembered ordering Varden to call in navvies from other parts of the line, from Warwick on the Birmingham & Oxford. By Sunday night he'd got nearly two thousand. They'd called themselves Brunel's army, and that's exactly what they'd become. He was commander-in-chief, his assistant engineers colonels of the regiments. The battle for Mickleton Tunnel was a military operation, highly organised and, with himself issuing orders from the midst of the mêlée, brilliantly executed.

'. . . the finest action of its kind to be fought in England since the Wars of the Roses!' said Saunders.

He smiled. Saunders disappeared. He sighed – and again there was nothing.

'You're awake,' said Mary.

He opened his eyes. He was lost – bewildered – but only for a moment. He was in bed, in his room, in Duke Street. It was daytime, late afternoon, he judged from the light; bright, but with that slightly hazy autumnal softness, a dustiness almost, real September sunshine. He felt weak and tired, desperately, desperately tired. Apart from that, all right.

Mary smiled down at him. She stroked his forehead, touched his right hand which lay outside the coverlet. He could feel her grip. But he could not return it. His arm was leaden. He could not move it. Nor could he move his right leg. His left leg, yes, and his left arm; but nothing on his right side at all. It was as if that part of his body no longer existed. When he found he could speak only with the greatest difficulty he knew at once what had happened to him. He also knew that his Great Babe had, after all, sailed without him.

After Brodie had been, passed judgement and departed, Mary came once more alone to his bedside.

'The doctor thinks you may soon be able to talk again. But you must stay quiet – and be patient!' she told him.

He acknowledged this with a slight, lop-sided smile. He had little choice but to be quiet. Patience, however, was something else. He questioned her urgently with his eyes. She understood at once what he wanted. It was almost as if she had read his thoughts.

Before bringing her stricken husband home from Deptford she had issued instructions to Brereton and Jacomb, who would together now deputise for him aboard *Great Eastern* during her trials, to have regular detailed reports forwarded to Duke Street with the greatest possible despatch. It was now the evening of 9 September. The latest had arrived only a few hours before and Mary was able to give Isambard all the information he craved. He listened avidly as she read.

With an escort of tugs and a following flotilla of both river and seagoing craft, *Great Eastern* had moved down river on Wednesday, the 7th, only a few hours behind her scheduled time of departure

314

from Deptford. On board were a host of prominent personalities, friends and families of the Great Ship Company directors, representatives from the press and from Messrs James Watt & Company, who had constructed and installed the screw engines. John Scott Russell, whose responsibility for the paddle engines had by this time been firmly re-established, was also on the ship.

At Purfleet she had undergone her first series of checks and trials, all of which she seemed to have come through with flying colours. There she had moored overnight, the following morning, cheered by milling crowds for practically every mile of the way, resuming her triumphant progress to the sea. Some minor difficulties in accurately calibrating compasses had led to a build-up of delays which had meant eventually anchoring overnight in the Nore. But all was now well Jacomb reported, and ready for the run to Weymouth. *Great Eastern* would weigh anchor at first light on the morning of the 9th.

The bedroom clock chimed, then struck six.

'They'll be well on their way by now,' said Mary, looking up from her papers. 'We won't hear again from them direct until when – the day after tomorrow?'

Isambard calculated quickly. He was relieved to find he could still think reasonably clearly. Assuming she'd achieved and maintained her trial speeds, his Great Babe would probably now be somewhere off Eastbourne. She would, of course, slow down during the night, reduce her average to something under ten knots, which would mean another fourteen to sixteen hours before she would drop anchor again. Today was Friday; yes, Mary was right, it would be about Sunday midday before another despatch could be expected. There would doubtless be a continuing spate of reports of sightings from observers on shore, Mary had more than enough already it seemed. But it was the ones from the ship which were important.

Forcing his reluctant tongue and stubborn lips to function more or less effectively, he managed to dictate a couple of letters to Mary. They were to the managers of the GWR works at Swindon asking for the men there to be given time off and arrangements made for them to visit the ship while she was at Weymouth.

Then Mary insisted he rest, and he slipped easily into a deep, and this time dreamless, sleep.

The first reports of disaster reached London late that night. *Great Eastern* had blown up! Immediately a rash of rumours erupted and spread like plague through the capital. A tremendous explosion had completely destroyed her. She had sunk within sight of land. All on board were lost, either killed in the explosion or drowned while trying to get ashore. It was the greatest single nautical tragedy ever.

The Times the following morning carried a brief but evocative account of what had occurred just twelve hours before:

> The forward part of *Great Eastern*'s deck appeared to spring like a mine, blowing the funnel up in the air. There was a confused roar amid which came the awful crash of timber and iron mingled together in the frightful uproar. Then all was hidden in a sudden rush of steam.
>
> Blinded and almost stunned by the overwhelming concussion, those on the bridge stood motionless in the white vapour till they were reminded of the necessity of seeking shelter by the shower of wreck – glass, gilt work, saloon ornaments, and pieces of wood which began to fall like rain in all directions.

The full facts, however, were not known until a hurriedly scribbled despatch from Jacomb, sent on by special messenger from Hastings, finally arrived at Duke Street.

With her screw engines making thirty-two revolutions per minute and her paddle engines eight, *Great Eastern* had attained her set trial speed within minutes of passing the Nore light. Though almost immediately thereafter she had encountered unseasonal and rather more than moderate westerly winds which had sent every one of the many craft still accompanying her scurrying for the shelter of Folkestone and Dover, she had maintained an imperturbable progress. The heavy swell inconvenienced this wonder of the seas not at all. Steady as a rock she had continued on her way so smoothly that those on board had marvelled at the miracle they were witnessing. It would take a full gale, a hurricane, they said, even to deflect this mighty ship from her course.

Below decks, however, unsuspected by the admiring passengers, things were far from satisfactory. The screw engines had given no trouble at all and were continuing to perform well. But from the time they'd left the Nore, the paddle-engine room had been a scene of unrelieved confusion which at times had bordered on chaos. Russell had placed Dixon in command of the engine room and was himself acting as observer on the paddle bridge, which left the boilers in the charge of McFarlane, one of McLellan's engineers.

Preheated water for all the ship's boilers was piped from special annular heat exchangers situated round the base of the funnels behind the elaborate panelling in the saloons. The arrangement served a two-fold purpose of utilising excess heat from the furnaces, that would otherwise be lost, and insulating these public rooms. As *Great Eastern* steamed westward the feed-water pumps serving the screw-engine boilers were all working perfectly. Those which served the paddle-engine boilers, for reasons at that stage unknown, were not. All McFarlane's efforts to maintain adequate water levels in his boilers had failed. Time and again the pumps had laboured alarmingly in scalding clouds of hissing steam. Finally they had stopped altogether. Which, if the paddle engines were to continue to function, left McFarlane with no alternative but to draw cold water direct from the boiler's reservoirs and bypass the annular heaters. As later became obvious, it was this action which made the ensuing disaster inevitable.

The annular feed-water heaters were equipped with stand-pipes to carry excess steam to the full height of the funnels before venting it harmlessly. It was thus impossible for any potentially dangerous pressure to build up inside the heaters should the clack valves through which pre-heated water was forced under pressure to the boilers become blocked or for any other reason fail to function – as when McFarlane's pumps had stopped working. But a week prior to the departure from Deptford it had been necessary to fit temporary stop-cocks to all five stand-pipes for a series of hydraulic tests to be carried out as part of the programme of final checks on the engines. This done, the stop-cocks should have been removed. They were and would be of no further use; never again would the need arise for the stand-pipes to be sealed. Indeed to do so at any time would be tantamount to setting light to the fuse of a bomb. Too late it was discovered that, for reasons which could not yet be explained, the stop-cocks on the stand-pipes of the heaters supplying the boilers for the paddle engines had not been removed. And not only were they still there; they were still closed. 'Yet another of John Scott Russell's many oversights,' commented Jacomb wryly.

The explosion had occurred at five minutes past six in the evening

317

of Friday, 9 September. *Great Eastern* had then been just off Dungeness. To the thousands of watchers crowding Beachy Head she had simply disappeared in a cloud of steam and smoke and flying debris. Understandably, it was from this source that the first rumours of total loss had emanated. But such was the amazing strength of Brunel's magnificent conception – the basic design having been proved by *Great Britain*'s ordeal on the rocks of Dundrum Bay almost thirteen years earlier – that an explosion which must have destroyed any other vessel had hardly shaken the *Great Eastern*. The saloon, fortunately deserted at the time, was, of course, totally wrecked. But in the adjoining library neither a book nor an ornament was so much as disturbed, not a mirror or a pane of glass cracked. Elsewhere even the noise was hardly heard. Nor had the ship faltered for an instant, or deviated from her course.

Beneath the uprooted funnel, however, the boiler room had been transformed into a scene from Dante's Inferno. From swirling mists of scalding steam there slowly emerged a ghostly procession of nightmarish phantoms that had once been men. Stripped of clothing and hideously blistered, some with leprous, lifeless flesh literally hanging from exposed bones, they had staggered or crawled into view before horrified deck crew and passengers. One poor wretch leapt overboard to be immediately caught by the floats of the still-turning paddle wheels. Three died within the hour. They were the lucky ones. Another three, still lingering in agony, had no chance of surviving.

Notwithstanding the terrible tragedy, Jacomb concluded, *Great Eastern* was continuing on course to Weymouth, at full power and at undiminished speed. Proved by disaster, she was indeed the greatest of all ships!

Isambard was much stronger when he woke. He could speak with comparative ease, and some feeling had returned to his paralysed limbs. It was, of course, impossible to keep him in ignorance of what had happened, and his first demand was for the latest information concerning his Great Babe.

Knowing full well this must be the blow he could not survive, Mary gave the news to him as gently as she could. Her heart was breaking, but she was calm and composed as she read Jacomb's report. He listened without once interrupting her. Then he questioned her closely, making her re-read again and again its most crucial passages, his mind all the while instinctively analysing information, grappling systematically with the host of new problems, looking, as always, forward.

But even as he did so Mary could see that the light in those still lustrous eyes, the last bastion of his still unconquered spirit, had already begun to fade.

There were times during the days that followed when it seemed, despite a slow but steady deterioration, that he might still rally, perhaps even recover. But late on Wednesday night he slipped at last into a rapidly deepening coma. Again he lay as if already dead. But beneath the smothering blanket of approaching oblivion Brunel's mind was racing once more.

Again there were voices, male voices, female voices, familiar voices; but none positively identifiable. Nor could he make out what the voices were saying; or where they were coming from. He could see nothing tangible. There was no colour. His world had become a maze of sombre shades of grey. It was peopled only by shadows.

After what seemed an eternity of this babbling confusion, the voices began to drown in a new and rapidly crescendoing sound – a sound he'd heard before, long, long ago, a sound he recognised instantly. It was the sound of water, rushing water, millions of gallons of madly rushing water, pouring under pressure through narrow tunnels, carrying all before it, smashing everything in its path, filling the passageways with wildly tossing debris, and with death. It was a terrifying, awe inspiring, monumental sound; a sound once heard, never forgotten; a magnificent sound to which even the sudden shattering drum-fire blast of cannon could not be compared.

'Jesus God above! The Thames is in again!' came the despairing wail he had somehow known must follow; the terror-stricken agonised cry echoing from nowhere to be lost again immediately in the all-consuming overwhelming thunder of the flood. Then he too, blind and blundering, was caught in that terrible maelstrom of buffeting suffocating blackness, his legs numb and useless, his arms hopelessly ineffective, his back feeling as if it had been broken. He was fighting for his life. But he knew he was trapped, helplessly trapped, unable to move, unable to breathe, unable to survive without assistance.

'Sam! Sam Ball! Collins!' He was shouting, screaming the names
with all the strength he could summon. But so deafening now was the
noise about him he could not even hear his own voice. Then,
miraculously, just as he was certain he could survive no longer, he
heard the hoarse whisper in his ear.

'Reach for my hand, Master Isambard,' croaked Sam Ball. 'Reach
out. Reach for it. Reach – for – my – hand.' Desperately, frantically,
he groped for the hand he could not see, the hand he scarcely hoped
to touch. It was there, somewhere, he knew, so near, so near – and
yet. . . .

At last he found it, touched it, held onto it as tightly as he could. It
felt strangely cold, like a hand long dead, and his own hand failed to
warm it. Rather he could feel his flesh growing likewise cold, a
creeping, paralysing, peaceful, sleep-inducing cold. In the familiar,
hard and horny comforting strength of a grasp he had known since
childhood, he knew now he would be eternally safe.

Again and again he sighed his relief in long, slow, shuddering sighs
that gradually took all the breath from his body. The noise of the
waters slowly grew less. Vaguely, in the distance, somewhere far
beyond the now fast-fading fury of the flood he could hear a clock
chiming – a mellow, measured muted mingling of crystal clarity with
blurred, mesmerising echoes.

Instinctively he began to count the ever fainter strokes that told
the hours – one, two, three, four, five, six, seven.

Then there was only silence.